THE LEGAL THRILLER HAS BEEN REBORN FOR A NEW GENERATION WITH THE "FRESH VOICE" (Robert Dugoni) OF

ALLISON LEOTTA

The former federal sex crimes prosecutor scores "a recipe for success: a vulnerable tenacious heroine, surprising twists and turns, and equal parts romance and danger" (*Library Journal*, starred review) in her acclaimed novels.

Praise for her debut novel
LAW OF ATTRACTION

Named One of the Best Legal Thrillers of 2010 by *Suspense Magazine*

"Riveting. . . . Leotta joins the big leagues with pros like Lisa Scottoline and Linda Fairstein."

—*Library Journal* (starred review)

"Engaging . . . far better than anything I've read from Grisham or the like."

—*Minneapolis Star Tribune*

"Intense and realistic. . . . Leotta is an up-and-coming literary giant."

—*Suspense Magazine*

"Realistic, gritty, and filled with twists and turns. . . . A great read for anyone who loves legal thrillers."

"Exceptional . . . intrigui

"A riveting page-turner. . . . Leotta turns her experiences into visceral prose."

—*Washington City Paper*

"An exciting legal thriller."

—*Milwaukee-Wisconsin Journal Sentinel*

"Leotta's expertise permeates every page. . . . An entertaining novel with psychological teeth. Don't pick it up if you have anywhere to go any time soon."

—*New York Journal of Books*

"A beautifully written and suspenseful debut. . . . A fabulous book!"

—Barbara Delinsky

"Gritty, suspenseful . . . strikes all the right chords. . . . Impressive."

—*Mystery Scene*

"Sexy, fast-paced. . . . Reminiscent of Linda Fairstein."

—*City Pulse*

"A great ride . . . a shocking end. . . . A stunning debut indicating a bright future."

—Robert Dugoni

DISCRETION

"A first-rate thriller. Leotta nails the trifecta of fiction: plot, pace, and character."

—David Baldacci

"Her experience shines through on every page. The result is a realistic legal thriller that's as fun to read as it is fascinating."

—Lisa Scottoline

"Beautifully crafted and frighteningly real."

—Douglas Preston

"An assured and authentic voice, and a highly entertaining storyteller."

—George Pelecanos

SPEAK OF THE DEVIL

Named Best Book of the Month by Apple and featured in the iBookstore

"Sexy and brutal . . . convincing and authoritative. . . . An author who knows what she's talking about."

—*Seattle Post-Intelligencer* (Editor's Choice)

"Leotta is on fire in the literary world."

—*Deadline Detroit*

"Taut and fast-paced . . . intelligent, probing . . . and very, very good."

—*Washington Independent Review of Books*

"*Speak of the Devil* comes to life in the most haunting and best way."

—Brad Meltzer

Books by Allison Leotta

Law of Attraction
Discretion
Speak of the Devil

ALLISON LEOTTA

LAW OF ATTRACTION

POCKET BOOKS
New York London Toronto Sydney New Delhi

Pocket Books
A Division of Simon & Schuster, Inc.
1230 Avenue of the Americas
New York, NY 10020

This book is a work of fiction. Any references to historical events, real people, or real places are used fictitiously. Other names, characters, places, and events are products of the author's imagination, and any resemblance to actual events or places or persons, living or dead, is entirely coincidental.

This Pocket Books paperback edition April 2015

POCKET and colophon are registered trademarks of Simon & Schuster, Inc.

For information about special discounts for bulk purchases, please contact Simon & Schuster Special Sales at 1-866-506-1949 or business@simonandschuster.com.

The Simon & Schuster Speakers Bureau can bring authors to your live event. For more information or to book an event, contact the Simon & Schuster Speakers Bureau at 1-866-248-3049 or visit our website at www.simonspeakers.com.

Cover design by Ervin Serrano
Cover photographs: rose © Jazzirt/E+/Getty Images; bullet hole © Jeroen Peys/E+/Getty Images

Manufactured in the United States of America

10 9 8 7 6 5 4 3 2 1

ISBN 978-1-4767-9370-2
ISBN 978-1-4391-9533-8 (ebook)

For Mike
my partner in crime

1

The courthouse coffee was terrible, but the morning after Valentine's Day was no time for a domestic violence prosecutor to go uncaffeinated. Anna poured the inky brew into a Styrofoam cup, took a sip, and grimaced. Scalding and bitter—a fitting start to a day of sorting through last night's crimes. At least she'd have help. Anna pulled out her cell phone and called her officemate.

"DV Papering," Grace answered in crisp singsong.

"Hey, I'm in the cafeteria. Want some coffee?"

"That'd be fabulous." Grace hushed her voice. "And grab a bunch of napkins. There's a woman bleeding all over your chair."

Grace had been a prosecutor for four months, but Anna was still new enough that the information jolted her. "Should we call an ambulance?"

"She's okay. A lot of scrapes and bruises, and a very messy nosebleed. Nothing life-threatening. I can cover till you get here. And can you snag me a muffin? I'm starving."

"Sure. Be right there."

Marveling at Grace's calm, Anna grabbed a muffin and got in line to pay. Three people stood in front of her: a tall guy in a dark suit, a man wearing a Redskins jersey over a blue collared shirt, and a buxom woman in fishnet stockings and a spandex miniskirt. Lawyer, Anna guessed of the first man. Then a policeman, hiding his uniform so courthouse visitors wouldn't ask him questions. And a prostitute, just getting off work, here to see her probation officer. The one thing Anna liked about the courthouse's grim basement cafeteria was its democracy. The cop might arrest the prostitute later tonight, and the lawyer might skewer the cop during cross-examination, but everyone had to wait in the same line to get their corned-beef hash.

After paying, Anna hurried to the napkin dispenser, but the tall lawyer who'd been ahead of her took the last ones.

She looked at him in dismay. "Actually, I really need those," she said, nodding at the napkins in his hand.

Something about the man's dark hair and lanky figure seemed familiar, but out of place. His tailored suit and buttery leather briefcase were common in the federal court next door, but marked him as several income brackets above the D.C. Superior Court crowd. He probably worked for some big Washington law firm, in one of the high-paying jobs she'd turned down to work for the government.

The man glanced down at her and suddenly grinned. "Anna Curtis! Hey! It's been a while."

"Hi, um . . ." She shook her head.

"Nick Wagner. Harvard Law School. I had a ridiculous beard? And hair down to here." He tapped his shoulder and blushed slightly. "Your team beat mine in the final round of Ames Moot Court. Kicked our asses, in fact."

"Nick! You used to play guitar in the Hark during Friday happy hour."

"You got it." His smile widened. "I guess you made more of an impression on me than I made on you."

"Sorry—I'm just in a rush, and focused on those napkins."

Nick placed them ceremoniously in her palm. "Some kind of food spill emergency?"

"Thank you. Bloody nose. Abuse victim in the Papering Room. So—I've got to go." Anna began to walk out of the cafeteria, looking over her shoulder with regret. "I'm sorry I can't really talk now."

Nick hurried along with her through the labyrinth of the courthouse basement. "So, you're a prosecutor—and you pulled papering duty on the day after Valentine's Day? What'd you do, run over the U.S. Attorney's dog?"

She had to laugh. Papering was the most despised assignment in the U.S. Attorney's Office, a task only the greenest prosecutors could be compelled to do. Anna would turn arrests from the last twenty-four hours into criminal case files: typing information into a computer, two-hole-punching police paperwork, condensing lifetimes of violence into slim manila folders. The tedium was broken only when a victim came to tell her sad story in person. And Valentine's Day was notoriously the worst time for domestic violence. People were two-timing each other, or paying too much attention to their baby's mother and not enough to their wife, or just plain forgetting a card. It was surprising how often a lovers' quarrel turned into a trip to lockup.

"I just started in January," Anna explained, "so I'm still in the hazing period."

"Well, we should catch up sometime."

"Sure," she said as they rounded a corner. A crowd of police officers lined the hallway outside the Papering Room. She'd never seen so many blue uniforms in one place before. It was going to be a long day.

"How about dinner tonight?" Nick asked.

"I don't know." Anna glanced sideways at him without slowing her pace. Despite the poor timing, it was a tempting offer. She'd been feeling homesick and disconnected in her new city. It'd be nice to talk with a law school acquaintance. She stopped in the doorway to the Papering Room and handed him her business card. "Call me. Let's see how things look later."

"I will."

He smiled at her: a warm, radiant smile. Despite herself, she felt a natural pull toward him. This might not turn out to be such a bad day-after-Valentine's Day after all.

That thought died as she walked into the Papering Room.

A tiny woman sat at one of the two sagging desks, flanked by Grace and a uniformed policeman. Blood had soaked the woman's white button-down shirt and spattered the gray linoleum at her feet. A few dark red drops flecked the bottom of the mint green cinder block walls. Her beautiful brown face was marred by two black eyes so swollen they were nearly shut. Raw red abrasions covered her left cheek in a messy cross-hatch pattern. She held a piece of bloodstained office paper to her nose and rocked herself back and forth, moaning softly.

Although Anna had read a lot of police reports describing gruesome injuries lately, she hadn't seen a woman this badly scraped up since her childhood. A wave of memories, guilt, and anger stunned her into a momentary paralysis. But today was her day to pick up cases, so this victim was her responsibility. Clenching her teeth, she strode over to the woman and held out a couple of napkins. "Here," she said gently. "Try these."

The woman swapped them for the paper at her nose.

"My name is Anna Curtis. I'm an AUSA, an Assistant U.S. Attorney. I'll be handling your case."

"Laprea Johnson," the woman said. Her voice was so soft it was barely audible.

Suddenly Laprea gasped. The pain on her face transformed into a puckered mask of rage. At first, Anna wondered what she'd said to infuriate the woman.

But she was glaring *past* Anna—at Nick, who stood frozen in the doorway. His face had turned an ashy white. The wounded woman spat her words at him.

"What the fuck are *you* doing here?"

2

Laprea Johnson couldn't believe who was standing at the door. She'd come all the way downtown to see *him*? What kind of sick joke was this?

"Laprea—oh no." Nick groaned and stepped into the office. "Was it . . ."

"D'marco?" Laprea stood up and stepped toward Nick. "You *know* it was."

"Oh shit, Laprea, I'm so sorry."

"You should be sorry!" She stood on her tiptoes, so close to Nick her nose almost brushed his chin. Her hand itched to smack his face.

The police officer put a gentle hand on Laprea's arm and backed her up a few steps. "Hey, hey. Easy, ma'am," the officer said. "Calm down."

Laprea yanked her arm away, but softened when she saw the sympathetic look on his face. Officer Bradley Green had been polite and kind since he'd come to her house in response to the 911 call. It was hard to be mad at him.

"I'm sure D'marco feels terrible about this," Nick said.

"He was feeling fine when his fist was in my face!" Laprea glared at Nick. In a way, this was his fault.

"Excuse me." Anna stepped between them. "How do you two know each other?"

"He's D'marco's lawyer." Laprea pointed at Nick.

Anna turned to him in surprise. "You represent the man who beat her up?"

"Allegedly," Nick said. "I'm with the Office of the Public Defender. I've represented D'marco Davis on different matters for two years." He turned to Laprea. "I really am sorry. I'll have a talk with him."

"He don't need no *talk*!" Laprea shouted. "He needs to be locked up!"

"Nick, I think you need to leave this office," Anna said. "Now."

"Right. Sorry." He started backing out of the room. "I should go to the cellblock anyhow, apparently. I'll talk to you later."

As soon as Nick was gone, Laprea's anger drained, leaving just pain and exhaustion. Her eyes throbbed, her cheek stung, and her arms ached. She collapsed into a chair. Now that she wasn't yelling, her chest started to tremble and her breathing became shallow gulps. She'd been bawling all morning; she couldn't seem to stop. Laprea put her head in her hands and cried as quietly as she could. She was ashamed to be here like this: a bleeding, sniffling mess, beaten up by the man who was supposed to love her. Everyone in this room must think she was such a loser. Her embarrassment just made her cry harder. She wondered where her mother was. She felt so alone.

Laprea was surprised to feel the prosecutor put an arm around her shoulder. Anna knelt down so they were face-to-face.

"It's okay," Anna said, patting her back. "You're safe here. It's going to be all right."

Grateful for the comfort, Laprea leaned onto the lawyer's shoulder. Anna kept holding her and murmuring soothing words. Laprea hoped she didn't get any blood on the woman's suit.

When she finally ran out of tears, Laprea lifted her head and accepted another napkin from the prosecutor.

Anna Curtis hardly looked old enough to be a lawyer. Real pretty, with honey blond hair and big, serious blue eyes. She had the tall, slim figure of an athlete on a Wheaties box. But the woman obviously did nothing to play up her looks. Hair in a tight ponytail, plain black pantsuit, sensible low-heeled shoes. Would this girl be any match for D'marco's lawyer?

"Did that attorney have something to do with all this?" Anna asked. She sat in her desk chair and faced Laprea.

"He just keep getting D'marco off," Laprea said, blowing her nose. "D'marco's gotta learn a lesson."

The woman at the other desk looked up from her computer. "What was Nick Wagner doing here anyhow?"

Laprea looked over at Grace, the woman who'd greeted her when she and Officer Green first came in. Was she a lawyer, too? She didn't look like she belonged in this sad little basement room full of mismatched furniture and old office equipment. The elegant black woman had the bone structure of Queen Nefertiti and the style of Oprah, in a gray silk suit and a string of giant pearls.

"You know him?" Anna asked Grace.

"Oh yeah. Whenever a local station needs to trot out an impassioned defense attorney, they call that guy.

He's always railing about police corruption on WTOP or denouncing something in the D.C. *Bar Bulletin.* The man's made quite a name for himself."

"I had no idea. We went to the same law school. Ran into him in the cafeteria—he gave me the napkins. I didn't know he was a defense attorney."

Didn't know? How inexperienced was this girl? Laprea wished the older black woman had her case. But Laprea understood how the government worked—she didn't have much of a choice. And she didn't want to hurt the younger woman's feelings by making a fuss.

Anna turned back to Laprea. "So tell me—when did this happen?"

Laprea struggled to put a time to the flurry of violence this morning. The kids had just left with Rose, and Laprea was getting dressed for work, so it must have been—

"Just after seven this morning, ma'am," Green answered.

"Almost an hour ago." Anna looked at the officer with surprise. "Why hasn't she been to the hospital?"

"Ms. Johnson refused medical treatment, ma'am."

"What? Why?"

"If we called an ambulance, she'd get charged for it. It's a couple hundred dollars a call."

At least the policeman understood the system. He looked pretty boyish, with his cropped light brown hair and scrubbed-pink baby face, but Laprea guessed he was around thirty. And he was cute—although he could probably lay off the Ben & Jerry's. The buttons on his blue uniform shirt strained against his stomach.

"Anyway," Green said, "she stopped bleeding before

I brought her over here. But she started crying again, and it got her nose bleeding all over again."

"We have a nurse here in the courthouse," Anna said. "Let's go upstairs."

Laprea didn't need a nurse. She would put some Neosporin on her cheek when she got home. For the rest of it, there was nothing a nurse could do. She'd been through this enough before. Her body just needed time to heal. She just wanted to go home and lie down in her own bed.

"No," Laprea said. "I want to get this done now."

Just then her mother walked into the room. Laprea exhaled with relief. "Sorry I'm late," her mother said. "I got somebody to watch the kids."

Rose Johnson wore her favorite pink tracksuit and a pained expression. Laprea had called her as soon as D'marco ran off. Rose was the one who had called 911, put an ice pack on Laprea's face, and shepherded the twins to the back porch so they wouldn't see their mother covered in blood. Rose was great in an emergency—but Laprea dreaded the lecture she'd get when they got home.

Anna introduced herself as Rose set her wide body down with a grunt. Rose kissed her daughter's head, then rested her elbows on her knees and leaned toward the prosecutor.

"What you gonna do about this, Ms. Curtis? D'marco Davis is outta control. You gonna keep him in jail this time?"

"I'll do my best."

"The *hell* does that mean? That man done this before and he just keep getting away with it! Does my daughter have to be dead before you people will lock him up? If he kills her, it'll be *your* fault!"

Anna grimaced, and Laprea felt sorry for her. Her mother was taking her anger out on the only available target. The person Rose really wanted to yell at was D'marco. Or her.

"We'll *ask* for pretrial detention, Ms. Johnson. But it's up to the judge." Anna paused to thumb through some paperwork. "Since D'marco's already on probation for a prior conviction, he'll probably be kept in jail until trial. Even if he's released, we'll get a restraining order so he can't contact your daughter."

"Piece of paper can't stop a fist." Rose harrumphed. But she sat back and let the lawyer continue.

Anna looked at Laprea. "I know this is hard, but I need you to tell me what happened. First, what's your relationship with D'marco Davis?"

A simple question, but Laprea didn't have a simple answer. What do you call the man who used to be the boy of your dreams? They'd been sixteen when they met. He was fine. All the other girls had been jealous when they saw him waiting for her after school. Back then, when D'marco got mad about her talking to other boys, it seemed romantic, a sign of how much he cared about her. She'd been crazy about him—heart-pounding, hand-sweating crazy. She got pregnant her junior year. She thought it would bind D'marco to her forever. Instead, as she got bigger and needier, his mean streak came out. He started hitting her when she was six months pregnant. Laprea realized—just a little too late—that they weren't going to live some modern fairy tale. Then the twins arrived. They were beautiful, and for a minute, everything was okay. But the reality of being teenage parents set in. D'marco didn't come by much. When he did come around, she needed so much from him: money for diapers and formula, baby chores, but mostly his attention. He pulled away. But the less D'marco was around, the more he thought she was with other men, even though she was stuck in a house with her mother and two babies. He started drinking more, and the beatings got worse. He always apologized afterward. He cried about how sorry he was; he begged her to forgive him. When he was apologizing, he was the nicest he ever was to her. He lavished her with attention and finally said all the things she wanted to hear. It was like he only realized how much he loved her right after he'd hit her. She always took him back.

Laprea put a hand to one throbbing eye.

"He's my babies' father," Laprea said at last. "We been on and off since D'montrae and Dameka was born. They twins—a boy and a girl. Four years old. Anyway, since D'marco been out of jail, we was on, I guess. I thought it'd be different this time."

Anna nodded. "What happened this morning?"

"I was getting ready for work. I'm a cashier at the Labor Department cafeteria."

Laprea looked at her watch. She was over two hours late for work. She would call them as soon as she got out of here. She hoped they'd understand. She needed that job.

"My mom left out—she was taking the kids to visit family in Baltimore. D'marco came over after she was gone. At first, I was happy to see him. But he was drunk and suspicious because I wasn't home last night, on

Valentine's Day. We didn't have no plans—I was just at my girlfriend's! But he ain't believed me.

"I told him he was being crazy, and that put him over the edge. He started hitting me. Once he started, he wouldn't stop. He was just punching me everywhere, my arms and chest and legs. I couldn't get away."

Her mother cut in. "Show her the bruises."

Laprea rolled up her sleeves to show the nasty welts on her arms. She spread apart her shirt's neckline, where a big bruise was forming on her chest. She grimaced as she remembered the thudding sounds D'marco's fists made as they landed on her body.

"He must've been hitting you very hard," Anna said.

"I think he been working out in jail." Laprea let out a short, bitter laugh. "I ran out the house, but he caught me right outside the door. He smooshed me right there, out on the front porch, for all the world and God to see."

"'Smooshed'?" Anna asked.

"To grab by the face and push, ma'am," Green said.

"It was so embarrassing," Laprea continued. "I wasn't even thinking about how much it hurt right then—I was thinking I didn't want my neighbors to see. I just wanted him to go away. So I told him I *should* see someone else, 'cause he don't deserve me."

Laprea began crying again. Anna handed her another napkin.

"Then he grabbed me and threw me against the side of the house and started punching my face. My nose was bleeding, and I couldn't hardly see out my eyes. He mashed my face into the brick wall so hard, I felt the skin on my cheek burning."

Laprea dabbed her swollen eyes delicately. The worst thing about this beating wasn't the pain, or the shame, or even the heartache. It was how she was going to explain her face to her kids. Other times, she'd told them she walked into a door or fell on the sidewalk. But they were getting old enough that they were questioning her "accidents." They had seen D'marco lay hands on her. It terrified them.

She swore to herself that they would never have to see that again. She would do whatever it took. For now, she just had to finish this terrible story. She took a ragged breath.

"He was holding my face against the wall, and he came in real close. He put his mouth to my ear, like he about to tell me some sweet nothing. And he whispered if he ever caught me with another man—he'd kill me."

3

At five-thirty that night, Anna and Grace closed up the Papering Room and walked across the street to the U.S. Attorney's building. Anna still had hours of work ahead of her, but at least she'd have quiet and privacy in the office she shared with Grace. As a rookie prosecutor, Anna was responsible for a caseload of about two hundred misdemeanors, the lowest-level crimes. Even cases like Laprea's were relegated to misdemeanorland. There was so much crime, the victim had to get shot or seriously stabbed for it to be considered a felony.

A wall of scuffed filing cabinets dominated their cramped office. Anna immediately began to file the twenty-one new cases she'd been assigned that day. Organizing her new files was the only way she could keep up with the caseload. Her officemate had a very different approach. Files, 911 tapes, and designer shoes covered Grace's desk and the floor around her desk. Despite her crisply tailored appearance, the woman was a complete slob. She was also the best friend Anna had in D.C.

Collapsing into her chair, Grace kicked her conservative courthouse pumps into a corner and pulled a pair of scarlet patent-leather stilettos from her desk drawer.

"Those shoes'll be doing something more exciting than I will tonight," Anna guessed.

"Charles is taking me to the opera."

"Nice!" Anna had to force the enthusiasm into her voice. She'd be alone tonight, as usual.

Grace's husband was a partner at a big law firm, and she could've spent her days lunching with ladies and organizing charity events. She'd chosen this job the way some women might take up quilting or belly-dancing lessons—because it was an interesting way to fill the time.

Anna had taken it as a form of penance.

"Don't work too late tonight," Grace scolded, as she headed out the door. "Get a pedicure, or watch *The Bachelorette,* or do *something* frivolous and girly."

"Have a great time! I won't be here much longer."

"Liar. But at least you're a cute liar."

Grace left a faint cloud of expensive perfume in her wake.

As Anna filed, she thought about Laprea's situation. Of all the cases Anna had seen in her short tenure, this one stuck out. Part of it was the age of Laprea's children. The other part was Laprea's injuries. Would Anna always be this upset when she saw someone with a gash on her cheek?

Anna shoved another folder into the drawer, channeling her anger into the act of filing. She wasn't a helpless little girl anymore. She was in a position to stop the violence.

Her thoughts turned to Nick Wagner. He'd seemed like a decent guy. How could he keep defending his monster of a client? She understood the system needed defense attorneys, but she couldn't get why anyone would want that job.

Sure, it was a coveted position. Public defenders often got a bad rap, but Washington's Office of the Public Defender was the most prestigious defender's service in America. Like the U.S. Attorney's Office, OPD had hundreds of applicants every year for a few openings. Both offices were famous for providing young attorneys with the best litigation training and trial experience in the country. Both organizations took their pick of graduates from the best law schools.

But brains alone didn't get anyone a job at OPD. The organization prided itself on being one of the most zealous defense shops in America. D.C.'s public defenders believed that the system was stacked against their clients; that the police were racist, fascist, or corrupt; and that mass imprisonment, not crime, was the real problem with D.C.'s poor communities. OPD lawyers were famously devoted to getting their clients off—in any way possible.

The result was bitter acrimony between OPD and the U.S. Attorney's Office. In other cities, it was common to have friendships between prosecutors and public defenders, casual softball games, happy hours. But not in D.C. They were adversaries in the tradition of cats and dogs, Montagues and Capulets, Angelina and Jennifer.

That morning, for just a moment, Anna had felt a real spark between them. Now Nick Wagner was just one of a hundred lawyers she had a case against. She would have no problem treating him just like any other defense attorney.

Anna's phone rang, and she stepped to her desk to pick it up. "Hello?"

"This is security calling from downstairs. A Mr. Nicholas Wagner is here to see you."

Her heartbeat sped up—which wouldn't have happened if it was any other defense attorney.

Damn.

"Come on in. Have a seat." Anna gestured to Grace's desk chair and pulled a box of 911 tapes out of the way.

"I like what you've done with the place," Nick said, stepping over a pile of Grace's shoes.

"We were going for a postmodern, deconstructionist look."

"If this was any more deconstructed, you'd need a FEMA trailer."

She laughed. They both sat down and faced each other across the cluttered office. "Seriously, to what do I owe the honor of this visit?"

"I just wanted to touch base with you, since we're going to be working together on this Davis case."

"Not together, exactly. More like against each other."

"Maybe so." He smiled. "But still, I wanted to check in. It was a rough morning. For everyone."

"Everyone except D'marco Davis." Anna's words were sharper than she intended.

"I know prosecutors don't believe this, but a day in the central cellblock is no picnic. It's a filthy, dangerous place. And now D'marco's behind bars for the next few months, at least until trial. I'd say that's a pretty bad day."

"I doubt a few more months in prison will mean much to a thug like him."

"He's a human being, Anna. He just hasn't had all of the advantages you and I have had."

"Oh, come on." Anna thought about the trailer home her family had moved into after they lost the house. What advantages did Nick imagine she'd had?

"There's another side to the story, you know," Nick said. "You saw how aggressive Laprea got this morning in the courthouse, just from seeing me. She could've started the fight with D'marco."

"Oh come on. I'll bet D'marco didn't have a scratch on him, did he? She's tiny! How much of a threat could she be to him?"

"All I'm saying is, she's no angel. She's got a criminal record that shows she can be violent."

Anna pulled D'marco's file out of the cabinet and handed Nick a printout showing Laprea's criminal history. "She had a couple minor arrests when she was a teenager. No convictions. Then she graduated high school and got a steady job. She's raising two kids with her mother's help—but not much help from D'marco. I wouldn't have a job if everyone in D.C. lived like Laprea Johnson. On the other hand, look at your client's criminal record."

Anna held up the thick rap sheet. D'marco had a string of drug-related arrests. He was on probation after serving a year in jail for armed drug dealing. He'd also been arrested for a series of escalating assaults on Laprea—but never convicted.

"Well." Nick sighed. He kicked clear a spot on the floor, stretched out his long legs, and laced his hands behind his head. "What are we going to do about this?"

Anna liked the way he said "we." Like they were

a team, working to find the answer to a tough problem together. She shook off the thought. There was no "we" here. She and Nick were in as adversarial a position as two people could be. Especially because she felt more invested in cases like Laprea's, where the woman was a longtime victim of abuse but kept going back to her abuser. Men like D'marco just got more violent. If he wasn't stopped, D'marco might very well kill Laprea.

"Your client could plead guilty," she suggested.

"Can't do that. He's on probation for that drug case. So if he gets convicted of assault, he'll get all the backup time in the old drug charge. In effect, he'll serve six years for a crime that carries less than a year. How 'bout a DSA?"

"He can't get a Deferred Sentencing Agreement with his record. You know that's our office policy."

"I guess we'll just have to fight it out in court then." Nick threw his hands up in the air. "Hate to do it—I still remember the trouncing you gave me in Moot Court."

"Hey, I just graduated from law school a few months ago. You've been doing this for two years. It'll be a fair fight."

"I *have* learned a few tricks." His eyes were laughing. What did he know that made him so confident?

Nick sat up suddenly, his attention caught by something on her desk.

"Are those Krispy Kremes?" he asked.

"You want one?" She held out the box and he reached for a chocolate frosted. "I bring snacks to Papering for the police officers. Especially the ones working midnights, who haven't been home yet in the morning. They'll wolf down cookies, candy, even week-old pizza. No one touched these, though."

Nick swallowed a big bite. "Bet it's the stereotype about cops and doughnuts. Mmm," he said, licking his fingers. "Their loss."

She laughed and chose a sugar-glazed.

"Don't fill up now," Nick chided. "You'll spoil your dinner."

"This *is* my dinner."

"Oh no, you're not getting away that easily, Anna Curtis. I asked you to dinner. You said yes. A prosecutor has certain duties of honesty in dealing with defense counsel. Backing out now would be prosecutorial misconduct."

Anna laughed. "I don't think people from my office have dinner with people from your office."

"I'm not trying to make a historic peace accord here."

"I'm just saying. I'm not sure I should go out with you."

"We're not 'going out.' I just want to catch up with an old friend."

She glanced at the clock to have a moment to collect her thoughts. It was just after six; she normally stayed at the office past nine. Having dinner with Nick was probably a bad idea. On a professional level, she was nervous about socializing with a defense attorney. On a personal level, it wasn't wise to spend any more time with an adversary this attractive. She found it hard enough to trust men who weren't on the other side of a criminal case.

"There's no rule that says a prosecutor and a public defender can't talk over food," Nick continued. "Anyway, we won't talk about the case. It's good to see another HLS grad who chose public interest over a firm, even if we are on opposite sides of the courtroom."

Anna thought about how quiet the office got after seven o'clock. Nick was right. There was nothing wrong with them having a meal together.

"What've you got in mind?" she asked.

They went to Lauriol Plaza, a popular Mexican restaurant in the Adams-Morgan neighborhood. Crowds of young professionals gathered there, still wearing their suits. Waiters steered trays of margaritas around clusters of people waiting in the bar area.

Anna and Nick scored a table by one of the big windows overlooking 18th Street. Their waiter arrived with chips and salsa and took their order. When he left, Anna scooped salsa onto a warm chip and smiled at Nick. She had spent so many nights alone at the office, immersed in the worst things that happened in the city. She was glad to be out for a change, surrounded by the happy chatter and bustle.

Nick, she noticed, looked a bit less lawyerlike with his suit jacket slung on the back of his chair and his tie loosened. Anna had draped her own suit jacket on her chair; underneath, she wore a sleeveless ivory shell. She noticed Nick's eyes skimming her bare arms. She looked away and smoothed back her ponytail, suddenly self-conscious.

"So," Nick said, taking a pull from his Corona. "How does a bright and beautiful lawyer from Michigan end up slaving away for a government wage in D.C.?"

She was more touched that he remembered where she was from than by his flattery. "I was never going back to Flint," she said. Too many bad memories. "I looked at a few cities and fell in love with D.C.—its American history, and the idealism of the people who follow politics like you might follow sports."

"But why not go to some fancy law firm? You have something against mahogany desks and six-figure salaries?"

She liked Nick too much to give her half-true stock answer about wanting to be in court instead of reviewing documents in a warehouse. But she wasn't ready to tell him the real reason yet. She guessed it would shock him.

"I wanted to do something good with my law degree," she said. She grinned at Nick as the waiter set down their food. "How 'bout you—did you grow up wanting to set criminals free?"

He didn't seem to take offense. "I like to think that I can see the good in everybody. If I give a voice to someone who might be going down the wrong path, maybe I can help him turn around instead of harden in prison. But let's not talk about work. I have a much more important question: How are those fajitas?"

She laughed. The fajitas were great. Their conversation moved to gossip about classmates and funny childhood anecdotes. Nick told her about mischief he and his friends had gotten into at St. Albans, a private school in D.C. Anna reciprocated with tales of the hearty Midwestern things that East Coast people liked to hear. She told him about GM's annual summer picnic, and how as a nine-year-old she'd gotten in trouble for galloping away on one of the ponies from the pony rides.

"That's when you needed a defense attorney!" Nick said.

They ordered coffee and kept talking long after their plates were cleared. When the busboys started stacking chairs on the tables, Anna noticed with embarrassment that they were the only diners still there. This was the best time she'd had since moving to this city.

Emerging from the restaurant into the cool winter night, Nick asked if he could walk her home. Telling herself they were just two old law school acquaintances reconnecting—certainly not a conflict of interest—Anna pointed Nick in the direction of her apartment, a few blocks away. Although it was a Monday night, Adams-Morgan was still busy. Groups of suited Capitol Hill staffers, interns in high-heeled boots, and Ethiopian men from the neighborhood all vied with each other for elbow room outside the bars and restaurants.

Anna and Nick walked comfortably side by side, talking and joking. She was surprised by how easily she let her guard down with him. Maybe it was the very fact that she was professionally prohibited from dating Nick that put her at ease. As long as they were on opposite sides of a pending case, he wasn't an option—so he was safe. In any case, Anna didn't want the night to end. Too soon, they turned onto Wyoming Avenue, a quiet street lined with trees and stately brick town houses. She pointed to one of the elegant homes.

"It was advertised as an 'English basement' apartment," she explained, pointing down a flight of steps to a subterranean entrance. "I was hoping there'd be fish 'n' chips."

"Nope, 'English basement' is just a fancy way of saying 'medieval dungeon.'"

Anna laughed and looked up at him. Although she was five eight, she still needed to tip her head back to meet his gaze. He had beautiful eyes, brown with green and gold flecks. "I had a lot of fun tonight. Thanks for getting me out of the office."

They stood facing each other, their breaths making cloudy puffs in the cold night air. She found herself leaning forward at the same time he did. Coming to her senses at the last minute, she stepped back and stuck her hand out to shake his. "I'm still not dismissing your case, though."

Laughing, Nick tried but failed to look hurt. He took her hand and held it for several beats longer than a handshake. "Fair enough, but how about dinner on Friday?"

She pulled her hand away. "I don't think so." Her skin tingled where his fingers had touched. She couldn't hang out with him anymore, that much was clear. "Call me if your client wants to plead guilty."

"Mm, not gonna happen. But I will call you when our trial is over."

"Good night, Nick."

She rushed down the little walk, down the three steps to her front door, and let herself in. When she was safely inside, she turned and looked back. He waved and walked away. She contemplated his receding figure. It was too bad they had a case against each other. She hadn't felt so attracted to anyone in a long time.

4

A week later, D'marco Davis sat at a table with his lawyer. D'marco felt calm and relaxed, ready to listen to Nick's advice. He wasn't happy to be back in D.C. Jail, no doubt, but unlike some of the younger men there, he wasn't spooked by his orange jumpsuit, the dull cacophony of other inmates talking outside, or the stale smell of bleach and urine that permeated the facility. He knew how to operate in this world, and he wouldn't be here long anyway. Not on this domestic bullshit. Nick had gotten him out of far worse.

The two men were sitting inside one of the tiny rooms reserved for attorney-client meetings. A small table and two wobbly chairs were the only furniture. The room would have felt claustrophobic except that all four walls were floor-to-ceiling panels of smudged Plexiglas. Identical Plexiglas rooms flanked both sides, all overlooking the jail's even less private visiting area. There, a long bench of young men in orange jumpsuits huddled into phones on one side of a wide pane of glass. Women of all ages—girlfriends, mothers, grandmothers—spoke into phones on the other side. A few children sat on their mothers' laps and sucked their thumbs or knocked on the glass. The men said "I love you" to the women they couldn't touch.

Nick tossed some paperwork on the table, sat back in his chair, and regarded his client coolly. "Couldn't you just be nice to Laprea?"

"She cheatin' on me!" D'marco tried to stoke the righteous fury he'd felt last week. But all he could muster now was sick regret. He hadn't meant to hurt her. She just pushed him over the edge sometimes.

"So leave her," Nick said.

"Naw, you don't understand." D'marco settled his massive arms on the wobbly metal table. "I love her."

"You've got a funny way of showing it. Try chocolates next time."

"Look, I'm sorry, a'ight?" D'marco flashed his most charming grin. "I do better, swear to God."

"Dammit, D'marco. It'd be hard to do worse." Nick held up a probation report. "And you're still on papers. You just had to keep your nose clean for a year."

D'marco snorted. "I ain't kept my nose clean for a year since I been eleven."

"Yeah, laugh. It'll be hilarious when you get convicted of this DV case, and they revoke you. You'll serve the five years left on your drug charge, plus whatever time you get for the assault."

D'marco paused. "Yeah?"

"Yeah. Just like I told you when you got released, not even two months ago."

"Hunh." D'marco grunted to appease his lawyer. But he didn't need a lecture. Nick's job was to get him off, not tell him how to live his life. "So, what's the plan?"

Nick sighed and inclined his head toward the bank of visitors. D'marco followed the lawyer's gaze. A woman was pressing her palm to the glass barrier separating her from her boyfriend; the boyfriend brought his hand against the glass so their fingers matched up. The woman gazed into his eyes, her face full of longing and hope.

"You know how this works," Nick said grimly. "The surest way out of this is if Laprea drops the charges. She loves you, and a big part of her wants to stand by you. You just need to give her a reason."

"Should I tell her not to come to court?"

"No, no." Nick shook his head. "If she reports you, it'll get you an obstruction charge. Don't go telling her not to testify, or to lie." Nick leaned forward and met D'marco's eyes squarely. "Look, you have to rekindle Laprea's good feelings toward you. It'll be harder than before, to do it from jail. But you still have phone privileges."

"What do you want me to say?"

"Just be nice. Remind her why she fell for you in the first place."

D'marco nodded with respect. The man knew what he was doing. The same old plan, but it had always worked before.

The homes on C Street SE were boxy, two-story brick duplexes across the street from Fort Chaplin Park. The park's dense trees provided a surprisingly wooded view for homes in the middle of the city. Inside one of the houses, Laprea sat on a couch between her twins, watching Dameka's favorite movie, *The Little Mermaid*, again. Through the living room window, Laprea could see her mother sitting on the front porch. Rose was talking to their neighbor Sherry, who sat on her own porch next door. The two old friends waved royally to passersby and gossiped about their neighbors: who had a baby on the way, whose boyfriend had made probation, whose son was back from Iraq. Laprea knew Rose wouldn't mention her own daughter's troubles.

The phone rang. "I got it," Laprea called as she picked up the cordless. A computerized voice asked if she'd accept a phone call from D.C. Jail. Laprea hesitated a moment before quietly saying yes. Then she walked into the bathroom, locked the door, and turned on the faucet.

D'marco's voice greeted her warmly. "Hey, baby. It's me."

"D." Wary, Laprea kept her voice neutral. It had been two weeks since the assault. "Why you calling?"

"I just miss you, shorty. I been thinking about you and the kids. How's D'montrae? He ask for me?"

"Every day." Not that he deserved to know.

"What about Dameka?"

"She doing real good in school. Got an award for spelling."

"She take after her mother." D'marco gave a low chuckle. "I miss you all so much. I'm so sorry about what happened, baby. I don't want us to fight like that."

"Me neither." She allowed a tinge of bitterness to her tone.

"Pree, I met this guy in jail, a pastor. We been talking

'bout families and the man's role. Kids need their father. I want to be that. I don't want them growing up without a father, like I did. I'm gonna change, I promise you. I'm not gonna drink. I'm getting job training. I wanna support you and the kids."

Laprea considered his words, wondering whether this time would be different. D'marco sounded sincere. She knew he wanted to be a better man. And she wanted so badly to believe that he could be—wanted the twins to have their father in their lives, wanted this man, the man she fell in love with, to cherish her.

Then she noticed her reflection in the mirror. The bruises around her eyes had faded into a sickly purplish green. The scrapes on her cheek were still pink.

"You hurt me, D. I don't think I can keep going through this."

"Please, Pree, gimme another chance. Every night I lie on the cot thinkin' how beautiful you look when you holdin' Dameka in your lap. How much I want to see that again and hold you." His voice cracked. "I love you, baby."

Laprea started to tear up. But before she could decide how to respond, Rose's voice bellowed through the phone. "D'marco Davis, how dare you call here!"

Great. How long had her mother been listening in? Laprea didn't need the receiver against her ear to hear Rose screaming from the kitchen.

"Don't you *ever* call this house again! If you try talking to my daughter again, I swear to God, I'll whup your sorry hide till you ain't got nothing left to feel pain with! Laprea, you hang up that phone right now!"

Laprea pressed End and threw the phone on the

counter. A moment later Rose was banging on the bathroom door, yelling for her to come out. The twins started shouting, too, their little voices full of excitement and fear. Laprea sat on the toilet, put her head in her hands, and cried.

The phone's insistent ringing tore Anna's attention from the brief she was writing. She looked at the clock: 8:30 p.m. Grace had gone home hours ago. Anna picked up, wondering who'd be calling now.

It was Rose Johnson, and she was furious.

"D'marco called Laprea from jail tonight, Ms. Curtis! I thought you got a stay-away order. What kind of system you running, where a man with a restraining order can call the woman he beat up?"

Anna tried to calm her enough to get the details. As Rose told the story, Anna heard the fear in her voice—the real emotion under her fury. She assured Rose that she would contact the jail and have D'marco's phone privileges revoked. She'd also get a recording of the call. Maybe they could use it against him at trial. In the meantime, D'marco would be stuck in jail with no way to contact Laprea.

"Thank God." Rose sighed in relief. "If he gets through to her, she gonna let him off, just like before."

As she hung up, Anna considered calling Nick and demanding that he instruct his client not to contact Laprea anymore. Would she do that with another defense attorney, or was she just looking for an excuse to call him? She hadn't spoken to him since their dinner two weeks ago. Although he'd called and left her a couple of friendly business-related voice messages, she'd responded with short e-mails addressing business and nothing more. She cringed remembering that she'd almost kissed him outside her apartment. She was a professional, not some tart. Professionally, she didn't need to call him now.

Instead, Anna spent the next hour sending e-mails and faxes to the D.C. Jail, working through the bureaucracy to cut D'marco off from the world. By tomorrow morning, he wouldn't be allowed to use the jail's phones or Internet services any longer. Would Nick be annoyed? Too bad.

When she finally left the office, Anna tried to push her work out of her mind. Grace was always telling her to take a few minutes a day to think about normal, fun, girl things, so Anna read the celebrity section of the *Express* during her subway ride home and tried to concentrate on which actresses had recently adopted children from abroad. When she emerged from the Metro, she made herself window-shop, skimming the fiction titles propped in the window of Kramerbooks and admiring the low riders displayed in the darkened Lucky Brand Jeans store.

But she couldn't stop thinking about D'marco's phone call to Laprea that night. Prosecuting this case, Anna wasn't just up against D'marco, or his lawyer, or the challenges in the legal system. She was in a very real way trying to protect Laprea from herself. Laprea had a history of taking D'marco back and refusing to press charges against him. If she did it again, a conviction would be nearly impossible.

As Anna pushed her apartment door open, her cat

ran over and threw himself against her legs, meowing and purring ecstatically. She scooped up the orange tabby and buried her face in his soft fur. The creature purred even louder. Raffles had been a neighborhood stray that Anna occasionally fed. He'd started meowing outside her door every night until she eventually relented, took him for a thorough deworming, and let him move in. Now she was glad for the company at night.

Most of the time, Anna loved having her own little place, but tonight she felt a wave of loneliness as she turned on the lights. She'd cheered up the basement apartment as much as possible. The small living room was decorated with a bright red couch, colorful Kandinsky prints, and a row of bookshelves sagging under the weight of her books. All the furniture was IKEA; Anna was proud of the fact that she'd put the pieces together herself. A few plants struggled to live in the stingy sunlight of the high half windows. On one of the bookshelves, a framed photo showed Anna, her sister, Jody, and their mother smiling in front of the carousel at the Michigan State Fair. That day was one of Anna's best childhood memories. Anna was twelve in the photo; her sister was ten. Anna held an enormous stick of cotton candy, its pink puff bigger than her head. Jody was in profile—for a decade, she turned her face just enough to hide her scarred cheek.

Anna remembered the bloody crosshatch of scrapes on Laprea's cheek where D'marco had mashed it into a brick wall. Would Laprea turn her face away the next time someone took a picture of her?

Anna looked at the clock, wondering if it was too late to call her sister: 9:55—just under the wire. She set the cat down, grabbed her cell phone, and padded to the galley kitchen at the back of the apartment. As the line rang, Anna rummaged through her pantry until she found a can of chicken noodle soup. She dumped it into a bowl and stuck it in the microwave.

"Hey, it's my long-lost sister!" Jody greeted her. They hadn't spoken all week.

"Sorry, I've been slammed at work. How are you?"

Jody told her Michigan had been hit with a snowstorm, but the GM plant stayed open so she'd made crazy overtime when others couldn't make it in through the snow. While they spoke, Anna ate spoonfuls of soup. They lived such different lives. Jody had cheered Anna through college and law school, and encouraged her to take her dream job in D.C. But Jody seemed content to stay in Flint, working on the General Motors assembly line, like many of their friends. Jody had always been the stronger one. She had nothing to prove to anyone.

Anna knew that much of her own drive was fueled by a need to atone for the unforgivable thing she'd done sixteen years ago in the kitchen of their trailer home. Jody had never berated her for it—in fact, they never spoke about it. Anna suspected they both avoided the topic for the same reason: their friendship might not withstand close scrutiny of what happened. Their relationship felt like the nuclear reactor built on the San Andreas fault line: a good and positive source of energy, always at risk of blowing up if the ground shifted.

"How 'bout you?" Jody asked. "Are you running Washington yet?"

"Hardly." Anna swallowed a mouthful of broth. "In

fact, it's a constant struggle just to keep my cases from falling apart." Anna told her about Laprea and how D'marco was trying to win his way back into her heart.

"Sounds familiar," Jody said somberly. "But is there anything you can do about it?"

"I'll call her tomorrow and give her the 'go team' speech. There's an advocate—she's like a social worker, she helps the victims get resources and support—I'll make sure she keeps in touch. And I'm getting the guy's phone privileges suspended. This won't be like the other times. He'll be totally cut off from her."

"Sounds like you've got it covered." Jody's voice held a smile. "Of course."

As they said good-bye, Anna felt reassured she'd done everything she could. She changed into soft cotton shorts and a tank top, washed up, and climbed wearily into bed. But sleep eluded her. The case kept running through her mind. She knew that however hard she worked, D'marco Davis's defense attorney was working equally hard on the other side.

The next Sunday, Laprea peered out the small window at the top of her front door and watched the MPD cruiser pull off. Rose had taken the children to Sunday school, so Laprea had a few hours to herself, the sort of alone time that was so unusual for a single mother like her. She brushed away a twinge of guilt and allowed a smile to creep onto her face as she replayed the afternoon she'd just spent.

Ten minutes later, as Laprea straightened up the kids' play area, there was a knock at the door. She peered out the window and narrowed her eyes when she saw who was standing there: Nick Wagner.

Laprea no longer felt like yelling at the man who'd so often let D'marco crawl out from under his mistakes without a scratch. Her anger had faded, like her bruises, to a dim memory. And D'marco's recent phone call had softened her. Curious to find out why he was there, she opened the door. The lawyer wore khakis and a light spring jacket instead of the usual suit and tie. He sure didn't want this visit to seem official.

"Hello, Ms. Johnson," Nick said pleasantly, cautiously. "How are you?"

"Okay."

"Ma'am, I'm sorry to bother you here in your home, but— Can I come in?"

"Mmm." Laprea led him into the living room and offered him a seat on the couch. She sat down in the La-Z-Boy and waited to hear what he had to say.

"I really appreciate you letting me in, and I'll try not to take up too much of your time. But I had to stop by because, well, D'marco misses you. And the kids. He's upset that he can't talk to you anymore."

Laprea nodded and kept her mouth shut.

"D'marco really cares about you," he continued. "And D'montrae and Dameka. You know I do, too. I've been involved with your family for a long time; I've seen you stand by D'marco through some pretty rough situations. But if he gets convicted of this assault, he's going to serve all his backup time, all five years. Plus up to a year for the charges in this case."

"So . . . D'montrae and Dameka would be, like, ten when he got out?"

"Right." Nick nodded. "That's a long time for your kids to go without a father in their lives."

"Hm." She hadn't realized that.

"It may be hard to believe, but I really think he's a changed man this time. He's working very seriously at his anger management classes. If he had your support, I don't believe he would do anything like this again. He loves you. He loves D'montrae and Dameka. He wants to be a good father to them. I think counseling, rather than jail, is the answer here."

Laprea wondered if Nick Wagner really believed his words or if he was just trying to chalk up another *W* in his win/loss column. But D'marco had said similar things on the phone. She wanted to believe he'd been sincere, that she could still work things out with the father of her children. Nick's words gave her hope that might happen. Against her better judgment, she let that hope creep into her heart, settle in, and start to grow.

Nick kept talking softly, telling her what made this time different, how their lives were going to be better if D'marco got out of jail this time. She was momentarily lulled by the words she wanted to hear. Then she shook herself out of the reverie.

"Ain't my fault he's in trouble. *He* hit *me*."

"Of course," Nick soothed. "But . . . you know that they can't even *have* a trial if you don't come to court."

She noticed that he didn't come right out and tell her not to show up for trial. Laprea had enough experience with the system to know lawyers could get in big trouble for doing that.

"Well, it ain't up to me," Laprea said flatly. "They sent a policeman with papers saying I gotta show up."

"A subpoena. So they may make you testify, whether you want to or not."

Laprea expected him to ask her side of the story then—but he didn't. Instead, he launched into the defense theory. "If it happened this way . . ." he started, and then he outlined different facts that would make a good defense for D'marco. None of them were true. She noted how deliberately the lawyer phrased things—never asking her to lie, but just telling her what might help D'marco, hypothetically, if that was what happened on the day of the assault. He was covering his own hide, she saw that—but she listened all the same.

Laprea wasn't making any decisions now. She just listened carefully, storing it all away for consideration at a later time. There were still weeks left before the trial.

The sound of a key rattling in the front door startled them both. Laprea stood quickly and looked around the living room as if she could find a place to hide the defense attorney. Rose walked into the house trailed by the twins, who were chattering about their Sunday school lessons. Rose stopped in her tracks when she saw Nick getting up from the couch.

"Get out." Rose didn't yell—probably didn't want to frighten the children—but there was no mistaking the steel in her voice, and no questioning her authority.

Nick slipped past Rose, murmuring apologies.

"Come back here again," Rose said, "I'll call the police."

As soon as he was gone, Rose turned toward Laprea. "What that man say to you?"

For just a moment, Laprea had been taken in by the

lawyer's smooth voice and pretty promises, but now that her mother demanded an explanation, she couldn't fool herself.

"Slick talk and lies," she said, going into the kitchen to fix lunch for the kids. "I don't even know why I let him in."

5

The morning of Laprea's trial, Anna couldn't find a single witness in her case. "Officer Green!" she shouted, trying to make her voice heard over the din of the witness room. Weary police officers stood gossiping with each other about last night's foot chase through the Sursum Corda housing complex. At the counter, four snot-crusted children clung to a fat woman waving a subpoena at the bulletproof Plexiglas and demanding to speak to the Attorney General. Less assertive civilians waited in rows of plastic chairs for prosecutors to call their names. Prosecutors rushed to talk to as many people as they could before the nine-thirty trial call, when they would have to tell a judge whether their witnesses were present and the government was ready for trial.

Anna finally found Brad Green in the hallway outside the witness room. He was absorbed in conversation with one of the newer DV attorneys, standing close to her and smiling deeply into her eyes.

"Officer Green, have you seen Laprea Johnson?" Anna didn't have time for pleasantries.

He shook his head. From their guilty looks, Anna guessed the officer and lawyer hadn't been talking about a case. She sighed. In the three months since they first met, Anna had learned that Green was something of a player, a cop who enjoyed the attention the uniform brought. Well, he could flirt all he wanted—on his own time.

Anna was heading to the desks behind the counter to call the Johnson household when she spotted Rose walking up the hallway. Relief turned to concern when she saw that Rose's eyes were red and she clutched a tissue. Anna hurried down the hall to greet her.

"Hi. What's wrong, Ms. Johnson?"

"Laprea's not coming. I begged that girl. She say she won't testify against her babies' daddy. She don't want to be responsible for him going to jail for five or six years."

"It wouldn't be anything *she* did that makes him go to jail. He's the one that hit her."

"*I* know that," Rose snapped through her tears. "I'm here."

Of course. It wasn't Rose who needed convincing. Anna nodded.

"Can't *I* just say what happened?" Rose asked. "Laprea told me. I can testify."

"I wish it were that easy. But you didn't see what happened yourself. Anything Laprea told you would be hearsay." Anna turned to Green. "Officer, I need you to go to Laprea Johnson's house and pick her up. If she's not there, go to her job, the Department of Labor cafeteria. Remind her that she's been subpoenaed. That's a court order. She has to come to court, or else she'll be arrested on a material witness warrant."

"Yes, ma'am," Green said happily. Some cops might

have grumbled, but he appeared glad to get out of the courthouse on an official mission.

Anna looked at Rose. "I hate to threaten her with arrest like that, Ms. Johnson, but it may be the only way to get her in here today. If she doesn't show up, the case will be dismissed."

Rose took a deep breath, then nodded. "Thank you, Ms. Curtis."

The seats were filling up as Anna and Grace walked into the courtroom. Anna couldn't resist glancing around for Nick Wagner. Since their one dinner together, she'd studiously ignored him in the courthouse except for the bare minimum of polite contact necessary for doing business. She had thought about him regularly, though, and knew some of her nervousness this morning was in direct anticipation of facing him head-on today. But she didn't see him in the crowded courtroom yet.

Friends and family of the various defendants eyed Anna and Grace hostilely or hopefully as the prosecutors wheeled their briefcases through the spectator section. The men wore baggy jeans and T-shirts. The women wore colorful acrylic fingernails, elaborate shellacked hairdos, and—fat or slim—skintight pants. Everyone showcased their tattoos. The days of wearing your Sunday best to court were gone. Every day in Superior Court was casual Friday.

A fleet of uniformed police officers sat scattered among the friends and family; there was no bride's or groom's side. A handful of probation officers and defense attorneys sat in the front rows, scanning their files before the judge took the bench.

Although D.C. Superior Court was the training ground for some of America's most renowned litigators, this windowless courtroom had seen better days. Yellow foam poked out through tears in the scuffed beige fabric covering the jury box and judge's bench. The thin brown carpeting had worn out in patches along the most trafficked areas. An irregular brown stain spread across several fluorescent light panels, where, according to legend, a rat had gotten trapped and died.

"All rise!" the courtroom clerk called.

There was a flurry of noise as everyone stood up. Judge Nancy Spiegel strode to the bench, her black robe flapping in her wake. She was an attractive woman in her midforties, with curly brown hair and a permanent vertical crease between her eyes. She appeared to be in no worse a mood than usual.

The judge began calling the cases that were up for trial that day. If the victim had shown up and was still cooperative—two big ifs—or if the prosecution could prove the case without the victim, Anna and Grace called "ready." All the "ready" cases would be tried later in the day. If they didn't have the necessary witnesses, they called "not ready," and the judge dismissed the case. The defendants in those cases were immediately released.

On the domestic violence docket, the prosecutors were "ready" about half of the time, an impressive number by national standards. By the time of trial, the vast majority of DV victims had gotten back together with their assailants and refused to cooperate with the prosecution. Prosecutors expected this, and tried to build cases they could win even without a victim willing to testify—but it was often impossible.

Anna knew that without Laprea's testimony, she couldn't make the case against D'marco Davis.

Anna glanced back into the audience to see if Laprea had arrived. She saw that Nick had taken a seat in the front row with the other defense attorneys. He smiled as Anna glanced over him. She tried to ignore the way her stomach dipped as if she'd reached the top of a roller coaster. She wondered if Nick was smiling because he was happy to see her or because he knew his client was about to be released. She nodded at him but didn't smile back.

"Calling the case of *United States versus D'marco Davis,*" the judge intoned. The deputy led the defendant out into the courtroom.

Anna took a hard look at D'marco. Although she'd been thinking about him for two months, this was the first time she was seeing him in person; because of her office's rotation system, other prosecutors had handled D'marco's prior hearings. The guy was enormous. Tall as his lanky lawyer, D'marco filled out his orange jumpsuit like a linebacker. His arms emerged from the short sleeves in a ropy clump of muscles, and his hands were big as dinner plates at the Outback Steakhouse. He wore his hair in cornrows running from his forehead to the back of his skull, where they fell in skinny braids that brushed the top of his shoulders. D'marco greeted his lawyer, then scanned the faces in the audience. He smiled. He knew what it meant that Laprea wasn't there. Then he turned to the judge, bowed his head respectfully, and said in a soft, polite voice, "Good morning, Your Honor." The guy was a pro.

The judge asked Anna the question of the day. "Ms. Curtis, is the government ready to proceed with trial in this case?"

Without Laprea, Anna couldn't call "ready" for trial. Her chest constricted at the idea that D'marco was going to walk away. She opened her mouth to say "no" when she felt someone tapping on her shoulder. Officer Green had returned. He whispered in Anna's ear and pointed to the last row, where Laprea was taking a seat. Anna heaved a sigh of relief.

"Thank you," Anna whispered.

"Go get 'em," Green replied.

"The government is ready for trial," Anna announced. She looked to see D'marco's reaction. He stared straight ahead, stone-faced.

As Green turned around to take a seat, Judge Spiegel looked up at the officer and smiled for the first time that day. "Ms. Curtis, I see you've called in the A team," she said without looking at Anna. "Good morning, Officer Green," she purred. If she didn't know better, Anna would've sworn the judge was batting her eyes at him. The officer returned the greeting and the two bantered for a moment.

Anna looked at Nick. A smirk played on his lips. He wasn't surprised by the camaraderie between judge and police; he was both amused and pissed off by it.

The judge finally turned back to her docket, noting

that D'marco's case would be the first trial of the day, beginning in about an hour. Grace covered the rest of the calendar call so Anna could speak to Laprea.

"I can't do it, Ms. Curtis. Please don't make me," Laprea pleaded with Anna. They were standing in the small meeting room off the entrance of the courtroom. Rose sat in one of the scuffed plastic chairs, her arms crossed on her chest, while Green hovered in a corner.

"Three months ago, you were begging me to get D'marco locked up," Anna said. "Do you really want him to walk out of here today? He'll just keep hurting you. And if he knows there are no consequences, the beatings will just get worse."

Laprea looked at the ground. Part of her understood that this was true. But today she was filled with hope.

"It's going to be different. He's in anger management. He's doing job training."

"Didn't he do that before?"

"I don't expect you to understand. But he's my babies' father. What good is it for my kids to have their father in jail? He just want to be there to see D'montrae and Dameka grow up. They need him."

"It'd be better for them to grow up without a father than to see him beating on their mother all the time," Anna replied emphatically.

"All due respect, Ms. Curtis, but you don't know my life."

Anna paused. She realized what Laprea saw when she looked at Anna: a white woman buttoned up in a suit, someone from a completely different world. Anna wanted to tell her it was all a veneer. *The suit, the law degree, they don't matter. Inside, we are more alike than you know.* But she couldn't find the words, and the moment passed.

"It's not all his fault," Laprea said softly. "I'm partly to blame."

"It is his fault!" Anna exclaimed in frustration. "No matter what you think you did, you don't deserve this!"

Rose spoke up. "I ain't never seen no bruises on D'marco."

Laprea turned to her. "Mama, you know how hard it is. Some men just want to get in your pants and then that's it, they done. D'marco want to be in my life. He want to take care of me and the kids. I am *not* gonna stop that."

Anna was brimming with frustration. She had to excuse herself and step out of the little room to clear her head. She walked to the back door of the courthouse and stepped out onto the concrete patio. It was early May, and she inhaled the scent of damp earth as she paced, oblivious to the smokers standing under the eaves.

Sometimes, Anna let a case be dismissed if a victim asked her to drop the charges. She considered doing that here. Laprea wanted it. Some people argued that it was paternalistic to pursue a case against the victim's own wishes. Anna didn't want to override Laprea's decision; it was important for the woman to feel that she had some control over her own life.

A memory flashed, unwanted. Anna saw her mother's face, the fear in her eyes when her father came home after another night at the bar. Alcohol seeped from his pores. Anna and Jody crouched under the table as their father held his belt, the one with the big pewter buckle, looped in a leather coil.

Anna shook off the image.

Laprea's children were four years old. Soon they would start internalizing their father's violence—and be more likely to replicate it. Dameka would be at risk of becoming an abused woman; D'montrae would be more likely to become an abuser. Anna wished someone had made her mother testify against her father back when Anna was four. Back when it could've made a difference.

She wasn't dismissing this case. She needed to protect Laprea, even if Laprea didn't want her protection at the moment. Anna believed she knew what was best for her, better than Laprea did herself.

Anna returned to the room where Laprea and her mother sat in stony silence. She crouched by Laprea's chair.

"I'm sorry," Anna told Laprea softly, "but I'm going to have to call you to the stand. I hate this part of my job, making someone do something they don't want to. But I saw what he did to you. I can't let this case be dismissed."

Laprea nodded in resignation. They would both do what they believed was right. But it wouldn't turn out as either of them intended.

6

Ms. Curtis, please call your first witness," the judge said.

They had already gone through opening statements, which were always short in a bench trial. In misdemeanor cases, where a judge decided the defendant's guilt, there was no place for the big speeches of a jury trial. Anna had just laid out the basic facts and charges: D'marco was charged with assault and threats for the post–Valentine's Day attack, and contempt of court for telephoning Laprea from jail. Nick reserved his opening statement, choosing not to tip his hand yet.

"The government calls Laprea Johnson," Anna said. Grace sat at the prosecution table next to Anna. She was on the record as cocounsel, but she was really just there for moral support. She smiled encouragingly at her friend.

Laprea climbed to the witness chair, raised her right hand, and swore to tell the truth. Anna led Laprea through the preliminary questions. Yes, Laprea knew a man named D'marco Davis. He was the father of her four-year-old twins. They had been seeing each other romantically, on and off, for the last five years. Yes, she saw Mr. Davis in the courtroom. Yes, she could identify him: there he was, sitting in the orange jumpsuit next to his lawyer. Laprea looked right at D'marco as she was asked to point him out. They smiled at each other across the courtroom. Anna should have known what would come next.

"Ms. Johnson, did something unusual happen between you and Mr. Davis on the morning after Valentine's Day this year?"

"Yes, it did."

"Please describe what happened."

Laprea paused for a few seconds before answering. She looked down at the microphone in front of her. D'marco stared at her intently. Nick was writing something on his legal pad.

"Well . . . we had plans for Valentine's Day, the night before. He was gonna take me out, but he never came around. I thought he was out with another woman. So when he came by my house the next morning, I was angry. We got to fighting. I grabbed a butcher knife and I said I was gonna kill him. He ran out the house and I chased after him with the knife. I caught up to him in the front yard and I tried to stab him. That's when he hit me, to stop me from stabbing him. I fell down and scraped my face on the ground."

Anna stood there, stunned. Although she hadn't expected happy cooperation, she hadn't expected Laprea to lie. Anna stared at Laprea. The young woman couldn't meet her eyes.

Anna looked around the courtroom, gauging everyone else's reaction. D'marco sat back in his chair, trying to conceal his glee. The judge looked unsurprised; this sort of thing happened in the DV courtroom all the time. Grace grimaced and shook her head. Nick continued writing.

Anna cleared her throat. Maybe she could still save the case. She would have to impeach her own witness. "Ms. Johnson, didn't you tell me and Officer Bradley Green, right after that incident, that you had not raised a hand to D'marco?"

"I made up that story because I was mad at D'marco. I was trying to get back at him because I thought he been with another woman. I lied to you."

Anna inhaled sharply. That answer wouldn't just tank this case, it would forever taint Laprea's credibility. If she were ever a victim again, a good defense attorney would obtain a copy of this testimony to show that she was an admitted liar.

Anna switched tacks. She wouldn't ask about the assault anymore, because Laprea would just continue lying. But Anna could still get D'marco on the contempt charge.

"Has the defendant been in touch with you since he went to jail in this case?"

Laprea looked at Anna, considering the question for a moment. There were some facts Laprea knew she couldn't avoid. D'marco's calls from jail were taped.

"Yes."

"And has he tried to get back together with you?"

"It's not just him. We *both* interested in working things out. For our kids."

"So, you want to continue your relationship with the defendant?"

"Yes."

"You love him."

Laprea looked at D'marco and smiled. "Yes, I do."

"You don't want to see him go to jail, right?"

"That's right."

"And you'd do whatever you could to help get him out of these charges?"

"I wouldn't lie."

Grace shook her head; Anna had gone one question too far.

"Ms. Johnson, the defendant called you from jail about a month ago, correct?" Anna was asking leading questions, which were usually prohibited during direct examination, but Nick wasn't objecting. Things were going too well for the defense.

"That's right."

"And you spoke to him for several minutes that day, isn't that right?"

"Yes."

Anna opened the case jacket and rummaged through the papers until she found the envelope containing the recording of the jail call. Her hands shook as she inserted the cassette into the tape recorder and hit Play.

D'marco looked amused as his voice saying, "Hey, baby," came out of the machine. The judge glared at him as his recorded voice tried to wheedle his way back into Laprea's heart. On the tape, Laprea was ambivalent. From the witness stand, she looked at her boyfriend tenderly, as his promises of love and devotion purred from the tape recorder.

Anna switched off the tape before it got to the part where Rose chewed him out. That wasn't relevant. "Ms. Johnson, at your request, there was a restraining order against the defendant, right?" Anna held a copy of the order up, so Laprea could see there was no getting out of this one.

"Yeah, that's true."

Anna read from the papers. "And that order said that he couldn't contact you 'in any way,' correct?"

"It did say that. But, actually, I wanted him to be able to call me. I missed him. So I visited D'marco in jail and told him the order had been lifted. It wasn't his fault. It was mine."

Anna felt as though the wind had been knocked out of her. She looked at Grace helplessly. They both knew that Laprea's testimony wasn't true, but there was no way to disprove it now. Grace motioned her hand in a slicing horizontal move: cut your losses. Every time Laprea opened her mouth, things got worse. "Nothing further." Anna sat down, defeated.

The defense had no cross-examination. Why would they? Everything they could have possibly wanted Laprea to say had come out during the prosecution's own questions.

Anna tried to salvage the trial, but it was a futile effort. Laprea's testimony had destroyed any chance of a conviction. Anna called Officer Green to the stand, but he couldn't say whether Laprea had pulled a knife or not. Although he could testify that she had told him a different story the day she received her injuries, he had no personal knowledge of what had actually happened.

With no other witnesses to call, Anna rested her case. Before Nick could even start his, the judge interrupted. The defense didn't need to put on any witnesses, she said. The prosecution couldn't possibly meet its burden of proof. There was no evidence to contradict Laprea Johnson's testimony. Based on that, the assault was in self-defense, there were no threats, and the defendant did not have the *mens rea,* the intent, to violate the restraining order because he reasonably thought it had been vacated.

Anna nodded miserably. This kind of ruling was not uncommon in a bench trial, where the case was decided by a judge rather than a jury. After hearing all the government's evidence, Judge Spiegel had concluded—reasonably, Anna had to admit—that there was no way the government could win. The court still had three more trials to get through today, so she was cutting this one off now.

"As such," Judge Spiegel concluded, "I have to find the defendant not guilty of the crimes charged." The judge looked at Anna. "Ms. Johnson's testimony today is obviously not what you believe to be the truth, but it leaves me no choice. Deputy, please return the defendant's personal belongings to him and release him immediately."

Anna splashed cold water onto her neck and looked at herself in the bathroom mirror. Pull it together, Curtis. She wouldn't let herself cry, but she needed a minute to calm down. She went into the only stall with a working lock and sat on the toilet, fully clothed. She rested her elbows on her knees, her head in her hands. She'd come so far—all that education, all that time preparing to be in a position where she could finally help—and she was still powerless.

After a few minutes, the restroom door opened and Anna heard the familiar clack of designer heels.

"Anna?" Grace called, concerned.

"I'll be right out." Anna tried to sound chipper. She flushed the toilet to make it sound like she'd been engaged in legitimate bathroom business. She stepped out and tried to smile at Grace. "What a mess, eh?"

"Total train wreck," Grace agreed sympathetically. "I have to hand it to your victim, though. That was some clever exculpatory testimony. Someone's been coaching her." She squeezed Anna's arm. "Are you okay?"

"Yeah, I'm fine." Women around here were built Ford tough; Anna would not admit that she'd come in here because she was too upset to stay in the courtroom. She headed to the door.

"Good. But do me a favor and fix your hair before we go out there."

Anna stopped and looked at herself in the mirror. No wonder she wasn't fooling Grace. Her hair stuck out like pieces of straw from her ponytail, and her forehead had two red marks where it had rested in her hands. She pulled out her hair band and shook her hair out. Grace chatted while Anna redid her ponytail.

"You know this was not your fault." Grace's voice was briskly soothing. "Eighty percent of domestic violence victims get back together with their boyfriends by the time of trial and recant their testimony."

Anna nodded wearily. She should have seen this coming.

She took one last look at herself in the mirror. Her hair was neat but there was nothing she could do about the pink marks on her forehead, like a steer that had just been dehorned. She turned to Grace, palms up.

"You look great," Grace lied soothingly.

They headed back to the courtroom, where they still had to handle three remaining trials.

"It's a badge of honor in some neighborhoods for a woman to lie for her boyfriend, to show how much she loves him," Grace mused as they walked. "Once Laprea decided to do that, there wasn't much you could do. She wanted him to get a walkaway."

"It's not what she'll want next time he uses her as a punching bag."

Nick was coming down the hall toward them. He wore a victorious grin. Great, Anna thought, I can watch him gloat. But when he saw Anna, Nick's smile disappeared. He walked over and stood in front of her like a schoolboy with an apple for the teacher.

"You did a good job," Nick said. "It takes guts to go forward with a recanting victim. Most prosecutors would have dismissed the case without trying."

"Thanks." She nodded at him and kept walking. She wasn't sure what was worse, Nick gloating or Nick politely not gloating. Either way, she couldn't talk to him now.

When Anna and Grace reached the lobby, Anna could see Laprea standing outside the glass entranceway, in the brick plaza in front of the courthouse. Anna froze midstride. D'marco, looking relaxed and confident, was walking out of the side door where prisoners were released. He had on the street clothes he'd worn the day he was arrested: a black North Face jacket, baggy jeans, and Timberland boots. Anna could see some dark stains on his jeans—dried blood from Laprea's face, Anna realized. But Laprea didn't seem to notice it. She smiled as her children's father sauntered over and embraced her. He held her for a long time, stroking her braids.

Grace shook her head. "Poor girl. The cycle of violence continues. I hate to say it, but you'll get him next time."

"I just hope next time isn't too late." Anna stood watching the couple, worst-case scenarios playing out in her head. "I should've found a way to protect her."

Laprea and D'marco turned together and walked toward the Metro, his arm draped around her shoulders, her arm hugging his waist. They looked like a nice couple. She gazed up into his face with hope; he looked down at her tiny figure with tenderness and gratitude. It was the last time Anna would see Laprea Johnson alive.

7

Tiny white lights twinkled from the trees inside the cavernous atrium, casting a warm glow on the white marble floor and pillars. An enormous bouquet of exotic flowers towered in the center of the lobby. The arrangement alone probably cost more than Anna's monthly rent. Scattered tables held silver warming dishes filled with miniature lamb chops and grilled asparagus, while white-gloved waiters walked through the crowd offering trays of hors d'oeuvres and glasses of wine. The lobby echoed with hundreds of well-bred voices, as young lawyers clustered in small groups to describe the powerful coattails they were riding. The Harvard Law School recent-grads happy hour was well under way.

Anna stood in a group of women, twirling her glass of white wine. She was half listening to a stunning redheaded lobbyist describe the advances of a lascivious congressman, and half gawking at her surroundings. The law firm of Arnold & Porter was hosting the happy hour, giving HLS alumni an opportunity to be impressed with their luxurious digs. Six blocks away from D.C. Superior Court, this was a different universe.

A waiter came up behind her and offered a tray of sushi. As Anna turned to take a piece of spicy tuna roll, she saw a familiar face. Nick Wagner stood one group away, smiling tentatively at her. Anna couldn't pretend not to see him. She raised her piece of maki in a fishy salute and turned back to her group. He had called her a few times since the trial, but she had ignored his voice-mail messages. She wasn't ready to talk to him. Moments later, he was standing behind her. Anna's chest tightened when she felt his presence.

"I was hoping I'd see you here," Nick said.

"Why?" She turned slightly to face him, but didn't move to allow him into her circle.

"I need someone to remind me why we work in Superior Court instead of signing on with Arnold and Porter. I don't know about you, but I could get used to sushi every night."

She didn't crack a smile. "Something about doing justice and serving the public, I think. Or, in your case, doing injustice and endangering the public."

Nick laughed. "I hope you're not still mad about that case, Anna. You did a great job. Laprea just didn't want her boyfriend to go to jail. She made that decision—it wasn't a decision you or I could make for her."

"How's D'marco Davis doing?" Anna asked sharply. She'd tried calling Laprea a few times since the trial, two months ago, but Laprea wasn't taking her calls. Laprea had no interest in talking to her.

Nick answered cautiously, knowing he was close to a danger zone. "He's actually doing well. He has a place of his own and perfect attendance at his job training and anger management classes."

"Has he been able to keep his hands off Laprea?"

"There haven't been any problems. I really think he's on the right track."

"Come on, Nick. You know he's not going to change. How could you defend him?"

"Everyone deserves a good defense."

"That's a nice idea in the abstract. You see what happens in real life."

"The whole system is stacked against these kids, Anna. I grew up just a few miles from D'marco Davis, but I probably got away with more as a teenager than he did. If a kid in Potomac smokes some weed, no problem, he goes to Princeton. In Southeast, the police are everywhere. The same kid with the same weed gets caught and now he has a criminal record. He can't get a job, so he turns to drug dealing. And a lot of the cops are brutal and dishonest. The system is just fucked up. Anything I do to help these kids evens things out a little bit. People need some leeway to figure out what's right and wrong without the coercion of a corrupt police state."

"Bullshit." Anna glared up at him, feeling her cheeks flush with anger. "If your father was beating the crap out of your mother, you'd be pretty damned happy if someone—anyone—stopped him. So don't tell me about 'coercion' and 'corrupt police states.' Those are naïve, anarchist ideas bandied about by people who have no idea about the reality of domestic violence."

She knew this was neither the time nor the place to talk about her family, but his smug superiority infuriated her. Nick was looking at her quizzically, obviously wondering what personal experience she claimed made her more qualified on the topic than him. Before Nick could reply, the redheaded lobbyist interrupted with a trill.

"Anna, introduce us to your cute friend!"

Anna tried to calm herself as she reluctantly allowed Nick into the circle and made the introductions. The women all turned to the newcomer eagerly. The lobbyist eyed Nick like he was another tasty little lamb chop. Anna felt a twinge of possessiveness, and was immediately annoyed by it.

The redhead tossed Nick the usual question Washingtonians ask when they first meet each other: "So, where do you work?"

"I'm a public defender."

That got a little "ooh" from the crowd. Nick grinned; Anna scowled.

"Wow!" The lobbyist widened her eyes. "Can that be dangerous?"

"The only danger is me boring my clients to death. Telling them about classes they can take. Anger management, job training, that sort of thing. A lot of these kids just need a little push in the right direction. No one's ever cared enough to give them that before."

Kids! He made them sound like orphans, not felons.

"Do a lot of your clients turn their lives around?" Anna asked sarcastically.

"Actually, you'd be surprised." He saw her raise her eyebrows. "You don't see the happy endings, Anna. You only get the cases when something goes wrong. When a guy goes straight, he doesn't have files at the U.S. Attorney's Office anymore. You guys just don't hear about him again."

Anna felt a bit chastened. She hadn't thought of that before.

"Even if a client doesn't reform right away, it's

important for me to be there for him," Nick continued. "These kids see the whole world stacked against them. It means a lot to know someone's in their corner."

"It must be so satisfying, helping poor kids like that!" The redhead looked like she wouldn't mind satisfying Nick, too.

"Yeah. It's not always pretty. But I love my job."

The women kept asking questions about his work, and Nick answered with eloquence and passion. Anna was skeptical of Nick's image of himself as a knight in shining armor, heroic defender of liberty. There were terrible, brutal men who didn't deserve liberty, who would only use their liberty to inflict pain on other people. But at least she was getting a glimmer of understanding about how Nick could do his job.

"So, how do you two know each other?" the redhead asked.

"Anna kicks my butt all around Superior Court." Nick smiled at Anna. "She's been schooling us defense attorneys since she got there. Get her autograph now; someday it'll be valuable."

The women murmured their approval. Anna smiled into her wineglass. She was still annoyed, but she wasn't immune to the power of a public compliment.

The group continued to chat, comparing their jobs, arguing politics, and dishing on local scandals. The redhead tried to flirt with Nick, but he was focused on Anna. Whenever a waiter with sushi passed, Nick flagged him down, making sure she had as much as she wanted. Her anger softened. The Curtis family history wasn't his fault. Neither was Laprea's decision to lie on the stand. Nick had just been doing his job. Anna accepted another glass of wine, feeling her cheeks grow warm as the alcohol took effect. She started to relax and enjoy herself. Their banter was clever and lighthearted, a break from the bleak facts she dealt with every day.

When a waiter offered Anna a third glass of wine, Nick turned to tease her.

"The secret to a good happy hour is equal parts alcohol and caffeine. You could use a cup of coffee. Maybe three cups. Come on."

Anna laughed. She could feel the women gazing at her back as she followed Nick to a table set up with a silver coffee urn and a pyramid of gold-rimmed porcelain mugs. Nick poured the coffee and they stood next to each other, cradling their mugs and surveying their opulent surroundings.

Anna turned toward him. "I'm sorry I jumped at you, Nick. I guess I'm still a little sensitive about that case."

"I'm sorry I gave a lecture on corrupt police states. Luckily, there will be no quiz."

"Forgive and forget?"

"It's a deal." Nick grinned. "Listen, you could use some real food. Are you willing to leave with a naïve, anarchist defense attorney—who doesn't have a case against you anymore?"

"I thought you'd never ask."

He took her to Bistrot du Coin, a charming French café in their neighborhood. They both ordered steak and fries and shared a nice bottle of red wine.

"I'm going to need a whole pot of coffee to maintain your alcohol-to-caffeine ratio," Anna said with a hiccup.

"I just said that to get you out of that crowd," Nick said, refilling her wineglass. "Now that we're alone, I think you should stick to wine."

She laughed. Nick told her the most scandalous courthouse gossip—he'd collected some great stories in his two years in Superior Court—letting her into a world she'd only glimpsed from the sidelines. He said there were rumors that Judge Spiegel and Officer Green were having an affair. They had worked on a case together a few years ago, before Spiegel was elevated to the bench, and were thought to be romantically involved then. Although Green had dated several women after that, he and the judge had remained close friends, maybe more. As Nick mimicked pillow talk between the judge and the cop, Anna couldn't stop laughing.

When they were done with dinner, Nick offered to walk her home. Her cheeks flushed with wine and laughter, she happily accepted. Anna tucked her hand in the crook of his arm and they laughingly stumbled toward her place. It was a warm summer night, and the streets of Adams-Morgan were even busier than usual. She felt some pride as people watched her walk by on the arm of the ridiculously good-looking attorney.

En route to her house, they approached a fancy new steel and glass condo building in the hottest location in the neighborhood, set a few meters back from the bars and restaurants of 18th Street. The ten-story structure loomed over the older brick town houses. Anna had heard that each unit cost over a million dollars. She wondered aloud who lived there.

"Actually"—Nick looked a little embarrassed—"I do." He paused, considering whether to ask his next question. Finally, he turned to her and smiled. "Would you like the grand tour?"

Anna understood that this wasn't an invitation to see how his kitchen was tiled. She gazed at Nick's face, the absurdly long eyelashes framing his hazel eyes, the chiseled cheekbones setting off his perfect smile. With his long, loping stride and mischievous grin, he looked like a cross between a young John Cusack and Jimmy Stewart. She loved Jimmy Stewart.

Her mind was fuzzy from the wine. But one thought stood out clearly and cleanly.

She wanted him.

She had for a long time. Although her sober self would have raised rows of mental hurdles—she shouldn't date a defense attorney, she didn't know him well enough to be alone with him, she should take this slow—the wine submerged these objections, leaving only her desire to answer the question of whether she wanted the "grand tour." The answer was simple.

She nodded.

Nick held the lobby door open for her, and Anna tried not to be overwhelmed by the space as she walked in. The lobby conveyed both Zen-like tranquility and pricey industrial chic. The floor and walls were black granite; the ceilings soared. An abstract steel sculpture towered in the middle. A wall of windows at the back framed a Japanese garden, where hidden lights illuminated a waterfall and koi pond. The male receptionist, dressed entirely in black, looked too much like a Calvin Klein model to possibly be straight.

The reception desk, opaque glass balanced on stacked rocks, held a bank of televisions, computers, and switches that suggested the building was equipped to make a landing on Mars. As they passed the desk, Anna caught a glimpse of herself and Nick walking by on one of the TV screens in the desk. His hand rested lightly, possessively on her lower back. They looked like a real couple.

"Heeey, Nick," the receptionist trilled, the singsong in his tone communicating that he found Nick's late-night company very interesting.

"Hey, Tyler." Nick ushered Anna into the brushed-steel elevator. He hit the "PH" button. "He's a nice guy," Nick whispered to Anna as the doors shut. "But he's not on the tour."

Inside, Nick's condo was like something from a modern architecture magazine, with gleaming wood floors, a two-story ceiling, and floor-to-ceiling windows overlooking the shining white obelisk of the Washington Monument in the distance. A floating metal staircase led to the second story. A fireplace made of stacked slate separated the living room from the kitchen, its rock walls going all the way up to the high ceiling. Black leather couches and an impossibly thick white rug were arranged in front of the fireplace.

"Did you kill a polar bear?" Anna asked, pointing at the rug.

"No, just a helpless little alpaca. I got it in Peru." He took her hand and led her to the hearth, where she bent down to touch the soft fur.

Nick pushed a button hidden in the slate, and flames whooshed up in the fireplace. Anna stood up, laughing.

"Do you have a mirror that comes out of the ceiling, too? Maybe a vibrating bed?"

"You think I'm putting the moves on you?"

Anna nodded. "Not that that would be such a bad thing."

Nick gently turned her to face him. He cupped her cheek with his hand, tracing her chin with his thumb.

"Anna, I've wanted to do this since law school."

He slowly brought his face to hers. His breath was sweet and warm. Anna's stomach flipped as his lips softly touched hers. All of her muscles tensed, then slowly relaxed. She melted into his body and drew him closer. He stroked her face with the back of his hand, then trailed his fingers down her neck and shoulder blades. She mirrored his touch, her tongue lightly exploring his, her hands wandering over the lithe muscles of his chest and stomach. Between kisses, Nick whispered that she was beautiful, stunning, exquisite, incandescent. She smiled and whispered back that he was a thesaurus.

She knew that his flattery, his wine-plying, his Rico-Suave bachelor pad were all part of a seduction game plan, and she wondered how many times he had used these moves before. Still, she was into it. She felt warm and tingly, relaxed yet excited, and very aroused. Warmth spread through her belly as he massaged the small of her back.

Kissing him, she pulled off his tie and unbuttoned his shirt. He deftly peeled off her clothes and then his own, so expertly she hardly noticed it, and lowered her onto the white rug. Anna giggled at the feel of fur on her back. She looked at Nick's body as he stretched out next to her. He was lean but athletic, with the long, sinewy muscles of a runner. His skin glowed golden in the firelight.

She closed her eyes again as he brought his mouth to hers. He trailed his fingers down her neck, over her clavicle to her breasts, where he traced butterfly-soft circles across her nipples. She moaned as his tongue followed and elaborated the trail his fingers had made. He covered her stomach with gentle caresses and flicks of his tongue, exploring the hollow of her belly, the gentle rise where her hip bones protruded, the downy-soft ticklish crease where her thighs met her hips. As his head went farther down, she pulled him up by his shoulders.

"No, Nick," she murmured, concerned not with her reputation or virtue, but when was the last time she'd had a bikini wax.

"Anna, I've been fantasizing about this for a long time. You wouldn't deprive a desperate man of his fantasy, would you?" He kissed her lips as his fingers stroked where his mouth had been headed.

Anna sighed and shook her head as waves of pleasure rippled up her spine. She relaxed and let him do what he wanted, which, it turned out, was exactly what she wanted. He slowly descended again, bringing his mouth between her thighs, using his tongue and fingers to explore her, first gently and then with building pressure and urgency. Anna arched her back and cried out as she climaxed.

Nick paused for a moment, letting her catch her breath.

"Do you have a condom?" she breathed at last.

"Don't worry," he whispered.

She looked down, and saw that he was already wearing one, although she hadn't noticed him taking it out. This man is a virtuoso, she thought, or some kind of evil genius. She pulled him up toward her, desperately wanting to feel him inside her. He smiled, resisted her pull, and lowered his head between her legs again. He made her come that way again, until she was clawing at his shoulders, begging him to come inside her.

Finally he did, covering her body with his own, saying her name softly as he slipped inside her. She gasped at the pleasure of his penetration. When she could breathe again, she opened her eyes. Nick was still, supporting himself on his elbows, cradling her head between his hands. Their faces were inches apart, and he was looking directly into her eyes. She felt a different kind of thrill as she gazed at him. It was a moment of perfect silence and connection, more intimate than anything that preceded it. Finally, he groaned, closed his eyes, and started slowly spiraling his hips. She wrapped her legs around his waist and moved with him, pulling him deeper inside of her. She let go of everything else—her crazy work and her crazy family and all the complications of living in the world—and just felt this: this pleasure, electricity, intimacy. They came together in a final explosive orgasm that left Anna breathless and shaky.

Nick rolled to his side, pulling her with him. They lay facing each other, foreheads touching, their long, athletic legs tangled like linguini. She became aware again of the soft rug under her skin, the crackling fire warming her bare back. Nick was stroking her hair, smiling at her drowsily. Her body was saturated with contentment, and gratitude, and a dozen other emotions she didn't have names for. Or maybe just too much wine. In any case, she knew that if she tried to say what she was feeling, she would sound corny and trite.

So she joked, "I've never been this close to an alpaca before."

8

Anna raised her head from the pillow, disoriented. This was not her bedroom. She looked around. This was way nicer than her bedroom. The floor was polished wood, the walls were ivory, the furniture was dark wood with modern lines. She was lying in a king-sized bed covered with a dark brown comforter. Light poured in through a sheer white shade that covered a wall of floor-to-ceiling windows; she could see the vague outline of the Washington Monument through the translucent fabric. Anna sat up and brought her hands to her throbbing temples. Her mouth felt and tasted like an old sweatshirt. As she recognized Nick's black leather briefcase in the corner, images from the previous night flashed back. She groaned.

Oh Lord, what had she done?

She heard the front door open and muted footsteps downstairs. Seeing him in the light of day was going to be awkward. She might as well get it over with. She slowly swung her legs off the side of the bed. Her whole body ached, and she didn't see her clothes anywhere. Damn. There was a soft white bathrobe draped on a chair next to the bed. Anna pulled on the robe and shuffled to the master bathroom.

It was bigger than her living room, and tiled in light

brown stone. A huge Jacuzzi sat under a skylight. She found a tube of toothpaste by the sink, put a dab on her finger and ran it over her teeth, then bent to the faucet and rinsed her mouth out. Her tongue still felt fuzzy but at least it was a minty fuzz. She ran her fingers through her tangled hair. It was the best she could do for now. Taking a deep breath, she walked out of the bedroom, emerging onto the landing at the top of the loft.

Nick looked up from where he was setting bags down on the kitchen counter below.

"Good morning, sleeping beauty," he called cheerfully. He was wearing khaki shorts, an orange T-shirt, and flip-flops, and was obviously less hungover than Anna.

"Hi." She suddenly felt shy.

"Come on down." Nick smiled. "The alpaca misses you when you're way up there."

Anna descended the steel staircase. "I wouldn't want to upset the alpaca."

Nick pulled out a stool and gestured for her to sit at the black granite countertop. "I figured you could use this."

He set a Starbucks cup in front of her. She smiled and sipped the latte, feeling her headache recede a fraction as the caffeine hit her bloodstream. It was exactly what she needed. She looked around the kitchen. It was gorgeous, all dark wood and stainless steel and granite. The floor-to-ceiling rock fireplace was at her back.

From one of his shopping bags, Nick pulled out a box with the words JULIA'S EMPANADAS written on it. It was from a little Salvadoran joint down the street. Anna smiled with delight as she selected one of the miniature meat pies.

"I love these," she said.

"Me too."

Nick watched her savor a bite. Then he settled next to her at the counter and they polished off the box of empanadas. Anna sat back at last, full and content, her hangover obscured by a cloud of happiness. She studied Nick. He looked adorably unlawyerlike with tousled dark hair and an unshaven face.

"So," Nick ventured. "Whatever happened to that guy you were seeing in law school?"

"Josh? We were talking about moving in together once we both got to D.C."

"I always thought he was a smart guy."

"But he got a clerkship in Atlanta. He's staying there."

"I always knew he was an idiot."

Anna laughed. "No, he's a good guy. It just turned out we weren't serious enough to change cities for each other."

In fact, Josh was one of the sweetest men Anna had ever met—which made him utterly undatable in the long term. Anna realized in college—when she was on the Dean's List and her boyfriend was getting expelled—that she had a tendency to fall for bad boys. Ever since, she tried to choose nicer men. With Josh, she'd oversteered. He was so nice as to be totally uninteresting. They'd parted ways exactly as they'd dated—amicably and without passion.

"What about you?" Anna volleyed. "I seem to recall that you had plenty of female attention at law school. All those groupies at your guitar gigs in the Hark. Has there been anyone special since then?"

"Not till last night."

She looked at him curiously, wondering if this was a standard line, as she was sure the "grand tour" was. Nick stood next to her stool and gazed down at her upturned face for a minute. He leaned down and kissed her. "Anna, I'm crazy about you."

Anna felt her body respond to his touch now and to the memory of the night before. She'd expected this morning to be awkward, but she felt natural with Nick, completely at ease. All traces of her shyness had disappeared. She deepened the kiss, pulling him toward her.

After a moment, he drew back an inch to ask, "What are you doing today?"

It was a Saturday morning. Although she'd planned to go to the office today and work on some files, she figured that could wait.

"Well." She regarded him mischievously. "You promised to give me the grand tour, right? But I think we only covered the rug and the bed." Anna ran her fingers down his chest and stomach to his shorts, where she caressed the growing bulge. He sucked in his breath and nodded, watching as she stroked him. "I don't think we hit that nice Jacuzzi in your bathroom." She let her bathrobe fall open as she gathered his T-shirt to pull over his head. "I'd like to be thorough."

If her life were a movie, Anna thought, the next few weeks would have been the falling-in-love montage. The time flew by in a dizzy whirlwind of late nights in the office interspersed with later nights with Nick. Most evenings, she would stop by her apartment long enough to give her cat some kibble and a pat, then rush over to Nick's place. When she spent the night with Nick, they didn't sleep much; they were too busy exploring each other's bodies. Between her long hours at work and overtime in Nick's bedroom, she was constantly sleep-deprived, but fueled by euphoria. After a few days, Nick ceremoniously presented her with her own toothbrush in the cup next to his bathroom sink. She never thought she'd be so delighted to receive the gift of oral hygiene.

They didn't advertise their relationship, and they were especially discreet at work. They both knew they would catch flack from their colleagues when it came out. Romances between the U.S. Attorney's Office and the Office of the Public Defender were unheard of. So Anna and Nick kept their interactions to after-work hours, and simply nodded at each other and tried not to smile too broadly when they passed each other in the courthouse. Grace sensed that something was up, but she didn't pry. She would wait until Anna was ready to explain why her cheeks flushed pink every time her cell phone buzzed with a text message.

Nick wanted to show Anna everything, to share his city and his life with her, and he ferried her all over D.C. like the enthusiastic host of a TV travel show. They went to the trendiest bars and the best restaurants, rushing home afterward to make love. He took her hiking at Great Falls, to a baseball game in his father's box at Nationals Park, to the Kennedy Center to see *Wicked*. They spent a weekend at St. Michaels, a resort town on Maryland's eastern shore, where they lounged on a sailboat, lazily ate crabs drenched in Old Bay, and then thoroughly christened the four-poster bed at The Inn at Perry Cabin. She hadn't known about this side of Washington—this happy, picturesque side, where beautiful people with perfect teeth played and relaxed. She hadn't known she could feel this strongly about someone in such a short time. She was falling in love with Nick.

They had no other cases against each other. Most of the time, she could forget that Nick worked on the opposite side of the courtroom. Once in a while, something reminded her with a thud.

One hot July day, they were driving to the Jefferson Memorial for a picnic by the Tidal Basin. Nick had lowered the convertible top of his BMW 650i, and Anna breathed in the fresh air. The whole city was carpeted with colorful flower beds, and her hay fever started to kick in. She opened the glove compartment, looking for tissues. Instead, she found a dull black handgun.

"Jesus, Nick!" She yanked her hand away as if it had been scorched.

Nick looked over, saw the glove compartment open, and stretched over her lap to shut it. She waited for him to say something, but he just kept driving.

"What are you doing with a gun in your car?" she demanded.

He sighed. He obviously didn't want to get into this with her. She kept staring at him.

"Look," he said, after a few moments of uncomfortable silence. "I have it for self-defense. When *you* go into Southeast, you get a police escort. I go by myself. I hadn't planned on getting a gun, but a client gave it to me, and it's been comforting to know it's in there when I have to go into a rough neighborhood."

"There's a law against carrying handguns in D.C."

"You've read *Heller.* The Supreme Court says that law is unconstitutional."

"It's still illegal to have an unregistered firearm."

"That's debatable. C'mon," he said, placing his hand affectionately on the back of her neck. "Are you gonna turn me in? Stop being a prosecutor for a minute."

"Nick," she said at last. "This makes me really uncomfortable. Can you please get rid of it?"

"Okay."

She studied his profile, wondering if he was just agreeing to shut her up. She decided to take him at his word. Of course she wouldn't turn him in—so long as he agreed to do the right thing now.

"Thank you. And one more favor. Don't let me stumble across any more of your work product, okay? The less I know about your job, the less likely we'll need couple counseling."

"You've got it."

Anna kept thinking about the gun, though, as Nick parked in a lot near the Jefferson Memorial; as they walked down the tree-lined path to a grassy spot by the Tidal Basin; as Nick spread out the blanket and their lunch. What was she doing dating a defense attorney? Their worldviews were too far apart. Anna tore a chunk off the loaf of French bread and absentmindedly broke off pieces, throwing crumbs to a family of ducks swimming by.

"Those are the most spoiled, overfed ducks in America," Nick teased. "You're contributing to the city's duck obesity epidemic."

"It's okay. I gave to the duck aerobics foundation."

He laughed and pulled her toward him. "Come here, you gorgeous duck philanthropist."

He kissed her, softly at first, then deeper. She forgot their differences. His lips lingered over hers as water lapped at their feet and the sun warmed her shoulders. She was filled with happiness.

Most of the time, things were so good, Anna didn't think about their jobs when they were together. They had a great time, even if they were just renting a movie and eating microwave popcorn. Nights were the best. She loved curling up with Nick after making love, feeling his chest rise and fall against her back while she drifted to sleep.

A few nights after their picnic, something woke her while it was still dark. She cracked open her eyelids and found herself lying in bed facing Nick. He was awake and looking directly at her. The streetlights outside his building cast a dim yellow glow in the bedroom and made Nick's eyes look bigger and darker than usual.

"Can't sleep?" she murmured, her own eyelids drifting downward again.

"The view's too good for me to be unconscious for it."

The words were his usual flirty teasing, but his tone was different. His voice was sincere.

She opened her eyes. Nick was gazing at her with absolute tenderness. His expression shook her. She thought of him as one of the "bad boys" she knew she should avoid, a charming game player who, at best, would use her until she stopped being fun for him. With Nick, she was like a chubby kid eating ice cream. She understood how bad he was for her—but he was so delicious. She'd rationalized that her present happiness might be worth the future pain.

Now, though—the way he was looking at her—she could see she had been wrong.

Nick loved her.

There was no question about that.

Anna felt a lump in her throat. She reached out to stroke his hair. As her fingers skimmed his temples, she felt a slight bump. She drew her hand away and saw a thin scar, two inches long, just under his hairline. It was a silvery line in the bedroom's dim light. She hadn't noticed it before.

"What's this from?" she whispered, touching the scar.

"Hm." His mouth turned down a fraction. "A car accident. I was eight."

"What happened?"

"My dad was driving through the city."

Nick paused.

"Did he hit another car?" she prompted.

Nick rolled onto his back and laced his hands on top of his head. Anna propped herself on an elbow so she could see his face. He was staring at the ceiling.

"No," Nick finally answered. His voice was soft but tight. "There was a kid on a bike. A black kid, maybe fifteen years old. He darted out from between a couple of parked cars. My dad braked hard and swerved. I wasn't wearing a seat belt, and my head went into the dash."

"Oh, Nick, that's terrible." She looked at the scar on his forehead. "You poor thing."

"I was all right. It was the kid who was hurt. We clipped him."

"Was he okay?"

"I'm not sure." Nick swallowed. He turned his head

so he was looking at the window. The city lights were dim halos through the sheer curtains. "The last I saw, he was lying in the street near the curb. My dad drove away."

It took a minute for Anna to process the information.

"Jesus. Did your father get in trouble?"

"Guys like my dad don't get in trouble for shit like that. He got his lawyer or somebody to get a copy of the police report. Saw that they didn't have his license plate or the make of his car. It was a bad part of the city. Nobody would be able to track him down. So he got the dents hammered out and the car repainted. And that was that."

Anna stared at Nick in horror.

"Did you ever find out who the kid was? Or what happened to him?"

"No. I was a kid myself." Nick closed his eyes. "I thought I saw him a couple times. Once when I was in the neighborhood for a case. Once in the hallway in Superior Court. But it was never him."

Anna's chest ached. Nick had been looking for that kid his whole life. Her understanding of Nick lurched for the second time that night. He wasn't just a pretty boy using his public defender podium to hold court at cocktail parties. He was trying to right his father's wrongs. He was doing the best he could to escape the mistakes of his family.

Just like her.

Anna wanted to heal Nick somehow, to make everything better for him, to protect him from the world.

She realized that she loved him, too.

She cupped his cheek, gently turned his face toward hers, and kissed his scar.

On a sunny Saturday in August, Nick told her he scored tickets to see Wilco playing a sold-out outdoor concert at Wolf Trap that night.

"Oh no, I can't go," Anna cried. "I have book club tonight."

"Book club? I'm with a woman who would give up Wilco for a night of reliving AP English class?"

"Well . . . we do have wine. And cheese."

"Oh, cheese—now it all makes sense. All right, I understand when I've lost to a bunch of women wearing trendy glasses. I'll let the tickets go. But for this afternoon, at least, you're mine. Pack for a day at the pool."

Anna wore a bikini under her tank top, and tossed a paperback novel, sunglasses, and a tube of Coppertone into a bag. Nick loaded some snacks into his car, lowered the convertible's top, and drove north on River Road into Potomac, Maryland. Her hair blowing in the breeze, Anna gawked as they passed mansion after mansion on sprawling, perfectly manicured lots. The front lawns, covered in elaborate flower beds and the occasional fountain, looked like cover pages for *Martha Stewart Living*.

Nick turned his car down a long, tree-lined driveway, which brought them to a huge house with a stately circular drive. The house was made of red brick, with a slate roof, blue shutters, and three chimneys. Anna supposed it would be described as a "colonial," although it was ten times larger than anything a colonist would have built. The lawn was the texture, color, and size of a football field. Centuries-old oak and maple trees bordered the property on both sides, and two deer were grazing on the lawn.

"My parents are in Europe for the summer," Nick said, as he began unpacking the car. "But I had the housekeeper open the pool. It's all ours today."

She gathered her beach bag out of the backseat. "Are you sure this house is big enough for us?"

He laughed and took her hand. "Come on."

Anna followed him into the house, trying not to reveal how out of her league she felt. She had recently seen a magazine spread with pictures of the interior of the White House; it could have been this home. Oil paintings hung in elaborate gold frames; Persian rugs lay under antique furniture; crystal vases perched on the mantel of a marble fireplace. Everything smelled of leather ottomans and lemon-scented furniture polish, and felt perfectly untouchable. Anna slowed down to look at photographs in silver frames atop a grand piano. She held on to Nick's hand, tugging him back to her.

"Is this you? You're so cute in braces!" she exclaimed, pointing to a picture of a coltish twelve-year-old Nick holding a lacrosse stick and flashing a silver grin.

"Ugh." He groaned. "That was not my finest hour."

He tried to pull her away, but she was fascinated with the photos. One showed young Nick wearing a child-sized tuxedo, standing with his parents. His father was a tall, bald man wearing his own tux and a Cheney-esque smirk. His mother looked like Grace

Kelly in her Monaco days, with chickpea-sized diamond studs and blond hair swept into an elegant updo. Anna scanned the other family photos: mom holding a tennis trophy, dad in a khaki hunting vest with a rifle crooked over his arm and a dead stag at his feet. Mostly, the pictures showed Nick's father with a series of politicians: shaking Ronald Reagan's hand; in conversation with the elder President Bush aboard Air Force One; duck hunting with a group of patrician gentlemen.

"What does your father do?" Anna asked as she studied the photos. She felt Nick's hand tense in her own. She straightened up and faced him.

"He exploits the poor and pillages the earth, at taxpayer expense. He's a lobbyist."

"I sense some hostility," Anna ventured softly.

"Fuck him," Nick said. "He's no fan of my work either."

Anna could sense the satisfaction Nick felt when he smashed his father's expectations by joining OPD instead of a corporate law firm. She glanced around at the untouchable furniture and the empty house. Maybe even wealthy kids could have tough childhoods. She squeezed Nick's hand.

Nick led her to the back of the house, through French doors that opened onto a broad slate patio. Cushy white lounge chairs were scattered around a deep blue pool. A sunken hot tub burbled next to a large stone cabana.

"Wow," Anna whispered.

Nick grabbed a couple of fluffy white towels from the cabana, and spread them on two lounge chairs he pushed together. "Make yourself comfortable," he said.

She pulled off her tank top and shorts, and kicked her sandals under the lounger. Nick whistled. She turned to him bashfully, suddenly embarrassed by the skimpy lavender bikini, although he'd seen her in less.

"You like?" she asked shyly.

"*Oh* yeah." Nick's eyes were round saucers of appreciation. Every yoga class and jog she'd ever taken was worth the look on his face.

He pulled out a couple of Diet Cokes and a bag of pita chips, and they settled onto the loungers. Nick paged through the *Washington Post* and munched on chips. Anna held her book on her lap, but didn't read it. She breathed in the clean, grassy air and looked at the beautiful yard. The sun warmed her skin, and the sound of the burbling hot tub lulled her into a drowsy haze. A dragonfly buzzed by her head and landed on her big toe. It fluttered its iridescent wings and then stilled.

Anna reached for Nick's hand, and he turned to look at her.

"Happy?" he asked.

"Completely blissed out."

He moved to the edge of Anna's chair and brushed a strand of hair out of her eyes.

"I love you," he said softly.

She smiled. She'd been thinking of saying these words for a while.

"I love you, too."

He leaned over and kissed her. She pulled him closer, losing herself to the feeling of the warm sunlight on her skin and Nick's chest pressed against hers. She wondered how much happiness one woman could take.

9

As Anna lounged on the deck chair a few miles away, D'marco Davis sauntered down the sidewalk to the corner store. It was a beautiful summer afternoon. Pigeons strutted in front of the Chinese takeout place that everyone called Mr. Wong's. Dandelions grew from cracks in the gum-stained sidewalks. Even the graffiti on the plywood of boarded-up row houses seemed cheerful. D'marco was in a good mood.

He'd meant it when he told Laprea he would change, and so far, he'd lived up to his word. He had stopped drinking, and now he didn't have to waterload when he went to give his urines. His probation officer had noticed his change of attitude, and said she'd help D'marco get a good job—data entry, behind a real desk—not the usual sandwich-making or barbering apprenticeship. Maybe D'marco would really get out of the drug business this time. He wanted to be around to see his kids grow up. He'd save up, he mused, move to a decent place, ask Laprea and the kids to come live with him. They would be a family. Today, anything seemed possible.

A bunch of guys were hanging out by the Circle B; like D'marco, they all wore long white T-shirts and baggy jeans. They stood talking and smoking; a few sipped from bottles wrapped in brown paper bags. D'marco shook hands with an older man in an electric wheelchair and greeted a few friends. Then he walked into the dim quiet of the little store.

Samir, the owner, recognized D'marco and waved at him from behind a wall of bulletproof glass. D'marco nodded back and strolled around, contemplating what to eat. The Circle B wouldn't give 7-Eleven a run for its money anytime soon, but it had a niche as the only convenience store brave enough to operate in one of D.C.'s worst neighborhoods. It was a narrow room with a concrete floor and three bare lightbulbs. A few flimsy metal racks held boxes of gum, candy bars and chips, and staples like soap, diapers, and shampoo. A coffeemaker sat on a foldout table coated with a sticky stratum of sugar and powdered creamer. Samir gave coffee free to cops, hoping to entice the police to hang around his store. Bottles of soda and colorful fruit drinks were lined up in the narrow fridge. D'marco grabbed a bag of potato chips and an orange soda.

When he got to the counter, Samir had already pulled down a pack of menthol ultra-lights and three scratch-off lottery tickets. D'marco appreciated that. "Anything else?" Samir asked through the microphone on his side. D'marco looked longingly at the bottles of liquor beckoning from the shelves behind the counter, but he shook his head. He was turning over a new leaf. He slid a twenty through the metal tray, and Samir returned the tray with the cigarettes, lottery tickets, and change. As an afterthought, D'marco pointed to a fabric rose in a clear plastic cylinder. He'd bring something nice for Laprea tonight.

As he walked out of the store, D'marco nearly ran into Ray-Ray, who was walking in. Ray-Ray greeted him enthusiastically. "D!" The two men clasped hands, touched shoulders lightly, and pounded each other on the back. They'd grown up a few houses from each other. They weren't blood relations, but they were so close, they were like family; D'marco considered Ray-Ray a playcousin. D'marco motioned for Ray-Ray to come outside with him, and the two men stood in front of a stoop a little ways away from where the other men stood. D'marco opened his pack of cigarettes and offered Ray-Ray a smoke. Ray-Ray took a cigarette gratefully.

D'marco studied Ray-Ray as they lit up. Same old Ray-Ray. He was as tall as D'marco, but where D'marco was thick with muscles and moved with a slow confidence, Ray-Ray was skinny as an alley cat and always hyped up on nervous energy. His dreadlocks were tied loosely back, revealing a few scars on his lean neck. D'marco knew the story behind each of those scars—but he didn't know Ray-Ray's given name. To D'marco and everyone D'marco knew, he was just Ray-Ray.

"You gonna hit it tonight?" Ray-Ray asked.

"What you talkin' about?" D'marco smiled and took a long drag on his cigarette.

"That rose." Ray-Ray pointed at the plastic container that D'marco had rested on the ledge behind them.

"It's for Pree. We back together."

"For real? After she got you locked up?"

"Nah, she did good. In the end. She testified that I ain't done nothin' to her."

"Man, I was you, I'd *fuck* that cop up."

"Man, he didn't do nothin'. He just doin' his job after she called the police."

"Nah, D, not *that* cop. The one who been fuckin' Laprea when you was locked up."

D'marco regarded Ray-Ray with slitted eyes. He blew smoke out of his nostrils in two thick gray lines. When he managed to speak again, his voice was low and full of danger.

"The fuck d'you just say?"

Ray-Ray nervously kicked an empty soda can back and forth between his feet. He hadn't meant to break any bad news. "You . . . uh . . . you ain't heard? Forget it. Can't trust no rumors anyway," he added lamely.

To Ray-Ray, it looked like D'marco stood silently for a moment, smoking his cigarette down to the filter and watching the traffic go by. But inside D'marco's chest, his heartbeat went from an idling car to a thundering steam engine. His body temperature rose four degrees; what had felt like a warm afternoon suddenly became a scorcher. Waves of heat shimmied in front of his eyes, blurring his vision. He felt sick and furious and dizzy. He dropped the cigarette butt to the sidewalk and ground it beneath his heel. Ray-Ray watched worriedly as D'marco stalked back into the Circle B.

Later that evening, Laprea sat on Dameka's bed with the twins snuggling on either side of her. She let D'montrae turn the last page of the book. There was a cartoon of a prince and a princess riding two white horses into a sunset. "And they lived happily ever after," Laprea read. "The end." Dameka sighed with happiness. D'montrae begged his mother to read *The Cat in the Hat.* "No, sugar, I was for real, that was the last one. Bedtime." She scooted D'montrae into his own bed and tucked them in, kissing both twins good night.

As she turned off the light, D'montrae called out, "Mommy? Are you gonna see Daddy tonight?"

"Yeah, baby, I am."

"Tell him I drew him a picture of us with the panda."

"That's so nice, sweetie. You can give it to him tomorrow, okay? Good night, baby dolls. I love you."

Laprea quickly changed out of her mommy clothes and into her girlfriend clothes: a shimmery pink T-shirt that stretched provocatively over her Miracle Bra, and a pair of tight black pants. She had to really suck in her stomach and pull at the fabric to close the pants' top button. She would go on a diet tomorrow, she thought. A scary idea slithered through the back of her mind. She paused, then pushed it aside. She'd deal with that tomorrow, too. She put on big silver hoop earrings and high-heeled silver sandals, then spritzed some perfume into the air and walked through the sweet cloud. She was excited. D'marco was taking her to a movie. She quietly jogged down the stairs and opened the front door to head out.

"Laprea?" Rose was sitting in the La-Z-Boy, knitting and watching television. Laprea sighed. She'd hoped to pass unnoticed.

"Yes, Mama?"

"You goin' to see that boy again?"

"You know I am."

"Humph."

Laprea hesitated, her hand on the door. Then she walked over to Rose and sat on the couch. "He's bein' so good, Mama! You wouldn't hardly believe it. He's sober now, and he's great with the kids." She leaned forward, full of enthusiasm. "We taking them to the zoo tomorrow. Will you come?"

"Humph."

Laprea looked at her mother for another minute. Rose didn't take her eyes off the television set. Laprea shrugged and walked to the door. "Bye, Mama," she called. She skipped down the porch steps.

As Laprea got to the sidewalk, a movement in the house made her glance back. Rose had gotten up from the television and was standing at the window, holding back the curtain to watch her only child walk away.

Laprea caught a bus and got to D'marco's building on Alabama Avenue a few minutes later. She wrinkled her nose as she walked down the hallway on the second floor. She'd been here a lot lately, but she still hadn't gotten used to the smell. Residue from years of cigarette smoke and frying food permeated the walls. Half of the hallway lights were out, paint peeled from dingy gray walls, and cigarette burns dotted the faded carpet where it wasn't worn out completely. The building was a dump, but tonight Laprea didn't care. D'marco was taking her out!

When she got to apartment 217, Laprea tapped on the door, practically dancing in place. D'marco opened it, looked down at her silently, and turned back inside without a word. He flopped down on the couch and stared at the TV, blaring an R. Kelly video. The living room of the one-bedroom apartment was sparsely decorated with a secondhand couch, a cheap coffee table, and a box of court documents in one corner. A huge flat-screen TV dominated the room. Laprea suspected how he'd gotten it, but she'd never flat-out asked. She didn't want to know.

"Hi, baby." She leaned down and gave him a kiss. Immediately, she smelled the alcohol on his breath. She pulled up sharply. "You been drinking?"

He gestured to a bottle of Wild Turkey on the table.

"Oh no, D, you was doing so good. What happened?"

He stared, expressionless, at the TV. "Heard you been seein' someone else."

The hairs on the back of her neck stood up. She should leave, now. She looked at the door. It was about fifteen feet away. She started backing toward it. "No, D."

He took a slug from the bottle. "I hear you was getting real cozy with MPD while I was locked up."

She shook her head and moved faster. "No. No, I wouldn't do that."

D'marco flew from his seat and grabbed her by the shirt. It was how he always started.

Ernie Jones glanced at his watch. "Damn," he muttered. It was 9:38 p.m. He was probably going to be late. He'd been working the janitorial graveyard shift at the Washington Hospital Center for thirty-six years, and he took pride in being on time to work. It seemed he was slowing up these days, though. Ernie supposed that made some sense; his sixty-first birthday was approaching and no part of him seemed to move as fast as it used to. But he didn't want an excuse—he wanted to be on time. He stuffed his keys into his pocket and hurried out of his apartment. If he didn't have to wait long for the bus, he could still make it.

The elevators were broken, so he headed to the stairwell at the end of the hall, shaking his head at the building's perpetual state of disrepair. As Ernie approached apartment 217, he could hear shouting and banging from inside. It was the new guy's apartment, and from the sound of it, he was having trouble with his girlfriend. That was none of Ernie's business. If he got involved in every bit of domestic drama in this building, he wouldn't have time to lead his own life. He didn't slow his stride.

Suddenly, the door to apartment 217 flew open and Laprea Johnson came flying out. Ernie stopped himself short as the woman ran out in front of him. She might be pretty if she wasn't so messed up, Ernie thought. Now, her braids were disheveled, her pink shirt was torn at one shoulder, and a gash from her forehead to her cheek had swollen her left eye shut. She didn't seem to notice Ernie.

"Liar!" she shouted at the man emerging from the apartment. "You promised me! You supposed to be in anger management!"

D'marco Davis emerged from the apartment. The enormous man was enraged. His hands were shaking with anger, and his nostrils flared. "You ain't supposed to be such a cheating bitch!" he roared. He held a bottle of Wild Turkey in one of his huge hands.

Laprea pointed to her face. "What am I gonna tell the twins? And my mother?" She was hysterical. D'marco took a step toward her, and she started beating on his chest with her tiny fists. He pulled back his hand, the one without the liquor in it, and backhanded her casually, like someone shooing a fly. His knuckles connected with her cheekbone with a sharp cracking sound. She collapsed to the floor.

"Hey, hey!" Ernie stepped between them. "They's no need for that."

"Get the fuck out the way," D'marco said, never taking his eyes off of Laprea. "This ain't none a your concern."

"Come on, now." Ernie put his hand on the man's elbow and tried to steer him back into the apartment. "It ain't worth all that, son."

D'marco furiously yanked his elbow away—and punched Ernie in the face. The older man staggered back, holding his cheek in shock and pain.

On the floor, Laprea caught her breath and started sobbing. Her other eye was swelling now, too. She stared up at D'marco, who glared down at her contemptuously. With effort, she pulled herself up to her feet. She tried to say something, but was so racked with sobs she could barely speak. Finally, she forced out the words between convulsions.

"That's it, D'marco. We done. I am calling the police and you going to jail this time. I don't care how much backup time you got. And you ain't never gonna see the kids again." She turned and fled down the hall to the stairwell. "Never!"

D'marco set his bottle down on the floor and walked

after her, glaring at Ernie. Ernie stepped back, holding up his hands to show he wouldn't get in the way anymore.

"Wait up, Pree!" D'marco called in a low, rumbling voice. "Come on, shorty! I didn't mean it." He jogged down the stairs. His calls echoed through the stairwell for a minute, then faded out.

Ernie pulled out his cell phone and dialed 911.

The next day, D'montrae ran through the house singing, "We're going to the zoo-oo! We're going to the zoo-oo!" He held aloft his drawing of the panda, letting it flap in the breeze he was creating. Dameka sat at the kitchen table with a box of Crayolas, drawing in her coloring book. Rose opened the oven and basted the pot roast she was making for Sunday dinner. Her eyes went to the clock for what seemed like the hundredth time that day. It was 2:00 p.m. Rose hadn't heard from Laprea since last night. The knot in her stomach twisted tighter.

Dameka looked up from her coloring book. "When are Mommy and Daddy coming to take us to the zoo, Gramma?"

Rose closed the oven and tried to smile reassuringly. "Later, baby. In a little bit."

She wiped her hands on the dish towel and looked out the window, considering what to do. She had already called Laprea's friends and checked with Sherry. No one had heard from her. Rose had even tried D'marco's phone, but he wasn't answering.

She knew something was wrong.

While the twins played in the kitchen, Rose picked up the cordless again. She walked out onto the front porch and closed the door so the children couldn't hear her. She dialed 311, the police nonemergency line, and cleared her throat as the operator answered. "I'd like to make a missing person's report," Rose said quietly. "It's my daughter."

Later that afternoon, Andre Hicks trotted through the parking lot with his friends, a rowdy bunch of nine-year-old boys. One of them tried to shove him into a parked car, and Andre laughed, punching the kid in the arm. Bored by the scant amusements in their apartment complex, the boys were taking a shortcut to the Circle B to get sodas and whatever action they could stir up.

They loped up the curb, into a scraggly wooded lot behind their apartment building. This shortcut had the advantage of passing a mountain of garbage heaped several yards back from the parking lot, in the middle of the reedy trees and brush. The garbage pile contained old chairs, broken appliances, worn-out toys, and hundreds of garbage bags. People threw stuff back here if it was too big for the trash chutes or when the chutes got too full to handle more garbage. A few times a year, someone would complain loudly enough, and the city would send the sanitation department to clear the debris. In the meantime, it was a treasure chest for the neighborhood boys. A few months ago, one of Andre's friends had found a stash of *Playboy*s in the garbage heap. That boy had been a hero for weeks afterward as they'd all pored over the pictures.

They'd almost passed the trash heap when Andre saw something pink glittering from a hole in a black garbage bag at the bottom of the pile. He slowed his stride, falling behind his friends as visions of *Playboy*s danced in his head. Andre stooped down to investigate. Was it some inexplicable contraption from Victoria's Secret? A toy? He grabbed the ragged edges of the hole and tore the garbage bag open. The pink thing was a lady's shirt. A small brown hand rested, motionless, on the shimmery cloth. There was still a lady inside the shirt. Andre started to scream.

10

As soon as Anna got to work Monday morning, she sensed that something was wrong. Everyone seemed to be staring at her as she walked in, as she waited for the elevator, as she headed down the hall to her office. Oh God, she thought, they know about Nick. Well, she'd known she would have to face the issue at some point. She supposed today was as good a day as ever.

As she walked into her office, Anna found Carla Martinez standing there, rummaging through a box labeled CLOSED FILES.

"Hi, Carla." Anna greeted the chief of the Domestic Violence and Sex Crimes Section with surprise. Carla had never been in Anna's office before. None of Anna's cases were significant enough to merit a visit from the chief. Oh no, Anna thought, even Carla knows about Nick. Still, as Carla straightened up, Anna had to admire her boss's peach suit, peep-toe pumps, and perfectly coiffed brunette bob. The woman always looked like she stepped off the pages of an Ann Taylor catalog. Anna's plain black pantsuit—which had felt so sharp and professional a minute ago—felt boring in comparison.

"Oh, Anna, I'm so sorry," Carla said. The chief

walked over to give her a hug. Anna accepted her boss's embrace with confusion and dread. Carla had never hugged her before; she didn't seem the hugging type. When she pulled back, Carla saw the puzzlement on her employee's face. "Oh dear," she murmured. "You haven't heard. Anna, I'm so sorry to have to tell you this. Laprea Johnson was killed over the weekend."

Anna sat at the big conference table in shock. People were talking, but she wasn't processing the words. This is my fault, she thought. The phrase kept running through her head. *This is my fault. If I'd done a better job on the case, Laprea would be alive.* That poor woman. And her poor children. What would their lives be like now? Their mother not only gone, but killed by their own father. Their tragedy was nearly incomprehensible.

Anna was in the formal conference room adjacent to the office of the U.S. Attorney. It was the nicest conference room in the office, decked out in top-shelf government decor. The table was made of polished stone and wood; the floor was covered in a plush blue carpet; an American flag stood next to the U.S. Attorney's seal on the back wall. Framed photos of postcard views of D.C. hung around the room.

Several of the photographs showed tourist sights Nick and Anna had visited recently. Anna wondered if Nick had heard. She tried to imagine how he would feel when he got the news, but she couldn't do the mental somersaults. The defense perspective was just too alien to her. For a while—when Laprea was safe and alive—Anna had been able to forget that she and Nick held such different viewpoints. But there was no getting around it now.

Would Nick feel any worse for winning the case than she did for losing it? He had just been doing his job, she understood that, but as a result of Nick's efforts, a vicious thug had been set free to kill. Anna had tried to put D'marco *in* jail, and she wasn't sure how she would live with herself. If she couldn't forgive herself, she thought, would she ever be able to forgive Nick? She wasn't sure.

The most senior members of the office sat around the long conference table. Joseph McFadden, the U.S. Attorney, sat at the head. Anna had spoken to him only once before, when she'd interviewed for the job. A political appointee heading an office of 350 career prosecutors, he didn't normally chat with misdemeanor AUSAs. He was flanked by the chiefs of his two most important Superior Court sections: Carla sat to one side of McFadden, and Jack Bailey, the Homicide chief, sat on the other. Anna didn't recognize the other lawyers. She slumped in her chair next to Carla and miserably studied Jack, who was looking at some papers. This was the worst way she could imagine to finally meet the renowned lawyer.

In an office full of the toughest trial lawyers in the country, Jack Bailey was known as the best. His improbable ascension from a kid in one of D.C.'s worst neighborhoods to the city's top homicide prosecutor made him a bit of a local legend. He was a tall African-American man with a cleanly shaved head and startling light green eyes. Jack looked younger than Anna had pictured; aside from the U.S. Attorney, the Homicide chief was the biggest cheese of all. Every new attorney tried to work her way up the office hierarchy, graduating from smaller cases to more serious ones, so she could eventually earn a position in Jack Bailey's Homicide Section. The last thing any rookie prosecutor wanted was to have one of her minor cases become part of Jack's Homicide docket. It meant something had gone terribly wrong.

Anna dreaded why she'd been called into this meeting. Were they going to reprimand her for losing Laprea's case? Was she going to be fired? She would understand if she was.

McFadden spoke, and the rest of the room fell quiet. "The *Post* called this morning about the Johnson murder. Turns out the victim was featured in the Metro section a couple years back; she graduated from some job-training program and got herself off public assistance. Now they want to know why this woman who climbed out of the proverbial garbage heap ended up in a real one."

Anna looked down at her hands. She didn't see the sympathetic looks aimed at her. She knew victims recanted in DV trials all the time, and this could have been anyone's case. But this was every DV prosecutor's nightmare.

"They want a comment from me," McFadden continued. "I'd like to tell them we have a suspect." He turned to Carla. "Do we have a suspect?"

"We do." Carla tapped the file from D'marco's last trial—the trial that Anna had lost.

McFadden turned to Jack. "Good. And we expect to charge him soon?"

Jack nodded. "Today."

"Excellent. This'll be a cautionary tale about domestic violence. But it has to have the right lesson: that it won't be tolerated."

"Absolutely." Carla folded her hands on the table and leaned forward to address the U.S. Attorney. "And the best place for that to happen is in the DV Section."

"I disagree." Jack's voice was deep and smooth, conveying a confident authority although its volume was low. "No one can prosecute a homicide like a homicide prosecutor."

"You've got all the rest of the homicides, Jack." Carla glanced at him with annoyance. "I've got a cadre of senior attorneys who want to work a homicide. Can't you spare one case?"

"There's a reason why my shop has all the homicides, Carla."

Anna knew what a tight ship Carla ran, and she bristled at Jack's words.

"Not only do we have the expertise in dealing with this *type* of family dynamic, but one of our prosecutors has already worked with this *particular* family," Carla said, putting her hand on Anna's arm. Anna's body tensed. She couldn't believe where this conversation was going. She wasn't here to be reprimanded—she was being used as leverage in a turf war. "Anna Curtis met the victim; she knows the mother. She already has a rapport with family members who will be government witnesses. She can work with a senior AUSA in my section. DV is the right place for this case."

Oh God, Anna thought. What about Nick? I can't be on this case!

Jack shook his head. "I respect the work done by the DV Section. But DV's expertise in family dynamics didn't secure a conviction back when this was a simple assault case."

Anna sank shamefully in her seat.

"Nothing against DV or Miss Curtis," Jack continued, glancing at Anna. "But you need a veteran homicide prosecutor on this case. It's the sort of case I'd handle myself."

"Okay, you've got it then," McFadden announced. "This case will go to the Homicide Section. That's the office policy, and we're going to stick by it. Jack, since you've offered, I'll ask you to take the case personally." Jack closed his eyes for a second longer than a blink. Jack had apparently planned to help initiate the case and then give it to one of his senior prosecutors. "But Carla makes some good points. I'm also going to assign Anna to work the case with the homicide team. Jack, Anna will be your second chair. Carla, you'll cut some of her responsibilities so she can devote the necessary time to this matter. Any press release will credit both the Homicide *and* the DV sections."

"Okay." Carla was not entirely satisfied, but she was still pretty pleased.

Anna gaped at her boss and McFadden. "But—I've never tried a homicide."

"You've got to learn sometime," Carla said, "and Jack is an excellent teacher."

Carla could be gracious now that she'd won.

Anna looked around the room. Should she tell these people about her relationship with the defense attorney? These were the highest-ranking prosecutors in her office, mostly stern silver-haired men. She couldn't imagine telling them the intimate details of her love life. But she wasn't sure she could accept the case and still stay with Nick.

She opened her mouth, but Jack protested before she could say a word.

"Listen, Joe," Jack said. "This isn't going to fly. Working a homicide case is a tremendous responsibility. It has to be earned. There are dozens of experienced attorneys who would love to handle this case. Besides, Detective McGee and I have already started it. SWAT's gearing up, and we're about to go execute warrants on the suspect's home."

"Good," the U.S. Attorney replied, standing up. The meeting was over. "I hope you brought a bulletproof vest in a size small. Take your second chair with you."

11

Anna trotted wretchedly after Jack as he walked out of the U.S. Attorney's Office and into the humid summer morning. He hadn't said a word to her. He strode across the brick plaza and up to a navy blue Crown Victoria parked at the curb. A man built like Santa Claus, but with skin the color of espresso beans, was leaning against the trunk of the car. The big man stood up as he saw Jack approaching.

"Hey, Chief," he called in a deep, gravelly voice. "What took so long?"

"We have an addition today." Jack turned and addressed Anna for the first time. "Anna Curtis, this is Detective Tavon McGee. McGee, this is Anna Curtis . . . my second chair."

"Second chair, huh?" McGee smirked at Jack. "They think you're losing your edge?"

"Something like that," Jack muttered.

"Nice to meet you, Counselor." McGee gave Anna a meaty handshake and a warm smile. She was surprised to see that his two front teeth were missing. The gummy grin gave him an endearing, babyish look, although he was probably in his fifties. He wore a black six-button suit with lime green pinstripes, a lime green shirt, and a shiny tie with a swirling lime-on-lime pattern. A black fedora perched on his head. In that outfit, he could only be a homicide detective.

McGee opened the car's front passenger door and ceremoniously gestured for Anna to take a seat. She shook her head quickly.

"No! Thanks, though."

On top of everything she'd done to piss off the Homicide chief, she wasn't about to claim shotgun. She climbed into the backseat. McGee made an even more elaborate Vanna White gesture for Jack to get into the front passenger seat. Jack sighed and climbed in.

As the unmarked police car careened onto the I-395 ramp, Anna tried to keep herself from sliding back and forth across the shiny faux leather seats. McGee started updating Jack on the Laprea Johnson investigation. From the backseat, the conversation was barely audible over the blaring sirens. Anna felt like a kid trying to listen in on her parents.

"Body turned up yesterday afternoon," McGee shouted over the sirens. "Coupla kids going through a trash heap behind Davis's building got the shock of their lives. Perp wrapped her body in black plastic garbage bags and dumped her in the heap."

"Cause of death?" Jack asked.

"Looks like blunt force trauma to the head, but we're still waiting on the ME's report. No obvious gunshot or stab wounds. She was beat up bad. Bruises all over her chest and arms, face looks like a war zone."

Anna felt sick.

"She didn't have any ID on her, so it took a minute to connect the body to a missing person's report from her mother."

"Did you find the witness who called 911?" Jack said.

"Yeah, guy named Ernie Jones. Good citizen—steady job, no record. Cooperative."

"Wonders never cease. How come there wasn't a police report?"

"Busy night." McGee swerved around a cluster of slower cars. "Uniform got there half an hour after the call. By that time, no one was around—turns out Jones went to work. There was nothing to report."

"Jury's gonna love that."

"They want better service, they should hire more cops."

"Positive ID on the body?"

"The mother, this morning."

Anna cringed at the image of Rose at the morgue, seeing her battered daughter laid out on one of the cold steel tables.

She vividly remembered the first time she'd met Laprea and her mother, in the basement of the courthouse. Rose had said that it would be Anna's fault if Laprea were killed. Anna agreed with that. The mantra that had been running through her head repeated itself: *This is my fault.*

She looked out the window as McGee drove. The drive from the sparkling downtown to the poorest section of the city always felt surprisingly short. As a matter of geography, the two neighborhoods were a few miles apart. As a matter of class, race, and economics, they were different worlds.

When the highway split, McGee veered onto I-295, leaving behind the wealthy Northwest quadrant of the city: the world of postcard-perfect white monuments, the centers of government power, the arrogant glass office buildings housing the country's most influential law firms, media outlets, and think tanks. The Anacostia Freeway took them over the muddy brown Anacostia River and into the part of the city that tourists on bus tours didn't see, the part that helped D.C. become "the murder capital of America" in the 1990s. Fancy condos became low brick apartment buildings, sagging public housing complexes, and modest row houses, some with plywood-covered windows, although they were occupied. Office buildings were replaced with pawnshops, check-cashing outlets, and liquor stores, or just boarded-up storefronts. The few working businesses covered their windows in metal bars and their counters in bulletproof glass. Children played in vacant dirt yards, alleyways, and between parked cars. These places were just as safe as the playgrounds, which were often controlled by drug dealers. Parts of Anacostia were like a slice of the Third World, steps away from the most powerful people and institutions in America.

As they pulled into a narrower street, McGee cut the sirens and turned off the police lights. The car sped silently through residential streets lined with squat brick apartment buildings. As the car rounded a corner onto Alabama Avenue, Anna's cell phone rang. It was Nick. She saw Jack looking at her in the rearview mirror.

"You need to turn that off," he said.

She quickly powered off the phone, glad the Homicide chief couldn't see who'd been calling.

In that instant, she knew she'd made a decision. She was going to prosecute the case, regardless of Nick.

There was no other way she could respond to the image of Laprea's shattered body—of Rose identifying the remains of her only daughter—of the two motherless children. Anna couldn't undo her mistakes, but she could make sure the killer was punished. She hoped Nick wouldn't defend D'marco; she hoped he would have the decency to decline the homicide case. If he did take it, though, she'd face that dilemma then. She wasn't going to tell anyone about their relationship—she wasn't going to say *anything* that would jeopardize her position on the case. She owed it to Laprea's family.

McGee pulled up behind two white vans. D'marco's apartment building was ahead on their right. The structure was replicated throughout this neighborhood: a low brick box surrounded by a chain-link fence. It was a quiet summer morning and few people were out. Most of the windows had their blinds pulled. It seemed inappropriate that birds were chirping, under the circumstances.

"SWAT's waiting on us." McGee nodded toward the vans.

Jack rolled up his shirtsleeves. He still wore his tie, but had left his suit jacket back at the office. He turned back to address Anna. "We'll be in the van during the police's initial entry into Davis's apartment. When SWAT gives us the all clear, we'll go in. When we do that, don't touch anything. Stay out of the officers' way. And stay with me at all times. Do you understand?"

"Yes, Mr. Bailey." She understood that he didn't want her here.

Anna followed the men out of the car, half running to keep up with them. A van door slid open and they climbed in. The van smelled of sweat and metal. Anna found herself in a tiny space crowded with men dressed in black paramilitary uniforms, complete with high-top boots, bulletproof vests, and helmets with the visors pushed back on their heads. The weapons holstered at the officers' sides and clamped onto the walls included the usual service revolvers, but also assault rifles and one shotgun. This was the Special Weapons and Tactics team—SWAT.

Someone handed Anna a black bulletproof vest with POLICE emblazoned in tall white letters across the chest and back. Anna watched how McGee and Jack fastened theirs and she did the same, pulling it over her black suit jacket. She tightened the Velcro straps as far as they would go, but it was still too loose on her.

Only then did it register what the officers were about to do—storm into D'marco's house to arrest him. The vest was because they thought he might shoot at them. Anna's head and neck suddenly felt very bare and exposed.

Jack showed his arrest and search warrants to the head of the SWAT team, a seasoned sergeant named John Ashton. Sergeant Ashton showed Jack the floor plans of the apartment. SWAT had done its homework. They knew which apartments were occupied and which residents had criminal records. They knew exactly where D'marco's unit was and how it was laid out. The two men grumbled about the fact that it was already so late in the morning. They preferred to serve warrants before dawn, surprising their sleeping target. Still, they agreed, it was better to do the search now than to wait another twenty hours.

At a signal from Sergeant Ashton, the SWAT team started moving in silence. The officers pulled down their visors, and one picked up a large shield mounted on one of the van's walls. They piled out of the vehicle, silently meeting a fleet of SWAT members pouring out of the second white van. Their movements choreographed, the men formed a snakelike column behind the man holding the shield. The man at the front of the line was peering through a narrow window in the middle of the shield, so he could see as he walked forward. The rest of the men walked crouching behind the leader. Anna stayed in the van with Jack and McGee as the SWAT team trooped into D'marco's building.

Sergeant Ashton led his men to the stairwell, which echoed with a dozen boots clomping up. They trotted to the second floor and marched through the shabby hallway straight to D'marco's apartment. Ashton knocked sharply on the door. "Police! We have a warrant!" There was no answer. "Police! Open up!" He waited several seconds. Then he tried the door—it was locked. He nodded to the two men holding a battering ram. They counted off quietly as they swung it at the door, gathering momentum with each swing. One . . . two . . . three! The officers slammed the ram into the door, breaking it down on the first hit, and then jumped back. Ashton threw a flash-bang grenade into the apartment and then pressed himself against the hallway wall.

Bam! An explosion shook the thin walls and a burst of light came from the doorway. The flash-bang didn't blow anything up, but would temporarily stun and disorient anyone in its vicinity. The officer with the shield rushed into the apartment, followed closely by an officer with a shotgun. The man with the shield stopped and rested the bottom of the shield on the floor; the officer behind him propped the shotgun on top of the shield. The men were protected behind the shield, and if there were a problem, one blast from the shotgun would take out many people.

The rest of the SWAT team poured in behind the shield, ready to grab anyone inside while they were still dazed from the flash-bang. Pointing their guns ahead of them, the officers yelled, "Police, put your hands up!"

But there was no one inside to follow their command. The man with the shield stepped aside. The officers looked in every room and closet, under the bed, behind every curtain.

The apartment was empty.

Back in the van, Anna sat on a fold-out bench across from Jack and Detective McGee. There was nothing they could do until they got the all clear from the guys inside. She looked around the van. Jack was absent-mindedly turning a knob on the SWAT radio. He appeared calm and unconcerned. In fact, he looked as tough as any lawyer she'd ever seen, with his shaved head and his broad chest filling out the police vest. Then Anna noticed a slight shimmer of sweat on his brown forehead. He must just be hot from sitting in the stuffy van, she decided. She couldn't imagine that Jack Bailey was as nervous as she was.

Anna wondered whether Nick knew that the police

were raiding his client's apartment. Just then, Jack's green eyes sliced to hers. Her heart skipped; she felt as if Jack had read her mind and caught her thinking about Nick. She blinked and looked at McGee, whose seat sagged under his weight. The detective was mopping sweat from his forehead with a lime green handkerchief. He winked and flashed her a grin. She nodded back, wondering what the story was behind those two missing front teeth.

The radio crackled to life. "All clear!" a voice yelled through the speaker.

Jack and McGee hopped out of the vehicle and strode toward the building. Anna wasn't surprised to see Jack move fast, but McGee was unexpectedly nimble for such a big man, especially wearing the heavy bulletproof vest. Anna hesitated. Jack turned back and looked at the young woman still crouching in the van. "Come on, second chair," he called, almost suppressing the note of amusement in his voice. Anna took a deep breath and hurried after them.

The SWAT team started searching the apartment as soon as McGee stepped into it. McGee was the point man; now that the apartment was cleared, his job was to coordinate the search and catalog every item the police seized. He pointed at an open box of documents in a corner, then to a woman's purse, sitting next to the couch. An officer photographed the items as they were originally found, then brought the items to McGee. McGee settled his big body into a chair at a small kitchen table and started sorting through the items, listing on a police form where they had been found and what was inside them. While he wrote, other officers started bringing him items from the other rooms: women's clothing from the bedroom, a bottle of Wild Turkey from the bathroom. McGee listed everything in neat round letters on the form, then he bagged the items in clear police evidence bags. He was meticulous and efficient, cataloging each item like a scientist on an archaeological dig. In between writing, he called out orders to the SWAT officers.

"Over there." McGee pointed at the couch. A couple of officers looked under the cushions. Finding nothing, they tipped the couch over, exposing the carpet underneath it. There were just a few coins and potato chip crumbs.

McGee emptied the purse onto the table and ordered the crime-scene technician to photograph the contents. Then he started writing everything down. One lipstick, CoverGirl. One package of chewing gum, Trident. One cellular phone, Nextel. One wallet containing $47.32, one D.C. identification card in the name of Laprea Keisha Johnson, two credit cards in her name, one family photo, and three business cards: one from Officer Bradley Green, one from Ebonique Nail Salon, and one from AUSA Anna Curtis. McGee carefully described every item in his police inventory sheet.

Anna looked at the contents of the purse over McGee's shoulder. She remembered when she gave Laprea her business card. She noticed Green's card even had his personal cell number scribbled on the bottom. Neither card had done Laprea much good.

Anna picked up the family photo. It was a recent Sears photograph of Laprea and D'marco, sitting with the twins posed on their laps. Laprea smiled broadly at her from the photo; they looked like a happy family. Anna hoped no one saw her wiping the tears from her eyes.

Jack came out of the bedroom and saw Anna holding the picture. "Anna, please don't touch anything," he said with barely concealed annoyance. She dropped the photo and backed miserably into a corner.

Jack walked toward the kitchen and stood watching the officers searching there. They were looking for black garbage bags, the kind Laprea's body had been wrapped in. The SWAT team emptied the drawers and cabinets, pulling out silverware and dishes, cans of soup and take-out packages of soy sauce. A silk rose in a plastic container sat on the counter. No garbage bags, though. The trash can was lined with a paper grocery bag.

McGee finished cataloging the evidence that had been brought to him and started walking around the apartment. His eyes didn't miss anything. When he got to the entranceway, he knelt down and looked at a pattern of rust-colored spots on the gray carpet. Bloodstains. "Crime Scene!" McGee bellowed. The crime-scene technician came over and nodded. The tech set a card with the number 1 next to the stain, and took photos of it from multiple angles before kneeling down to cut patches of the stained carpet and put them into a sterile brown paper bag.

McGee stepped outside the apartment, and looked for more stains in the hallway. A pattern of rusty spots was visible on the filthy carpet. McGee pointed it out to the crime-scene technician. The tech put down a card with the number 2 by the patches and repeated the process. They would test all of these swatches to determine if they held Laprea's blood.

It was a small apartment, and after an hour, they'd found everything they were going to find. The search was done; now they just needed to execute the arrest warrant. Jack turned to Sergeant Ashton and they started talking about how to locate and arrest D'marco Davis.

"A few officers will stay here and stake out the building," Ashton said. "A few will try his grandmother's house."

"Good," Jack said. "I spoke to his probation officer. Davis has an appointment on Thursday. In the unlikely event that he shows up, he'll be arrested there."

Deliberately not touching anything, Anna gazed out the window. A brawny man in a white T-shirt and baggy jean shorts was walking up the driveway. He was carrying an orange soda and a small plastic bag from the Circle B. Anna recognized him immediately. Her heart started racing.

"There he is!" she said excitedly, pointing out the window. "It's D'marco Davis!"

Sergeant Ashton strode to the window and looked to where she was pointing, then made a quick hand gesture. The other officers instantly dropped to the floor or flattened themselves against the walls, pulling their guns up to their chests. Jack shot his arm across Anna's chest, pushing her away from the window and pressing her against the wall. "Get down," he whispered. They sank to crouching positions next to the window. Ashton gestured to his colleagues, and he and six other SWAT officers trotted silently from the apartment. The others started to fan out along the hallway.

Moments later, seven officers burst from the front

door of D'marco's building, guns drawn. D'marco was about twenty yards from the building. "Police!" Ashton yelled, pointing his gun at D'marco. "Get down! You're under arrest!" D'marco took one look at the men in black paramilitary uniforms—and sprinted in the other direction. The officers lowered their guns and ran after him; they couldn't shoot at someone who hadn't threatened them. They shouted commands without much hope that D'marco would obey.

"Hold up! Hold up! Hold up!"

"Stop! Police!"

"Get the fuck down!"

Up in the apartment, pressed against the wall, Anna heard the shouts and then the retreating thuds of running footsteps. Jack drew his hand off of Anna's chest, looking embarrassed to find it there. Anna stood up and peered out the window. A dark swarm of SWAT officers was chasing D'marco down the street. She watched until they turned a corner, out of her sight. Jack stood next to her and looked out the window, the planes of his face drawn tight with tension.

"Will they get him, Mr. Bailey?" Anna asked.

"We'll see." The Homicide chief turned to her. He seemed to notice her, really notice her, for the first time today. "Good eye. You can call me Jack."

12

Sergeant Ashton sprinted after D'marco Davis, down the sidewalk of Alabama Avenue. The other officers were at various distances behind him. Ashton was running flat out, as hard as he could. D'marco had a clear advantage—unlike the SWAT officers, he wasn't encumbered by twenty pounds of police gear—but Ashton was still gaining on him. It was his job to outrun criminals, and he was good at it.

A few citizens watched the chase from the windows of the apartment buildings, but no one came outside. They would come out after the suspect was apprehended, but they didn't want to get in the way of any stray bullets now.

Ashton chased D'marco past several public housing complexes, and then the suspect turned onto a street lined with brick row houses. As he followed the suspect around the corner, Ashton was breathing hard, but feeling good. The distance between him and D'marco had closed to less than fifteen yards. His legs were a black blur, his arms fired like pistons. He was flying over the sidewalk, closing the distance. He felt a hard, relentless satisfaction. This was his favorite part of his job.

Then he saw D'marco cut into an alley between row houses. Shit, Ashton thought. Not this again. He raced into the alley, swerving to avoid crashing into a rusty Dumpster. Not the fire escape, he thought. Not the fucking fire escape.

In defiance of Ashton's mental command, D'marco scurried up the ladder to the black metal fire escape bolted to the brick building. The ladders were supposed to be kept elevated to avoid people coming up from the ground like this, but they often didn't follow that code. "Shit," Ashton said aloud this time. All the thugs were doing this lately. He stopped at the foot of the ladder and pulled his radio off his belt. "Fan out!" he called into it. "Fan out! Target's going on the roof!" He clipped the radio back onto his belt and followed D'marco up the ladder, which then became black metal steps. As Ashton ran up them, he could hear the metal rat-a-tat-tat of people following him. He glanced down. Two of his officers were following him up; the other four must be spreading out around the block. Good.

When he got to the rooftop, Ashton stopped and looked around, pointing his gun across the roof as he looked for the suspect. The roof stretched out for half a block, the length of six row houses. It was covered in blacktop and there was a tall chimney in the center of each house's roof, six chimneys in all. Piles of garbage dotted the roof, as well as scattered needles, empty bottles, used condoms, and one soggy mattress. D'marco wasn't anywhere in sight.

Ashton waited until the two other officers made it up to the roof. Keeping his gun pointed ahead of him, he gestured with his chin to the first large chimney. It was four feet tall, big enough for a man to crouch behind. The other men nodded and pointed their guns ahead of them. Ashton went to the left of the chimney, the other two went to the right, quietly approaching it with their guns drawn.

Ashton's movements were controlled, but he knew what danger he and his men were in. They didn't know where the suspect was; they didn't know whether he was armed. But the officer was used to this kind of risk. He was in the superalert state of someone experienced in harnessing his adrenaline rush. He heard every note of his feet crunching softly on the blacktop, he smelled the tar of the roof and the grass below, he heard a car starting several blocks away. And then he saw the shadow move on the other side of the chimney.

"Freeze!" he yelled, pivoting around the chimney. D'marco bounded up like a sprinter out of the blocks, running wildly across the rooftop. The officers grunted and ran after him. They passed chimney after chimney, until they were approaching the edge of the roof.

Ashton wondered what the guy would do. Was he a jumper? The distance between this roof and the next one was about seven feet. A narrow alley ran between this set of row houses and the next. They were three stories up. A fall from this distance could kill a man. As they reached the edge of the rooftop, D'marco didn't slow down, and Ashton knew what the other man would do a few seconds before he did it. D'marco sprang off the edge of the roof.

Ashton pulled himself to a skittering stop at the edge of the roof, and held his hands up to make the other officers stop. He held his breath as D'marco flew over the abyss. D'marco landed with a crashing thud, half on, half off the other rooftop. His chest and arms were on the roof, but his legs dangled off the side of the building, kicking without finding purchase. D'marco grunted and tried to scramble up. His fingers reached for something to grab, and found nothing. For a moment, Ashton thought the man was going to fall to the alley below. But then D'marco somehow leveraged his huge arms and heaved himself onto the roof. He lay there, crumpled and panting, for a moment. Then he picked himself up with effort and kept running away from them, limping now.

The three officers stood at the edge of the roof, panting, watching the suspect trot away in a jerky, uneven lope. They were a good team, these officers, but they weren't insane. This was an alley you jumped only if your life or your freedom depended on it. Theirs did not. And they each had twenty pounds of police gear strapped onto their bodies. Sergeant Ashton wouldn't risk his own or his men's lives foolishly.

There were men below who might still be able to catch D'marco when he went down. And they had other tools. Ashton brought his radio to his mouth. "I need a helicopter," he barked.

Back in D'marco's building, the remaining SWAT officers were leaving the apartment to help their colleagues search for D'marco. Anna heard the radio traffic and understood that D'marco had gotten away. The officers would keep searching the neighborhood, but from the sound of the grumbling officers in the apartment, it didn't seem like anyone thought the prospects of catching him today were good. Anna felt a shiver of unease run down her spine, knowing Laprea's killer was still on the loose.

Jack and McGee took off their bulletproof vests. McGee gestured for her to do the same, but Anna hesitated. Seeing her face, McGee smiled. "Don't worry, Counselor," he said. "There's one place that D'marco Davis won't be coming today, and that's right here." She took a deep breath and unfastened her bulletproof vest. They handed their vests to the last SWAT officers heading out the door.

"Come on." Jack beckoned McGee and Anna into the hallway outside of D'marco's apartment. "It's gonna be a long day."

McGee turned to Anna. "We'll talk to the neighbors, see if anyone heard anything on Saturday night. We've gotta do it now, before people start forgetting. Memories are short around here." Anna nodded, it made sense, but she couldn't believe they were doing this with D'marco lurking out there somewhere. She glanced nervously around the hallway.

McGee caught the nervousness in Anna's glance and smiled. "It's a homicide case, sweetheart, not a bake sale." His voice was joking, and his eyes were kind. "Don't worry." He patted a lump under his lime pinstripes. "I'm a good shot. Most of the time."

Jack knocked on the door to apartment 215, the unit right next to D'marco's. The walls in this building were thin; the resident who lived here might have heard some of D'marco and Laprea's fight. Anna stood behind Jack and McGee. She could hear somebody shuffling around the apartment, but no one answered the door. Jack knocked again, more forcefully this time. Finally, the door opened two inches. A single brown eye peered at them suspiciously from the crack. The chain lock was still fastened.

"What?" the eye's owner asked. From the sliver that Anna could see, it was an older woman, with slicked-back gray hair and smoke-stained yellow teeth. The single eye was bloodshot, and its owner had dragon breath. The woman had obviously lived a hard life; she looked like she was in her sixties, but was probably just pushing forty.

"Good morning, ma'am," Jack said with quiet authority. "I'm Jack Bailey, from the U.S. Attorney's Office. I was hoping to talk to you about an incident that took place Saturday night."

"I don't know nothin'," the woman said. She started to push the door shut. McGee stepped forward and jammed his foot against the door, his enormous body easily bracing it open.

"Hey now, purty lady. Ain't no call fo' that." McGee smiled as he slipped into a perfect Southeast street dialect. "How'm I supposed to ax you out, if you be slammin' this door in my face?"

The woman favored him with a small smile, which turned to a frown when her eye flicked to Anna. But Anna hardly noticed. She was looking at the detective in surprise. When he'd spoken to Anna and the other police officers, McGee had used a newscaster-bland accent. She realized he had the capacity to effortlessly switch dialects. He sounded like a different person here, and she wondered which was the real McGee. Both, she concluded after a minute. McGee was a little bit of both worlds. That was part of what made him a good detective.

"Many witnesses don't realize that the little bit they do know is important," Jack said pleasantly. "I don't expect you'll be a star witness." No one who lived in this building would want that. "But if you have time to talk for just a moment, it would be very helpful."

"I ain't gotta talk to you."

"That's true, you don't. But I would appreciate it."

"No." She turned to McGee. "And getcho damn foot out my door."

Jack sighed. "Just a moment." He pulled a form out of his briefcase and quickly scribbled on it. He handed the paper through the crack in the door.

"Waddis?" she asked angrily.

"A subpoena. It's a court order telling you to come to my office this Thursday to testify in the Grand Jury. You don't have to talk to me now, but you will have to answer some questions there."

"I ain't comin' down to the snitch building!"

"I'm sorry, ma'am," Jack said quietly, "but you don't have a choice. If you don't come, they'll send the marshals to arrest you."

"This's fucked up! I ain't done nothin', and you harassin' me!"

"We're sorry for the inconvenience. You'll get forty dollars to compensate you for your time and travel expenses."

"Yeah?" Her voice softened. "I know lots a things 'bout a lot of people. I might have to come down a coupla times."

"I'll look forward to seeing you on Thursday. Have a good day."

Jack nodded at McGee, who pulled back his foot. The door slammed in Jack's face. He looked down the long hallway and sighed. They would knock on every door in the building "One down, fifty to go."

"Hope you brought a lot of subpoenas," McGee said.

"Do you want me to take some?" Anna asked Jack. She was over her nervousness, or at least she wasn't going to let it slow her down. If this had to be done, they might as well do it efficiently. "I could knock on some of the doors."

Jack considered her offer for a moment. She could see the calculations in his head: dozens of doors to knock on, hours saved, versus giving this responsibility to an unseasoned prosecutor.

"No," he said at last. "Thank you, though. Just stick with me." She was an unproven quantity. He might be forced to have her tag along, but he didn't have to let her do anything.

They moved to the next door.

It was almost seven by the time they finished at D'marco's building. No one had let them into their apartment except Ernie Jones, who seemed to feel guiltier than Anna, if that was possible. They gave the rest of the residents subpoenas through doors that differed only in how far they were cracked open. Ernie would be a great witness, McGee told Anna, but they shouldn't expect much out of the other residents' testimony.

And they would have to work with the warrant squad to help find D'marco. A few hours earlier, Sergeant Ashton had called Jack to say that D'marco had gotten away. He could have hidden on a rooftop, or jumped to another building, or gone down into someone's house, or just slipped off a fire escape that wasn't being guarded. SWAT would get him, the Sergeant promised—eventually. The prosecution could help by questioning witnesses about his friends, family, and hangouts. The SWAT team would use the information to locate him. Anna was doubtful. They were having a hard enough time convincing anyone to talk to them at all, much less to disclose where their murderous friend was hiding out.

As they piled back into McGee's car, Anna looked around the street half expecting to see D'marco behind a dark tree or a parked car. But the street seemed to be empty. She settled into the backseat, feeling more exhausted than she ever had in her life.

"Can I drop you at your home, Counselor?" McGee asked her from the rearview mirror as he started the car.

Although he had been engrossed in his work throughout the day, McGee had made a point of being nice to her, explaining things as they went along. She got the impression that now that she was on his team, McGee would look after her like a loyal watchdog.

"I should go to the office," Anna answered. "I'll start a chain-of-custody log for the evidence you seized today."

"No," Jack cut in. "It's been a long day. Go home. The evidence will be there tomorrow."

"I want to get started," she protested. It had been a

long day, but she hadn't done much except watch the officers search. She knew she had a long way to go to prove herself.

Jack turned to face Anna in the backseat and shook his head. "This is a marathon, not a sprint. I expect another long day tomorrow." Jack turned to McGee. "Can you swing by Anna's house, and then mine? I need to relieve the nanny."

McGee nodded and eased the car onto I-295. Anna sat back and closed her eyes, secretly relieved that Jack insisted that everyone go home. She was bone-tired, emotionally drained, and dreading the next thing she would have to do.

As they crossed the bridge back into Northwest, Anna's cell phone vibrated silently with a new call. Speak of the devil, she thought. It was Nick. He had called several times today. She pressed the button to decline this call, too. A minute later, the phone buzzed with a new text message. She opened it. Nick had written: "Call me as soon as you get this. It's important."

She glanced up. Jack was gazing out the window; if he'd noticed her buzzing phone he gave no indication of it. Anna flipped the phone closed and slid it back into her purse. She would wait until she left the police car to face the looming crisis in her personal life.

13

An hour later, Anna sat at her kitchen table, staring at the phone in her hand. The microwave beeped for the fifteenth time, vainly trying to remind her that the dinner she reheated was getting cold. Anna tried her sister's number yet again, but there was still no answer. She had hoped to talk to Jody before confronting Nick, but she'd run out of time. She would have to figure this out herself. Nick would be here any minute.

Raffles rubbed against Anna's leg and mewled for attention. Anna picked up the cat and scratched him behind the ears. She once had a case where a woman threw a cat out of a sixth-story window after the woman learned that her husband's lover had given it to him as a gift. Not what you'd think of as a federal crime. Because Washington, D.C., was a federal city, federal prosecutors handled the street crimes that would have gone to the local District Attorney's office anywhere else. Before Laprea's death, Anna thought that the Washington U.S. Attorney's Office held the best of both worlds: she could have the prestige of being a federal prosecutor while fighting violent crime. Now, Anna wished she was an AUSA in any district except D.C., just a regular federal prosecutor handling a tidy

Medicare fraud case rather than a player in this horrible bloody world where nice women were killed by the men who were supposed to love them.

There was a knock at her front door. Anna wished she had more time to think, but this was it. She put her hand on the doorknob, steeled herself, and opened it.

Nick stepped into her living room and pushed the door shut with his elbow. He wore a suit and a tortured expression. He immediately wrapped his arms around her and buried his face in her hair.

It felt both natural and completely wrong to be in his arms. She stood frozen as he held her. He inhaled deeply at the nape of her neck.

"Oh, Anna," he whispered.

She let him embrace her for a moment. She hadn't planned to, but it was such a comfort to be held. She wondered how to start. Before she could, Nick pulled back and looked at her. He held her arms steadily.

"I have to tell you something terrible," he said softly.

"I know," she said, and started crying.

Once she started, she couldn't stop. Her shock and grief from Carla's announcement this morning, the frustration building throughout the day as D'marco's neighbors slammed their doors in her face, her guilt and regret—all of it came pouring out in noisy, hacking sobs. Nick gently drew her closer. Anna cried into his chest as he stroked her hair. She cried like her heart was breaking—because it was, and because she knew it was only going to get worse.

When her crying finally subsided, Nick cradled her head in his hands, and kissed her gently. She let him—or, rather, she let herself. For a moment, she savored the taste of his mouth, sweet through the saltiness of her tears, his clean scent, the warmth of his chest pressed to hers. She consciously took in every part of him, trying to memorize each detail, knowing she would play them through her head in the months to come. Then she drew back.

"I heard about Laprea's murder this morning," she said. She took a step back and drew a deep breath. "I'm prosecuting the homicide case."

"What?" Nick was stunned. He didn't seem to know where to begin. "You can't, you're in the misdemeanor section."

"I'm second chairing. It's because I know the family. From our case."

"No, no, no." Nick ran his hand through his dark hair and turned from her. "Fuck," he whispered. He paced across her small living room. There wasn't much space; his long legs covered the length between the sofa and kitchen table quickly before he stood in front of Anna again. He put his hands on his hips and looked at her with grim determination.

"Anna, you can't do it. Tell them you have a conflict."

Now she had to walk away, moving herself out of his gravitational pull. She went to the window at the front of her apartment. The basement window started at the height of her nose; her view was level with the sidewalk outside. She watched two pairs of feet go by: a woman's in Mary Janes and a man's in bowling shoes.

Nick walked up behind her and put his hands on her hips.

"What about us?" he asked softly.

It was the question she had been struggling with all day. Her tears had dried and now she just felt the gritty residue of salt on her cheeks.

"Are you going to represent D'marco Davis in the murder case?" she asked, turning to him.

"Of course I am. He's my client, he has been for years. He needs me now."

"Then there can't be an 'us.'"

His voice was almost a whisper. "Why are you doing this, Anna?"

"No, why are *you* doing it?" she cried, pushing him away. "You got him off—you *fought* me to get him off—and now he *killed* her! And you're going to try to get him off *again*!"

"That's my job!" Nick shouted back.

"It shouldn't be! Not if you have a heart! This isn't some law school competition—these are real people. Now Laprea is *dead*, and it's *our* fault! Her children lost their mother! Don't you feel any responsibility for that?"

"I feel terrible! But there's nothing I can do about that now. I can't make her not dead. But I'm a defense attorney. In America, everyone deserves the best defense. That's what I do. I defend people from the government."

"You work to set criminals free!"

"He's innocent until proven guilty! You don't think he should get a defense. It'd be a lot easier if you could just presume him guilty, wouldn't it, but guess what? He gets a trial by jury and a lawyer."

"Don't fucking lecture me about criminal procedure! This isn't about 'does he get a lawyer'—this is about *you*! And me, and Laprea and D'marco. I didn't protect her—I failed. You got him off—you succeeded. I don't know which one of us is worse. But I know I'm not going to lose this time."

"Anna, this is ridiculous." He narrowed his eyes at her. "Don't blame me because *you* couldn't convict D'marco Davis."

Anna inhaled sharply. She felt like he'd just kicked her in the stomach. It was the worst thing anyone had ever said to her.

"You asshole," she whispered.

"You're upset right now," Nick said, lowering his voice and putting his hand on her arm. "That's understandable. But try to calm down. You just need to recuse yourself from this case."

"*I* need to recuse *my*self?" Her voice was an unnatural screech she'd never heard before. She yanked her arm away. "I can't be with you anymore, Nick. I'm prosecuting your client for murder. And it's not just the conflict of interest. I can't be with someone who would defend a man like D'marco Davis. I don't know how you live with yourself—but I know I can't." She strode to her door and opened it. "Now get the fuck out of my house!"

He stared at her, so angry he was unable to form a response.

This was not how she'd wanted this to go. If they were going to break up, she'd hoped to do it as two people of goodwill who understood that circumstances beyond their control were pulling them apart: reasonably, logically, sadly but nobly. She'd had a vision, herself in a long hoop skirt standing at the rail of an ocean liner sailing out to sea, waving a lace handkerchief at Nick while he remained standing on the wharf. A civilized, romantic leave-taking. Not this screaming, name-calling fight in her basement apartment. In some distant corner of her mind, she was vaguely aware that she would come to regret sending him away like this. But she was seething now, unable to take back what she still felt. She stood at her doorway, glaring at him.

Nick stalked out without another word. Anna shut the door and watched through the window as his feet strode angrily down the sidewalk. When he was out of sight, she stumbled to her bedroom, threw herself onto her bed, and cried herself to sleep.

14

The first indication that something was wrong came from the autopsy.

Dr. Danielle Laroche checked the name on the corpse's wristband: Laprea Johnson. The body lay naked on a stainless steel gurney. Dr. Laroche wheeled the gurney out of the cooler and down the hall to the autopsy room, passing several other bodies laid out on carts lining the hallway. Some were covered with sheets, others were naked. Every size and color of the human spectrum was represented: young and old; men and women; black, white, and brown; bloated and emaciated; tattooed and unscarred; hairy and bald; well-endowed and not—all lying stiffly in the pale pallor of death. One infant's body looked tiny on an adult-sized gurney.

The Office of the Chief Medical Examiner was responsible for investigating every suspicious death in D.C. With more than 4,000 investigations each year and not enough pathologists to conduct them, the office was running a bit of a backlog. But Laprea Johnson's case had gotten some press, so they'd immediately assigned it to Dr. Laroche, their best pathologist. Dr. Laroche was a pretty black woman with a set of dimples that dotted her cheeks when she smiled. Juries loved her.

The doctor pushed the cart into the autopsy room, an enormous space flooded with bright fluorescent lights. The walls were lined with stainless steel sinks and counters covered with glass jars and beakers. The white tile floor, scrubbed with a strong antiseptic solution every day, gleamed despite the messy work done around it. The middle of the room held a dozen autopsy bays, where eleven other bodies were already laid out. Pathologists and orderlies hovered over them in various stages of examination. Each bay had its own set of power tools and hoses hanging on cords from the ceiling.

In one corner of the room lay an in-ground scale, slightly bigger than the rolling table. Dr. Laroche pushed the gurney onto the scale, which automatically subtracted the standardized weight of the cart. The doctor noted the weight of the body by speaking into a handheld tape recorder: "One hundred and four pounds." Her voice had a trace of a lilting Caribbean accent, a remnant of her childhood in Jamaica. Eventually, she would turn her tape-recorded notes into a written autopsy report.

The pathologist pushed the cart into the vacant autopsy bay to continue her examination. She noted her findings into the tape recorder.

"The body presents as a slight twenty-one-year-old African-American woman, five feet one inch tall. Small, round bruises, approximately two inches in diameter, consistent with finger marks, cover both upper arms, the left shoulder, and chest. There are bilateral subdural hematomas in the orbital sockets," she said, noting Laprea's two black eyes. "These injuries, while visually remarkable, were not fatal."

She noted Laprea's bruises on a triplicate form with a figure of a woman, coloring in marks on the figure to correspond with Laprea's injuries. The doctor looked at the large dent in the left side of Laprea's head. No bullet holes, no knife wounds. Plain old blunt-force trauma to the skull. Before she made a single incision, the doctor knew that this was the cause of death. Still, everything had to be examined and documented.

The pathologist used her scalpel to make a long cut starting behind Laprea's right ear, running over the crown of the head, and terminating behind the left ear. After the exam was over, the doctor would sew the incision back up, and it would not be visible during an open-casket viewing. Dr. Laroche peeled the skin away from both sides of the incision, pulling it backward behind Laprea's head and forward over her face, revealing the top of the skull. To a layperson, it would look as if a red cloth covered the lower part of Laprea's face, but that *was* her face, inside out. Dr. Laroche could now examine the exposed skull. It was deeply fractured on the left side, a wide crevice running from the temple to the base of the skull.

Dr. Laroche slid on a clear plastic face shield and pulled down the Stryker saw hanging from the ceiling. The handheld power saw had a round, revolving blade, which would cut through bone but not soft tissue. She turned it on and the tool whirred in her hands. She sawed a line around the equator of Laprea's skull, making one triangular notch in back so that when they put the skullcap back on, it would not slide off the bottom half. She pulled off the top of the skull, now the shape and size of a large soup bowl, exposing the brain that was encased within it.

Dr. Laroche cut the spinal cord and lifted the brain easily from its cavity. It was grossly bruised where the skull had been fractured. This was the cause of death. She noted this into her tape recorder. The doctor then hung the brain from a string in a jar of formaldehyde solution. In two weeks, the tissue would be fixed by the chemicals, allowing easier handling and a more thorough inspection.

The pathologist then turned to the trunk of the body, using her scalpel to make a deep, Y-shaped incision in Laprea's torso, the branches of the Y starting at the shoulders and meeting under the breasts, the stem going down to the pubis. There was little blood, as the body had no blood pressure now except gravity. The doctor peeled back the skin from the Y and used bone-cutting shears to break through the ribs, removing a large, neat square of ribs and sternum. This opened the body cavity so the doctor could cut out the internal organs—heart, liver, intestines, stomach, kidneys, uterus—in a single large block, hefting the mass onto a separate table. Each organ was then separately weighed, dissected, and examined.

The results were unremarkable until she reached the reproductive organs. Dr. Laroche sliced open the uterus along both sides, bivalving the pear-shaped gray organ. She stopped when it lay open. Inside the uterus nestled a human fetus the size of a peach.

• • •

Jack rubbed his temples as the paralegals filed out of his office. He'd spent most of the day trying to douse a flare-up of support staff drama. The paralegals claimed that the secretaries weren't doing their share of the filing; the secretaries were mad that the paralegals got to work a flextime schedule; and everybody was angry at Jack for forbidding them to play DVDs on their computers during the workday. Finally, at four o'clock, he could concentrate on the Davis case.

He had almost gotten through Laprea Johnson's preliminary autopsy report when his phone buzzed. He groaned. Once, he would have ignored it, but now any call could be an emergency that only the Homicide chief could address. He picked up the phone.

It was Anna, asking if he was free "sometime this afternoon." Sure, he agreed distractedly. He had barely put down the receiver when she appeared, legal pad in hand, hovering in the doorway. He waved her into the office.

"Hi, Mr. Bailey. Um, I mean Jack." She walked in and stood nervously in front of his desk. He gestured for her to have a seat.

Anna's anxiety reminded Jack of his days as a rookie prosecutor. He had been similarly intimidated—though he'd hidden it better—by the Homicide chief at the time, a burly Irishman whose capillaries flared red when he yelled at his lawyers. Sometimes it was hard for Jack to believe he was sitting on this side of that desk now.

While he empathized with Anna's nervous deference,

he didn't try to ease it. It was good for the young lawyer to be a little frightened of him. That fear would not only keep her on her toes, it would serve as a fence between them, keeping their relationship formal and well defined. He was her boss, not her buddy. That line was particularly important now that they were co-counsel on this case. It was necessary both for the public perception of their relationship and for his own peace of mind.

Especially, Jack thought, with a young woman this attractive.

Anna sat in the chair on the other side of his desk and crossed her legs. Nothing in the way she dressed was seductive or designed to call attention to herself: she was wearing a black skirt, a blue silk blouse, and low-heeled pumps. Nevertheless, Jack couldn't help noticing that she had great legs.

He brought that thought to a screeching halt. He avoided thinking about the women he supervised in that way. It couldn't lead anywhere but trouble. With a conscious effort, Jack looked at Anna's face and not her calves.

Anna pointed at the pictures of Olivia sitting on his desk, the only personal decoration in the room. "Your little girl is beautiful," Anna said.

"Thank you. Luckily, she takes after her mother."

He gestured to a picture of a beautiful woman sitting on a playground swing, holding a beaming, toddler-sized Olivia on her lap.

"Is she a lawyer, too?"

"She was a police officer. She passed away."

Jack had gotten to the point where he could say this without grimacing.

"I'm so sorry."

"Thank you."

In the awkward silence, Anna handed him a stack of papers. "I thought you might want the *Jencks* materials to turn over to defense counsel," she said, "so I got Detective McGee's notes and reports together, and redacted the witnesses' home information."

Jack glanced at Anna's neatly organized papers. The prosecution was required to give the defense any prior statements of any government witness. Anna was getting a jump on things—they wouldn't need a *Jencks* package until the preliminary hearing, and there wouldn't be a preliminary hearing until D'marco was arrested—but this would eventually save Jack an hour of paperwork. The young woman was making herself useful.

She handed him another sheet of paper, a to-do list she'd made for herself. "I was thinking of a few things I'd like to do on the case. I just wanted to run them past you before I get started. Make sure I'm on the right track."

He nodded, sighing. His attempt to minimize Anna's role by simply ignoring her was not working.

"I want to track down every police report and 911 call that's ever come out of Laprea's house," Anna said. "I'll find every time she reported that D'marco hit her. A good 911 call could be powerful, like her voice talking from the grave. We're allowed to introduce evidence of past abuse—the jury can infer that since D'marco beat Laprea on other occasions, the same interaction prompted him to kill her this time."

"Okay." Jack would have assigned a paralegal to get the 911 calls, but if Anna wanted to pursue it, that would save him some time. "Go ahead and get the calls. We'll have to argue about getting them in. The Supreme Court's been cutting back on evidence like that."

"I know, I read *Crawford* and *Giles*. But I think we may have a good argument here. I'm also going to call every hospital in the city, and see if Laprea was ever treated there. I'll subpoena any medical records. I did some research on the rule against hearsay. There's an exception for statements made during medical treatment. If she ever told doctors she was there because D'marco hit her, it will be admissible."

Jack tried not to smile as the young prosecutor continued to elaborate the bullet points on her to-do list, describing legal tactics he had been using for ten years as if she were Columbus finding America. At least she was headed in the right direction.

"Basically, I want to get every piece of evidence that will give Laprea Johnson a voice," Anna concluded. "She can't speak anymore, she can't tell the jury what happened the night she was killed. But we can tell the story of D'marco's abuse through the bits and pieces she left behind."

"Great." Her to-do list would free him up to talk to witnesses and put them in the Grand Jury. That was the meat of a homicide case. She could cook up all the side dishes she wanted.

"And I wanted to let you know I'm going to go to

Laprea's funeral on Friday." Despite her deference to him, Anna said this as a statement, not a request.

"Are you sure you'll be welcome there?" Jack asked quietly.

"No. But I have to go."

Jack saw the determined set of her chin. "Okay," he sighed. "But you can't go alone. You know you can never speak to a witness on your own, right?"

A prosecutor always needed an officer or someone with her to observe any conversation with a witness, in case the conversation came into dispute and someone had to testify about it later. Otherwise, the prosecutor might become a witness in her own case, and would have to recuse herself from it.

"Actually, I hadn't thought of the funeral like a witness conference," Anna admitted. "I wasn't planning on bringing anyone else. But I'll find an officer to go with me."

"Bring McGee. And I'll come, too." Jack wasn't letting her talk to witnesses without him, even at the funeral. Especially at the funeral, where emotions would be running high, and excited words might be exchanged.

Jack noted Anna gulping nervously. She didn't want him to go, Jack surmised. She understood that Laprea's family might yell at her, and although she was prepared to take it, she didn't want Jack to see it. At least she knew what she was getting herself into, Jack thought. It took a certain amount of courage to walk into that situation.

"You came by at a good time," Jack said, deciding to

share some information with Anna. "I was just looking at the preliminary autopsy results."

He pushed the report across the desk. Anna scanned the papers blankly. Jack had felt the same way the first time he'd tried to read an autopsy report. To a layman, it was incomprehensible, full of medical jargon.

"It takes a while to understand those," he told her. "Cause of death is blunt force trauma to the skull. Laprea Johnson died of a single blow to the left side of her head with a hard object. Davis had to hit her with something harder than just his fists. Time of death is estimated at eleven thirty p.m. on Saturday, August sixteenth."

Anna nodded. "But Ernie Jones saw Laprea and D'marco fighting around nine thirty that night."

"The estimated time of death is just that—an estimate." He wondered how often he would have to explain elementary things like this to the rookie prosecutor.

"Oh, okay."

"They can tell from the blood pooling that the garbage dump behind D'marco's building was not where she was actually murdered. Her body was placed there sometime after her death."

Anna nodded. With the body wrapped in garbage bags, that had seemed obvious even before the autopsy report.

"The trace evidence unit vacuumed her body," he continued. "There were a few hairs, but from an animal, nothing human. Probably a pet."

"I don't think the Johnson family has any pets. We didn't see anything pet-related at D'marco's place."

Jack nodded noncomittally. "Maybe a wild animal or a stray, touching the corpse. There was one more thing," he said. "Laprea Johnson was pregnant when she was murdered."

Anna's eyes got big, then closed in pain. "Oh no. Poor Laprea. Poor Rose." Jack watched her with sympathy. The news had also hit him in the gut, compounding the scope of this tragedy. Anna finally opened her eyes and stared out the window. "Does D'marco know that he also killed his own baby?"

"Don't know. They still haven't caught him."

"I see." Anna blew out a breath and slumped back. She looked sick. "How pregnant was she?"

"Hm," Jack said. He wasn't sure. He flipped through the autopsy report. "Let's see. Sixteen weeks."

Anna looked down in concentration. "That would make the baby's conception . . . in mid-April." Surprised, she looked back up at Jack. "D'marco Davis was in jail awaiting his trial for the Valentine's Day assault then."

Jack rocked back. He hadn't caught that. The girl might be a rookie, but she was sharp.

"Someone else fathered that baby," he murmured.

"Who?"

He shook his head.

15

As they drove through Anacostia, Jack and McGee took turns pointing out landmarks from their prior cases. Anna listened from her usual position in the backseat. Their stories were completely incongruous with the sunny summer afternoon.

"See that community center?" McGee nodded at a low concrete building. "I had a case where this lady got jumped in that parking lot. They stuffed her in the trunk of her car, took her to Fort Dupont Park. Gang-raped her, beat her, left her for dead. She managed to crawl to a house."

"Yeah, I heard about that," Jack said. "What'd the ringleader get? Thirty years?"

"Life," McGee said proudly.

Jack pointed to a park next to the community center. "My first AWIK happened there," he said, referring to his first assault with intent to kill. "Father of four was mugged and beaten with a tire iron. He was a vegetable after that."

"Mm." McGee conveyed a lot of sympathy in a single low grumble. "Remember the Clarence case?"

"Sure."

McGee looked at Anna in the rearview mirror. "Guy

killed his baby mama and cut her heart out of her chest." He pointed to a dirty brick apartment building.

"Yikes," she said. So many grim landmarks. Once you were a prosecutor, how could you ever look at the city the same way again?

McGee slowed the car as they crested the top of a hill. Jack pointed out the side window. "Look," he said to Anna. Her gaze followed his index finger. He was pointing toward a bare dirt lot littered with broken glass, used condoms, and needles. Beyond the lot was a postcard view of downtown Washington, D.C. The Capitol building, the Washington Monument, and the Lincoln Memorial stood like white model buildings on the green lawn of the National Mall. Anna could see the sprawling lawn of the White House, and the avenues of glittering office buildings surrounding it. It was an incredible view of the city where some of the most powerful people in America worked, where decisions that affected the entire world were made.

Then they were driving down the other side of the hill, and the view was blocked by boarded-up buildings again.

"I grew up a few blocks from here," Jack said. "It hasn't changed much."

As they drove into the parking lot of Mt. Calvary First Baptist Church, Anna tugged uneasily at her skirt. She had managed to put aside her nervousness on the drive over, but now it hit her full-on. How badly would Rose lash out at Anna for her role in Laprea's death? No matter how furious Rose was, Anna wouldn't blame her. She felt that she deserved the full force of Rose's wrath. But she also knew the only reason she was second chair on this case was because of her supposed relationship with the family. She wondered if Jack would use this as an excuse to get her kicked off the case.

As they walked into the church, they were surrounded by the thrum of hundreds of voices. The sanctuary was packed. People sat in the pews, stood in the aisles, jostled for space at the back. Men wore suits and ties; women mostly wore black dresses and black hats, although a few women were dressed in all white. Almost everyone was African-American; Anna's was the only white face in the crowd. The sanctuary was large but simple, with a high ceiling, pure white walls, clear windows spaced at even intervals, and a big wooden cross at the front. Laprea's shiny white casket was flanked by enormous bouquets of pink lilies at the front of the church.

"How do you want to do this?" Jack asked Anna loudly, raising his voice so he would be heard over the noise of the sanctuary.

"I want to find Rose."

Jack and McGee exchanged a glance, but they followed Anna as she wended her way up the center aisle.

Rose was sitting in the front row, wearing a black dress and a hat with a black mesh veil. She was surrounded by women: standing in front of her, sitting beside her, crowded into the pew behind her. All the ladies were reaching out their arms to touch Rose while they murmured soothing words. Laprea's mother was like the center of a flower, and her friends and relatives were the petals.

As Anna approached, one of the women noticed her

and nudged the other women. The women murmured and then parted, creating a passageway with a formidable wall of church ladies on either side. Anna stood looking at Rose, and Rose sat looking back at her. The rest of the church buzzed with conversation, but everyone around them was silent, watching the two women as they faced each other.

Anna thought she was ready for anything that Laprea's mother could dish out. But Rose greeted her in a way Anna was not prepared for. She stood up, walked over to Anna, and stood in front of her. Then she raised her arms and pulled Anna into a tight, cushiony hug. Her arms were warm and soft. Anna felt a rush of sorrow—and relief. Her eyes stung with tears as Rose held her, just as Anna had held Laprea in the Papering Room only six months before. Rose started crying, too. Rose's friends let out a collective sigh and closed in again, but now Anna felt their hands on her back, too, their voices soothing her as well as Rose. Jack and McGee stood awkwardly to the side, hands in their pockets, looking down at their feet as the women embraced in shared grief. Finally, Rose patted Anna's shoulders and pulled a handkerchief out of her pocket. She dabbed at Anna's wet cheeks before wiping her own.

"Here, sugar, sit down." Rose steered Anna to the pew, where they sat side by side.

"I'm so sorry, Ms. Johnson," Anna said, sniffling softly.

"Ain't nothing for you to be sorry about." Rose patted Anna's hands. "This's been building for years and years. You the only one ever came close to stopping it."

"I wish I'd done a better job."

"No use blaming yourself. Only one to blame's D'marco Davis."

"We're going to get him, Ms. Johnson, I promise you."

"Thank you," Rose said simply. She smiled at Anna through her tears. "It means so much to me that you're here."

"Of course." Anna introduced Rose to Jack and Detective McGee.

"I'm sorry I can't really talk to you now," Rose said. "But I do want to hear how the investigation's going. Could you come to my house next week?"

"How about Monday afternoon?" Anna glanced at Jack. He nodded, and they chose a time. Rose gave her a final hug. As Anna walked away, the church ladies enfolded Rose again.

McGee pointed to some free seats and the three of them slid in. After a few minutes, the service started with the choir launching into "I'll Fly Away."

The pastor stepped forward and raised his arms. "We're here today to celebrate the homegoing of Laprea Keisha Johnson!" he proclaimed.

"Hallelujah!" the crowd roared back.

There was an inescapable grief underlying the entire service, but the gathering was not about grieving. The congregants were there to celebrate the life of the woman they loved, and to rejoice in their faith that she had gone home to join her Father and Creator.

Anna thought about her own mother's funeral, so different in tone from this one. She closed her eyes. Feeling the wooden bench pressing against her shoulder blades, she mused that the bench in that church in

Michigan had felt exactly the same. She had been in law school when she'd gotten the terrible phone call from Jody. Her mother had died in a car accident, hit by a drunk driver who'd sped through a red light. The tragedy had knocked the breath out of Anna, but even as she'd sat crying in the corner of her dorm room, and then at her mother's church, Anna knew that, in some ways, she had gotten more than she had a right to expect. Those last twelve years with her mother, away from her father and his raging violence. Twelve good years, free of fear and pain.

But what Anna had done to get those years was unthinkable. Unforgivable.

She opened her eyes as a woman in front of her stood up spontaneously, raised her arms, and called, "Amen, brother!"

Anna liked this service. Although her mother's death had been the result of an accident rather than human malice, the funeral at her Lutheran church had been more somber than this one. Anna remembered the strained, tight faces of everyone who came to pay their respects, the prescripted call and response they intoned with gray, obligatory inflection. This felt better, she thought. It was a positive and personal affirmation that their loved one was now in a better place.

She wondered what Nick would think—and then realized that she wouldn't be able to talk to him about it, not later tonight, probably not ever. She had experienced jolts like this over the last several days. As this one passed, Anna leaned back on the wooden bench and exhaled deeply. Despite missing Nick, she felt a small but real sense of peace for the first time since

Laprea's death. Rose's forgiveness had given her that. If they could just catch D'marco, she thought.

He was closer than she would have imagined. On the street in front of the church, D'marco Davis sat in the eleven-year-old Toyota Corolla he'd chosen to steal because it had dark-tinted windows. A screwdriver was still punched into the ignition. He reclined in the driver's seat and watched the church, as he had all morning, noting who was coming and going. A small bottle of Wild Turkey sat beside him; it was still mostly full. He wasn't far enough into it yet to do anything foolish. He was still in control. He sat quietly, patiently, biding his time.

D'marco was still driving the Corolla with the tinted windows three days later. He was sober when he turned the car into the alleyway behind Rose's house. With some effort, he had restrained from drinking this afternoon. He would need to think clearly for what he was about to do.

He drove down the alley, a narrow concrete drive bordered by the backs of row houses and their fenced yards. It was a quiet, hazy summer afternoon, and no one was out. A dog barked in the distance, but no human seemed to notice D'marco parking the stolen car a few houses before Rose's yard. He pulled the long black screwdriver out of the ignition and put it into the pocket of his baggy jeans. A wall of humid heat hit him as soon as he climbed out of the car. The buzzing thrum of insects was all around.

D'marco shut the door quietly and walked to Rose's

chain-link fence. He could see Dameka and D'montrae playing on the back porch. Rose would be inside, making dinner or talking on the phone. D'marco took a deep breath. He had to do this.

He climbed over the fence, landed softly in Rose's grass, and crept stealthily to the screened porch. The twins were pushing Matchbox cars around a curving track, narrating a car chase. Rose wouldn't let them play Grand Theft Auto on the Xbox; she thought it was too violent. This was the closest they could get.

"D'montrae," he called softly. "C'mere. Quiet now." The little boy turned toward the sound of his father's voice.

"Daddy!" he cried, running over to him.

"Shhh," D'marco said, putting his fingers to his lips. Dameka ran over, too, and they both knelt down to their father. The porch was chest-high on D'marco. He reached up so that his hands were pressing theirs through the screen. He could feel the warmth of their little fingers through the mesh. "Quiet," he whispered.

"Why quiet, Daddy?" Dameka whispered back.

He paused, waiting to see if Rose would come to the window at the back of her kitchen, or whether the door leading from the porch into the kitchen would open. Nothing happened.

"It's a surprise," he said softly. After another minute, D'marco climbed up the steps and opened the screen door quietly. Keeping low, he crept to the back corner, where Rose could not see him from inside. He crouched in the corner, then waved the children over. They ran to him, their faces full of delight at this game, their eyes unclouded by fear or apprehension. They were just glad to see their father. They had heard whispers about their mother's death, but people had been discreet; the twins did not yet understand the role their father had played in it.

As D'marco knelt in the corner, they pressed into either side of him, throwing their little arms around his neck. Dameka was leaning on his leg, pressing against the pocket where he had stashed the screwdriver. He could feel the tool digging into his thigh. He pulled her closer.

"How's my li'l boo?" he asked softly.

"Oh, Daddy—" she started to launch into a story, but then he heard the doorbell ring inside the house.

"Shh," he said again, putting his finger to her mouth. He pulled the twins tighter to him so they would be still.

He could hear Rose greeting someone at the door. He heard footsteps coming into the house, and a few people's voices. He remained crouching with the children for a moment, considering his options. He hadn't counted on anyone else being there. Keeping his hands on the children's heads, D'marco slowly stood up and peered over the ledge of the kitchen window. There were bars over the window, but the window itself was open, allowing a breeze into the house through the screen. He could hear the voices inside.

"Thank you so much for inviting us over today," a woman was saying.

"Of course," Rose replied. "Thank you for coming."

If he squinted, D'marco could see through the screen into the house. Beyond the kitchen, Rose was sitting on the couch in her living room. A young white woman sat next to her. D'marco couldn't see the rest of the people in the house, but he heard male voices, too; apparently, some men were sitting in chairs outside of his sight line. It took D'marco a moment to recognize the woman as the prosecutor who had tried to convict him last time.

D'marco quickly squatted down again. His breath was fast and shallow, and his hands suddenly felt moist. He gripped the screwdriver in his pocket for reassurance. After a moment, he realized that this could be an opportunity for him. He smiled at the twins.

"Shh," he whispered.

16

They all sat in Rose's living room, Anna next to Rose on the couch, Jack and Officer Brad Green in chairs flanking the coffee table. Jack had asked Green to come with them today instead of McGee, telling Anna that Rose might feel more comfortable with an officer she already knew. He was right. Rose had greeted them all warmly, but had been especially happy to see Green, greeting the officer with a big hug and instructing him to sit in a cushiony La-Z-Boy chair, obviously the choice seat in the house. Then she had pulled out a photo album and sat next to Anna on the couch. Rose flipped through the album, showing Anna the pictures of Laprea growing up: Laprea doing an Easter egg hunt in Sherry's front yard; Laprea in a hot-pink dress standing before an airbrushed cloth background at her junior prom; Laprea in the hospital after she'd given birth to the twins. Green shifted in his chair and Rose looked up.

"I'm sorry, boys, I been running off at the mouth. You could use something to drink, coming out here on such a hot day. There's lemonade in the fridge. Brad, you know where the cups at, right? Could you get four of them and the lemonade?"

Green nodded and went to the kitchen, obviously

relieved to have an assignment. Rose turned to Jack. "He's a good officer. Always looking after us, stopping by to make sure everything all right."

Jack nodded. "Officer Green's an excellent community policeman."

"He came up around here, right?" asked Rose.

"Well, I wouldn't say around *here*." Jack smiled wryly; Anna recalled that Jack had grown up in this neighborhood himself. "I think Officer Green came up in the 'burbs—maybe Silver Spring? He played football for the University of Maryland for a year or so."

Rose leaned forward, interested. "For real?"

"Yeah, he was the kicker during my senior year."

"I bet he was good."

"He *was* pretty good. I remember when he scored the winning field goal against Virginia Tech in the last few seconds. The team carried him off on their shoulders. He was something of a local celebrity after that. Till he got injured—tore his ACL, I think. That was the end of his football career."

"Mm," Rose murmured, looking toward the kitchen, smiling. The idea of Green as a football hero clearly appealed to her.

Anna followed Rose's gaze and watched Green puttering around the kitchen. He didn't look like a football hero now. Although he still had bright blue eyes and plenty of cropped light brown hair, he also had that little potbelly straining against his uniform shirt, and his pink face was getting puffy, cushioned under an expanding layer of fat. Time had taken its toll. Anna guessed how hard it must have been for Green to suddenly lose his star athlete status—and how being a cop had probably filled some of that void. The MPD uniform wouldn't attract anything near the glory of a Terrapin football jersey, but it did get the attention and respect of many women, and garnered a lot of perks from the shops and businesses where an officer patrolled. Green had probably been an indifferent student, Anna thought, somewhat lost in the huge campus when he was no longer a football player—but as a police officer he could still be a local hero.

Jack turned the conversation to the subject they'd come here for. "I'd like to talk to you about our investigation. Anna and I will be following all possible leads. As part of that, we'd like you to come to the Grand Jury next week."

"Whatever I can do to help." Rose nodded nervously. "Do you think you'll catch D'marco soon?"

"The police are doing everything they can."

Hearing this, D'marco smiled, even as he crouched lower. He could hear the police officer opening the fridge on the other side of the brick wall. D'marco nudged the kids back to their toy cars. He didn't want their silence to get Rose's attention.

"Go on and play," he whispered. "I'll watch."

Inside, Jack was explaining Rose's role in the case. "We'll need you to establish the time that Laprea left the house the night she was killed. And where she was going."

"She said she was going to D'marco's house," Rose answered quietly.

Jack nodded and continued asking questions about that night. Despite her grief, Rose was clear and concise, easily remembering the details.

"I know this is hard to talk about," Jack said. "But you're doing great. You're going to be a fine witness."

"We might also have you talk about the previous times that D'marco hit Laprea," Anna added. "There's a good chance the prior assaults will be admitted at the trial."

"Plenty of those." Rose shook her head. "I was always afraid this would happen. I don't know why that girl couldn't stay away from that man. Probably the same reason I couldn't stay away from her father."

"If you don't mind me asking, what was her father like?" Anna asked.

"A lot like D'marco. In and out of jail. Charming when he wanted to be. Mean when he drank. He would smack me around, in front of Laprea sometimes. He's in prison now, won't get out till 2020 or something."

Anna nodded at the familiar story. Green came out of the kitchen with a carton of lemonade and four plastic tumblers filled with ice. He set them on the coffee table. Rose poured lemonade into the cups and handed Anna one. Anna took a sip, formulating her next question. There was no delicate way to get around it.

"Ms. Johnson," Anna asked, "do you know whether Laprea was dating anybody besides D'marco?"

On the porch, D'marco sat up straighter and strained to hear. That was why he'd come here, to ask the twins that very question. This could be the jackpot.

"No, I sure don't," Rose said as she handed cups to Jack and Green. On the porch, D'marco slumped back against the brick wall in frustration. "Not that she would've told me. Why do you ask?"

Anna paused and looked at Jack. Someone had to

tell Rose that Laprea had been pregnant. Anna dreaded doing it. Poor Rose! One blow after another. But she had to know. Jack nodded: Anna was the best person to break the news.

"Laprea was sixteen weeks pregnant when she died," Anna said gently. "The timing makes it impossible that D'marco was the father."

Rose's eyes got wide and her hand froze with the juice carton in midair. "Oh, Lord," she said at last, thumping the carton to the table. Her eyes brimmed over with tears. Anna squeezed Rose's arm.

On the porch, D'marco stared blankly ahead, in shock. The twins, who weren't paying attention to what was being said inside, were playing with their cars. Finally, he turned to Dameka.

"Baby girl," D'marco said softly, "you know if Mommy had any friends? Man friends?"

Dameka stopped moving her car along the track and looked at him nervously. She knew that talk of other men never led to anywhere but trouble in her house. She shook her head silently. D'Montrae mirrored her movement.

Inside, Rose was wiping her eyes with a tissue. "Can you do a paternity test and find out who the father was?" she asked.

"It's not that simple," Jack explained. "The scientists can't just look at the fetus's DNA and determine who the father was. They need to compare the child's DNA to a suspected father's DNA. We'll have the FBI determine Laprea and the baby's DNA profiles, and then run them through CODIS—that's a national database of the DNA profiles of convicted felons. If the child's father is in CODIS, we'll be notified that there's a match. But if he's not, then DNA doesn't tell us anything until we have a potential father to test."

"I see."

"How are the twins doing?" Anna asked, to direct the poor woman's thoughts away from the grandchild she'd never meet.

"They okay. I'm not sure they really understand she ain't coming back."

"They're so lucky to have you," Anna said softly.

"I'll call them in." Rose turned to the kitchen window. "Dameka! D'montrae! Babies, come inside!"

On the porch, the twins stood still, looking at their father, wondering what to do. D'marco pushed the children toward the kitchen door. "Go on," he whispered, trying not to panic. "Just don't tell your gramma I'm here." He held the screwdriver tightly beside his leg.

The twins walked uncertainly into the house. D'marco closed his eyes for a moment and leaned his head back against the brick wall. A thin trickle of sweat dripped from his forehead into his eye. He should run, he knew it. But he wanted to hear what the police and prosecutors said.

"Say hello to Miss Curtis, Mr. Bailey, and Officer Green," Rose instructed the twins as they filed into the living room. Dameka and D'montrae obeyed, giving the visitors shy glances and quiet hellos as they hovered by Rose's legs.

"Hey, I have something for you," Green told them. He pulled two colorful patches with the Metropolitan Police Department seal out of his pocket. He held them out, and the twins ran over to him. "Here you go."

"Cool!" D'montrae exclaimed, grabbing his MPD patch.

"Wow!" cried Dameka. She turned to the back of the house and ran toward the kitchen. "Daddy! Daddy!" she cried. "Look what I got!"

Anna, Jack, Green, and Rose looked at each other for a stunned second. Daddy? Then Green was on his feet, running through the living room, knocking two cups of lemonade off the coffee table as he rushed past Dameka.

As Green threw the kitchen door open, Anna could see D'marco running through Rose's backyard, flying over the small lawn like an Olympic sprinter. By the time Green's feet flew down the porch steps and hit the grass, D'marco was jumping over the fence into the alleyway. Anna and Jack followed Green through the porch.

Green got to the fence as D'marco threw himself into the driver's seat of the Corolla. D'marco jammed the screwdriver in the ignition, frantically trying to hit the sweet spot. The car roared to life. Green stopped a few feet in front of the car. He braced his feet wide apart, pulled out his Glock, and pointed the gun at the windshield.

"Stop!" Green yelled. "Police! Get outta the car!"

D'marco threw the car into gear, ducked his head down, and floored it. The Corolla hurtled toward the officer.

Green held his ground and squeezed the trigger, firing several shots at the approaching car. Four percussive blasts echoed through the alleyway. *Pop! Pop! Pop! Pop!*

Anna and Jack, who had reached the lawn, dove to the ground. The shots cracked D'marco's windshield in two places and blew out a tire, and the car started swerving. But no bullets hit D'marco. He kept the gas pedal pressed to the floorboard. Green leaped out of the way of the speeding car at the last minute.

The car fishtailed as it passed Green. Anna raised her head from the ground and watched in horror as the car's trunk swung toward the officer. A moment before the trunk slammed him into Rose's fence, Green jumped back, avoiding the swerving vehicle. The screech of metal scraping metal pierced the air and the fence buckled into a crooked V. D'marco hit the gas even harder and managed to keep the car going, although now it was swerving wildly because of the blown-out tire. He accelerated the old car as fast as it would go down the alleyway.

"Fuck!" Green cursed under his breath. He clambered back over the lopsided fence into Rose's yard and sprinted back to the house. Jack and Anna ran after him. "Call 911!" Green shouted to Rose as the three of them ran up her porch and through her house. The officer slipped on the lemonade and ice cubes spilled on the wood floor of the living room, but Jack put out a hand to hold him up, and Green stayed upright.

The three of them ran out of the front door to Green's squad car, as Rose picked up her kitchen phone and punched in 911. The children stood leaning against each other in the kitchen looking back and forth between the front and back doors with astonished, wide-eyed stares.

Green chirped the police cruiser open. His hand

closed over the driver's door handle a moment before Jack's was on the passenger's and Anna's was on the back door. "Stay here!" Jack shouted to Anna, but she was already throwing herself into the backseat as Green started the car.

Green screeched away from the curb, leaving black skid marks on the pavement and the smell of burning rubber in the air. Anna was thrown across the seat; she had to use the metal cage separating the backseat from the front to pull herself upright.

The cruiser's sirens blared, as Green yelled for backup on his radio. He careened the car around the corner onto Texas Avenue, toward the mouth of the alleyway that D'marco had been driving out of. As they rounded the corner, Anna could see D'marco's car ahead on Texas Avenue, speeding down the street, swerving wildly between the four lanes as he struggled to keep the damaged vehicle under control.

Green raced after him. D'marco's car veered back and forth on the street, scraping a car parked on the right side of the road and then careening toward an SUV driving toward them on the left. The Corolla swerved in time to avoid the oncoming truck, but then bashed another car parked on the right. It looked like he was playing bumper cars.

Anna caught a glimpse of Green's face as he steered the police cruiser around the debris left in the Corolla's wake. He wore a look of extreme concentration—and complete joy. The sirens blasting, the car barreling down the street, the radio squawking as other officers barked that they were on their way—he was loving it.

The Corolla turned suddenly off the main artery

onto a smaller street. Green spun the steering wheel around to follow him. D'marco blew through several stop signs, then turned again. He was trying to lose them in the labyrinth of small streets, but he wasn't able to build up enough speed in his battered car.

As another turn sent her skittering across the backseat, Anna went to buckle her seat belt, but remembered there weren't any back here. She braced her hands against the cage in front of her and briefly wondered what the hell was she doing here. She was a lawyer, not a cop; she should be back at Rose's house, calling 911 and waiting to make a police report. That thought evaporated when D'marco's car seemed to pull farther away from them.

"Faster!" Anna yelled to Green. "Go! Go!"

They were coming up on an open yard near a public housing complex; a bunch of kids in white T-shirts were hanging out on either side of the street. When they heard the sirens, the younger kids yelled, "Po-po! Po-po!" A few boys threw ziplock baggies to the ground or walked quickly in the other direction. But when they saw that the police cruiser was chasing another car—that it wouldn't stop for them—they gathered at the curb to watch.

As they drove past the kids, Green slowed down, and Anna saw that the boys were screaming, waving their arms, cheering and booing. They seemed to be rooting for D'marco, she thought. That was confirmed when an aluminum can struck the cruiser's windshield.

"Fuck you, 5-0!" a kid yelled.

Then a bunch of the kids were throwing stuff at the police car, rocks and glass bottles and trash. It was a small thunderstorm of garbage and curses. Anna ducked as a rock hit the side window near her face, spreading a web-shaped crack along the glass. Green kept driving, and then the kids were behind them.

They tailed D'marco through a few more turns, then they were heading back in the direction they'd just come from, and the side street was about to end at the intersection of Texas Avenue. When D'marco reached the big street, he tried to turn left. Green yanked the wheel to follow him. But D'marco's maimed car couldn't handle the sharp turn, and it spun out in the middle of the intersection.

Green hit the brakes, but couldn't stop in time. The cruiser smashed squarely into the passenger side of the Corolla, T-boning it, plowing the car to the side of the road, where the concrete curb stopped it. There was a screeching crash of metal as the two vehicles crumpled into each other.

Anna was thrown forward by the impact. Her chest and face hit the metal cage despite her braced arms, and she landed halfway between the seat and the floor. Then there was stillness.

Anna sprawled, dazed and disoriented. The only sound was the hissing coming from the police cruiser's engine. With effort, she pulled herself up. Her breath was knocked out, but she wasn't hurt. She looked to the men in the front seat. No one had been wearing a seat belt. Green was lifting his head slowly from the steering wheel, and Jack had a bleeding cut over his left eye.

"Are you okay?" Jack slowly turned back to ask her.

"Yeah." She took a deep breath. "You?"

Jack nodded, then closed his eyes.

Green shook his head to clear it, and looked at the Corolla ahead of them. As the officer tried to focus on the car, D'marco bailed out of it and started limping down Texas Avenue. Green cursed, climbed out of the police car, staggered for a moment, and then hobbled after the suspect.

D'marco looked back and broke into a limping run. Jack groaned and climbed out of the car, heading to follow Green. Anna tried to get out of the backseat, but she was locked in. She banged on the window and Jack turned back and opened her door.

Anna climbed out of the police cruiser and looked down Texas Avenue. D'marco and Green had picked up speed and were jogging down the street. "Come on!" she yelled to Jack, and ran after Green. After a moment of surprise, Jack ran after her. D'marco Davis and Officer Green were already two blocks ahead of them.

The street had small homes on the left and a wooded park on the right. As D'marco ran left onto Ridge Road, Jack grabbed Anna's arm and steered her up the driveway of a house on their left. At the end of the drive was a dirt track through the trees behind the houses. Anna never would have noticed it herself.

The track opened into the backyards of some single-family homes on Ridge Road. Anna and Jack ran to the side of a house, where Jack stopped and put out his arm for Anna to stop, too.

Jack's eyes darted around the side of the house until they landed on a couple of metal trash cans. He pulled the lid off one of the cans and gestured for Anna to press herself up against the brick wall so that D'marco, running up from the right, wouldn't see her. Then Jack crept up the driveway of the house, using the cars parked in the driveway to shield him from D'marco's view. Jack crouched behind a car that was parked by the sidewalk.

Anna strained to hear anything, but only heard the shouts of some kids playing down the block. She wondered if D'marco had veered off in another direction. Then she heard the faint sound of irregular running footsteps crunching up the sidewalk from the right. The footsteps grew louder and more distinct until she could hear D'marco's heavy breathing. Jack lifted the garbage lid to his shoulder, sprung onto the sidewalk, and braced himself.

D'marco crashed into the makeshift shield with a clanging thud. Both men went flying to the ground in opposite directions.

Green was just a few yards behind D'marco. He ran up to the sprawled man, used his foot to flip D'marco onto his stomach, and dug his knee into his back. The officer yanked D'marco's arms behind him and slapped the handcuffs on.

"You have the right to remain silent, asshole," he panted with a smile. The officer was obviously enjoying this.

D'marco groaned. He was exhausted, injured, and now in police custody.

Anna ran over to where Jack was gathering himself up off the sidewalk. She held out her hands to help him up, but he waved her off. He stood up—slowly, but on his own.

"Are you hurt?" she asked.

"Yeah. But it was worth it, right?" He grinned,

rubbing his shoulder. "Usually, an exciting day at the office is when the printer jams."

She laughed. "How did you notice that dirt track?"

"I used to live around here. I must've taken that shortcut a hundred times when I was a kid."

For a moment they just stood there grinning at each other, recognizing the strange position they were in: two lawyers standing on a hot summer sidewalk in the middle of a workday, a couple of crumpled cars in their wake and a wanted felon getting handcuffed at their feet.

Green continued to recite D'marco's *Miranda* warning. "You have the right to an attorney. If you cannot afford an attorney—"

"I know my rights," D'marco interrupted, spitting blood onto the sidewalk. "I want my lawyer. Nick Wagner."

"Yeah," Anna replied, meeting D'marco's narrowed eyes. "We know him."

17

Anna had always prided herself on her ability to quickly assess a problem and decide on a solution. Today, however, she stood in front of her closet for ten minutes, unable to decide what to wear. She was torn between wanting to look fabulous and wanting to look like she'd put no particular effort into how she looked. She eyed a periwinkle silk jacket with a Chinese collar. It was a rare bit of color and funk in her otherwise drab prosecutor's wardrobe, and people always complimented her eyes when she wore it. She touched the sleeve, tempted, then shook her head. She should just wear her usual courthouse uniform—albeit her best version of it. She pulled out her favorite black pantsuit, the one whose sleek cut made her look especially long and lean, and a pink blouse. She would indulge in high-heeled shoes.

Today was D'marco Davis's detention hearing, which meant Anna would be seeing Nick for the first time since their breakup, ten days earlier. They would be sitting on opposite sides of a courtroom, adversaries in the most high-stakes case of her career. There was nothing wrong with wanting to look her best, she told herself, as she blow-dried her hair for the first time in weeks. She and Nick were done, obviously. But she didn't want him to think she'd fallen apart since their breakup, she reasoned, as she dug through a drawer to find her long-neglected mascara.

When she was done primping, she headed out of her apartment into the already steamy August morning, joining a stream of young professionals in drab suits flowing toward the Metro. She wondered how many of these clean-cut twentysomethings were lawyers. Probably 80 percent. How many had the biggest case of their career against a lawyer whom, a few weeks ago, they were sleeping with? Surely she was the only one.

She wondered how she should behave when she saw Nick. What would "Ask Amy" say? Anna decided she would be professional but cool. Impeccably polite but detached. As she walked down the steep escalator into the cavelike recess of the Dupont Circle Metro station, she practiced greeting him. "Good morning, Counselor," she whispered. Maybe that was too formal? She didn't want to tip off Jack by being overly stiff. "Hello, Nick," she tried. Her ex's name came off her lips a bit too breathlessly; it sounded like she was greeting him as he brought a tray of French toast to her bed. She sighed. This was impossible.

She'd just keep her mouth shut and make herself as unobtrusive as possible.

She kept worrying throughout the subway ride to work, skimming the same article in the *Express* three times without comprehension. What if Nick outed their relationship? She didn't think he would—he'd be just as embarrassed—but what if he said something inappropriate? What if Jack suspected something? Her secret was uncomfortable, like a prickly tag that kept scratching her neck. She wished she'd just told Jack in the first place. Now, too much time had passed.

When she got to her building, she headed to Jack's office. He wasn't at his desk, but his secretary, Vanetta, pointed down the hall to a little conference room, a space Jack was starting to call their "war room." Anna thanked her.

The war room started out as a convenient place to have the guys from Closed Files deliver the boxes containing D'marco's old cases. Over the past week, Anna and Jack had also started to pile on the conference table the police and autopsy reports, medical records, photographs, phone records, and stacks of legal research. Recently, both prosecutors had spent as much time in the war room as in their offices.

Now Jack was sitting at the table reading an outline she'd left on his chair the previous night. He looked up as she entered.

"Hey, this isn't half bad," Jack greeted her, holding up the document. She had drafted an outline of a direct examination of Detective McGee for the preliminary hearing today. Jack would be asking the questions, but she'd wanted to help.

"Hey, don't go crazy with the praise. It'll go to my head." She smiled at him—but something was wrong. "Is everything okay?" Anna asked. "You're looking at me funny."

"I'm sorry," he stammered. "It's just, uh—did you do something different with your hair? I mean, it looks nice."

"No, well, kind of, I guess—" She touched her unusually sleek hair and cursed herself for being so transparent.

Jack quickly changed the subject. "You put the *Jencks* package together, you prepared the questions—why don't you handle the prelim today?"

"Really?" She had hoped for his approval, but hadn't expected this vote of confidence.

"Sure. It's the same procedure as the misdemeanors you've handled. Don't be nervous just because the case caption has the letters FEL instead of MSD. You're supposed to be learning from this case, right? So, learn. If you screw up, I'll just have to fire you."

She smiled at Jack. His words were gruff, but this was the first time he'd asked her to do anything important on the case. She hoped it meant he was starting to trust her.

"And if I do well?"

"I'll tell you how McGee lost his two front teeth."

"Oh, the stakes are high."

An hour later, as they walked into the courtroom, her good mood was replaced by jitters. Her eyes skimmed the courtroom as she walked to the prosecutors' table. Nick wasn't here yet. That was both a relief and an extension of the torture. Seeing him was going to be hard, but waiting might be harder.

This courtroom was laid out the same as the misdemeanor courtrooms where Anna had tried so many cases, but the details told her that she was practicing law at a different level. There was no foam poking from under the fabric of the jury box. The prosecutors' desk had one case file on it—hers—instead of dozens. And the people in the audience actually seemed to be sitting up straight, paying attention, knowing that this was important.

She wasn't sure who all these people were, however. Some were D'marco's friends and family, some were Laprea's, but a handful looked like lawyers wearing suits, except that they were toting backpacks instead of briefcases.

"Who are these people?" Anna whispered to Jack.

"Press," Jack replied. "Don't say anything to them." He motioned for Anna to sit in the chair closest to the jury box, where two sketch artists were already drawing the layout of the courtroom on big creamy tablets. "This way, you'll be in the picture."

This was Anna's first official appearance in this case, the first time she would say *anything* in a felony courtroom, and she suddenly realized she would be doing it in front of a bunch of journalists. She hoped they couldn't see the sweat beading at her hairline.

McGee sat behind the journalists, reading a newspaper, which he would hastily put away when the judge took the bench. He was wearing a blue seersucker suit and a tie with enormous yellow sunflowers. He was ready.

There had been one previous hearing in the case of the *United States v. D'marco Davis,* the initial appearance, three days earlier. Jack had handled that minor hearing alone; she'd been stuck in a misdemeanor courtroom. D'marco had been temporarily detained based on the arrest warrant, but if the government wanted to keep D'marco in jail until the trial, they needed to present live testimony now to prove that they had sufficient evidence that he committed the murder.

The courtroom's door swung open behind her, the reporters shifted and murmured, and Anna stopped breathing for a moment. She knew who it had to be. She turned around to see Nick striding up the aisle, smiling and nodding at the reporters. As he entered the well of the courtroom, his eyes met Anna's.

Against her will, Anna felt happy, feathery, and warm at Nick's gaze. The sight of him still sent happy signals to the pleasure centers of her brain. She had to consciously remind herself that he wasn't walking in to kiss her hello, but to fight her to get a murderer off—for a murder he allowed to happen. She should hate him. She looked at Nick, wondering if he felt as conflicted as she did. His mouth curved into a smile. He looked good.

Suddenly, she remembered Jack and the packed courtroom. She turned away from Nick, but it was too late. Nick walked right up to her.

"Hello, Anna." He paused, then reached out to shake her hand.

"Hi, Nick." She swallowed and lifted her hand to meet his. She felt his warm palm press against her own, like it had many times before, under such different circumstances. They were standing so close, she could practically feel the heat emanating from his body.

"You look nice," he said softly.

His hazel eyes were tired but sincere. She gazed at them, feeling something like homesickness. Then she realized he was still holding her hand—and she jerked it away. She held that hand a few inches away from her thigh, fingers splayed, as if she had been burned.

"Thank you." She strained to keep her voice light and casual. Had the crowded courtroom noticed their nanosecond of intimacy or her scandalized reaction?

Her eyes darted around. If the sketch artists had perceived it, at least they weren't drawing it.

Then she turned to Jack. He had noticed. He was looking coolly at Nick.

"Don't you think I look nice, too?" Jack asked Nick sarcastically. "I wore this tie special."

"Sure, Jack." Nick's eyes cut to the Homicide chief. "You always look . . . the same."

The click of the judge's door interrupted their greeting. "All rise!" called the clerk. Nick nodded and walked to the defense table as Judge Nancy Spiegel came in. As the judge took the bench, Jack glanced at Anna quizzically. He wanted to know what was going on between her and the defense attorney. Anna looked down at her papers, hoping he couldn't read what she was feeling. Her heart was thumping.

"Good morning, everyone," Judge Spiegel said, banging her gavel lightly. "Please be seated." The judge seemed to have lost some of her usual snap, and the vertical crease between her eyes appeared particularly deep today. Anna wondered if the judge also felt bad for the part she had played in letting D'marco go a few months ago.

In the three months since D'marco's misdemeanor trial, the courthouse had done its annual judges' rotation, and Judge Spiegel had landed a coveted Felony 1 docket, where she now presided over the most serious cases: sex offenses and homicides. There were three other Felony 1 judges; Judge Spiegel had been chosen by lottery to preside over this case. It was not unusual to have a jurist sit on a case where she had seen the defendant before. Anna thought this judge was a good draw for the prosecution—maybe the judge would give them some breaks out of regret for her earlier ruling letting D'marco go. Anna wondered if Nick would ask the judge to recuse herself. On the other hand, maybe he liked a judge who had previously declared his client not guilty.

A deputy U.S. marshal led D'marco out of a side door. Anna was glad to see him back in an orange jumpsuit, and clinking with each step. His hands were manacled in front of him, his feet were chained together, and a chain connected the restraints at his hands and feet. In front of a jury, he would be unshackled and allowed to wear civilian clothes; for everything else they would keep him visibly declawed. The marshal brought D'marco to stand next to Nick.

"I'm sorry to see you again, Mr. Davis, under these circumstances," said the judge sternly. "Very sorry indeed."

Anna heard the scratching of pencils as the reporters scribbled the judge's words in their notebooks. Judge Spiegel paused to let them get their quote. Then she turned to the lawyers.

"Identify yourself for the record, please."

Anna glanced at Jack. This is your show, his look said. She cleared her throat.

"Anna Curtis for the United States of America."

"Nicholas Wagner for the defendant, D'marco Davis."

Anna felt proud every time she introduced herself in court. She represented the interests of the entire country. That usually meant putting the bad guys away—but not always. She had a duty to be fair. If she thought the police had violated the Constitution, it was her job not to use the tainted evidence—and to train the police not to do it again. If she thought a defendant hadn't committed the charged crime, her job was to drop the case. Her duty wasn't just to win, it was to do justice. And this time her role had a more personal meaning to her.

She thought about Nick in his narrower, opposing role. His duty was to his client alone. He had no obligation to seek justice or serve the community's needs. If he knew his client was guilty, he still had to defend him as best he could. The criminal justice system needed defense attorneys, but Anna felt bitter that Nick had chosen that role over hers.

Anna didn't look at Nick as he addressed the court, but he hovered at the edge of her peripheral vision. Standing a few feet away from him like this, separated by impassable circumstances, felt wrong to her. They'd once been as close as two people could be. Now they had competing goals, and only one of them could win.

"Ms. Curtis, you may call your first witness," the judge intoned.

"The government calls Detective Tavon McGee."

As McGee took the stand, Anna picked up her outline of questions, not to read it, but to have something to do with her trembling hands. She steadied herself with the usual introductory questions.

"Good morning, sir. Could you please state and spell your name for the record."

"Detective Tavon McGee. T-A-V-O-N M-C-capital-G-E-E."

"What is your current rank, station, and duty assignment?"

As Anna talked McGee through his background and experience, she felt herself relaxing. She had learned in law school how to build a case in court, and she was good at it. She put up with all the dreck—herding uncooperative witnesses, xeroxing police reports, two-hole-punching intake forms—to have the opportunity to try cases. And Detective McGee was an ideal witness—he was smart, he would tell the truth, and he was on her side.

As she led him through the story of D'marco and Laprea's violent relationship, she found herself forgetting Nick's presence at the table next to hers and the reporters scribbling behind her. She focused on telling the story through her questions and McGee's answers. McGee's testimony was all hearsay, but hearsay was admissible at this pretrial hearing. Once she had set the stage, Anna directed McGee to the night of Laprea's murder. McGee described Rose's last conversation with her daughter, and how Laprea was headed to D'marco's house.

"Without telling us the person's name," Anna said, "is there a neighbor at D'marco's building who saw the defendant with the victim on the night of her death?" They would keep Ernie Jones's identity secret for as long as possible to protect the witness, but today McGee could relate hearsay about what the janitor had seen.

"Yes. I'll call that person Witness One." McGee described how the witness had seen D'marco hit Laprea and how D'marco even assaulted the witness. They moved on to how the body was discovered by a nine-year-old boy the next day. The reporters' pens scratched away.

Anna had McGee recite D'marco's home address, and then she asked him, "What was the address of the building where Laprea Johnson's body was found?"

McGee paused for dramatic effect. "The same."

"Can you describe the injuries to the body?"

"Ma'am, there were so many, I'm not sure where to start."

The detective was playing it up for the reporters. "Let's start with her head, detective." McGee nodded and launched into a detailed recital of Laprea's injuries.

"Did the medical examiner have a conclusion regarding the cause of death?"

"Blunt force trauma to the head."

"And did the ME have a conclusion regarding the manner of death?"

This was a standard question, but McGee milked the moment, pausing before answering in a low, ominous voice.

"Homicide."

Anna continued asking questions until the whole story was out. This case sounds pretty strong, Anna thought as she finished up. "Nothing further." She sat down with relief and satisfaction.

But she was only half done. Now she had to watch her ex-boyfriend cross-examine the detective.

Nick walked to the podium between their two tables. He didn't waste any breath on polite niceties but began straightaway trying to destroy her case.

"Detective, you don't have a single eyewitness to how Laprea Johnson actually died, isn't that right?"

"That's right," McGee conceded.

"Or to how her body came to be in the lot behind

the fifty-unit apartment building where my client lives, true?"

"True."

"Did anyone besides Witness One see or hear anything unusual that night?"

"So far, we haven't spoken to any other neighbors who admit they saw or heard anything."

"Fifty units, and not one person saw the alleged murder? How many of the residents have you spoken to?"

"Objection," Anna asserted as she stood up. Typically, she wouldn't object to this line of questioning, and she was aware that Nick had sat through her entire direct examination without objecting. But now was not the time to do him any favors. Nick wasn't entitled yet to details about who the government had spoken to or when they'd spoken to them. Later, she'd have to turn everything over. For now, she just needed to put forth enough evidence to show that D'marco Davis had committed the crime. "This doesn't go to probable cause and it's beyond the scope of the direct examination."

Nick glanced over, as if surprised to see her standing there. Her objection had broken the rhythm of his questioning. He almost looked hurt. Sorry, Nick, she thought, but this is how it's gonna be.

"Sustained." The judge broke their tension without realizing it. Anna sat down.

"Very well," Nick said. He shuffled some papers, gaining a minute to get himself back on track.

Anna listened carefully as Nick moved to his next question. She was on full alert now. She couldn't let him get away with anything just because she still cared about him. Especially because she still cared about him. As soon as Nick asked another technically objectionable question, she was on her feet. She knew she was being unusually aggressive with her objections. Better to be too aggressive, she thought, than not aggressive enough.

Finally, Nick was done. Anna sat back, satisfied. She had kept him to the bare minimum of information he was entitled to at this hearing.

Nick sat down and shot Anna a look; she was surprised to see that it was a little grin. He knew that any other prosecutor would have been more relaxed, and her zealousness amused him. His smile was infectious, and she had to fight back her own grin. She imagined the teasing he would have given her tonight—if they were still talking.

"I find there is probable cause to believe that the defendant committed the charged crime," the judge was saying. "And because this crime was committed while he was on probation, there are no conditions I can impose that would guarantee the safety of the community. The defendant will be held in jail until his trial next spring."

As the marshal led D'marco back to the holding cell behind the courtroom, the reporters turned to wait for the lawyers in the hall. Anna caught a glimpse of one of the artists' sketches. She'd been portrayed as Barbie-Goes-to-Court, with big melony breasts straining the buttons of her suit. She looked down at her chest with amusement, as if the sketch artists might have noticed something she'd missed all these years.

When she looked up, Nick was standing at the prosecution's table, addressing Jack. Nick wanted something, but he understood now that he would not get a sympathetic audience with Anna. He handed an envelope to Jack.

"That's my initial discovery request," Nick said. "It's the usual stuff. And I'm requesting that the fetus's DNA profile be run through CODIS."

So, Anna thought, Nick had also realized that his client couldn't be the father of the baby. Like the prosecutors, he wanted the baby's DNA profile to be compared to those in CODIS, the database of convicted felons, to see if the father was in that group. If the father wasn't in there, Nick would be in the same position the prosecutors were—having to use old-fashioned methods to find out who Laprea had been dating. Only then could anyone initiate DNA testing on a suspected father.

"We've taken the steps to get that started," Jack replied. "Of course, you'll get the results as soon as we do."

"Good." Nick nodded. "And I wanted to talk about a plea deal with you. What kind of offer would you be willing to make?"

"If he takes a plea now," Jack replied, "we could do manslaughter. If we have to indict this, we won't offer anything lower than second-degree murder."

"Manslaughter would be fair, under the circumstances," Nick replied slowly. "My *client* just needs to understand that. This might be a good case for one of your come-to-Jesus talks."

Jack nodded. It wasn't uncommon for a defense lawyer to see that a plea was in the best interest of a client, even when the client initially refused to consider it. Sometimes it helped to have the prosecutor tell the defendant how strong the case was. The prosecutor could be a lot more aggressive than the defense attorney because he didn't have to build a relationship with the defendant.

"Okay," Jack said, gesturing for McGee to come join them. Jack needed a witness in case the conversation ever came into dispute. The big detective followed Jack and Nick to the door that led to the holding cell. Anna trailed after them.

The door led to a different world. Carpet became filthy linoleum, wood walls became scuffed white cinder block. The scent of urine stung Anna's nose. The narrow hallway opened onto a small cell with a single bench lining the back wall. Metal bars coated with peeling orange paint separated the lawyers from three prisoners in the cell. Two of the prisoners slumped on the bench, but D'marco was pacing, agitated from the hearing he'd just left. He looked up, surprised, as the prosecutors lined up outside his cell.

"Hey, D'marco," Nick greeted his client softly. "The prosecutor wants to talk to you."

"Good morning, Mr. Davis." Jack stepped forward and stood inches from the bars. D'marco crossed his arms and regarded Jack with open hostility. Jack ignored the enmity and spoke as if they were having a beer together. "I'm here to tell you why you should man up, and quickly. I can tell you're angry, and I know I'm the last person you want to be talking to right now. But I want to tell you how this case looks from where I'm standing, and what I think the jury's going to see. Your lawyer can correct me if I'm wrong, but I think he agrees that this is something you should listen to."

D'marco looked at Nick, who nodded. D'marco took a small step toward the Homicide chief.

"There's a long history of you fighting with Laprea. A lot of trips to the emergency room. And there's nobody else who ever hurt her like that. The jury's gonna hear all of that. Right out of the gate, they're gonna want to convict you."

D'marco's chin lowered a fraction as Jack's point hit home.

"First, Laprea's mom will take the stand. She hates you. She'll tell the jury about the times you beat her daughter before, and the last time she saw her daughter alive—when Laprea was going to visit you. She's a strong lady, but she'll be crying when she shows the jury the pictures of her two grandkids whose mother is dead. Then the jury looks at you. What do you think they're thinking?

"Next, an officer testifies that Laprea's corpse was found in a garbage pile behind your house. The medical examiner testifies: blunt force trauma to the head. The cops raid your apartment—and they find her purse still there. They see you and you run, like you know you're a guilty man. Christ, a few days later, you tried to run over Officer Green! By this point, the jury knows what you did. They can probably picture it in their minds.

"But they don't have to picture it. Because our last witness saw you beating her, moments before she was killed. You were in a rage. You backhand her across the face. He tries to calm you down, but you're so enraged you slug the Good Samaritan. I've got a picture of him with a big welt on his face. He's not in love with you, Mr. Davis. You can be sure he's gonna testify against you.

"You chase Laprea down the stairwell and the

Samaritan calls 911. It's a good call—you'll hear the tape. But the cops get there too late.

"Mr. Davis, I've been doing this a long time. After the jury hears this evidence, when I play that tape again in my closing argument, when they picture Laprea Johnson running down that stairwell, the mother of those two children running for her life, running from you, and the police arriving moments too late—some jurors will be crying. The rest will want to kill you themselves."

D'marco let out a deep breath.

"I'm willing to give you a plea of manslaughter now," Jack responded. "Maybe you killed her by accident or in the heat of passion. You'd have to take the Unauthorized Use of a Vehicle charge for the stolen Corolla, but I'd be willing to drop the Assault with a Dangerous Weapon/Car—for trying to run over Officer Green—to an Assault on a Police Officer. With your record, the sentencing guidelines would call for six to twelve years on the manslaughter, and one to three years on the UUV and APO—so we're talking about a range of eight to eighteen years with this plea.

"Your lawyer will tell you that's a generous deal. You'd likely be in your thirties when you got out, you could still have a life. I'll tell you the truth: I'm not offering this for your sake. I'm doing it for Laprea's family, to save them the grief of the investigation and the trial, of having this whole thing dragged out. I don't want her kids—your kids—to have to go through that. I expect you don't want that either.

"But if you don't take this deal, and I have to spend more of the government's resources on this, my next offer is going to be worse for you. If we have to go to trial, you'll be convicted of murder. That carries the possibility of a life sentence."

D'marco paused as the options sunk in, then shook his head and crossed his arms on his chest. "I ain't pleadin' to nothin' I ain't done."

"D'marco." Nick's voice rang a warning. "Don't say anything. We're still asserting your right to remain silent. Mr. Bailey is here to *give* us information, not to take it."

Jack nodded, then continued. "In ten years, I haven't met a single defendant who admitted what he did—at first. Let me show you something."

Jack pulled some photos out of a folder and handed them through the bars to D'marco. The first few showed D'marco's house the day of the search warrant—the whiskey bottle, Laprea's purse, the bloodstains on his carpet. The next photo showed her body lying in the garbage pile behind his building. The final one was from the autopsy, a close-up of her face, her two bruised eyes, the crushed, bloody dent on the side of her head. Laprea's eyes were closed and she seemed to be grimacing; she looked like she was having a nightmare. D'marco twitched, but managed to keep a neutral expression. Nick paled and looked away. Anna also turned her head from the photos. Jack hadn't shown the worst ones, from the end of the autopsy, where Laprea's stiff body had a gaping cavity in its torso, and glossy organs were laid out in full color on a table next to it. Anna had seen all of them before, but refused to look at them anymore. They'd given her nightmares.

"Imagine what the jury is going to think when they see these pictures," Jack said. "And the judge. I don't think Judge Spiegel wants to do you any favors. If you plea now, I'll agree to cap the sentence. You wouldn't be at the mercy of a judge who wants to see you rot in prison for life."

Nick looked at D'marco, as if saying, *Do you get it now?* D'marco was scowling. "I think that's enough," Nick said to Jack. "D'marco and I will talk it over and get back to you."

But D'marco was agitated. He tossed the pictures back at Jack, scattering them on the floor outside his cell. "Man, I ain't done it! I hit her, okay, but—"

"Stop right there!" Nick spoke loudly. "Don't tell them anything."

"I wanna tell 'em!"

"I want to hear it," Anna said, stepping forward and meeting D'marco's eyes.

The men all turned to her, surprised. D'marco was the most surprised, but he stepped forward eagerly and put his hands on the bars.

"A'ight, so here's the—"

"Mr. Davis, listen to your lawyer." Jack pulled Anna back and stepped between her and the prisoner. "Ms. Curtis is not in a position to advise you or elicit information from you."

"Fuck that, man! Fuck you!" D'marco shouted, hitting the orange bars with dull metallic thuds. The lawyers all stepped back, like tourists who had gotten too close to the lion's cage. The door to the courtroom swung open and the marshal came striding in to see what the commotion was about. D'marco was pacing between the bars and the bench at the back of the cell, kicking the bench loudly when he got near it. The other prisoners scooched into the corner. "You all come back here tellin' me what to do, talkin', talkin', but you ain't gonna listen to what I got to say? That's fucked up! Fuckin' lawyers! Fuckin' MPD! I got rights! I got—"

The marshal herded the lawyers out of there, calling into his walkie-talkie for another marshal, warning that they might have to restrain D'marco or separate him from the other prisoners. Nick tried to stay back with his client, but the marshal wouldn't let him.

As the lawyers walked back into the courtroom, Anna could hear D'marco yelling curses at the marshals and banging around his cell. The people still left in the courtroom looked toward the door, wondering what was going on in the cellblock. Anna smiled weakly at them, hoping that if she looked calm enough, they wouldn't realize that the commotion was her fault.

Anna and Jack walked quietly back to the office through the soupy-hot August morning. Anna didn't know if it was the humidity making her sweat or the tension of unspoken issues between her and Jack. Jack had noticed Nick's familiarity with her. What did he think? She didn't want to talk about that, so she addressed her more obvious blunder instead.

"Hey, Jack, I'm sorry I asked D'marco to talk to me. I shouldn't have done that after Nick told him not to."

"Not unless you want to get disbarred," he replied mildly. "It's okay. He didn't say anything of substance. Forget about it."

It was an error, but he knew she understood her

mistake; there was no need to hammer away at it. She was grateful.

Jack pointed to the Firehook Bakery on the corner. "Got time for a cup of coffee?"

"Sure."

They stepped inside the coffee shop, welcomed by the smell of brewing coffee and baking muffins. The barista greeted Jack by name. He ordered an iced coffee, and Anna held up two fingers. As she was pulling out her wallet, Jack paid for both drinks, so she just tucked a couple of dollars into the tip jar.

She followed Jack back out into the late morning sunlight. He strolled to a waist-high flower planter and leaned back on it, sipping his coffee and gazing out toward the courthouse. After a moment's hesitation, Anna perched next to him and looked out at the crowd. Judiciary Square swarmed with lawyers hurrying to court, homeless guys hawking shoeshines, and thugs lined up at hot-dog carts to buy half-smokes before their court hearings. One wild-eyed man was pacing and muttering about the radio transmitter the CIA had implanted in his teeth. A kid was playing an impromptu percussion set on some plastic buckets. Despite her worry that he would ask her about Nick, Anna was happy to be sitting here with the Homicide chief, who was treating her as an equal. Then Jack turned to her with a serious expression, and Anna tensed.

"McGee lost his teeth in a foot chase," Jack said.

"Aha." Anna smiled and relaxed. "Go on."

"It happened before my time, but the story's legendary. Give any cop a few beers and he'll tell you about it. When he was in his twenties, they had McGee doing undercover SLIP work. You know what that is?"

"Solicitation for a Lewd and Immoral Purpose. He was posing as a john, propositioning prostitutes?"

"Exactly. So one day, he's out on the track—you know, the street where the prostitutes hang out to pick up their 'dates'—when this guy comes running out of an alley, being chased by a hooker who's yelling, 'He just raped me!' So McGee chases him, and—this is over twenty years ago—McGee is fast as lightning, and after a block or so, he tackles the guy onto the sidewalk.

"But now all the prostitutes run up, and they're furious. It's a big hazard of their job—prostitutes get raped all the time, and sometimes worse. So they start beating on the guy.

"McGee tries to stop them, and now they think he's *with* the rapist or he *is* the rapist or something—he's in civilian clothes and there's a lot of confusion—and they start beating on *McGee,* tearing at him, kicking him with those big high-heeled platform boots. There's, like, a dozen hookers, all in short-shorts and fishnets and wigs and what have you, and they just give McGee this epic beatdown. By the time his arrest team gets over there and breaks it up, McGee's passed out, his shirt's torn clean off his body, his wrist is broken, his lip is split, and his two front teeth are lying on the sidewalk next to him."

"Whoa."

"He spent a couple nights in the hospital. The guy he caught turned out to be a serial rapist who'd been terrorizing the city that summer, specializing in prostitutes and drunk college girls leaving bars. McGee got a medal of honor for it."

"That's quite a story. But . . . why doesn't he get his teeth fixed?"

"I've never straight-out asked him. But I think he's proud of them. Cops know the story, they see him, and they know it's him. Plus, I suspect he thinks it's just funny."

Anna nodded, smiling. That sounded like McGee. She leaned farther back on the edge of the planter, trying to picture a young, skinny McGee getting beaten by a mob of furious prostitutes.

"So, how do you know Nick Wagner?" Jack asked casually.

Anna took a sip of her coffee to hide her gulp. She'd known that the question was coming, but he'd still caught her off guard. She hadn't decided how to answer it. The question raised so many issues: her duty to this case, her desire to have Jack think well of her, her reputation, her privacy, her obligation to Jack, to Rose, to Laprea.

"We were in law school together," she found herself saying. It was the truth. Maybe not the whole truth, but their relationship was over, and it wouldn't affect her work. She was just beginning to earn Jack's respect—she couldn't bring herself to tell him she had dated an OPD attorney. She didn't think she had any duty to disclose it. Still, she felt a pang of guilt at her evasion.

Jack nodded, looking out at the pedestrians. He didn't press her further. "Wagner's got his hands full," he said. "He obviously wants a deal, but his client won't go for it. If D'marco doesn't plead, Wagner's going to lose. He hates to lose a high-profile case."

"It doesn't have to be that cynical, does it?" Anna

asked. "Maybe he's just recommending a plea because it's D'marco's best option now."

"Maybe. But I don't think Nick Wagner is your typical OPD true believer. He's a spoiled rich kid who enjoys playing defense lawyer. He likes to talk about working in the trenches while he's nibbling on shrimp at cocktail parties. He doesn't like to take weak cases to trial, especially high-profile cases. He must think this one's a real loser."

"Defense attorneys must be used to losing, though."

"Sure. But he'll do whatever he can to win. And he has a big bag of tricks."

Anna's mind wandered back to the alpaca rug in front of Nick's fireplace. She was familiar with a few of his tricks. Jack took a sip of his coffee and studied Anna's face as she gazed at the passersby.

"What I'm saying is: Be careful dealing with him, Anna. Be very careful."

Anna turned back to Jack. She couldn't read his poker face. She didn't agree with his assessment of Nick, but she wasn't going to debate him about it. Especially since the tone of his advice made her wonder if he meant it on a more personal level.

"I'll be careful," she said, and she meant it. She couldn't change the past, but she would be wiser in the future.

Anna and Jack tossed their empty coffee cups and headed back to the office. The conversation had been much easier than she had imagined. With any luck, her relationship with Nick wouldn't come up again. Anna relaxed in the comfort of her hopeful naïveté. Now she could forget her liaison with Nick and concentrate on building a case to keep his client in jail as long as possible.

18

Ray-Ray sauntered through the yard of the D.C. Jail with the authority of a CEO walking past a row of cubicles. The other prisoners waved and called greetings to the tall, skinny man, and Ray-Ray nodded back, greeting a few by name. Meanwhile, his eyes continually skimmed the yard.

He was hoping to see D'marco here today. Ray-Ray had heard that his old friend was back in jail. He still felt guilty for being the one who broke the bad news to D'marco the day that Laprea was killed. Ray-Ray knew it was probably his big mouth that had sent D'marco over the edge that night. He wanted to see how D'marco was hanging in there, and if there was anything he could do for him.

But until Ray-Ray found his playcousin, he wouldn't miss any opportunities to do business.

Midway around the basketball court, Ray-Ray slowed and called, "Yo, Peanut." A short man lounging on a concrete picnic table hopped up and met Ray-Ray by the court. They clapped hands languidly and said a few quiet words. Then Peanut went back to the table and Ray-Ray continued to walk casually downcourt, flipping his dreads over his shoulder nonchalantly. The entire transaction took less than five seconds. To anyone watching, it was just a handshake between jailhouse friends. Only the closest observer would have seen Ray-Ray slip a tiny ziplock bag filled with white powder into Peanut's hand as Peanut slipped a twenty to Ray-Ray.

Smuggling contraband into the D.C. Jail had always been a lucrative business. Most of the prisoners were accustomed to seeking happiness through drugs, women, and the occasional fight over drugs and women. Their habits didn't evaporate just because they were in lockup. Just the opposite. In jail, they needed the obliterating relief of a rock of crack or the protection of a knife more than out on the street, where pleasure and protection were more easily acquired. So the prisoners were willing to pay high prices for anything that made it inside. The jail's voracious appetite for contraband was surpassed only by the creativity of the entrepreneurs who satisfied it.

Ray-Ray was one of those entrepreneurs. He was a weekender, the magical status sometimes conferred on petty offenders who held a steady day job. After Ray-Ray was convicted of shoplifting for the third time, the judge sentenced him to sixty days in jail, but allowed him to serve the sentence on weekends so he could keep working as a busboy during the week. The judge hadn't intended it, but this arrangement also allowed Ray-Ray to run a profitable side business of filling orders from prisoners who weren't furloughed Monday through Friday.

Ray-Ray's method of import was as effective as it was low-tech. He wrapped his contraband in cellophane, coated the plastic with Vaseline, and shoved the package so far up his rectum that the probing, latex-covered fingers of the guard conducting a Friday-afternoon strip search wouldn't reach it. The items could then be gingerly retrieved Friday night, wiped off, and sold to prisoners whose cravings made them overlook the method of transport. Ray-Ray's specialty was heroin, although he would occasionally take orders for crack, vials of PCP, and, once, some tightly rolled-up pages of *Hustler.* He charged four times the street price for drugs. Ten times for the porn, which had not been a comfortable experience.

His business was booming. In the six weekends he'd served so far, Ray-Ray had earned more than he had in six months of bussing tables. He knew he could be making even more. For every customer he had, there were three who wanted to buy from him. But Ray-Ray couldn't bring in enough supply to meet the demand. He'd tried to think of a way to increase his wares, but finally, sadly, concluded that his business had no room for expansion. His profits were limited by the size of his colon.

Ray-Ray walked through the yard and made a few more transactions with some of his steady customers. By the time he reached the far side of the basketball court, he was three zips away from being sold out.

Ray-Ray leaned against the wall and fished a package of Newports out of his pocket. He looked around as he lit up, scanning for any additional clientele. The yard could feel disorienting sometimes, cut off as it was from any reference point in the outside world. It was an inner courtyard of the jail, an asphalt square surrounded by four high walls of pinkish stone. A basketball court dominated the center of the yard, and some concrete tables lined the sides. There were a few scattered pieces of stationary workout equipment, but no free weights; the jail had gotten rid of them a few years ago after the prisoners started getting too big. A difference in muscle mass between prisoners and guards could have serious security implications in a facility where the guards didn't carry guns.

As Ray-Ray scanned the yard, his eyes rested on a big man working out on the dip bar. It was D'marco Davis. Ray-Ray grinned and strode over.

"D!"

D'marco glanced over, saw Ray-Ray, and released himself mid-dip. He landed with muscular grace on the blacktop and strode over to his friend.

"Ray-Ray."

The two big men in orange jumpsuits greeted each other with a loud, back-thumping half handshake, half embrace. Ray-Ray was delighted to have found his friend, and to find him looking good. They stood watching a basketball game while they talked and caught up. Ray-Ray filled D'marco in on what was happening in Anacostia, and then asked D'marco what was going on in the jail.

"You ain't gonna believe this," D'marco said softly. "There's a . . . a business opportunity you gotta see."

Ray-Ray followed D'marco to the back of the prison yard. The yard was formed by the rectangular courtyard created by four adjacent jail buildings, but there was one corner where two of the buildings did not touch each other. There was an opening between the two buildings at that corner of the yard, wide enough to drive a car through. That space was sealed off by a large steel double door that led directly to the street outside. The prisoners never saw anyone open the door or use it for anything; it appeared to be welded shut, its original purpose lost to history.

D'marco pointed to the door.

"Yeah, man." Ray-Ray shrugged, disappointed. Like every other inmate, Ray-Ray had given this door a serious once-over when he first came out in the yard, and quickly concluded there was no getting around it. It went up about eight feet, ending in a wide, flat concrete ledge. There was a slight gap above the ledge, then a sheet of metal ran six stories up to the top of the two buildings. The metal walled off the opening between the two buildings. "So what? You can't get out there."

"True. But you can get stuff in."

D'marco pointed to the eight-inch gap between the top of the door and the bottom of the metal sheeting. Through that gap, they could see the sky.

"Other side of that is Nineteenth Street."

"Huh." Ray-Ray looked at the door with renewed interest. Ray-Ray's eyes were wide when he turned to D'marco. "You know what we can do with this?"

"Yeah, man," D'marco replied, laughing quietly.

D'marco sat Ray-Ray down at one of the cement tables and they got down to business. The men spoke in low voices, their elbows on their knees, leaning toward each other to hear. D'marco explained his proposition; Ray-Ray listened with growing excitement, then pitched a few ideas of his own. They came to a detailed plan.

Ray-Ray left the jail on Sunday feeling like he'd just won the lottery.

The very next day, Ray-Ray returned to D.C. Jail—but this time on the outside of the walls. The 96 bus dropped him off at the corner of 18th and Massachusetts Avenue SE. Ray-Ray walked down to 19th Street. The big structure of the jail was on his left; a vacant lot was on his right. It was amazing, Ray-Ray thought, how close the jail was to the street. From this side, it just looked like a big ugly office building.

Between the sidewalk and the jail was a little strip of grass and then a waist-high brick wall, which couldn't stop a child. There wasn't a chain-link fence here, or the swirls of barbed wire that surrounded some other sections of the jail. On this side of the facility, the thick walls of the jail itself provided the outer layer of security. Except that Ray-Ray knew there was a chink in it.

Ray-Ray walked along the enormous pinkish stone building until he saw the strip of metal running up from a thick steel door. You couldn't tell from the street, but that metal strip was the back corner of the prison yard.

Ray-Ray crossed the grass and stood by the little brick wall. He was less than twenty feet away from the jail. He could hear the prisoners talking and shouting on the other side of the metal door, and if he strained, he could even hear the rhythmic thump of a basketball hitting the asphalt court. Most important, Ray-Ray could see the eight-inch gap between the bottom of the metal sheeting and the ledge on top of the door. He would have to be precise. Ray-Ray checked his watch: 3:30 p.m. He looked across the street, at the vacant lot. No one else was around. He glanced at the jail itself, sure he would see a watchtower with a guard looking out at him. But there was none.

He was alone on the street and no one was looking at him.

Ray-Ray reached into his pocket and pulled out the brown paper package of heroin. He took a deep breath, clenched his fist around the package to steady his arm, and took aim.

Inside the yard, D'marco looked at his watch: 3:30. He stood up from his place at the concrete table. As he did, he nodded at two men on the opposite side of the yard. The two men nodded back at him and turned to each other.

"Fuck you, mothafucker!" the first one screamed, and shoved the second man.

"Fuck me? Fuck you!" The second man grabbed the first by the lapels of his orange jumpsuit. They started brawling. A crowd quickly gathered around them, yelling and egging them on.

The four guards in the yard ran over to the fight and pushed their way through the crowd. "Break it up! Break it up!" The guards grabbed at the thrashing men, trying to get them under control.

Perfect. D'marco nodded to Peanut. They were standing at the corner by the big metal door. The ledge above the door was about eight feet off the ground. Peanut locked his fingers together, forming a stirrup with his hands. D'marco put a foot in the stirrup and Peanut boosted him up with a grunt. D'marco's head was level with the gap above the door. He peered out and saw Ray-Ray walking quickly away on the sidewalk outside. D'marco looked at the wide concrete ledge above the door. A small brown paper package sat right in the middle.

D'marco swept his arm across the ledge and grabbed the package. He hopped down from Peanut's hands. D'marco slipped the package into his pocket and walked casually back to the table where he'd been sitting; Peanut walked the other way.

The guards were hauling away the two inmates who'd been fighting. Those prisoners would get some mild discipline, but it would be worth it for the heroin D'marco would give them later. D'marco raised his chin at them as they were led away. They'd done their jobs. The guards had been distracted by the fight, and hadn't seen D'marco retrieve the package from above the door.

D'marco settled back at his seat at the table. His fingers stroked the package nestled inside his pocket. He let out a sigh of pleasure, and felt something close to love as he fondled the solid feel of powder wrapped in plastic and paper.

They would make several thousand dollars on this package alone. This was a gold mine.

But it wasn't just about the money to D'marco. Cash could get him a few perks in the jail, but he understood the limits of money inside these walls. It couldn't buy him a comfortable bed, a flat-screen TV, a night out on the town. It wouldn't let him sink his fingers into the soft curves of a woman's body. No matter how much money he had in here, he would still have to sleep in a concrete box that reeked of shit and bleach. And if he got convicted, they'd ship him off to a federal prison, which could be anywhere in America. D'marco had grown up with a guy who was now serving twelve years in a federal prison in Kansas.

That's why he needed to take this opportunity now. To D'marco, this package of drugs wasn't just a way to make money. It was a way to get Ray-Ray used to throwing things into the jail. Once Ray-Ray got casual about smuggling drugs in like this, D'marco would ask him to get a gun. And then things could really start to happen.

19

Anna sat back in her chair and stared at the files stacked on her desk. She was combing through the prior cases where D'marco had been charged with assaulting Laprea. In each of these cases, the charges had been dropped after Laprea went back to him. Why? Anna wondered. Why did she keep doing it? Why didn't Laprea just leave him the first time he hit her?

But Anna knew why. At least, she knew all the theories. Experts talked about the "cycle of violence." After a beating, the man is repentant and sweet. He promises to change. He tells the woman he loves her, he needs her. And he does need her—no one else needs her like that. No one who doesn't hit her. So she goes back to him, hoping for the best, and for a while everything is fine. Until the next fight, when he beats her again, and the cycle starts over.

Rose had mentioned that Laprea's father was abusive, too. That explained a lot. Something happened to little girls who grew up watching their mothers being hit—something that created an internal compass steering them into their own abusive relationships. Anna had seen the same history in so many of her cases. It was a peculiar law of attraction. Each woman subconsciously tried to re-create the relationship she'd seen between her parents.

To understand her own family, Anna had taken classes about domestic violence in college; she'd read all the literature. After she learned how often abuse was passed down through the generations, she vowed that she wouldn't accept the inheritance of violence. That determination impacted every relationship she'd had since then.

For a moment, her thoughts turned to Nick, and how easily and naturally she'd fallen in love with him.

She wrenched her mind away from the defense attorney and focused on her computer. She needed to finish this *Drew* motion, in which she was arguing to admit evidence of the past violence in Laprea and D'marco's relationship. As part of the motion, Anna had to summarize all of their prior DV cases. It was depressing work. Anna reread a police report and started typing.

> On October 14, 2004, at 10:15 p.m., two MPD officers responded to a radio run for a family disturbance at the home of Laprea Johnson. When they arrived at the home, the officers found Ms. Johnson standing on her front porch. She was crying, shaking, and bleeding from a small cut above her eye. As the police approached her, Ms. Johnson pointed to a man walking down the street and shouted, "My boyfriend just hit me! I want him locked up!"

Anna's phone rang. She glanced at the incoming number; it was the receptionist transferring a call. Anna pinned the receiver to her ear with her shoulder but continued typing, trying to finish the paragraph before she lost her train of thought.

"Anna Curtis," she answered distractedly.

"Hey, Miss Curtis, how you doin'? This D'marco Davis. I gotta talk to you."

Her fingers froze on the keyboard.

"I'm sorry, this is *who*?"

"D'marco Davis."

She pulled the phone away from her ear and stared at it, wondering if this was a prank. But she recognized his voice.

"Hello?" he said.

"Mr. . . . uh . . . Mr. Davis." She tried to pull her thoughts together as she brought the receiver back to her ear. "I'm sorry but I can't talk to you."

"You busy now? I can call later." He was annoyed but trying to sound friendly.

"No, it's not that. It's—you can't call me."

"Why not?" he demanded. D'marco paused, and she could feel him struggling to get his anger under control. When he spoke again, his voice was soft and sugary sweet. "I just wanna tell you a coupla things. 'Bout my case. They important."

"I'd like to hear anything you want to say, but your lawyer needs to be there. We can meet, all of us together, or you can tell your lawyer anything you'd like the government to know, and he can pass it on."

"That ain't happening," D'marco replied with growing frustration. "That's why I called you. I already told my lawyer—"

"Mr. Davis!" She cut him off. "Don't tell me anything

that was said between you and your lawyer. That's attorney-client privileged."

"What if I don't want no attorney-client privilege?"

"I can't advise you about that. You should talk to your lawyer if you want to consider waiving that privilege."

"I'm tryin' to tell you! I don't wanna talk to my lawyer—"

"Mr. Davis." She spoke over him again. "Really, I can't speak to you. I have to go now."

"This's fucked up! I wanna give you information—you gotta take it! What about my rights, bitch?"

She hung up.

Anna stared at the phone as if it might bite her. She fielded crazy phone calls every day. Sometimes the family and friends of men she was prosecuting called, asking her to go easy on their loved ones, or cursing her out if she had not. Sometimes people called thinking she had the power to do all kinds of things, like take care of the rabid pit bull that lived down their street. But this was the first time she'd gotten a call from a defendant himself. Her heart was pounding from being cursed at by a furious prisoner, and her mind was filled with questions.

Why had he called her? What could he want to say that Nick wouldn't let him say?

She was sorry she had to hang up on him. If it were up to her, she would have listened to anything he wanted to say. But the rules were clear. Prosecutors weren't allowed to talk to defendants who had a lawyer, except with the lawyer's permission, and she certainly didn't have that. The rules were meant to protect the accused, to prevent the government from going behind a defense attorney's back to get information that a defendant with the benefit of good legal advice wouldn't reveal. They were fine rules, Anna thought. But she'd hated to hang up when D'marco clearly wanted to tell her something.

She dialed Jack's number, and he picked up on the first ring.

"You're not going to believe this," Anna began. "I just got a call from D'marco Davis."

Jack was in her doorway a minute later. "You're kidding," he said.

"Nope. Come on in, make yourself comfortable."

Jack stepped easily around Grace's files, which were stacked at irregular intervals on the floor. He was used to navigating their messy office by this point.

"So, what happened?" he said as he sat in Grace's desk chair.

Anna told him about the phone call. He listened with quiet concern.

"You doing okay?" he asked when she was done.

"Sure. It was just a little surprising, is all."

"I'm sorry that happened to you. If D'marco's going to harass anyone, I'd prefer him to choose me."

"It comes with the territory, right? This is a homicide case, not a bake sale." Anna tried out McGee's words, sounding tougher than she felt. "You can't worry every time an AUSA gets a little harassed, right? You wouldn't have time for anything else."

"Sure, sure." Jack shifted uneasily in his chair. Anna wondered if he was this protective with the other attorneys he supervised. "Anyway, you did a good job handling that phone call."

"I didn't do anything."

"Exactly. You refused to talk to him. That was the right thing to do. It'll make our follow-up a lot easier." Jack pointed to her phone. "We need to call Nick Wagner and inform him about this."

"Oh."

She just sat there, staring at Jack, trying not to panic. Jack smiled at her and nodded toward the phone. She smiled back weakly, but still didn't move. Jack walked to her desk, hit the speakerphone button, and dialed the main number for OPD. He asked the receptionist for Nick Wagner, then sat down at Grace's desk again as the line clicked over. Anna hoped the defense attorney wouldn't pick up.

"Nick Wagner," he answered.

Jack nodded to Anna; he expected her to take the lead. She cleared her throat and tried to sound normal.

"Hello, Nick, this is Anna Curtis."

"Anna." Nick's voice softened. She hadn't called him since the case started. "It's good to hear your voice."

"I'm sitting here with Jack Bailey," she rushed ahead. "You're on speakerphone."

"Hi, Nick," Jack called, with forced cheer.

"Oh. Hello, Jack."

"You'll be happy to know that Ms. Curtis is looking nice again today."

Nick paused a beat. "I am happy to know that. Is there anything else you wanted to tell me, or is that the reason you called?"

Anna needed to get this call over with.

"Listen, Nick, we just wanted to let you know that your client called me a few minutes ago. He wanted to talk to me about the case."

"Christ. What did he say?"

"Nothing, I wouldn't let him talk. I told him that I'd be willing to listen to anything he wants to tell me, but only through you. Do you want to set up a meeting for that?"

"No."

"No, I didn't think so."

"We'll send you a letter documenting all this," Jack said. "I'm also sending you a copy of the results from the CODIS search—we got the report yesterday. The father isn't in CODIS."

"Fine," Nick said curtly. The news didn't surprise anyone. The father of Laprea Johnson's baby was not a convicted felon. That got them pretty much nowhere. It could be anyone else in the world.

"Listen . . ." Jack hesitated. "I don't want to tell you how to do your job—"

"Then don't."

"Just make sure your client doesn't call Anna again."

"No kidding."

The line clicked as Nick hung up.

"Asshole," Jack muttered. "Anyway, write up a memo to the file about Davis's call. Then call it a day. Go home, get some rest for once, forget about Davis."

"I don't want to rest. I want to be helpful."

"You're more helpful than I could have imagined when you were assigned to this case." He smiled at her. "I'm being selfish. I don't want you to burn out. I know you've been working late nights on this case. Tonight, I want you to go home early, rent a movie or—I don't know—go rollerblading or clubbing, whatever it is you kids do these days."

"Okay, Gramps." She laughed, feeling some of the tension from the phone call drain from her shoulders.

"Gramps!" Jack huffed with mock indignation. "No more back talk from you, missy, or you're grounded."

Anna laughed. Jack was only ten years older than her, and he certainly didn't look like anyone's grandfather. His shaved head conveyed a tough hipness, and he was trim and athletic, moving with a lean elegance. With his tall stature, smooth mocha skin, and striking green eyes, Anna supposed Jack would do pretty well with the ladies at a club himself. She was surprised at the thought. She'd always seen him as her stern, demanding boss, but she suddenly recognized that Jack was actually a young man.

"In the meantime," Jack added, "I'm getting Davis cut off, for good. No more phone calls for him."

"That should be tattooed on his forehead. 'No phone calls for me.'"

As Jack walked out, she turned back to her computer, humming without realizing it. She was in a better mood than she'd been in for a while.

A few weeks passed without another word from D'marco. Jack thought the issue was closed, until one night in late September, when he sat at his desk, flipping through that day's mail. It was the usual stuff: reports from the FBI, memoranda from MPD, D.C. *Bar Bulletins*. Then he saw an unusual envelope, light blue and slightly crumpled, with his name and address handwritten in bold, slashing strokes. Jack looked at the return address: D'marco Davis's name, prisoner ID number, and the address of the D.C. Jail. Jack shook his head. Without opening the envelope, he walked it down the hall to the war room.

It was a Wednesday night, and Jack knew he could find Anna there now. He stopped walking halfway down the hall, though, and looked down at his feet. He was still wearing his galoshes. There'd been a thunderstorm this morning, and he'd put the rubber boots on for his walk to the subway. Then he'd gotten so busy he'd forgotten about them and worn them all day. Now he noticed that they looked goofy, like clown feet sticking out of his suit trousers. Jack turned back to his office and pulled the galoshes off of his dress shoes. As he walked out again, he felt both better and sheepish. If he were going to see anyone else, he wouldn't have thought about his footwear.

Anna was sitting at the conference table, taking notes as she read a transcript. She was deep in thought and didn't notice Jack. Her suit jacket was draped over a chair, her shoes sat on the floor next to her, and her feet were tucked under her as she worked. Her hair hung in a blond curtain around her face. She pulled it back as she read, distractedly pinning it behind her head with a pencil, exposing the soft nape of her neck. Jack blinked and looked away. He rapped his knuckles on the door frame.

"Knock, knock," he said. Anna looked up, startled. "Sorry, I didn't mean to scare you."

She smiled when she saw it was Jack. "Hazard of the job. You sit around reading about the bogeyman all day, you start to jump at shadows."

He sat down in his usual seat across from her. They

had spent hours in this room, sitting across from each other as they pored through reports and evidence. They both had other duties, so they worked on this case in the mornings before court, and then after court finished in the evenings. They'd spent many late nights in the war room, both because there was a lot to do and because they enjoyed each other's company—the chance to bounce ideas off of each other instead of toiling away in their own separate offices. Besides his daughter and the nanny, Jack realized, Anna was usually the first person he saw every morning and the last one he saw each night. He didn't mind. She was easy company.

Jack slid the envelope across the table to her.

"Tell me if you can guess what that is," he said.

She picked it up and studied it.

"You've gotta give D'marco points for persistence," she said with a puzzled smile.

"Or something." Jack stuffed D'marco's letter, unopened, into a larger manila envelope.

"What are you going to do with the letter?" Anna asked.

"I'll send it to his lawyer. And we'll write another letter to both Wagner and the judge explaining this. It all has to be on the record."

It was a hassle for Jack. They had to document everything in fairness to the defense attorney, and to cover themselves, in case anyone ever accused them of improperly contacting the defendant. But, Jack said, the one who would really be inconvenienced by this was Nick Wagner, who clearly couldn't control his client.

"It makes you wonder what's going on in that lawyer-client relationship," Jack said.

Anna nodded, but then changed the subject. "Do you have time to talk about medical records?" she asked. Jack nodded. "I'm having a hard time getting some stuff from Greater Southeast Hospital."

"Sure."

Jack relaxed in his chair as she described the problem. It was just one of a hundred logistical issues that came up with every criminal case. But Jack enjoyed talking about it with Anna, the two of them hashing out challenges in the war room, surrounded by the quiet office. He hadn't admitted it to himself yet, but this was becoming his favorite part of the day.

D'marco paced the length of his cell, fuming. His lawyer had visited him earlier today, and yelled at him for writing to the prosecutors. The fucking prosecutors had sent his letter to Nick! Without even opening it! Nick had given him an earful. When D'marco tried to explain, Nick had just gotten angrier, and walked out on him. Now D'marco was the furious one.

The system was stacked against him.

No one respected him.

He knew what he had to do.

This weekend, when Ray-Ray was in again, D'marco would tell him to toss a gun onto the ledge. Ray-Ray might be a little nervous about it, but he would do what D'marco asked.

D'marco would get his gun—and he would use it to escape from the jail. And then he would find that lady prosecutor. All he needed was five minutes with her.

20

Ray-Ray wiped the damp rag indifferently over the dark, shiny wood of the four-top table. More crumbs fell onto the white marble floor than into the dirty tub of dishes he'd been aiming for, but he ignored them. He wasn't going to get any awards for being the busboy of the year—and he didn't care. He held on to this job for one reason: so he could report steady employment to his probation officer and keep his cushy gig as a weekender in the D.C. Jail. Meanwhile, if the Center Café wasn't completely spick-and-span, it wasn't Ray-Ray's problem. He knew the manager would follow after him with a broom, sighing and grumbling—but she wouldn't fire him. That was all he really cared about here.

The restaurant where Ray-Ray worked was a chic café inside the central hall of Union Station, and one of the most visited tourist spots in Washington. Union Station's central hall was massive and beautiful, with gleaming white marble floors, huge white pillars, and a soaring, barrel-vaulted ceiling of carved golden panels. Towering statues of nude Roman legionnaires guarded the ceiling, looking stern and dignified despite their strategically placed modesty shields. The huge lobby was lined with tourist shops and fancy stores.

Right in the middle of the lobby was the Center Café, Ray-Ray's workplace. The restaurant was a circular, double-decked structure made of dark wood, open to the historic hall it sat in. Although the café was two stories, the soaring ceiling of Union Station still towered high above. The restaurant had no walls; it was set apart from the lobby by wooden planters filled with flowers and ivy, giving it the feel of an outdoor sidewalk café. Every table had good views of the comings and goings of Union Station.

The hallway echoed with the voices of dozens of people walking around outside the café. Union Station had a little something for everyone: it was a historic site and a shopping mall, it had a food court and a movie theater in the basement, and beyond the beautiful main hall, it held a teeming train station. All kinds of people passed through here: millionaire law firm partners, nose-ringed nonprofit interns, tourists in shorts and knee socks, and thugs of every degree.

The Center Café's patrons tended to be the more upscale types. Ray-Ray didn't think anything of the man wearing a suit and tie who walked up as he was clearing off a table.

"Excuse me," the man started.

"Hostess's over there." Ray-Ray inclined his head without making eye contact.

"Actually, I was hoping to talk to you. Ray-Ray, right?"

Ray-Ray looked up, suddenly suspicious. It was never a good sign for a white man in a suit to be asking for him. And since Ray-Ray had agreed to smuggle a gun into the D.C. Jail for D'marco, he'd been feeling anxious. He wondered if this guy was here because the plan had somehow gotten out. Ray-Ray hadn't bought the gun yet—he was so uncomfortable with the idea that he'd been putting it off. He couldn't be in trouble just for *talking* about it with D'marco—could he? He met the man's eyes nervously, but didn't say anything.

"My name's Nick Wagner. I'm D'marco Davis's lawyer." Nick held out the identification card clipped to his belt loop. It had his name and the words OFFICE OF THE PUBLIC DEFENDER printed on it.

"Oh, hey, man." Ray-Ray exhaled with relief. This guy wasn't here to get him in trouble. He was on D'marco's side. Ray-Ray set the tub of dirty dishes on the table behind him, wiped his hands on his apron, and reached out to shake the attorney's hand. "What can I do to help? Here, have a seat."

Nick and Ray-Ray sat at the table Ray-Ray had just been cleaning.

"Thanks for your time," Nick said with a smile. After a few minutes of small talk, the lawyer got to the point. "D'marco tells me that you might know who Laprea was dating right before she died."

Ray-Ray winced. He still felt bad for telling D'marco that rumor. And the worst of it was that he didn't have any more information.

"Aw, man. Wish I did. But I just heard some stuff on the street. Just talk, y'know. Some folks seen a police cruiser hangin' around outside her house a coupla times, seen the same cop goin' in and out. I heard it was a white cop. Ain't never seen him myself."

"Do you know anyone who did see him?"

"Nah. I don't even remember how I heard it. There was just talk."

"What made folks think they were dating? I mean, were they ever seen out together or anything like that?"

"Nah, man. Nothing 'pecific. Rumors is rumors."

"How do you know the police officer wasn't just investigating her case?"

"Ha. You know how many cases in that neighborhood? Robberies. Beatdowns. Dealing. How often's a cop stop by just to 'investigate' a misdemeanor assault? Never. You call 911, they slow up, take they report, and go. Or don't even take a report."

Nick nodded. "Do you know anyone else she was seeing romantically?"

"Uh-uh." Ray-Ray remembered what D'marco had told him: that Laprea was pregnant with someone else's child when she died. D'marco had acted like it was no big deal, but Ray-Ray could tell that the news hurt D'marco badly. "You tryin' to find that baby's father?"

"Doing the best I can, but we're not having much luck."

"Oh." Ray-Ray felt sorry for his friend. Nick seemed to read his face.

"It's actually better this way. If the father's unknown, I can argue to the jury that someone else was close to her, and it could be *anyone*—and maybe that other guy killed her. Maybe that's reasonable doubt. If the father were identified, the prosecutors would interview him, bring him to court, and what if he has an alibi? Or he's some putz that wouldn't hurt a fly? Unless the father happened to have a longer record than D'marco—and we know he doesn't, because he wasn't in the police DNA database—we're much better off with a mystery man."

"Mm," Ray-Ray replied, not entirely convinced. "You gonna get D'marco a good plea, right?"

"Yeah, but the case against him is strong. No matter what, he's gonna have to serve some serious time. He needs to start coming to terms with that."

Nick stood up, pulled a business card out of his suit jacket, and handed it to Ray-Ray. "Let me know if you hear anything else."

"Okay, I will. Good luck, man."

"Thanks." The lawyer walked out into the main hall and merged with the crowds of people.

Ray-Ray carried the tub of dirty dishes back to the kitchen and set it down by the slop sink. He lifted a dirty plate and held the sprayer to it while he thought. He rinsed the same plate for five minutes, thinking about what the lawyer had just said, and what a tough spot D'marco was in. Ray-Ray wondered if Laprea might still be alive, and D'marco out of jail, if he'd just kept his mouth shut. In a way, Ray-Ray knew, D'marco's troubles were Ray-Ray's fault.

He would get the gun tonight, Ray-Ray decided. And he would throw it to D'marco tomorrow, along with the usual three-thirty package of heroin. He owed his friend that much.

"Are there any further questions for this witness?" Anna asked.

She looked at the blank faces of the grand jurors.

The jurors stared back, bored. A few hadn't looked up from their newspapers during the whole presentation.

"Shall we excuse the witness then?" she asked.

The jurors murmured their acquiescence. Anna opened the waist-high door to the witness box to help D'marco Davis's cousin step down.

"With our thanks," Anna said, as the man walked out of the room with a scowl. Anna glanced at Jack, who nodded at her. She'd done just fine.

When Jack first invited her to assist him in the grand jury, she had been intrigued. Misdemeanor cases didn't go through the grand jury, and Anna had never been inside one. The whole grand jury process was filled with an air of mystery.

Everything that happened in the grand jury was secret. The jurors and the prosecutors weren't allowed to talk about what happened inside the grand jury to anyone outside of it. That was designed to protect the integrity of ongoing investigations. A witness could bring their own lawyer, but the lawyer had to wait outside the grand jury door while the witness testified inside. There was no judge and no defense attorney. It was just the prosecutor questioning the witnesses, with the occasional question from a juror. If, after hearing all the evidence, the grand jury found that there was probable cause to believe that someone committed a crime, it would return an indictment, an official charging document that sent the defendant to trial. It was a tremendous power, and unlike almost every other part of the criminal justice system, it was a power exercised entirely behind closed doors.

Anna had almost expected the grand jury to look like the all-white Krypton courtroom from the opening scene of *Superman*.

She had been slightly disappointed the first time Jack had allowed her into the grand jury room. Instead of a whirring crystal fortress, the grand jury room looked like a college seminar room, but with the rows of Formica tables and plastic chairs curving around a witness stand instead of a chalkboard. A tired-looking court reporter sat to the side of the witness stand, typing on her stenographic machine and periodically opening an old tape recorder to flip the tape. The jurors themselves were random civilians who had been mailed letters instructing them to report for jury service. Many of them didn't want to be there. And in cases like this one, they were quickly bored.

It was November—three months after Laprea's murder—and Jack and Anna had called more than fifty people to testify before this grand jury so far. Most of those witnesses didn't know, or at least claimed not to know, anything relevant to D'marco's case. But because so many people wouldn't talk to them voluntarily, Jack and Anna used their subpoena power to get people to talk to them in the grand jury. They had put dozens of D'marco's neighbors on the witness stand, each of whom claimed not to have seen or heard anything unusual on the night of the murder.

The prosecutors had also begun to subpoena D'marco's friends and family, to see if D'marco had confessed anything to them or had any kind of alibi. So far, Anna had learned nothing. At least her questions nailed down their stories about what they were doing on the night of the murder. D'marco's buddies wouldn't be able to provide a false alibi for him later.

The jurors were getting tired of the parade of irrelevant witnesses. Anna was sorry to bore the jurors, but the job had to be done. And she was grateful to be getting this experience. Under Jack's watchful eye, Anna had examined a few minor witnesses, like the cousin she'd just excused. She was glad that Jack's faith in her abilities was growing.

And she thought the jurors might be more interested in their next witness. Anna opened the grand jury door and peered out to the waiting area.

"Ms. Davis, we're ready for you," Anna said.

The big woman sitting next to Detective McGee looked up from her magazine. She wore a gray security guard uniform and a gravity-defying salt-and-pepper beehive. She frowned at Anna, but followed her into the grand jury room. Anna showed the woman to the witness stand, then sat in a free chair. This witness could be too challenging for a rookie to handle. Jack would be asking the questions.

The foreman swore the woman in. She glared at Jack as she answered the usual introductory questions. Her name was Jeanne Davis; she was fifty-three years old. She lived in Southeast D.C. and worked as a guard in an office building in Northwest. Yes, she knew a man named D'marco Davis. He was her grandson.

The jurors sat up straighter and murmured to each other. Newspapers were lowered. The defendant's grandmother? This might be interesting.

"What was your role in bringing up D'marco Davis?" Jack asked.

"I raised him up since he's seven." Jeanne crossed her sizable arms and glared at Jack with open hostility.

"How did he come to live with you?" Jack ignored the attitude and spoke mildly.

"They took him away from my daughter."

"What's her name?"

"Tawanna Davis."

"How old is she?"

"Thirty-six."

"Did Tawanna care for D'marco until he went to live with you?"

"Kinda." Jeanne didn't want to be there, and she didn't want to give them anything they could use against her grandson.

"What do you mean?"

"She got issues."

"What issues?"

"Crack." A few of the grand jurors hummed in understanding. Some of them had similar issues in their own families. Jeanne looked over at them and seemed to soften a bit. She spoke toward an elderly woman in the front row. "Stealing to pay for the crack. Selling herself to pay for the crack."

"How old was D'marco when he was removed from Tawanna's care?"

"He was six."

"Did he come to live with you right away?"

"I couldn't take him at first. I had three other grandkids in my house."

"Where did D'marco go then?"

"Foster homes. Then a group home. I don't even wanna know what happened to him there." The elderly juror nodded sympathetically. "The social worker came and said he had no place to go. So I took him in."

"Was that difficult?"

"You do what you gotta do. I raised up my kids best I could. Now I'm raising their kids. By myself."

"How long did D'marco live with you?"

"Till he was twenty."

"What happened then?"

"He caught a drug charge. He been arrested before, but it was all bullshit. 'Scuse my language. This time he got locked up for a while."

"When he was released last December, did he return to your house?"

"Nah, I was full up. He took a place on Alabama Avenue."

"Which is where he was living on August sixteenth?"

"Yeah."

"Do you know where D'marco's parents are living?"

"We ain't seen his father since he was a baby."

"What about his mother?"

"She took to the streets. I ain't heard from her in years." Jeanne tried to keep a poker face, but Anna could see how much this pained her.

Jack asked about other friends and relatives, and he jotted down Jeanne's answers. Those folks would also be receiving grand jury subpoenas.

"Did you ever meet a woman named Laprea Johnson?"

"Yeah, I knew Laprea." Jeanne wrinkled her nose as if the name left a bad taste in her mouth. "She was his baby mama."

"What was she like?" Jack wanted to see if Jeanne

would insult Laprea. It would give them evidence of bias if she later tried to testify at trial on D'marco's behalf.

"She okay. She let me see the kids."

Jack tried to get her to elaborate on her relationship with Laprea, but Jeanne knew this was the important part. She gave one-word answers wherever possible.

"Did you ever see your grandson and Ms. Johnson fighting with each other?"

"No."

"Did you ever see him strike her?"

"No."

"Did you hear about any fights between them from anyone else?"

"No."

"Did you ever see Ms. Johnson with injuries?"

"No."

She's lying, Anna thought. But Anna understood that. Jeanne was trying to protect her family. Anna noticed Jack was treating her gently—more gently than other witnesses who had obviously lied. Few people would blame a grandmother for trying to protect a grandson she'd raised.

"Have you spoken to Mr. Davis since August sixteenth?"

"A few times, on the phone, since he been in jail."

"Have you talked with him about the death of Laprea Johnson?"

"No. Not at all."

Jack glanced ruefully at Anna. They were getting nowhere. The only thing left to do was to lock her out of lying for her grandson at trial.

"Ms. Davis, what were you doing the night of August sixteenth?"

"I was at home," she answered. After a pause, she continued. "With D'marco. All night."

Jack looked up, surprised, but only for a moment. If anyone was going to provide the defendant with a false alibi, it was this woman. Even criminals without a friend in the world could usually cough up a mother or grandmother willing to perjure herself to protect him.

"What do you mean by 'all night'?"

"He came over for dinner. He didn't leave till the next morning."

"When you say he came over for dinner: What time did he arrive?"

"I'm not sure exactly. I'd say around six p.m."

"Was it still light outside?"

"Yes, definitely."

Jeanne was making up a story to protect D'marco, but she didn't know the evidence they already had against him. She didn't know that her story was totally incompatible with what Ernie Jones saw in the hallway of D'marco's building.

"And you say he didn't leave until the next morning. When was that?"

"I'd say around eight a.m. Right before I went to work."

"What were you two doing all that time?"

"We watched TV after dinner. And he played some video games."

"He has his own apartment, right?"

"Right."

"With his own bed?"

"Yes."

"So why did he stay over at your house that night?"

"It just got late. He didn't feel like walking home. He just went to sleep on the couch; he does that sometimes. I woke him up there the next morning. He didn't go out all night. I know that for sure."

The jurors were openly glaring at her. They'd initially had sympathy for Gramma—but no one likes to be lied to. They'd already heard testimony from Ernie Jones, and they'd also heard Ernie's hysterical 911 call saying D'marco had just hit him and Laprea. The jurors knew that D'marco had been at his own house, beating up Laprea, around 9:30 p.m. They knew Jeanne Davis was lying.

"Ma'am, what shows did you watch on TV that night?"

She paused. "I don't remember."

"What video games did Mr. Davis play?"

"I'm not sure. I don't play those things," she replied haughtily, as if Jack had personally invented the scourge of computerized games.

"Have you spoken to your grandson about what you would say concerning where he was that night?"

"No, sir." She arranged her face into a look of outrage, as if Jack had shocked her with the suggestion that she collaborated with her grandson about his alibi.

"Have you spoken to his attorney, Nicholas Wagner, or a defense investigator about where your grandson was that night?"

"That's confidential."

"No, ma'am. Mr. Wagner is not *your* lawyer. Your discussions with him are not protected by the attorney-client privilege. I'm instructing you to answer the question." Jeanne's eyes radiated pure hatred. "Or risk being held in contempt."

"The lawyer came to my house. He wanted to know if Laprea been seeing anyone besides D'marco. I told him I don't know, just like I told you."

"Did you also tell Mr. Wagner that D'marco had been with you on the night of Laprea Johnson's death?"

"I told him exactly what I just told you."

"And what did he say?"

Anna tensed up. It was strange to hear Nick discussed this way. She no longer spoke to him directly, but they were still inescapably tied to each other: both of them circling this case, tracking down the same witnesses, trying to find out what the other knew and to anticipate the other's strategy, all in preparation for a final showdown against each other.

"He thanked me for telling him," Jeanne replied. "But he said he didn't think it would be something they could use at trial."

Anna felt her shoulders relax. If Nick had considered using this obviously false alibi, her opinion of him would have plummeted. But he had done the right thing, Anna saw, with a relief she wouldn't have admitted to feeling.

"You love your grandson, right?" Jack was asking. He would lock in Jeanne's bias.

"Yes."

"You don't want to see him go to jail, right?"

"Course."

"Nothing further. Are there any questions for this witness?"

A few jurors raised their hands, and Jack allowed them to ask their questions. Most of the queries went something along the lines of "Do you seriously expect us to believe your ridiculous alibi story?" Jeanne answered as best she could, but by the end, she knew she wasn't fooling anyone.

When the jurors ran out of questions, Jack excused the witness. He looked at the clock. It was 4:45.

"All right, you're all excused for the day," he announced.

A small cheer went up, and the jurors streamed out of the grand jury room, bidding the prosecutors good night as they fled to their own lives.

Anna and Jack rode the elevator to their offices. "Well, that's one person who believes D'marco did it," Jack said, after the elevator doors slid shut and they were alone.

"Yep," Anna replied. "Gramma doesn't know where D'marco was that night, but she knows her grandson well enough to understand that he needs an alibi."

As Jack was questioning Jeanne Davis in the grand jury, D'marco was walking casually around the prison yard, holding a gun concealed in the pocket of his denim jacket. He didn't know that his grandmother had been summoned to speak in the grand jury that day, and if he had, he wouldn't have thought about it much. He knew she couldn't save him. He knew that if he wanted to get out of jail, he had to take matters into his own hands. Which was what he was doing now.

D'marco shoved his hands deeper into his jacket's pockets, comforted by the weight of the gun in his hand. He glanced at the other prisoners in the yard. There was the usual hubbub of men talking, smoking, playing basketball. No one paid him particular mind. No one suspected what was about to happen.

21

D'marco walked past a group of prisoners standing in a clump, arguing about last Sunday's Redskins game. It was a chilly gray November day, and the men huddled into their thin prison uniforms. They were all wearing the same orange jumpsuits and prison-issue denim jackets as D'marco. A few called hello to him, but D'marco just nodded and kept walking toward the basketball court.

An intense game of two-on-two was going on, and a crowd had gathered around the court to watch and bet. D'marco made his way to the back, so the crowd blocked him from the view of the guards.

D'marco was patient. He stood with his hand in his pocket, feeling the weight of the Glock 17 semiautomatic pistol hidden in there. Ray-Ray had picked a good gun. D'marco liked the fact that he was using the same firearm that the police did. He rested the grip in his palm and let his thumb play over the serrations on the rear strap. He didn't worry about leaving fingerprints, knowing that, contrary to popular belief, the police were rarely able to lift usable prints from guns. His index finger rested lightly on the side of the trigger. The safeties were off. He was just waiting for the right moment now.

Finally it came: a big move on the basketball court. The guy with the ball charged past a defender, knocking him down, then flew up to the basket for a loud slam dunk. The crowd erupted, men shouting in appreciation or yelling foul, depending on which way they'd bet.

D'marco discreetly pulled the gun out of his pocket, then slid it into the front of his jacket. Holding the weapon flush against his chest, with the fabric of his jacket covering it from view, he laid the muzzle carefully against the edge of his left bicep. Then he fired a single shot into his own arm.

The reaction from the other prisoners was immediate. These were men who recognized the sound of gunshots. The basketball dropped to the blacktop as the players fled the court. The spectators dissolved in a riotous mass, shouting, shoving and running in all directions.

D'marco was stunned by the pain for a moment, but kept his presence of mind enough to let the gun drop through his jacket to the asphalt. No one noticed the gun fall. He felt a twinge of regret as the weapon dropped away, but he couldn't risk being frisked and having it found on him. Once he was out of here, he could get any weapon he wanted on the streets. He staggered away from the gun.

"I been shot! I been shot!" he screamed. When there was enough distance between him and the gun, he allowed himself to collapse to the blacktop.

D'marco lay on his back as men ran all around him. He hoped no one would step on him. He was probably in more danger from the stampeding crowd than the gunshot wound, he thought, although his arm really hurt. He hoped the bullet had taken the best possible route: through flesh, but no bones. In and out.

The guards were screaming at each other and the prisoners, trying to forge order out of the chaos. D'marco draped his injured bicep across his chest. He felt a warm stain of blood spreading over his torso. There seemed to be a lot of blood—soon the stain covered his entire chest—which was perfect. He needed to look as gory as possible. Between the blood and the bullet hole he'd fired through the front of his denim jacket, he hoped it would look like he'd been shot in the chest.

There was still one finishing touch. He lifted his bleeding bicep to his face and let the blood fill his mouth. He held the blood in his mouth, not swallowing, breathing through his nose. The mouthful of his own blood was disgusting—warm, salty, and nauseatingly thick—and D'marco forced himself not to gag. He just needed to keep it in his mouth until the guards came.

Soon, the prisoners were cleared out and the yard was silent. D'marco peeked at the gray November sky. He wondered if they might not notice him for a while, and whether he might be at risk for freezing to death if he had to lie here bleeding for a long time. A moment later, the crunching of guards' footsteps on the asphalt was a relief. D'marco closed his eyes as the guards gathered around him.

"Jesus," one said. "Is he dead?"

Someone kneeled next to him and laid his fingers on D'marco's wrist.

"No, there's a pulse."

D'marco used that moment to gargle and choke on the blood in his mouth. He felt the blood spatter his forehead and drip down both sides of his mouth.

"Oh God!" a younger guard screamed, jumping back.

"Call an ambulance!" another shouted.

A few minutes later, the paramedics trotted into the yard. D'marco heard the snap of rubber gloves being put on, and then an EMT was kneeling over him, checking his vital signs. D'marco kept his eyes closed but let out a soft groan, expelling the remaining blood from his mouth.

He was lifted gently onto a stretcher. He lay completely motionless as the paramedics carried him to the bay where the ambulance was waiting.

By the time the stretcher was being loaded onto the ambulance, the guards were murmuring nervously. The city had recently been sued after a prisoner died in jail. Would they be held responsible for this prisoner getting shot? Would they each have to get their own lawyers if they were sued? As the doors slammed shut, one paramedic was unrolling an IV drip while the other was starting the truck, and a single guard was riding shotgun. No one had handcuffed him.

D'marco had to force himself not to smile. This was going to be easier than he'd expected.

22

Anna jogged down the trail, her breath coming out in quick, cloudy puffs. The days were getting shorter, and it was already dark outside. Still, Rock Creek Park was full of runners jogging down the asphalt path that followed the creek through the wooded park. Cars swished by on the parkway that paralleled the running path. Their headlights flashed over the bare branches of trees and the water rushing through the creek. The frigid air seared Anna's throat and drew rosy circles on her cheeks and nose. It felt good after the dusty, forced heat of her office. She felt her head clear and her thoughts sharpen as the cold air circulated in her lungs.

The Taft Bridge came into view, signaling the end of her run. She rallied herself into a sprint, her arms chopping the night air, her legs flying over the pavement as she ran up the hill that took her out of the park and toward the busy street. It was a pleasure to move her body, to feel her feet come in sharp contact with the earth, to make contact with the physical world in a way that she didn't as a lawyer. She pushed her lungs and legs to the limit, until she felt like she couldn't possibly go any farther—and then she made herself go a little more.

When she reached Connecticut Avenue, she slowed

to an exhausted walk, gulping for air, her heart racing. Hands on her hips, head down, she passed the concrete lions guarding the bridge, which took her back over Rock Creek Park. Anna ignored the whooshing cars and the people passing her on the sidewalk—she was losing her Midwestern instinct to nod hello to everyone she passed—and gazed out at the park beneath her, dark and quiet amid the glowing bustle of the city. Her thoughts drifted to whether she would order Thai food or heat up the remains of a burrito from last night.

By the time she turned onto her own quiet street, her breathing was mostly back to normal, though her throat was raw from the cold air. She coughed and stretched her arms out in front of her. There were fewer cars and people here than on busy Connecticut Avenue, but there was enough activity that she didn't pay any attention to the tall man sitting on a bench on the other side of the street.

As she approached her house, her cell phone rang from within her hip pack. She unzipped the small pouch, rummaged past some tissues and ChapStick, and dug out the phone. She looked at the incoming number. It was Jack's office.

"Hello?" Her voice was raspy and a little breathless from her run.

"Anna, hi, it's Jack. Sorry to bother you at home, but you're never going to believe this."

"It's no bother." She'd left the office earlier than usual today, feeling like she needed a good long run. Now she was unexpectedly pleased to hear Jack's voice. "What's up?"

"D'marco Davis escaped from jail this afternoon."

Anna was so surprised she stopped in the middle of the sidewalk. A couple had to walk through a bed of ornamental cabbages to get past her.

Jack continued, "It looks like another prisoner shot him."

"You're kidding." Anna shook her head and started moving again. She reached her house and trotted down the three steps to the door of her basement apartment. Cradling the phone to her ear with her shoulder, she dug through her hip pack for her keys. "Wait, did he get shot or escape?"

"Both. He was so badly injured, they couldn't treat him at the jail's infirmary, so they were transporting him to the hospital. The guard didn't restrain him because, apparently, it looked like he was dying. When one of the paramedics turned his back, D'marco just sat up and walked out of the ambulance."

"Geez. Should I be doing something? Do you want me to come into the office?"

Frankly, Anna wouldn't mind going back to the office and spending the evening with Jack. She pulled her keys out and fumbled to insert her house key in the door. Her fingers, numb from the cold, felt large and clumsy.

"No. There's nothing we can do. There's a BOLO out on him."

"BOLO?"

"'Be On the Lookout' for him. It's been distributed to local police. They'll find him. Eventually."

"Great." Anna groaned as she finally got the key in the lock and pushed her door open. She reached her hand inside and flipped on the lights so she could peer into the mailbox mounted outside her door. She pulled out a couple of bills and flyers, juggling her keys and mail as she kept the phone pressed to her ear with her shoulder. "He's probably at Gramma Jeanne's house, playing video games."

She stopped talking abruptly as she heard footsteps running up behind her. Anna spun around and saw a large man barreling down the walk to her apartment. In a flash of horror, she recognized D'marco Davis as he rushed toward her. With a gasp, she darted into her apartment and tried to slam the door, her keys and mail scattering around her. But D'marco braced himself against the door and shoved it inward; the momentum sent Anna flying back into her house, into a sprawl on the floor. Her phone shot out of her hands and skidded away on the wood floor.

Anna screamed and reached for the phone, hoping that Jack was still on the line. "Oh my God, Jack! He's here! It's D'marco—"

D'marco kicked the door shut, scooped up the phone, and snapped it shut. Only then did Anna notice the blackish-brown stain covering D'marco's denim jacket, the way that his left arm hung limply by his side, bandaged with some sort of makeshift tourniquet, and the intense focus of his eyes. He took two steps over to where she was sprawled on the floor. She tried to scramble away from him, but backed into a wall.

"Help!" she tried to scream, but her throat, already raw from her run, constricted with fear as D'marco loomed over her. Instead of coming out as a scream, it came out as a squeaky rasp. "Help!"

Her eyes locked on D'marco's as he reached his enormous hands down to her face.

23

Jack heard Anna's screams, and was on his feet before the phone went dead. He grabbed his cell phone and ran down the hallway, dialing 911 as he ran. The office was empty; there was no one else to help him. He ran past the elevator bank and flew down the stairwell, descending five stories in a few seconds. The 911 operator answered the phone as he was running out of the stairwell into the lobby.

"Nine-one-one. Police, fire, or ambulance?" she answered in singsong.

"Police!" Jack shouted as he ran to the front doors. "An escaped prisoner is at the home of a federal prosecutor! We need all available units to respond to her house immediately!"

"Please calm down, sir."

He stopped running and stared at the phone. The operator was treating him with the condescension reserved for hysterical callers. He cursed to himself.

With exaggerated slowness he said, "Okay. I'm calm."

"What's the location of the offense?"

Jack froze with his hand on the front door. He didn't know. He'd been with McGee when they dropped Anna off a couple of times, but he didn't know the address.

"I'm not sure of the house number," he said, knowing how weak the answer sounded. "It's Wyoming Avenue Northwest, under the name of Anna Curtis. See if you can look it up." He told the operator he was the chief Homicide prosecutor. He couldn't tell if she believed him or cared. She said she would send the police.

Jack's mind raced as he ran outside. Hell, he could call his own team to the scene. He dialed McGee's cell, and to his relief, McGee answered. Quickly, Jack told him what was happening.

"But I don't know her address!"

"Anna's address," McGee said slowly. "Let's see . . . Nineteen eighty-three Wyoming Avenue Northwest, Apartment B."

"Thank God for the memory of a Homicide detective," Jack breathed.

"Not exactly. She's listed in the phone book. I'll meet you there."

Jack ran down the street, fruitlessly searching for a cab on the deserted streets around Judiciary Square. He kept running toward Chinatown, where people would still be out having dinner or drinks and taxis would be more likely. He finally hailed one at the corner of 7th and F. Jack dove in and barked out Anna's address. The driver turned slowly north on 7th Street.

"Look, this is an emergency situation." Jack flashed his U.S. Attorney's Office credentials as if they were a badge, exactly what the credentials were *not* to be used for. "You'll get a commendation from the mayor if you can get me there in three minutes."

The cabbie smiled at Jack. "What am I gonna do with a commendation from the mayor?"

Jack opened his wallet and counted the cash he had in there.

"I have a hundred twenty-two dollars on me. It's yours if you can get me there in three minutes."

The driver hit the gas, pressing Jack back against the seat as the cab screeched through a yellow light.

"Ssshhh," D'marco said as he leaned down to cover Anna's mouth. His hand was enormous; his palm covered the entire lower half of her face. Anna thrashed her head from side to side, but couldn't get out of his grip. She opened her mouth until his hand slipped in a little, and then bit down as hard as she could. Her teeth sunk into the webbing between his index finger and thumb. She tasted his blood in her mouth and hoped he wasn't HIV positive.

D'marco howled in pain and jerked his hand away. Anna used the moment to scramble out from under his legs and run to the front door. Her hand was on the doorknob when D'marco grabbed her by the arms and pulled her away from the door.

"Nuh-uh," he grunted.

She struggled to get out of his grasp, twisting and thrashing, but he held on effortlessly, like she was a leaf turning in the wind. She tried screaming again, and this time her voice was louder.

"Help!" she shouted. "Someone help me!"

He jerked her to him, so her back was pressed against his stomach, and covered her mouth with his hand.

"Shut up," he hissed.

This time, he kept her chin clenched shut, so she couldn't bite. He hauled her, kicking and fighting, across her living room. Anna tried to break out of his grasp, but he held her in an unbreakable bear hug. She realized how much bigger he was than her. He was almost a foot taller and probably double her weight. He dragged her to the red couch.

She thrashed in his arms, terrified. Was he going to rape her? The printout of his criminal history flashed through her head: a bunch of domestic assaults, drug distribution while armed, but no sex crimes. Still, there was a first for everything.

She fought with renewed effort. Anna remembered from a women's self-defense course that the human knee could withstand only ten pounds of pressure. She lifted her foot and brought it back as hard as she could in the direction of his knee. She didn't hear the sound of a kneecap popping out of place, as she'd hoped, but it was enough to make him yelp in pain and let go of her. Anna bolted in the other direction, toward the back of her apartment, where the door of her kitchen exited to the back alley.

"Goddammit, woman!" he roared.

She glanced over her shoulder as she ran. He was running after her, moving fast, faster than her. She wasn't going to be able to open the back door, which was locked three different ways, before he caught up. Desperately, she scanned the kitchen for a weapon. The only thing in reach was the wooden dish rack, covered with bowls, coffee mugs, and silverware.

Anna grabbed the rack and swung it at D'marco, just as he was coming up on her. The rack crashed into the side of his head; bowls and mugs hit his skull and each other with resounding cracks. He slammed back into the refrigerator. Magnets, pictures, and coupons scattered all over the floor. D'marco slumped back against the appliance, dazed, and Anna turned to the back door.

She threw open the dead bolt, slid the chain lock out, and started fumbling with the key in the doorknob. She turned the key—too late. D'marco came up behind her and covered her wrists with his huge hands. He pulled her off the doorknob, and turned her to face him. Her back was pressed against the door, and her hands were caught in his viselike hold.

She looked at the huge man looming above her. He was breathing heavily and bleeding from cuts to his head where the dish rack and dishes had hit.

"Lady—" he said.

She kicked him in the groin. He folded over with a grunt and pitched forward onto her. She stumbled backward under the weight of him, and they ended up crumpled in a pile against the door, his body half covering hers.

Anna tried to squirm out from under him, but she was like the Wicked Witch of the East caught under Dorothy's house. Grunting in pain, D'marco grabbed her wrists, and pinned them on either side of her. With effort, he sat up and straddled her, keeping her arms pinned to the kitchen floor.

She was trapped.

Anna stared up at the escaped prisoner. A mixture of sweat and fresh blood was running into his eyes and dripping onto his denim jacket, where old blood had already dried into a black stain. He was breathing hard and grimacing, his face contorted in pain.

She had never been so terrified. She was too scared even to cry. If he was going to kill her, she hoped it would be something quick.

Keeping her pinned, he took a moment to catch his breath. Finally, he spoke.

"You one hell of a hard woman to talk to," he said.

Anna stared at him.

"I'm just wanting five minutes with you," he said. He shifted, securing her arms with his knees so he could wipe the blood from his forehead onto his sleeve. "You always play this hard to get?"

She looked at him in disbelief. Finally, she said, "You could've just made an appointment."

"Shit, I tried that, Ms. Curtis." Davis practically laughed. "You ain't takin' my calls. You sendin' my letters to my lawyer without readin' 'em. What's a felon supposed to do?"

Anna wondered if it was possible he was joking with her. No, she thought, feeling the hard kitchen tile pressing against her skull and shoulder blades, this was definitely not a joke.

"I ain't killed Laprea," he said. "I loved her."

"Oh—okay," she said, as earnestly as possible, like that was the end of it. Prosecution over.

"I know how it look," he said, surprisingly matter-of-factly. "I ain't never treated her right. I hate that. I'm gonna carry that the rest of my life. She was my babies' mother, and I loved her. I just get kinda crazy when I drink."

Anna nodded, trying to convey empathy. Is he going to let me go, she was thinking. Are the cops coming? How long can I humor him?

"Look, Ms. Curtis, I did hit Laprea that night. Okay? But I ain't killed her. Last I saw, she was runnin' down the street, away from my building. I stayed there, went back to my apartment, drank too much, and passed out on my couch."

"I see," Anna said, still not understanding why he was telling her this.

"I know that sound crazy," D'marco said, reading the confusion in her face. He rearranged himself so he wasn't pressing so hard on her arms. "But I heard she was fuckin' a cop—sorry, having relations with a cop. That's what we was fightin' about. After she run down the stairs, I told her, she should just *keep* running, and don't come back without that cop, 'cause I'd peel his wig. She said she *would* get him, and then I'd be done. That was the last time I ever seen her. She musta gone to him, to that cop. You gotta find him, Ms. Curtis. He's the one that killed her."

"Who's the cop?"

"That's why I'm here. I want you to find out."

"D'marco, I'm the *prosecutor.* Just tell your defense attorney this; I'm sure he'll work on it." She bit her tongue. She should be humoring him, telling him she'd do whatever he wanted.

"You think I ain't done that already?" D'marco raised his voice in frustration. Calming himself, he continued, "My lawyer's good—but he ain't never had an innocent client. He don't believe me. He's working on this, but only 'cause I keep telling him to, and he ain't gettin' nowhere. His heart ain't in it. He thinks I should just plead." D'marco shook his head. "Even if he did believe me, no cop's gonna talk to him. Police hate defense attorneys. But they talk to *you*. And you can pull MPD records and shit. I know it ain't your job to get me off, see. But you were the only one wanted to listen to me that day after my hearing, in the cellblock, till your boss stopped it. And I know you cared 'bout Laprea. You want to find out who really killed her. Even if you hate me."

Anna opened her mouth with the reflexive female instinct to deny that she hated him, but she never got a chance.

24

A crash from the front of her apartment startled both D'marco and Anna. She looked up to see two young men wearing sweatshirts and jeans running in and pointing guns around her house. *What now?* she thought. Then she saw the badges hanging around their necks. They were police officers.

The two cops yelled almost in stereo, "Police! Put your hands in the air!"

D'marco sprang off of Anna and bolted for the back door. He wasn't going back to jail voluntarily. The officers raised their weapons and aimed at his heart. *Shit,* Anna thought, scooching herself into the corner. *It would really suck to survive D'marco only to get shot by the cavalry come to rescue her.*

The officers didn't take the shot; she was too close. D'marco threw open the back door, ready to run into the alley behind her house. He would disappear into the city.

Except when D'marco opened the door, he found Detective McGee pointing his gun a few inches from his face.

"Not this time, Princess." McGee smiled at D'marco. "Lie on the ground, hands behind your head."

D'marco didn't move.

"I know about your jail break today, Mr. Davis," the big detective purred. "When *I* shoot you, I promise you'll be too dead to escape from another ambulance. Now get the fuck down!"

D'marco lay on the kitchen floor.

Jack burst in through Anna's front door, and his eyes flashed around the apartment, sizing up the situation. He saw that McGee had D'marco under control; he saw the two other officers lowering their weapons and going over to help McGee; he saw Anna crouched in the corner, frightened but alive. He blew out a breath and strode over to her.

"Anna, are you okay?" Jack knelt down in front of Anna and gathered her hands into his.

"I'm fine," she said, watching the felon being handcuffed on her kitchen floor. "I'm fine. I'm fine. I'm fine," she repeated, reassuring herself as much as Jack. She looked at the Homicide chief. "Will I get a Special Achievement Award for this?"

Jack laughed as he helped her to her feet and looked her over. His eyebrows knit together at something on her stomach. She looked down at herself. Her T-shirt was dotted with bloodstains; so was her kitchen floor.

"It's his blood, not mine," she explained.

She could feel her hair sticking out of her defunct ponytail; she could smell her own sweat from her run and the struggle. She was a mess. But she was alive.

The terror of what happened finally caught up with her. Adrenaline had propelled her when she'd thought she was going to die, but now that the danger was gone, she started to shake uncontrollably.

Jack opened his arms and she gratefully stepped into

them, resting her head on his chest as the fear worked its way out of her system. She was glad that Jack didn't say anything, just wrapped his arms around her while she caught her breath and slowly stopped shaking.

As she calmed down, she became conscious of Jack's chest under her cheek. His muscular pecs rose and fell as he breathed. He felt strong and solid. Anna's fear drained away, replaced by the desire to stay in the safe circle of his arms as long as possible. She remained pressed against him for another minute, feeling his hands gently stroking her back, the warmth of his body flush with hers. She closed her eyes and heard his heart thudding under her ear. Jack had been scared, too. She looked up at him. Perspiration beaded his forehead.

"You okay, kiddo?" he asked gently.

"Yeah."

Their faces were closer than they'd ever been. She wondered if the butterflies in her stomach were from what had just happened with D'marco or from Jack's nearness.

A clanking, shuffling sound made Anna look away. The two sweatshirted cops hauled D'marco to his feet and led him toward the front door. McGee was reholstering his gun and looking at Anna and Jack curiously. Anna became acutely aware that this was her usually stern boss she was pressing against. She let go of him and quickly stepped back.

"How did you get here so fast?" She tried to normalize her voice as she spoke to Jack. "Who are these officers?"

"After I heard you screaming, I started calling officers I knew lived or worked near here. These guys live around the corner. And McGee must have broken every traffic law on the books."

"Thank you so much, Officers," she called. "Thank you, Detective McGee."

"Anything for a little overtime," McGee deadpanned.

She walked toward the sink to get a drink of water, but hobbled a step, crunching over the broken dishes and surprisingly unsteady on her feet. Jack kicked a chunk of a mug to the side, steered her to the kitchen table, and made her sit down. He asked her where her cups were and filled a glass with water. "Drink up," he instructed. She gulped down the whole thing. She felt like she could drink all of Lake Superior, she was so thirsty from her run and the struggle with D'marco. Jack refilled the glass and handed it to her again.

She was bringing the glass to her mouth when the sound of sirens pierced the air. A moment later, two uniformed police officers came running through her open front door.

"Police!" they yelled, pointing their guns around the apartment. The uniformed officers looked around in surprise at the apartment full of men. There was a tense moment, with everyone yelling that *they* were the police, until McGee and the two cops in sweatshirts held up their badges, and one of the uniformed officers recognized McGee. Greetings were called; guns were lowered.

"Those must be the officers that 911 dispatched," Jack said. Then, under his breath: "Fucking 911."

Anna rarely heard him swear. She realized Jack was more upset than she was.

25

It took a while to clear everyone out of her house. There was paperwork to be done, photos to be taken, a crime scene—surreally, her apartment—to be processed. Anna watched the strange sight of a technician lifting bloodstains from her kitchen floor. She had to give a statement to the detective who was investigating D'marco's escape and assault. So, Anna thought wearily, this is what it feels like to be on the other side of a PD-252, the victim statement form. She was exhausted. Part of her wanted all of the officers to get out of her house so she could get some rest; another part was dreading the moment she'd be left alone.

Finally, everyone left except Jack. She was grateful for his company as he helped her clean up her apartment. He worked quietly by her side—sweeping up the broken mugs, mopping D'marco's blood off the floor, checking that her locks were all working—until her house was back in order. When there was nothing left to be done, she slowly walked him to the door. She didn't want him to go.

"Thanks, Jack. For everything."

"Don't thank me anymore." He put a hand lightly on her shoulder. "Are you going to be okay here tonight?"

"Yeah, sure." She tried to sound nonchalant.

"Tonight's probably the safest I'll ever be. After the neighborhood saw all those police officers leaving my house, no one's going to mess with me."

"Okay," he said slowly. "Good night, Anna."

"Good night, Jack."

He squeezed her shoulder and turned to walk out. She was sorry when his hand left her arm. She took a deep breath, steeling herself for the moment she would be alone in the apartment. She would call Jody, she thought, and keep her sister on the phone as long as she could. Everything would be fine, Anna knew. There was no danger. But she was still spooked.

Maybe he saw the look on her face. Jack turned back to her.

"Look, Anna, I don't feel right leaving you here alone like this. I have to go now—Olivia is waiting and the nanny needs to go home. But I have a guest bedroom. Would you like to stay there tonight? I think it might be better for you than being here by yourself."

Anna paused. She wanted Jack to think she was tough and fearless; she was reluctant to admit that she was nervous. Then she glanced at the empty house behind her. The memory of D'marco pinning her to the back door was fresh and raw. She felt a vague sense of menace from the suddenly quiet apartment. Now was not the time to put on a tough-guy act. She smiled up at him.

"Actually—that'd be great."

Jack lived in Takoma Park, a sylvan neighborhood straddling D.C.'s northeastern border with Maryland. As the cab drove Jack and Anna through the streets, she gazed at the colorful bungalows and Victorians.

"The homes are like dollhouses," Anna murmured. She glanced at a sign. "Historic district?"

"A lot of the houses were built around the turn of the century. They were summer homes for people living downtown. Back then, this was the boondocks." Jack pointed to a house flying a UN flag, a rainbow flag, and a peace sign flag. "This became a bit of a hippie enclave in the seventies. Some people still call it Granola Park. The city declared itself a 'nuclear-free zone' and has its own policy prohibiting trade with Burma."

"I'm sure Burma's really upset about that."

"Yeah." Jack laughed. "Now the activists are being replaced by yuppies like me, who just want a neighborhood near the Metro that's safe enough to raise kids in. Some of my neighbors were suspicious when they learned I'm a prosecutor. That makes me The Man. But I joined the board of the organic food co-op. I compost. And Olivia's just too cute for anyone to resist. Now my neighbors accept me as another local character, That Prosecutor Fella."

"It's a cute neighborhood. I pictured you living in the city."

Why? Jack thought, suddenly wary. Because I'm black?

"Because you're the Homicide chief," she said quickly. "Not some law firm partner. I expected something less gingerbready, more gritty."

Fair enough, Jack thought.

"I had enough of 'gritty,'" he admitted quietly. "I wanted to raise Olivia in a neighborhood where she could play on the streets. I grew up in Anacostia. Every couple years, a kid I knew would get killed in some urban gun battle or something. I wanted something better for my daughter. Someplace like where you must have grown up, Miss Midwest Corn Princess," he joked.

"I grew up in Flint," Anna retorted. "We've been in a recession for twenty-five years. My dad worked on the line at the General Motors plant. When he got laid off, we lost our house and moved into a trailer park. So don't bring out that tiara just yet."

"I'm sorry. I just assumed you were a trust fund kid, coming from Harvard Law School and being so—" He stopped abruptly.

"So what?"

So beautiful, he thought.

"So smart," he said.

Jack directed the cabdriver to a yellow Victorian house at the end of a quiet street. The home and all the trees around it were strung with multicolored Christmas lights, and a tall plastic snowman lit up the yard.

"Excited about Christmas, Jack?" she teased. "We haven't even had Thanksgiving yet."

"If it was up to Olivia, we'd start celebrating Christmas in June," Jack said, handing the cabbie a twenty.

As Jack pushed open the front door of the house, Olivia came running through the foyer. She wore pink pajamas and pigtails and dragged a teddy bear behind her. "Daddy! Daddy!" She hurled herself into his arms, and he scooped her up, flinging her into the air. She shrieked with delight, then threw her arms around his neck and covered his face with kisses. "Did you get the bad guy?"

"We sure did, pumpkin."

A plump, smiling Latina followed Olivia into the foyer. "She was excited to get to stay up late," the nanny told Jack. She stopped when she saw Anna. Her eyes narrowed. "A lady friend! You said you had to work. An emergency, you said."

"Luisa, thank you so much," Jack said, walking her to the door. "I *was* working. This is Anna—from work. I'll put the overtime in your next paycheck, okay?"

"Sure, Mr. Jack, no problem. Good night, *cosita*." The nanny kissed Olivia as Jack opened the door. "Good night, Miss Anna From Work. Don't work him too much later tonight."

"Good night," Anna called, choking back a laugh as Jack shut the door behind the nanny.

With her arms still wrapped around her father's neck, Olivia turned to Anna. The little girl had gorgeous mocha skin and Jack's green eyes. "Hi," she said brightly. "I'm Olivia." The five-year-old stuck out her hand and shook Anna's.

"Hello." Anna smiled at the precocious girl. "I'm Anna."

"This is the lady I've been working with," Jack told his daughter. "Anna has nowhere to stay tonight. Do you think she could stay here?"

"Yeah. You can use my bear," Olivia said, handing Anna the stuffed teddy. "You're pretty, just like Daddy said."

"Well, thank you." Anna blushed and looked everywhere but at Jack. The living room, painted a cheerful buttery yellow, was brimming with toys. A big Christmas tree stood in a corner. Beyond the living room,

Anna could glimpse the kitchen, decorated with finger-paint drawings and noodle art.

"Okay, you," Jack said, with embarrassed laughter. He set her on the floor. "Bedtime. Go upstairs and choose the book you want to read before bed."

"Mm . . . how about three?" she asked, with the sweet, bossy authority of a five-year-old girl who knows she has her father wrapped around her finger.

"Two," he conceded. It was always a negotiation. Olivia ran happily up the stairs, knowing she'd won. Anna watched the scene wistfully. Jack was the kind of father she'd always wanted.

Half an hour later—after Olivia had her books read, her bedtime prayer recited, her glass of water brought, her teddy bear reclaimed and tucked in, and several kisses—Olivia was finally in bed.

"That's quite a bedtime ritual you've got there," Anna whispered as Jack led her down the hallway.

"I know, but I can't sleep if I forget to tuck in the teddy bear," Jack whispered back. He turned on the light in the guest room.

Anna set her backpack on a daybed covered with a colorful quilt. A toy chest, rocking horse, and child-sized table and chairs took up one wall. This was a playroom when guests weren't staying over.

"Jack, I need to tell you what D'marco said when he came to my house. I think we have to look into something."

"We'll talk about that tomorrow. You should get some rest now."

He showed her the little bathroom attached to the bedroom, and took a towel out for her. She couldn't wait to shower off the dirt and sweat from tonight. She was glad she'd be doing it here in this friendly house, with the tough-as-nails Homicide chief down the hall, instead of in her lonely basement apartment. She knew this was a place where she would be completely safe.

Anna followed Jack back to the doorway of the bedroom. He turned, and they stood facing each other.

"Jack, thank you. For everything," she whispered, keeping her voice low so she wouldn't wake Olivia. "I didn't realize how much I needed to be around people tonight. Your daughter is beautiful and so is your house. Thanks for letting me come over."

"Of course. You had a tough night. Maybe you're fearless, but anyone else would be pretty shaken up. I'm just glad there was something I could do to help."

He was standing with his hands clasped behind his back, like a soldier at attention. Something about his formality made Anna realize they were a man and a woman standing alone together in a bedroom.

"Is there anything else I can do for you?" he asked quietly.

Anna almost laughed. He hadn't meant a double entendre, and she felt sophomoric to have assigned a sexual meaning to his question. But it got her thinking about how his chest had felt under her cheek earlier that night, the rhythmic thump of his heart beating under her ear. Her eyes skimmed over his face, resting on his mouth. He had beautiful lips, full and sensual. Strange that she'd never noticed that before. If she stepped forward now, she wondered, would he fold her into his arms again? Or more?

She cut off the thought, bewildered by it. It was ridiculous—absurd. He was her boss. Her stern, no-nonsense, straight-arrow boss. She must be seriously overwrought—she was turning a simple, nice gesture into something it wasn't. She shook her head no.

"Okay." He stood in the doorway for a second longer. Anna wished she could know what was going through his head. After a moment, he smiled at her politely. "Good night, Anna."

"Good night," she whispered to his back.

Anna awoke to the feel of a hand patting her foot. She opened her eyes. Morning sunlight glinted through the cracks of the curtains. Olivia stood next to the bed, one hand on Anna's foot and the other holding an African-American Barbie doll. She was still in her pink pj's.

"Hi," the little girl said with a shy, flirty smile. "Will you pour me a bowl of cereal?"

"Sure."

Anna sat up, getting her bearings. The sound of running water came from Jack's bathroom. He must be taking a shower. Anna stood up. Olivia grabbed her hand and pulled her down the hallway. Anna laughed and stumbled along, wiping the sleep from her eyes. Olivia led her to the kitchen and pointed up to the cabinet that held the Cheerios. Anna poured some into a bowl with milk, and they sat down at the kitchen table. Olivia munched away happily. Anna looked around the kitchen and living room. There were few surfaces that weren't covered with toys.

"That's nice." Anna pointed to the Barbie Dream House set up next to the couch.

"Thanks! Look at these!" Olivia popped out of her chair and ran to the living room, where she scooped up a few toys in her path: another Barbie, an electric toy drum, and a sticker book. She dumped the toys proudly on the kitchen table before taking her seat and another slurpy mouthful of cereal.

"Wow. That's good stuff." Anna pressed a button on the drum, which made it play an island rhythm. Anna stood a Barbie on top of the drum, bouncing the doll up and down to the beat. "It's a dance party," Anna said.

"Dance party!" Olivia cried. She grabbed the other Barbie and bounced it on top of the drum next to Anna's doll. Olivia sang along as the dolls danced.

When the music stopped, the little girl called, "More!" and pressed the button again. This time the drum played a catchy salsa tune. Olivia stood up and grabbed Anna's hand. "Come on, it's a dance party!" Anna held Olivia's hand and twirled the giggling girl around the kitchen.

When Anna looked up, she saw Jack leaning against the kitchen doorway. He wore his suit pants, a white undershirt, and a look of supreme amusement. She was suddenly cognizant of the fact that she was dancing around her boss's kitchen in a tank top, shorts, and bare feet. She froze, but Olivia ran over and grabbed her father's hand. "Come on, Daddy! It's a dance party! Dance!"

Jack stepped into the kitchen and easily obeyed, moving his feet expertly to the salsa beat, spinning his daughter around and around. Anna laughed and clapped her hands with delight. Jack smiled at her as Olivia passed under his arm. It was the biggest smile she'd ever seen on his face.

An hour later, Jack and Anna emerged from the house, lawyers again. He wore a dark suit and tie; she had changed into the gray skirt suit she'd brought. Her clothes from last night were stuffed in her backpack, slung over one shoulder. Olivia stood next to Luisa on the porch and waved at them enthusiastically. "Bye, Daddy! Love you! Bye, Anna! I hope you beat the bad guys!"

"Me too!" Anna turned back to wave at the adorable girl. Jack smiled as they walked down the sidewalk toward the Takoma Metro station. He looked at Anna's suit.

"You don't have to come to the office today. You can take the day off."

"I've never taken a sick day. I'm not going to give D'marco the satisfaction of starting now."

Jack nodded. He would have been the same way.

"So, when are you auditioning for *Dancing with the Stars*?" she teased.

"Don't get me started, Britney."

"Britney? Come on. I was going for Madonna, circa 1992."

"Were you even born then?"

"I was eight," she said, feigning indignation.

"I graduated from high school that year." He shook his head in disbelief.

"Oh, did they have high schools back then?"

"Mercy." He put up his hands in laughing surrender.

"Now that I've got you on the ropes"—her voice turned serious—"let's talk shop."

He nodded.

"D'marco didn't come to my apartment last night to hurt me," she explained. "He wanted to tell me something." She described what D'marco said about the night of Laprea's murder. "He admitted that he hit her, but he swore the last he saw of her, she was alive and running off to see a cop."

Jack shrugged. "So that's going to be his defense? I've seen defendants blame the police, but that's ridiculous."

"I hear you. But he walked away from an ambulance after he'd been shot just to tell me that. That's probably why he was calling and writing letters."

"Anna, every man in the D.C. Jail swears he's innocent. Denial is a natural human instinct. You could have him committing the crime on videotape and he'd tell you it was his evil twin."

"Okay—but—what if Laprea *was* seeing a cop? What if it was Brad Green?"

"Green?" Jack looked at her incredulously. "Are you sure you didn't hit your head on something last night?"

"I know, I know. But hear me out. Laprea *was* seeing somebody else, right? She was pregnant with another man's child when she died. So, who's the other man? Rose didn't know of anyone else that Laprea was dating—but she did say that Green stopped by the house a lot. And when we visited . . . Green knew where they kept everything in the kitchen, he was all friendly with the kids. Rose said Green was always 'looking after' the family. What if it was more than that?"

"I don't think Green was Laprea's type," Jack said gingerly.

"Stranger things have happened. . . ."

"True. But if Laprea was dating Green, why did she keep it a secret from her mother?"

"Maybe Laprea didn't want to deal with the fallout unless the relationship really became serious. Maybe it would be controversial to date a cop. Maybe Rose would disapprove of the interracial aspect of it."

Anna glanced at Jack, gauging his reaction to her last comment. She'd found herself thinking about interracial relationships a fair amount lately, wondering if it was still an issue for anyone who lived in a modern, cosmopolitan city. Wondering, more specifically, if it was an issue for someone like Jack Bailey, or his friends and family. But Jack's face remained neutral and he didn't respond to her last point.

"Come on, Anna. First Davis wants us to believe he was home all that night with his grandmother, playing video games. Now he wants to blame the police for killing this woman that an eyewitness saw him beating. Gimme a break. No jury's gonna buy that."

"But the way D'marco said it—I think he really believed it."

"No offense, but you were hardly in a position to judge his credibility. That was a traumatic situation."

Anna knew Jack was right. But something about Green had nagged at her from the beginning—and made D'marco's story ring true. She couldn't just let it go.

"Well, how about this," she proposed. "What if we just get a paternity test? Let's see if Green is the father of Laprea's baby. Then we can put it to rest one way or the other."

"What?" Jack was looking at her as if she'd just claimed to have seen Bigfoot.

"If it turns out Green is the father, then we've uncovered the truth, and we'll deal with it, hard as it might be on our case. That's our job. If it turns out to be nothing, great. It just makes the case stronger. It shows that the government investigated D'marco's allegations, we took steps to confirm or deny it. It shows we're acting in good faith."

"That's exactly wrong," Jack countered. "If we DNA-test Green, it will just suggest we might believe Davis's bullshit story. And when it comes back negative, that won't disprove Davis's story, unless you plan on DNA-testing every other police officer on the force. Are you going to swab every officer on the Metropolitan Police Department? And how would you even do that? With thirty-five hundred search warrants? Based on a street rumor Davis claims he heard? You don't have probable cause for any of them—you don't even have PC for Green."

Anna nodded. It was a valid point.

"Look, Anna," Jack said gently. "We know who did it—and so does his attorney. There's no way Nick Wagner would be trying to plead his client guilty if he had any kind of a viable defense—especially one involving a police scandal. Wagner would be all over that. If there were any truth to that story, he'd be pounding the table, demanding to interview police officers about where they were the night of Laprea's death, and leaking it all to the press. He'd make a whole sideshow of it. But he's not. He's telling D'marco to plead guilty. That tells you how meritless this claim is. I understand you're shaken up by what happened, but don't get suckered into wasting your time and energy on this. You have enough to do without chasing down Davis's fantasies that his own lawyer can't be bothered with."

Anna walked silently next to Jack. She had also wondered why Nick wasn't making a big deal of the police angle, since his client apparently told him about it. She concluded that he didn't know what she knew—he hadn't seen how friendly and familiar Green had been at the Johnson house. He had no reason to suspect Green.

She considered Jack's arguments—they were all fair points and she understood his reasoning. But she just couldn't get the possibility out of her mind.

26

When they got to the office, Jack and Anna were greeted like celebrities. As Anna badged her way through the lobby turnstiles, someone among the morning bustle cried out, "There she is!" The entire lobby seemed to turn toward her.

"Hey, Anna!" exclaimed a vaguely familiar lawyer from the district court section. They'd never spoken before. "How're you *doing*?"

"Okay," she replied cautiously, walking to the elevator bank.

"Good for you, for coming in today," said a secretary carrying a McDonald's bag.

"Um, thanks."

Anna turned to Jack, wondering how everyone had found out. He shrugged. They rode the elevator up, and he walked her protectively to her office. Grace was already there, poring over a newspaper spread on her desk. When Anna walked in, Grace sprang out of her seat.

"Hey, can I get your autograph?" Grace hopped over the files scattered on the floor and grabbed Anna into a tight hug. "I'm so glad you're okay," she whispered.

"How'd you hear?" Anna asked when Grace let her go.

"You're famous."

Grace pointed to the front page of the *Washington Post*'s Metro section on her desk. "Federal Prosecutor Attacked in Her Home," the headline read. Anna picked it up with astonishment. Jack stood behind her and they skimmed it together. As Jack read the paper over Anna's shoulder, Grace noticed how close together they were standing and arched her eyebrows.

The *Post* had a picture of Anna's house, with D'marco's mug shot and her law school yearbook picture inset in it. The article hit all the highlights, talking about how D'marco escaped from the ambulance, forced his way into her home, but was caught before anyone was hurt. The paper didn't mention that the first cavalry that came galloping in was Jack's ragtag group of off-duty cops. Anna tossed the paper back onto Grace's desk.

"That was fast," Anna said.

"But not surprising," Jack replied. "There was a lot of activity on the police scanners. This is big local news. There are murders every week, but a full-fledged prison escape and attack on a prosecutor only happens every few decades." Jack looked at his watch. "I have to be in court soon." He turned to Anna. "D'marco will be arraigned on the new charges this morning. Escape, Assault, B&E, et cetera, et cetera."

"Should I come, too?"

"Only if you're ready for your close-up. There will be press." She shook her head. "Then stay here. You obviously won't be assigned to the new case—you're the victim of it."

"Right."

"Now, I want you to take it easy today. Nothing more strenuous than redacting witness statements. Grace, I'm counting on you to make sure she relaxes."

"I'm not sure that's possible," Grace said. "But I'll give it my best shot."

Jack smiled and walked out.

Grace ceremoniously cleared a path through her piles of paper and Jimmy Choos, and Anna sank gratefully into her desk chair. Grace was dying to hear the details, so Anna told her everything that had happened last night. Grace oohed and aahed over the story. It sounded a lot better in the telling than it had felt in the happening. Anna realized she had her first great war story.

"So," Anna concluded. "After all the dust cleared, I was left wondering if Officer Green might be the father of Laprea's child."

"Girl, that cop is a dog," Grace said. "I wouldn't be surprised if he put the moves on Laprea *and* her mother." Anna was heartened that Grace didn't think she was crazy for suspecting Green. "But you're not concentrating on the most interesting part of your story. You were a modern-day damsel in distress. Only your Prince Charming rode in to save you in a Yellow Cab."

Anna felt her cheeks reddening.

"So . . ." Grace looked at Anna coyly. "How are things going with Jack?"

"Good." Anna could put on a neutral voice even if she couldn't control the blood flow to her cheeks. "He's an excellent lawyer."

"I know that, my dear. What I'm asking is: How are things going with Jack?"

"Okay, Miss Nosy Pants. If you must know—"

"Yes?" Grace leaned forward.

"Nothing's going on."

"Oh, come on! A good-looking single man, a beautiful single woman, hours spent alone together, and . . . nothing?"

"Nope."

"Is it because he's your boss?"

"Yes, it's because he's my boss! Haven't you watched the sexual harassment video? He's a supervisor. I'm not even allowed to give him a gift worth more than ten dollars."

"Actually, he's not your boss," Grace corrected her. "Carla is. Evaluations, promotions, everything goes through Carla. Correct?"

"Actually, that's . . . that's true."

"He doesn't have any supervisory authority over you."

"Hm. Maybe you're right."

"Of course I'm right. Now, you might catch a little flack from the sisters for taking a good black man off the market. But it won't be too bad, I would think. And I can give you some cover there."

"Okay, enough matchmaking!" Anna protested, laughing. "Remember, I'm the victim of a crime. I'm traumatized. I need a seaweed wrap and a Swedish massage, not an interrogation about my love life."

"That's my girl!" Grace said proudly; she'd introduced Anna to the concept of seaweed wraps.

Grace picked up the phone, dialed a number she knew by heart, and made an appointment at the Red

Door Spa for the two of them that weekend. When she hung up, she handed Anna a Post-it note with their appointment time written on it.

"Just let me know if anything develops," Grace said. "Personally, I would love to see it happen—you and Jack are two of the best people I know."

"Thanks, Grace."

Anna loved her friend fiercely in that moment.

At nine o'clock, Grace had to go to court. Anna sat back and gazed around her empty office. It was the first time she'd been truly alone since D'marco had pushed his way into her house. She felt less shaken than she'd thought she would. Being at Jack's last night had taken the edge off of her jitters.

She pulled out some witness statements and a thick black marker. She would black out the witnesses' home addresses and personal information before turning the papers over to the defense. Redacting this kind of paperwork was an important part of protecting witnesses, but it was mindless work. She knew Jack had her doing it today to give her a break.

But she couldn't concentrate on the work. Her mind kept going back to D'marco's words, and Officer Green. It just wasn't sitting right.

Okay, she decided after she read the same police form three times without processing it, she would do a little research. There was no harm in that.

She got up and quietly shut the office door. It took only a few minutes on the Department of Justice intranet to find the phone number for the FBI's DNA laboratory. A brisk female voice answered. Anna explained that she was an AUSA, and that she needed to talk to a

DNA analyst. The line was transferred, and a man with a nasal voice answered.

"Hi," Anna started, then paused. She had never dealt with DNA before—it was too expensive and complicated to be used in misdemeanor cases. She wasn't sure where to start. "I have a case where I want to find out who's the father of a child. Actually, the father of a fetus, an aborted fetus. How would I go about doing that?"

The analyst explained that Anna would need to send samples from the fetus, the mother, and the suspected father to the FBI laboratory. They would determine everyone's DNA profile. Then the profiles would all be compared, and the FBI could tell to a near certainty whether the man had fathered the child.

"The FBI already determined the DNA profile for the mother and the fetus," Anna explained.

"If we already have the mother and the child's profile, then you'll just need a sample from the possible father."

"A blood sample?"

"No. Paternity tests used to require blood. But these days, we just need a buccal swabbing."

"What's that?"

"It's a fancy way of saying you run a Q-tip over the inner cheek. To collect saliva. If we have the man's saliva, we have his DNA."

"And how long does the whole process take?"

"There's a bit of a backlog. I'd say three to four months."

That sounded long to Anna. They seemed to get it done a lot faster on *CSI*.

Anna thanked the analyst and hung up. She sat back in her chair and gazed out the window, chewing the end of her pen while she thought. How could she get a buccal swabbing from Green, without a warrant? Anna's mind raced through the possibilities, all of which seemed unlikely. Then she took the pen out of her mouth and held it in front of her face, rolling it around in her fingers as she studied it. A patina of spittle glistened on the cap.

She had an idea. She picked up the phone again.

An hour later, Anna sat waiting at a little table in the Firehook Bakery. The coffee shop was midway between her office and the courthouse, a perfect meeting spot. But the waiting was giving her time to second-guess her plan. Was she really going to do this? It didn't violate the man's rights. But it was sneaky and not in the spirit of people who were supposed to be on the same team. He was a nice guy. Still, she reasoned, it wouldn't hurt him physically, and the only way he would ever find out was if he had actually done something wrong. Anna was somewhat comforted by the fact that Grace agreed that her suspicions were reasonable.

Her cell phone rang. She looked at the incoming number with surprise. It was Nick. He hadn't called her cell phone since this case had started. She certainly couldn't talk to him right now. She let the call go through to voice mail. But then, as she continued to wait, she couldn't suppress her curiosity. She dialed in for the voice message.

Nick's voice sounded beaten. "Hi, Anna. I just got

out of D'marco's presentment. I heard about everything that happened last night. I'm so sorry." His voice cracked. "I'm just so damned sorry. I'm going to the Irish Times now. Will you come meet me? Please. Let me apologize in person."

She didn't have time to process Nick's message beyond making a mental note of where he said he'd be—the Irish Times was a restaurant and pub down the street from the courthouse—because she spotted Green walking toward the shop. She dropped her phone back in her purse. She felt a twinge of guilt just seeing the officer. Could she really go through with this? She stood up and got in the line to order drinks. She'd soon find out.

She had just reached the cash register when Green opened the door, letting in a blast of cold November air.

"Hi, Officer Green," she called to him as he walked in. She was surprised at how natural her voice sounded. "Cuppa joe?"

"No thanks," he answered. Anna realized that he got so much free coffee as a cop, her offer held little temptation for him.

"I can't drink alone," she said, trying not to sound desperate. "What'll it be?"

He shrugged. "Small coffee."

She ordered two small coffees. When she handed one of the hot paper cups to Green, she felt like the witch handing the poison apple to Snow White. He thanked her and took it over to the table with all the fixings. Green poured two Equals and lots of skim milk into his cup. Anna wondered if he was trying to lose weight.

"So, how *are* you?" he asked as he stirred his coffee. His usual smile was tinged with concern.

"Fine, fine."

"I heard what happened last night." He put the lid back on and clapped her on the shoulder. "What a scare! I'm really glad you're okay."

"Thanks."

Oh, man, she thought, he was being nice. It made her feel guiltier.

Anna pointed to the little table where she'd been sitting. "Do you have a second? I'll tell you about these subpoenas."

"Sure."

"Thanks for agreeing to serve them," she said as they sat down. She pulled out four folders with subpoenas for four different misdemeanor cases. She could send the subpoenas out in the mail, but they weren't enforceable unless the witness was hand-served. Any officer could serve them, but this was her excuse to get Green here—and to get him to put his mouth to the lid of that cup.

Green wasn't drinking his coffee, though. He was looking out the window, watching a paralegal in a short skirt walk by the coffee shop. Anna tried not to stare at his cup. He *had* to drink his coffee. She would keep him here until he did. She started telling him about the witnesses he would deliver the subpoenas to.

"This guy works midnights," she said, sliding a folder across the table, "so you'll have to catch him early in the evening." She picked up another. "And this lady is really old. Give her a lot of time to answer the door."

Green returned his eyes to hers and wrapped his hands around the cup of coffee for warmth—but he still wasn't drinking. Anna tried not to fidget as she willed the officer to pick up his cup. Desperately, she described the entry system of one apartment building. Green nodded, but didn't take a sip. She told him one of the homes had a dog that would bark but not bite. He murmured about being able to handle dogs, but didn't bring the coffee to his lips. Finally, she ran out of things to tell him.

Green glanced at his watch and stood up. "Okay, got it. I'll bring the returns back to you next week. I gotta run now. They'll be calling my prelim any minute."

He grabbed the folders and his coffee and walked toward the door. Anna slumped back in her chair. He was taking the coffee to go. That wouldn't work. Her plan was a bust.

As he reached the door, Green tried to juggle the folders of subpoenas and the coffee, all while opening the door, and the papers started slipping out of his arms. He sighed and set everything on the fixings table. He straightened out all the papers. Then he picked up his cup of coffee. Anna was watching him so intently, his movements seemed to go in slow motion. He brought the cup to his mouth, put his lips on the plastic lid, tipped his head back, and took a sip of the coffee. Then he tossed the almost-full cup into the garbage hole built into the fixings table.

Anna practically jumped out of her seat. She forced herself to wait an excruciating few seconds until Green gathered up his papers, walked out, and crossed the street toward the courthouse. Then she walked over and peered into the circular hole where Green had tossed his used coffee cup. The receptacle was full of garbage. Green's coffee cup was on top, just an inch below the hole. She took a brown paper lunch bag out of her purse. Ignoring another customer's surprised glance, she used a napkin to gingerly pluck Green's coffee cup out of the garbage can. She used the napkin to remove the lid, stuffed the lid into the paper bag, rolled up the bag, and stuck the whole package into her purse.

Anna heaved a sigh of relief and hurried out the door before anyone would ask her about what she'd just done. A sample of Brad Green's DNA was safely stashed in her purse.

27

Anna was back in her office, alone, when her cell phone rang again. It was Nick, calling her for the second time today. This time, she answered his call.

"Hello, Anna!" Nick's voice was somewhat blurred but relieved that she'd picked up. She could hear glasses clinking and people chatting in the background. "It's Nick."

"Hi, Nick." For a second, it felt like before, when they would call each other several times a day. Anna deliberately pushed that feeling away.

"I'm so glad to hear your voice," he said softly. "I was so worried. How are you, Anna?" It was the question of the day, but Nick asked it with such concern, it took on a different meaning. He cared more about her answer to the question, he felt more personally responsible for it, than anyone else who would ask after her today.

"I'm fine. Your voice sounds funny. Where are you?"

"I'm still at the Irish Times. I needed a drink."

"You're drinking already? It's not even four o'clock."

"Already?" He laughed. "I've been drinking for four hours. Come over here, Anna. Have a drink with me."

"I don't think that's a good idea, Nick."

"Please. I have to tell you something. I have to apologize in person. I have to see with my own eyes that you're okay."

She hesitated. A large part of her wanted to go meet him.

"I'm sorry, Nick. I can't. I—I have a lot of work to do."

"Okay. But will you be home later? Can I at least call you tonight?"

She hesitated. "Okay."

When they hung up, she turned back to her computer. She started writing her cover letter for the evidence submission form she was sending to the FBI.

"Come on, I'm taking you all out to dinner."

Anna and Jack looked up from their usual seats in the war room. McGee was standing in the doorway. He wore brown snakeskin boots, a beige suit with brown pinstripes, a brown shirt, and a beige, brown, and fuchsia paisley tie. He smiled at them, baring the gummy gap that used to be two front teeth. "You both need a change of scenery. Your butt cheeks are gonna grow into those chairs."

Anna smiled at the detective; she knew this was McGee's way of looking after her, after D'marco's visit last night. She glanced at Jack to see what he would say. It was almost six o'clock. He usually worked until seven, went home to play with Olivia until her bedtime, and then worked from home. Jack checked his watch, looked at Anna, and raised his eyebrows in an unspoken question: Did she want to go? She nodded. She would like to go out, anything to stay around people and delay going back to her apartment for the first time since D'marco's visit.

"Okay," Jack said to McGee. "But it'll have to be quick. I have to leave by seven."

"Then there's only one place we can go," McGee replied. Jack rolled his eyes; he knew what was coming. McGee clapped Anna on the back as she stood up. "Get ready for the culinary sensation of your life!"

Ben's Chili Bowl was packed. The red pleather booths lining the walls were jammed full, and lobbyists sat next to street kids on stools at the long silver counter. Behind the counter, a short-order cook in a white apron stood over a sizzling stovetop. The smell of frying potatoes filled the air.

While they waited for a table to open up, Jack told Anna about the diner. It was located on U Street NW in a historically black neighborhood that was rapidly gentrifying. Ben's had been dishing out chili dogs and cheese fries to a loyal crowd for fifty years, even as the crowd changed with the neighborhood. To fans like McGee, Ben's was as much a D.C. landmark as the Lincoln Memorial.

After a few minutes, they snagged a booth. McGee and Jack sat at opposite sides of the table. Anna hesitated for a moment before sliding in next to McGee. She was the only one who picked up one of the laminated menus wedged behind a jar of ketchup. Within seconds, a harried waitress came over to take their order.

"Chili dog, cheese fries, and a Coke," McGee ordered happily.

"The same," Jack said.

"Make it three," Anna said dubiously, putting down the menu unread. When in Rome.

McGee picked up his glass of ice water and held it in the air. "I'd like to make a toast," he said with exaggerated formality. He grinned. "To maximum security lockdown!"

D'marco would now be experiencing the highest level of supervision the D.C. Jail had to offer. They all clinked glasses and drank.

Jack raised his glass for another toast. He smiled at Anna and McGee. "To the best team I could hope for. Cheers."

The waitress returned with a tray overloaded with food. She plunked down plates piled high with grease-soaked fries and chili-soaked dogs. McGee smacked his lips, tossed his tie over his shoulder like an aviator's scarf, and eagerly dove into his cheese fries. "Mmmmm," he said. He was practically purring. Anna tentatively took a bite of her chili dog. It was delicious. They all wolfed down their food, chatting between bites.

"Hopefully, we can rest easy now," Jack said, as he wiped his mouth and threw the crumpled napkin on his empty plate. "No more surprises for a while."

Anna smiled as McGee sopped up every last drop of chili with his bun. But Jack's sentiment made her pause.

"Actually—I should tell you something. So there are no surprises for you either."

"What's that?" Jack asked, smiling.

"This afternoon, I asked the FBI to determine whether Brad Green was the father of Laprea's baby."

"Ha!" McGee threw back his head and laughed like it was the funniest thing he'd ever heard. His big belly bounced up and down.

"I'm serious."

"You did what?" Jack asked. The smile vanished from his face.

"I had the FBI's DNA laboratory initiate a paternity test."

"How?"

"I sent a cup that Green had used and thrown away. The FBI said they can use that for his saliva sample. You don't need a warrant to take someone's garbage from a public place."

Jack and McGee were looking at her like she'd just shot the president. "Son of a bitch," McGee said softly. He put his hand deliberately on top of his glass of Coke and made a show of sliding it away from her.

It hadn't dawned on her that she would upset other officers by investigating one of their own. Anna looked to see Jack's reaction. The only movement in Jack's entire body was the muscles in his jaw, clenching and unclenching. She knew by now that meant he was furious.

Uh-oh, she thought.

"Anna, I had forbidden you to do that." Jack's voice was so slow and soft that Anna knew he was struggling to keep it under control.

"You didn't forbid it," she said defensively. "We disagreed. You said I was too shaken up, and I shouldn't waste my time and energy chasing shadows. This isn't because I'm shaken up, and I didn't mind putting in the time and energy."

"We investigate the bad guys, Anna, not the police."

His voice was getting louder, straining against his self-control.

"Well, what if you think one of the police could be a bad guy?"

"Then you send the matter to Internal Affairs, and you go through the proper channels to start an investigation in our office."

"Okay, let's do that."

"Are you kidding me?" he exploded. "You have no basis to accuse him of anything! Absolutely nothing indicating that Green has *ever* done *any*thing wrong!"

"I felt like there was something weird there, for a while—even before D'marco said anything. The way Green acted at Laprea's house, the—"

"We don't investigate a man based on feeling 'something weird'! You're putting the man's reputation, his career at stake just by making the accusation. An accusation based on nothing! I can't believe you would treat a police officer this way! A respected officer, with ten years on the force, who's working on your case! Deceiving him while he's doing you a favor!" Jack stared at her for a long moment. "What were you thinking?"

She held his gaze. "I was thinking this is a search for truth."

"There's a difference between a search for truth and a wild-goose chase! I've been a prosecutor for ten years. You've been one for . . . how many months? When I tell you to do something, you do it! You don't argue about it, or go behind my back when we disagree. Don't you see all the issues this raises? Is Green under investigation by our office now? Do I tell Green? He obviously can't investigate this case anymore. Do I have to disclose to defense counsel the fact that we're doing paternity testing on Green? Our own officer? Nick Wagner's gonna have a field day with this!"

"Look, Jack, I'm sorry! If it's that terrible, I'll tell the FBI not to process it."

"You're damned right you will! Dammit, Anna, I told you not to be working when you were too upset to be thinking straight!"

"This isn't because I'm upset, Jack!" Her voice contradicted the sentiment she was trying to communicate.

"It has to be. You're an intelligent person. The only reason I can think that you'd do something like this is because you're overwrought." Jack stood up. He pulled on his coat and threw a couple of twenties on the table. "This is my fault. I shouldn't have let you come in to work today. Go home, Anna. Take a couple days off. I don't want to see you at work tomorrow."

"There's nothing wrong with me! I don't need a sick day!"

Jack turned to the detective. "McGee, can you give Anna a ride home? I've gotta relieve the nanny."

McGee nodded, but didn't look happy about it. Anna watched miserably as Jack walked outside. It was starting to snow, and a few flakes danced in the triangle of street light that illuminated Jack as he climbed into a cab. Her chili dog rumbling uncomfortably in her stomach, Anna realized that she had managed to alienate both men in one night.

In her living room later that night, Anna sprawled on her couch in soft cotton pajama pants and a tank top. She mindlessly flicked through the channels. She had eaten a handful of Tums, but she knew it wasn't her dinner that was making her stomach roil. She felt terrible about her fight with Jack. It wasn't just being yelled at by a senior lawyer. He was also her friend, her mentor, the person she saw on a daily basis more than anyone else. The idea of disappointing him lodged as an uncomfortable lump in her throat.

A knock on her door interrupted her thoughts. Anna's breath caught hopefully. Maybe it was Jack. Maybe he had come over so they could talk about this. She could apologize for her misstep, and they could try to figure out how to resolve everything. She turned off the TV and padded to the door. She took a deep breath, then peered out.

She could hardly believe what she saw.

28

Standing with her eye pressed to the peephole, she had to admit that some part of her had always hoped that Nick would show up on her doorstep to apologize and tell her he loved her. That she meant more to him than any client or ideology. That he was sorry to have chosen defending D'marco over being with her. Maybe if he said those things, they could be together again.

If now was going to be that moment, Nick Wagner was off to a very disappointing start.

He was drunk. Very drunk. An amber stain marred his half-untucked shirt; his tie was askew; his eyes could only open to half-mast. He swayed back and forth, one hand on her doorknob for support, the other clutching a box to his chest. Bewildered and concerned, Anna slid aside the dead bolt. Whiskey fumes hit her as soon as the door was open. She wondered how Nick was still standing.

"Nick! Are you okay?"

"Hello, Anna." Nick's head lolled to one side. It seemed to be a struggle for him to straighten it and bring his bloodshot eyes to focus on hers. "I brought these for you."

He held out the box to her; it was from Julia's

Empanadas. She did not reach for the box. In addition to being intoxicated, Nick didn't look well generally. He had soft blue circles under his reddened eyes, and the sparkly mischief they'd always held was gone. His tailored suit hung a bit loosely. He was losing weight. Still, he was extravagantly handsome—in fact, his new leanness made his cheekbones more chiseled and his chin a strong, sculpted square. That, and a day's worth of stubble, made him look like a Hollywood bad boy. Anna felt physically drawn to him, as she always did when he was near. She consciously took a step backward.

"Why are you here?" she asked. Too many thoughts and emotions were running through her head for her to parse them all: the continuing anger and hurt at how their relationship had ended, astonishment at his appearance on her doorstep, affection at the sight of his tousled dark hair, anxiety about the impropriety of this visit, and a twinge of fear at the sight of a very drunk man at her door. She pushed the last thought aside. Nick was not her father. However drunk he got, she knew, Nick would not hurt her.

"I told you, I have to see you." He started to walk into her house, slowly, with the careful, exaggerated steps of the truly intoxicated, but without hesitation, as if the past three months hadn't happened.

"No, Nick. Stop." Her voice was soft, but the hands she put on his chest were firm. She gently pushed him back onto the concrete landing outside her front door. "I don't think you should come in now. And when you sober up, you'll agree." She slid on a pair of shoes and walked outside with him. She grabbed his arm and tried to pull him up the three steps to the sidewalk. "I'm going to call you a cab."

"No." He sat on the middle step. She tugged on his arm, but he didn't move.

"Come on, Nick!"

A few passing pedestrians glanced over and chuckled. A little drunken drama was not an uncommon sight in Adams-Morgan; the bars were just a few blocks away from her house. She sighed and let go of Nick's arm. She walked to the street, leaving vague footprints in the thin layer of powdery snow on the ground. She hailed a cab and motioned for the driver to roll down his window.

"Hi." Anna leaned down to talk to the cabbie. "I need you to take my friend home. He lives just a couple blocks from here, but he's a little tipsy. Can you make sure he gets home in one piece?" The driver nodded. Anna went back to the defense attorney on her doorstep. "Okay, Nick. This nice taxi driver is going to make sure you get home okay."

Nick shook his head, but didn't move any other part of his body.

"Come on. You've gotta go." She gave a tug on his arm. He sat stubbornly still.

"I don't want to go home." He turned toward the cab and raised his voice so the driver could hear. "I feel sick."

She looked helplessly to the cabbie, hoping he would help her bring Nick to the car. The driver shook his head and drove off. He didn't want someone who was going to vomit in the backseat. Anna stamped her foot in frustration.

"Nick!"

He reached for her arm, trying to get her to sit on the step next to him, but she brushed him off. She was freezing and not in any mood to play games. Fine, she thought. If Nick wanted to stay here, he could. She didn't have to do anything about it. She brushed past him and walked back down into her house, locking the door behind her. He could find his own way home.

She went to the bathroom. She combed her hair and put it up in a ponytail. She took her time brushing her teeth and washing her face. She flossed, then gargled with mouthwash. She trimmed her nails and rubbed moisturizer onto her hands. When there was nothing else she could possibly do before going to bed, she walked back to her front door and peered out the peephole.

Nick was still sitting on her steps, the box of empanadas on his lap. His head rested on the brick wall, and his eyes were closed. A few flakes of powdery snow were sitting in his dark hair, like confectioners' sugar atop a chocolate cupcake. Anna shook her head, wondering what to do. She couldn't let him freeze to death out there. But he was too big for her to force him to go home. She tried to think of someone she could call to help her. Grace? Jack? But they would ask why the defense attorney was camped out on her steps. Ditto the police. She still hadn't told anyone about her relationship with Nick, and she didn't want to start like this.

The best she could do, she thought, was to bring him inside, sober him up, and then send him on his way. She pretended that this reasoning was not influenced by her desire to hear why he'd come here tonight. She opened the door and walked outside.

"Wake up, Nick," she said, shaking his shoulders. "Nick!"

His eyes opened, disoriented for a moment. He focused on Anna's face and smiled.

"Come on." She hauled him to his feet. "Get inside before someone sees you here."

He followed her into the house, no longer a stubborn mule but a happy, obedient puppy. He set the box of empanadas on the table next to the front door. She pointed to her red couch, and he sank down. She stepped away from him and stood in front of the couch, crossing her arms on her chest.

"Why are you here?" she asked.

He leaned his head back against the couch and closed his eyes. "I spent the morning representing a man who broke out of jail to attack my girlfriend. I wanted to make sure she was okay."

"I'm not your girlfriend," Anna snapped, although a traitorous part of her heart thrilled to hear him say it.

He opened his eyes. "I know." He tried to straighten his tie, but only pulled it farther off center. "You look beautiful," he said, patting the couch next to him.

"And you look like you were mugged by Jim Beam." She sat in the chair across from the couch.

"Naw, he didn't mug me." Nick laughed mirthlessly. "We've been good friends since this case started. I've been hanging out with him just about every night. Mostly, I tell him about you. I can't stop thinking about you, Anna. And this case. This fucking case!"

His face contorted with a pain so sharp it sliced through several cushioning layers of whiskey.

"I didn't know it affected you that much," she said cautiously. Anna didn't like to see anyone hurting, but she felt something close to relief to see Nick like this. She'd wondered if he had a conscience at all, whether Laprea's death meant anything to him or if it was just an unpleasant footnote in his defense playbook. In a way, it was good to know that it had touched him. That he was human.

"Affected me?" His voice cracked. "It's the only thing I think about. I can't believe it's gotten this crazy. That you were in danger. I could never forgive myself if anything happened to you."

He covered his eyes with a hand. He didn't seem to be breathing. "Nick?" she asked. He didn't move. She got up and walked over to him uncertainly, then pulled his hand gently away from his eyes. His face was twisted with regret, his eyes brimming with tears. He wrapped his fingers around her wrist and pulled her to sit on the couch. His eyes searched hers, seeming to beg her for help.

"I know this is all my fault, Anna. I can't keep living like this."

She looked at him sadly—and then with growing hope. Did this mean he realized that representing D'marco was the wrong choice for him? For them? That he wasn't going to do it anymore? Was he getting off the case—choosing her over his client?

"It's going to be okay, Nick." She squeezed his hands. "It's not too late. Whatever choices we've made in the past, they're not irreversible. There's still time to do the right thing."

"Promise?"

He cupped her face between his hands and leaned in to kiss her. She jumped back before his lips touched hers, but not before she felt his warm, whiskey-scented breath on her neck.

"Jesus, Nick. No." She bolted from the couch. "I'm going to make you some coffee," she announced briskly. "Then you have to go."

She fled to the kitchen, pulled a bag of coffee out of her cabinet, and willed her heart to slow down. She wasn't sure whom she was more furious at: Nick, for trying to kiss her, or herself, for almost allowing him to do it. Herself, she decided. She was sober; she had no excuses.

While the coffee brewed, she stood in the kitchen, as far from Nick as her apartment permitted. The sounds of percolating coffee almost drowned out the whoosh of blood rushing through her ears. When it was ready, she poured a mugful, took a deep breath, and brought it out to Nick.

He was passed out on the couch, slumped sideways on the cushions. A soft snore wheezed from his mouth. She set the coffee on the table and knelt by him. "Nick," she said, poking his arms. He didn't move. She shook his shoulders vigorously. "Nick!"

He was out.

She allowed herself a moment to gaze at him. His face had smoothed out; he was peaceful at last. She brushed a lock of his hair out of his eyes. His eyelashes, dark and ridiculously long, curled on his cheeks, giving him an angelic look that she didn't think he deserved. She gazed at his beautiful, slumbering face for a long time. She was simultaneously furious at and aching for him.

She decided not to wake him. She rationalized the decision: it was her first night in her apartment since D'marco had come here. It felt safer with Nick on her couch—even if he was passed out. And she didn't have much of a choice anyway, she told herself—he was unconscious.

She tugged off his shoes and pulled his legs onto the couch. Nick groaned softly. "Buddy, if you think you feel bad now, wait till morning," she said, as she slid a cushion under his head. His moaning quieted to soft, steady breathing. She spread an afghan on top of him and turned out the lights.

Anna went to her bedroom and climbed into her own bed. She lay on her side, facing her door, which she'd left cracked open. She could hear the faint sound of Nick's breathing from the living room. Except for the distance between them, it sounded like it did when they used to sleep together, curled into each other's bodies. She craved that feeling now. It was so close.

She stared at the crack in her bedroom door for a long time. Why? she wondered. With all the men in this city, why did she have to fall in love with this one?

29

Jack swore as another car cut him off. This drive made him remember why he always took the Metro to work. It wasn't even 8:00 a.m., and the morning rush-hour traffic into the city was already horrendous. Sixteenth Street was practically a parking lot. Instead of a pleasant walk through a nice neighborhood and a ten-minute chance to read his newspaper on the subway, he was fighting idiots to move his Volvo station wagon forward by inches. The snow from last night didn't help—this city panicked at the sight of the white stuff. This commute filled him with a general sense of frustration at the world. But he wasn't going directly to work this morning, and it didn't make sense for him to take the subway for this trip. He would just have to fight the congestion.

He felt terrible about his fight with Anna. He didn't want to argue with her. Especially the day after D'marco Davis attacked her in her own home. When he'd thought about it, later, he knew that what she'd done wasn't a disaster. Anna would cancel the paternity test. Jack had already told McGee not to mention it to anyone. Green would likely never find out, and this would blow over without notice. Jack shouldn't have blown up at her.

He knew he wouldn't have reacted that way with any of his other attorneys. Lawyers often disagreed, they had different strategies—Jack didn't yell at them. Folks made mistakes—he'd never benched anyone before. Jack took pride in his calm during crises, his ability to handle any situation with quiet, focused precision. He hadn't understood why this time was different. At least, he hadn't last night at Ben's, while it was happening. He did now. He'd lain awake for most of the night, unable to sleep, thoughts spinning through his head. The conclusion had finally hit him around 3:00 a.m., stunning both in its simplicity and his ability to ignore it for so long.

He was attracted to Anna.

When she'd rejected his idea, he'd taken it as a personal rejection, and he'd overreacted.

Jack turned right onto Columbia Road, and then turned left, down 18th Street, the heart of Adams-Morgan. Now the challenge was parking. He looked for an open space as he slowly drove down the street.

He'd fought against his feelings for Anna for a long time. He'd tried to convince himself that it was fatherly protection or dutiful mentoring. But no. He knew what it was. He wanted her.

And, he thought, there was a chance she felt the same way. He'd caught her looking at him a few times, across the war room table, for no particular reason—just studying his face or his hands. She stayed in the war room a lot, even when she was working on her other cases. Maybe she wanted to be near him, just as he wanted to be near her, even if they were just silently working side by side.

And two nights ago, at his house—as they were standing in the guest bedroom—he was pretty sure she'd wanted to kiss him. He had stepped away, because Olivia was in the next room, because he didn't want to be the sleazy boss from the sexual harassment training video, because he wouldn't take advantage of a young woman who'd just survived a harrowing night. But he had seen the flash of desire as her eyes flicked over his face—he was certain of it.

A spot opened up on 18th Street, and Jack parked in it.

He should have kissed her. Dammit. Who knew if that moment, that perfect moment, would ever present itself again? Instead, a day later, he was chewing her out in front of a detective. From possible lover to asshole boss in one day. He had to make it right.

He got out of the car, avoiding the dirty puddles where last night's snow was melting. There was a pretty flower shop on the corner of 18th and Wyoming. *Should I bring her flowers?* he wondered. *Would that send the wrong message—or the right one?* He paused in front of the shop. He wasn't sure how to handle this. He hadn't dated anyone since Olivia's mother died; he hadn't been interested in anyone else. And he certainly didn't know how to handle this particular dating situation, fraught with workplace issues, race issues, age issues, issues he probably hadn't even spotted yet.

After a moment's hesitation, he pushed all that aside. He would handle it like any other problem: he would confront it head-on. He would tell Anna how he was feeling, and give her a chance to respond. It might be controversial, it might be messy, but it would be out in the open and they could deal with it honestly. Let the chips fall where they may. He stepped into the shop and bought a bouquet of deep purple irises.

He knocked on Anna's door a few minutes later, flowers clutched in his hand, his heart beating in his throat. The chain inside clanked, the door swung open, and Anna was standing in front of him. She was still wearing pajamas. Her blond hair was in a ponytail, and her face was clean and makeupless. She looked natural and beautiful and very young. Her eyes widened when she saw him on her doorstep, and then widened even more when she saw the flowers he was holding by his side.

"Hi, Anna," he greeted her.

"Hi," she gulped.

"I'm sorry to just show up like this, but I wanted to apologize to you. I overreacted yesterday. What you did wasn't so bad. It's just a blip, and we'll handle it. I don't know what's gotten into me. Actually, I do know. That's what I wanted to talk with you about. Can I— Do you have a minute?" He gestured toward her house.

Her cheeks went from a light pink to a deep rose. She looked acutely uncomfortable. She'd initially opened the door a few feet. She didn't open it any farther now. In fact, the opening seemed to narrow a bit. She glanced back into her apartment.

"Well—uh—actually—" she stammered. There was a moment of uncomfortable silence.

Suddenly, Jack got it.

"Do you have company?" he asked.

"Um—yeah."

He felt like he'd been punched in the gut. It hadn't

occurred to him that she might have a boyfriend. How did she have time for a boyfriend, he thought fleetingly, when she was always at the office? But it didn't matter how. She did. The flowers in his hand felt incredibly heavy.

"Who's at the door?" a man's voice called from inside her apartment.

"Nobody!" she cried back. Her face was panic-stricken.

Jack's head recoiled as if she'd slapped him. She saw it.

"No, Jack, I didn't mean that *you* were nobody. I just meant that, it wasn't anyone that needed to be—that had to have a—what I meant is . . ."

As she stuttered out the incoherent explanation, a dark-haired man wearing an untucked shirt and wrinkled pants came to the door. As Jack saw the other man's face, he felt a strange sense of recognition. He knew who he was looking at, but the person was so far removed from his normal place in the world, so out of context, that his appearance just didn't make sense at first, and Jack didn't fully comprehend who it was.

Then his brain caught up to his eyes. It was Nicholas Wagner. In rumpled clothing. In Anna's house. At 8:00 a.m. Jack's blood froze, then boiled.

"Nobody, huh?" Nick said mockingly, blinking his eyes in the bright winter sunlight. He stood behind Anna and looked at Jack venomously over her shoulder. "I think we've met."

"What are you doing here?" Jack asked him slowly. His jaw started to clench.

"The same thing as you, apparently," Nick said. He

reached past Anna and took the flowers from Jack's hand. "Thanks, she'll love these."

"Nick, no!" Anna cried. She spun from the man behind her to the man on her doorstep. "Jack, it's not like that!"

Jack turned and strode back up the steps to the street. His chest was a tight, raging battle between abject humiliation and wanting to punch that Wagner kid. He had to get out of here before he became a number on today's lockup list.

Jack shook his head as he strode down the sidewalk, barely able to comprehend the enormity of his miscalculation. Everything he'd thought was wrong. Anna wasn't interested in him at all. She was dating the defense attorney.

He became aware of a pattering of feet behind him. "Jack, wait!" Anna cried. She was racing up to him, barefoot on the wet sidewalk. He didn't break his stride, but she caught up and trotted next to him. "It's not like that—he was drunk, he just needed to stay over."

"You were out drinking with the defense attorney?" His legs were longer than hers; she had to jog to keep up with him.

"No, he came over, unannounced. He was stumbling drunk and feeling guilty about getting D'marco off the first time. I felt sorry for him. I just let him sleep it off on my couch."

"He acted an awful lot like your boyfriend."

"Well, we were . . ." She slowed and fell a few inches behind Jack. He stopped and turned to her. They stood facing each other in the quiet gray morning, an odd couple: he in his suit and trench coat, she in bare feet and pajamas.

"You were what?" he asked.

"Not while the case was going on . . ."

"What?" he demanded.

She swallowed. "Dating."

"When?"

"Between the first case and our investigation." Jack turned and walked even faster toward his car. She ran to catch up. "I was going to tell you!"

"When were you going to tell me?"

"Okay," she admitted. "I wasn't going to tell you."

"You lied to me."

"No!"

"You said you knew him from law school."

"I did know him from law school. I just—all this happened after law school," she finished weakly.

A thought suddenly struck him. He wondered if she could be that treacherous. He slowed his step and narrowed his eyes, searching her face.

"Is that why you're investigating Officer Green instead of D'marco Davis?"

"No! Jack, no! I would never try to sabotage our case!"

"You see how bad this looks, Anna. How am I supposed to be able to tell what side you're on? How can anyone?"

"You know me, Jack. Jack! Look at me!" She grabbed his arm with a strength he wouldn't have guessed the slim woman had. He spun to face her. They were inches apart, her hand grasping his arm. She looked up at him—a direct, courageous look—but her lips were quivering. "You *know* me. I wouldn't try to hurt our case. Jack, I'm on your side."

Her big blue eyes pleaded with his. They were beautiful eyes, he thought. Beautiful and traitorous. When he spoke again, he had reined in his anger, hurt, and humiliation. His voice was cold and emotionless.

"This is textbook misconduct, Anna. You've betrayed this case."

"No, I'm committed to it!" Her voice became more hysterical as his became flatter. "It's been over between me and Nick for a long time! It won't affect my work on the investigation!"

"There'll be no more of your 'work' on this investigation."

"What do you mean?"

"This is a conflict of interest." He turned to his car and unlocked it. "You're off the case."

"Jack, please—" She put her hand on his arm again.

"Enough!" he thundered.

Anna flinched and stepped back. Jack stood still for a moment, bracing himself on his car. He looked over at her, shivering and barefoot, tears brimming over her eyes. A fleeting instinct told him to put his arm around her shoulders, to draw her into an embrace, that she would welcome it. A few minutes ago, he had been hoping for just such an opportunity. But he couldn't trust her anymore. He took a deep breath and lowered his voice.

"This is not negotiable."

Jack wrenched the door open and climbed into the driver's seat. All the hopes he'd held this morning were destroyed. He didn't look at Anna again as he started the car and pulled off.

30

With dismay, Anna watched from the snowy sidewalk as Jack's car drove away. She couldn't believe what had just happened. Jack had come here to apologize and—she thought of the flowers—to tell her something more? Instead, he'd found Nick Wagner hanging out in her living room. She groaned. How Jack must have felt! She thought of the look on his face when he slammed the car door. The possibility of forgiveness was nowhere on it.

And Anna hadn't just lost Jack—she'd been fired from Laprea's case. She'd reneged on her promise to Rose and the debt she owed Laprea's children. The purpose that had driven her days was suddenly gone.

When her bare feet became so cold that the pain turned to numbness, she turned and trudged back to her apartment.

As she walked in, Nick came out of her kitchen holding a cup of coffee. He offered the mug to her. She ignored the offer, put her hands on her hips, and looked at Nick furiously. She thought she saw a trace of a smirk on his face, but it quickly became a look of rather unconvincing regret.

"What the hell was that all about?" Anna's voice was a decibel below a shout.

"Anna, I'm sorry—"

"You're sorry? You wouldn't have to be *sorry* if you hadn't been such an asshole! You came to my house drunk! I let you stay here so you wouldn't freeze to death—and this is how you repay me? By flaunting yourself to my boss? Why did you come to the door? Why did you take those flowers? What the fuck were you thinking?"

"It wasn't right! He was coming on to you—and he's your supervisor. That's sexual harassment!"

"Not if it's wanted!"

"Was it?" His voice quieted. "Wanted?"

"That's none of your business. Nick, I can't believe what you just did!"

"I'm sorry, but I saw this guy here, trying to win you, and I just reacted. It was an instinct, you know. To fight for my girl."

"I am not your girl!"

"I know that!" he shouted back. Coffee sloshed out of the mug. "I am very aware of that!"

"You were a dog peeing on a fire hydrant! I am not your territory!"

"Do you think this is easy for me? Seeing you sitting next to him in court? Getting phone calls from the two of you? Knowing all the time you're spending with each other, the long nights with your heads together, planning how to beat me? We never even talk anymore. Okay, we can't date—but we're not even *friends*. Look." Nick lowered his voice and put his hand up in a gesture of peace. "I didn't want to get you in trouble. I got up this morning and I passed your room, and there you were, sleeping, and

I just wanted to climb in with you. I thought I did a pretty good job of restraining myself."

Anna felt some of her fury dissipate. She understood what Nick was saying; she had felt a similar nostalgia just last night.

Seeing her face relax a bit, Nick continued to plead his case.

"All I wanted to do this morning was apologize—sober this time—for what D'marco did to you. I just wanted to make it right."

"Great job, Nick." The anger had left her voice, replaced with exhaustion. "You got me kicked off the case."

"Christ."

Nick set the coffee mug on her kitchen table and stepped cautiously toward her. He approached her with his arm outstretched, slowly, carefully, like a wrangler approaching a wild mustang. He laid his hand gently on her bare arm and looked down at her. An electric warmth radiated down her arm from where his fingers lay. She looked at his face. His hazel eyes held a spark they hadn't last night.

"I'm so sorry, Anna."

"You don't seem sorry. You seem glad."

"Maybe I'm a little bit of both," Nick acknowledged softly. "Because this could actually be a good thing. There's no conflict now. We can be together. If you're honest with yourself, you'll admit that you want it, too. Come back to me, Anna."

He moved his hand slowly up her arm.

She looked at his face, momentarily confused, thinking that she must be misunderstanding what he was saying. She remembered what he'd started to say last night, before he passed out.

"No conflict *now*?" she asked slowly. "Are *you* still representing D'marco Davis?"

"Not in the case involving your assault. I decided I can't do that. But on the homicide—" He grimaced. "Yes."

She backed away from him in astonishment. He was asking her to get back together with him—not because *he* was getting off the case, but because he had gotten *her* kicked off. She felt her fury growing in a hard, tight knot in her chest.

"I don't have a choice," Nick said. "Please, try to understand, it's not about you—"

"You selfish asshole. You come to my house drunk, flaunt yourself to my boss, get *me* kicked off of Laprea's case—which, by the way, you're going full steam ahead on—and then you expect me to fall sobbing into your arms with gratitude? Get out," she said, pointing to the door. When he didn't move, she grabbed his coat, opened the door, and threw it out onto the wet concrete steps. "Get out!" She pushed him through the door and slammed it shut.

She just wished she'd done it nine hours ago.

She leaned back against the door, breathing as hard as if she'd just run a sprint. Her anger felt like a hot itch over all of her skin. She looked at the side table. The box of empanadas and the bouquet of irises sat there next to each other. But she was alone.

Three hours later, Anna sat uncomfortably in a chair in front of the U.S. Attorney's desk. Her anger was gone, replaced by a nervous tightness in the pit of her stomach. The U.S. Attorney was looking at her like she was an interesting but worrisome specimen he'd found growing in a petri dish. Carla Martinez sat protectively next to her, and a gray-haired man whom Anna recognized as the Chief Muckety-Muck of Something or Other sat on the brown leather couch to their right. Anna's legs were crossed and her ankle in the air was jittering nervously. She noticed the jittering, stopped it, and shifted, nervously awaiting their verdict.

After she'd thrown Nick out, Anna had decided that she had to tell Carla everything immediately, before Carla heard it through the grapevine. So Anna had showered, put on her most serious dark suit, caught the Metro, and marched herself into Carla's office. Anna confessed the whole story—or most of it, at least. She didn't mention Jack's flowers or the possibility that he had come over for anything other than professional reasons. Carla listened quietly and asked a few questions, but she didn't jump up and down or scream. Carla seemed to take the whole thing as a setback, but not, as Anna had imagined, the most horrendous thing that had ever happened. Anna realized that the chief of the Domestic Violence and Sex Crimes Section had seen plenty of scandals in her time.

"I appreciate you coming here and telling me. That took guts," Carla said when Anna was done. "Let me ask you this: Is your relationship with Wagner over?"

"Yes. It has been since this case started."

"Did your past with him affect your work on the Davis case at all?"

"No."

"Between you and Jack, I assume Jack made all the charging decisions, plea offer decisions, and the like?"

"Yes."

"Okay." Carla sighed and paused for a moment, reflecting. "I think we have a chance to muddle through this. But it's not going to be pretty." Carla picked up the phone. "The front office has to be informed."

A few minutes later, Anna found herself sitting here, in a guest chair in the U.S. Attorney's office, as Carla summarized her story.

"I see." McFadden pressed his fingertips together when Carla finished. He studied Anna for a moment, then picked up his phone and dialed Jack's number. Jack didn't answer. McFadden replaced the receiver, then turned to the muckety-muck on the couch. "Donald, what do you think?"

Donald didn't look at Anna. "Well, Ms. Curtis is still in her probationary period."

"Meaning?"

"Her employment can be terminated at any time, for any reason, without notice."

"Hm."

Anna sat up in her chair. Donald, whoever he was, was recommending that she be fired. She opened her mouth to respond, but Carla spoke first.

"No way," Carla said firmly. "That is not an option."

"Carla, you have to admit, this is a serious ethical issue," Donald said gravely.

"No, I don't believe that's true. Anna told me that her relationship with the defense attorney was over before this case began and did not affect her judgment or the team's decisions in the Davis case. I believe her."

McFadden sighed. "We all do. But we still have to report this situation to the Ethics and Professionalism Office. In turn, they might notify D.C.'s Office of Bar Counsel."

Anna's mouth opened. Just being referred to these committees was scandalous. EPO enforced ethics rules at the Department of Justice. If EPO found that she violated the rules, she would lose her job here. Worse, if they referred her to the D.C. Bar, her license to practice law could be revoked altogether.

"Why?" Anna asked. "If you believe me?"

"It's not about whether *we* believe you, Anna." McFadden's tone was stern but not unsympathetic. "It's about doing things by the book. We're the prosecutors. We try to put people in jail every day, to take away people's liberty. To do that, we have to stand on the moral high ground, and hold ourselves to the highest of standards. If you were seeing Mr. Wagner romantically during the time that you were opposing counsel, it would be an ethical violation. In this type of situation, it's better if we allow an objective party to look into this and make the final call. I'm sorry, but there will have to be an inquiry."

The last word hung in the air, conjuring images of the Star Chamber.

"Frankly," Donald ventured, "it might be easier for everyone involved—including Anna—if we just let her go now."

"No," Carla retorted. "If you feel you need to refer

her to EPO, so be it. But don't pretend that you're firing her for her own good. Being fired is never helpful on a résumé. Look, this young lady is an excellent prosecutor, and we're short-staffed as it is. With the budget what it is, I haven't been able to hire a new prosecutor in a year, and I've lost two to attrition. And believe me, crime isn't going down. I simply can't lose her. You owe me this."

Anna watched Carla's steely speech gratefully.

McFadden narrowed his eyes for a moment, then sat back in his chair with a smile of surrender.

"Okay, Carla," McFadden said. "If it means that much to you, we'll let Anna stay on. But we can't have her appearing in court while EPO is investigating her."

Anna felt a wave of relief—until she realized that she was qualified for only one position in this office that wasn't a litigating position.

"Sure," Carla answered easily. "Until this is cleared up, I'll assign Anna to our Papering Room in the courthouse."

Anna realized her ankle was jittering again. She pulled both feet under her chair. She was grateful for Carla's efforts and relieved not to be fired. But papering was the worst job in the office. It was awful even on a once-a-month basis, possibly madness-inducing for longer.

"Full-time?" Anna asked.

"Until this is cleared up," Carla said.

"What about my cases?"

"Someone will take over your caseload. Thank you, Joe, for your time."

Carla stood up and motioned for Anna to do the

same. She wanted to leave before McFadden changed his mind.

Anna followed her boss down the hallway. They walked to Anna's office, and Anna turned to Carla in front of her door.

"Carla, thank you for that."

"Of course. They won't fire you, I'll make sure of that. But they may keep you in Papering so long that you'll be tempted to leave on your own. Frankly, they probably hope that you'll do just that. Think of it as a test of will." Carla gave her a small, sad smile. "Why don't you take a few minutes to pack up your personal effects and take them to the Papering Room in the courthouse. They need a hand in Papering today anyhow."

Anna nodded and wistfully watched her boss walk away. On top of everything else, she understood how much she'd disappointed Carla.

Anna's office was empty; Grace was probably in court. Anna looked around the room. She'd never thought she would feel sad to leave this office: cramped, dingy, and full of mismatched furniture and Grace's piles of shoes. But she'd always assumed she would leave when she was promoted to a felony section, to a private office with fewer scuff marks on the walls, to a world of bigger cases and more responsibility. Now she was leaving shamefully, to be a glorified typist in a windowless cellar for an interminable time, cut off from her friends and cases, while she awaited an "inquiry" into her sex life. By comparison, this cramped, dingy shared office seemed great.

Anna glanced at the file cabinets. All of her

misdemeanor cases were in there. They would go to a new attorney. It felt like leaving a beloved pet dog at the pound. She hoped the new owner would care for them well.

Then Anna's gaze fell to her desk. Three redwells rested on the corner. Besides the boxes in the war room, these were her working files on Laprea's case. Anna ran her hand across the files. Her fingers paused on the manila folder that she'd marked PATERNITY TEST yesterday. Last night, Jack had told her to cancel it, but she couldn't do that now. She was off of this case, in no uncertain terms. Jack would do it. Jack would be doing everything from here on out. She hoisted the files and walked them down to Jack's office. His door was uncharacteristically closed.

"He's in a meeting, hon," Vanetta called. "Can I help you?"

"Um." Anna looked at the door, then back at the secretary. She wondered if Jack was really in a meeting or if he just didn't want to talk to her. It didn't matter. Anna handed the files reluctantly to Vanetta. "Can you let him know I dropped these off?"

"Sure."

Anna walked despondently back to her own office and started packing up her things.

Half an hour later, she pushed out of the front doors of the U.S. Attorney's office. She was holding a single box filled with scrunchies, Clif Bars, a package of knee-highs, her mug, and miscellaneous other stuff. A few passing people looked at her curiously. This was the grown-up version of the "walk of shame," Anna realized, walking out of your office in the middle of the day, clutching a box of hastily packed personal effects.

She looked at the courthouse to the left. If she wanted to keep her job, she had to go to Papering, in the basement of the courthouse. Then Anna looked at the Metro entrance, to her right. She could simply head down the escalator and catch the next train home.

Everything Anna loved about the job was gone now. Quitting would save her a lot of grief, and unlike being fired, it wouldn't destroy her résumé. There would be no EPO inquiry if she didn't work here, and no subsequent referral to the D.C. Bar. She would keep her license for sure. And she wouldn't have to work in Papering for months, praying to be cleared, while her colleagues whispered about her demotion. With her qualifications, she could easily get a job at a law firm. She could go make a ton of money, have an office with a view, eat sushi every night. Get a clean slate. Start over.

It was tempting.

She stood standing there for a long time, looking between the courthouse and the Metro station, wondering which way to turn.

31

The route from Detroit Metro Airport to Flint was a flat line through snow-blanketed farmland. The November landscape was all browns and grays: pewter sky, bare trees, the stubble of dead grass poking through snowdrifts. Near the highway, the white fields were bordered with dirty snow and pockmarked piles of sooty ice that had been plowed into heaps along the shoulder. As the city of Flint drew closer, the farmland was replaced with warehouses, strip malls, box stores, and fast-food chains. The fields became parking lots planted with rows of road-salted SUVs, the metal crops of the modern Rust Belt.

Anna sat in the passenger seat of her sister's GMC Yukon, her backside pleasantly toasted by the built-in seat warmer. Everyone around Flint worked in the auto industry and bought fully loaded cars at a steep discount. The SUV's big leather seat felt luxurious compared to the plastic seats Anna had gotten used to on Washington's subway. But she had also gotten used to the District's elegant embassies, its pruned flower beds and reflecting pools, the stately museums and monuments. She hadn't missed this gritty suburban sprawl.

She had missed her sister, though.

She gazed at Jody, who was steering the truck down

the wet gray streets. Looking at Jody had once been like looking in a mirror. Although Jody was two years younger and a little taller, they had the same honey blond hair, the same high Germanic cheekbones, the same pink-cheeked smile that Anna now associated with Midwesterners. Now, however, the sisters' different lifestyles were carving their physiques into different shapes. Anna was thin from jogging, yoga, and the constant stress of her work, while Jody was built more solidly, her muscles forged by installing instrument panels into the cabs of trucks. Jody's palms were calloused and her nails cut short; Anna had soft hands and a French manicure from her day at the spa with Grace.

Yet the one thing that used to differentiate them had mostly faded. Anna studied Jody's cheek. The long scar running from her mouth to her ear was barely visible now.

"It's so good to see you, Jo," Anna said.

"You too." Jody took her eyes off the road and grinned at Anna's camel-hair coat. "You look good. Like a real grown-up." Jody was wearing the same puffy red ski jacket and hiking boots she'd had in high school.

"I'm glad I can fool *someone*."

They were approaching a small, run-down trailer park. Anna grimaced as she saw the neighborhood where they had once lived, so long ago. A battered sign announced MAPLEVIEW PARK: A MOBILE HOME COMMUNITY. The rusting trailers might be called "mobile" homes, but none had moved an inch since being parked. The trailers, and many of their occupants, were stuck there. There weren't any trees in view either, despite the Mapleview name. It was just a flat patch of dirty snow with a strip mall on either side and a stubbly cornfield behind it.

"They're talking about tearing it down and building a Meijer there," Jody said quietly.

"Good riddance." Anna closed her eyes and pressed her forehead against the cool glass.

They continued driving until they got to Swartz Creek, a suburb of Flint with small houses, neat yards, and several cars in every driveway. American flags hung from many porches and UAW bumper stickers adorned most vehicles. Although a lot of jobs had gone to Mexico, there were still enough left here to support this quiet suburb, at least for now.

Jody pulled the Yukon into the driveway of a little white ranch house with a green door. After years of diligently squirreling away her money, she had accumulated enough for a down payment and bought the house this summer. Anna had seen photos online, but this was her first visit.

"Home sweet teeny-tiny home," Jody said cheerfully.

"Are you kidding me? In D.C., this house would cost half a million dollars. My apartment would fit in your garage."

Jody laughed and helped Anna carry her things inside. Anna toured the house, oohing and aahing over the rooms, which Jody had painted herself in bright funky colors. Anna ran her hand over the multihued purple walls in the bathroom.

"Nice work with the sponge painting."

"Yeah, I was a Benjamin Moore poster girl for a while there."

Jody made hot chocolate and the sisters curled up

next to each other on the couch as the sunlight faded. Jody dished the latest news about the troubles of the auto industry and the gossip about their high school friends.

Anna sipped her cocoa and listened for a while, then interrupted her sister. "Okay, enough about everyone else's love life. Tell me about yours. How's that guy you were dating? Doug. Is he a keeper?"

"Ugh, no. What a jerk. We're done."

"What happened?" Anna asked. "You said he was so cute."

"Yeah, when he was sober. Johnny Depp by day, Johnnie Walker at night. I'm done with dating."

"Oh, come on," Anna chided. "You just have a talent for picking the bad ones. If there are ten guys asking for your number, you give it to the one with the mean streak."

"You should talk!" Jody laughed. "What about that guy you dated, the one who ended up defending that murderer? Talk about not being able to sort the good from the bad. I'm glad you got rid of him."

Anna paused for a minute, then looked down at her cocoa. She wrapped her fingers around the warm mug and took a deep breath.

"Oh no," Jody said. "Don't tell me you got back together with him."

"No," Anna insisted. "But—it's complicated."

"What's going on?" Jody asked suspiciously.

Anna wasn't sure where to begin. "Do you have a computer here?" Moments later she was surfing the Internet on Jody's big old Dell, which was set up on a folding card table in one of the spare bedrooms. Anna pulled up a legal blog: Above the Law: A Legal Tabloid. Below the banner were chatty articles about legal gossip.

Anna scrolled down to a recent post, titled "A Superior Sex Scandal." Photos of Anna and Nick were inset in the text. She stood up and looked at Jody while her sister leaned in to read the article. Anna had practically memorized the piece since it came out a few days ago.

> The juiciest story of the day concerns a young blond AUSA named Anna Curtis, who has been romantically linked to defense attorney Nicholas Wagner. You might not think this is such a big deal—until you learned that they are opposing counsel on one of the biggest homicide cases in D.C. this year. Curtis is a prosecutor on the D'marco Davis case, which recently got some serious press after the defendant escaped from jail and assaulted Curtis in her home. Wagner is Davis's lawyer. A reliable source tells us that Curtis and Wagner have been dating for an unspecified period. We tried to reach Curtis at work, but got a cryptic voice message saying that she had been "reassigned." Rumor has it that she may have been fired or placed on administrative leave. Wagner, who is still working at OPD, was unavailable for comment, and spokespersons from both offices did not get back to us. So we must turn to you, our good

readers. If you have any information about this, e-mail us. We'll keep you posted as the news comes in.

Beneath the story was a section where people had posted comments with varying levels of schadenfreude. Some seemed to be from attorneys in her office.

Curtis never deserved to be put on this case in the first place. She only had a few months in the USAO. That's what happens when you let a rookie prosecute a murder case.

I thought she was getting it on with the Homicide chief, not the defense attorney.

Anna Curtis is an intelligent and hardworking attorney with high ethical standards. It is a travesty that her name is being dragged through the mud like this.

whatever. she's hot.

The comments continued for three pages. Jody straightened up and looked at Anna. "Oh no, Annie," she said, shaking her head.

Anna told her about Nick's drunken visit, Jack bringing flowers, Nick coming to the door and grabbing the bouquet. She found herself choking up as she described her efforts to explain it to Jack, and watching him drive away. Anna told Jody how Jack had kicked her off the murder case, how she had reported it all to Carla, and how she was demoted to Papering.

"At least you weren't fired," Jody said, steering Anna back to the living room couch, where they sank down together.

"No." Anna was surprised that she almost felt sorry instead of relieved. "They don't fire you. They reassign you to some crap job in the basement and wait for you to quit. I'm tempted."

That was why Anna was here. She'd taken a few sick days at work. She needed to get away, escape the whirlwind of gossip, get some perspective, and figure out what to do next.

"Have you spoken to Jack since that morning?" Jody asked.

"No. There's nothing else I can say. He's the only truly good man I know, and I humiliated him. He must hate me."

Jody put down her cocoa and pulled Anna close. "Oh, Annie, what a mess," she said. When Jody pulled back, she swept her arm grandly around the living room. "Consider this your anti-spa getaway. A long weekend in Swartz Creek is guaranteed to make you feel better about your own life," she joked. "Did I mention you're sleeping on the couch? I don't have an extra bed yet."

"Can I expect mints on my pillows at night?"

"No, but if you look under the cushions, you can probably find some leftovers."

"Ew."

"Wait till you see the mud bath."

Anna felt her mouth begin to curve into a smile for the first time in days.

Anna spent the rest of the week immersing herself in her sister's life. They went shopping; they met old friends at Scooter's, the local watering hole; they went cross-country skiing. They celebrated Thanksgiving with a huge supper and a trip to the cemetery to lay flowers on their mother's grave.

Throughout it all, Anna thought about what she should do next; but she could neither come up with an answer nor put the question out of her head. Nighttimes were the worst. Whenever Anna closed her eyes, images of Laprea, D'marco, Nick, and Jack blended with images of the trailer park where her family had lived when she was ten.

She spent her last night in Michigan sleeplessly on Jody's couch, flipping around every few minutes. The clock read 4:42 a.m. when Anna finally gave up trying to sleep. She sat up on the sofa, wrapped the blanket wearily around her shoulders, and stared at Jody's black windows.

In the dark predawn hours, exhausted but unable to sleep, she made her decision. She would quit and get another job. She didn't need to hang on to a job where she wasn't wanted, just to battle other people's nightmares. She had plenty of her own.

But the decision didn't bring her peace, and she still didn't sleep.

Her mind kept ricocheting between three terrible,

shameful memories. Standing in the doorway of her apartment with Jack, flowers in his hand, when Nick walked up. Outside the courthouse after losing the first D'marco Davis case, watching Laprea walk away with him. And hiding under the table in their mobile home, the last night Anna's father beat her mother.

She couldn't recall now how the argument began. Dad was drunk, of course. And he was yelling at Mom about something. It could have been anything, really. He wasn't working anymore and the fights were getting worse and more violent. Anna climbed down off her chair and left her homework on the kitchen table as the yelling got louder. She stood next to Jody, hoping it would blow over.

Anna remembered wishing Mom would give in, just apologize for whatever wrong Dad had imagined. Just to calm him down. Sometimes that worked. But this time, whatever Mom said just angered him more.

Anna remembered the crack as Dad slapped Mom across the face, and the sharp gasp of her mother's breath as she staggered backward. Mom bent over, bracing her hands on her thighs, trying to get her breath back, like she always did when Dad hit her like that. From that position, Mom's head was at the same level as Anna's. Anna remembered catching her mother's eye—and the fear and shame in her mother's expression.

Maybe it was the shame that made Mom stand up this time and face down Dad, and do something she had never done before. She stood up and pushed him back.

It was a disaster.

Enraged, Dad caught Mom's arm and twisted

it—then pummeled her straight in the face. She staggered back against the countertop.

Anna remembered his shouted curses as he took off his belt, the one with the big pewter buckle, and started whipping Mom with it. Anna and Jody shrieked and dove under the kitchen table to escape the flying buckle. Dad hit Mom's head, her shoulders, her stomach; the belt curled itself around her torso like a wicked, whizzing boa constrictor with each blow. The metal buckle met skin with sharp thwacks and dull thumps. Mom crumpled to the floor and curled into a ball, covering her face with her arms.

Anna and Jody screamed as they huddled under the table, watching the belt strike Mom over and over. Welts flared on her arms, neck, and hands. The sound of violence filled the room—their mother's cries, their father's yells, the girls' shrieks, the whoosh and thwack of the belt.

"Stop! Dad, stop!" Anna cried. He was in a frenzy. Handsome and charming when he was sober, he was monstrous now, a horrible, furious, thrashing creature.

Anna's fear was a metal taste in her mouth, a warm trickle down her leg, a thumping in her ears louder than her mother's screams. Jody yelled, "He's killing Mommy!" Anna had to do something—but the fear wouldn't let her move. Dad raised the belt again. In her desperation—in her fear—Anna *had* done something. Something terrible.

As her father brought the belt down, Anna shoved her little sister out to their mother.

Jody stumbled into the middle of the kitchen. For an instant, she looked like she would run back under the table. Her eyes were terrified. But then the eight-year-old girl straightened up, put her arms out to shield their mother, and stood her ground.

It all happened in a millisecond, but in her mind's eye, Anna could still see her father's half-conscious rage, her mother's expression of horror, and the perfect arc of the belt—right before the metal buckle struck Jody in the face. It caught the corner of her mouth and ripped through the soft flesh of her cheek, tearing a path to her ear.

The room was suddenly silent. A flap of Jody's cheek hung from her face, the wet pink inner layer turned inside out. Anna could see her sister's molars through the laceration; it looked like she wore a crazy lopsided grin. Blood poured from the wound, soaked her shirt, spattered and pooled on the floor at her feet. Jody stumbled and fell. She crawled over to their mother and put her arms around her, still protecting her from their father.

The belt hung limply in Dad's hand, its momentum spent. He blinked, confused by the sudden appearance of his youngest daughter with her face ripped in two, slowly realizing what he had done. Then he opened his fist and let the belt fall to the floor. It landed in a coiled heap next to the dark red puddle of Jody's blood. He stumbled out of the trailer home.

It had been so long since Anna had allowed the memory to play out fully in her conscious mind. The force of it started her crying, soft little gasps that quickly built into long, gulping sobs. Anna buried her face in the arm of the couch and tried to stifle her bawling with the pillow.

"Annie." She felt a hand rubbing her back. "Annie, what's wrong?"

Anna sat up and found Jody standing over the couch, sounding very worried. Anna rarely cried in front of her sister.

"Oh no, I woke you up." Anna started crying even harder. She couldn't do anything right.

"Stop, stop, it's okay." Jody flicked on the light. Anna blinked in the sudden brightness. "What's going on?"

Anna squinted up at her sister through tear-blurred eyes. She had never talked to Jody about what happened that day sixteen years ago. She was afraid to.

Anna suddenly understood why her memory of her mother's last beating had been mixing with images from Laprea's case, why the two scenes kept her from sleeping this night and so many nights before. Anna had failed Laprea—just as she'd failed her sister years ago. That's why she wanted to quit now. That's why she'd come home to Michigan to figure it out.

She quieted her crying and wiped her eyes on the sleeve of her T-shirt.

"I was remembering," Anna said at last. "The last time Dad hit Mom."

Anna looked at her sister, waiting for the anger to come. But it didn't. Instead, Jody's face softened with . . . what? Anna realized that it was relief. To finally be talking about this.

"Tell me about it," Jody said softly, sitting down next to her.

"I'm so sorry, Jo." Anna's voice trembled. "For what

I did to you that day. For this." Anna reached out and touched the fading scar on Jody's cheek. "I pushed you, out into the belt. That scar . . . the stitches . . . those stupid kids calling you Frankenstein—it was my fault."

"Oh, Annie. It wasn't your fault. It was Dad's fault."

"I was such a coward."

"Come on—you were ten. I don't blame you. I'm *glad* you did it," Jody said earnestly, as she pulled a section of Anna's blanket over her own legs. "I was too scared to move on my own, and Mom needed our help. If he hadn't hurt *me,* Mom never would have called the police, she never would have left him, she never would have pressed charges. If it wasn't for this scar, she would have just taken him back, like she did so many times before. We wouldn't have gotten the next twelve years, those good years, with her. I'm proud of this scar, Anna, because it set Mom free. It set *us* free."

Anna bit her lip as Jody embraced her. It was true; they had been free of their father after that. He pled guilty and served a year in jail. Anna and Jody had seen him only a few times afterward—during court-supervised visitations in which both girls refused to talk to him. Finally, after all those beatings, their mother refused to take him back. He eventually gave up and moved out of the state, looking for another job. Their father's departure was the best thing that could've happened to them. Anna, Jody, and their mother moved in with a pair of great-aunts until their mother completed job training as a medical assistant and moved them into their own little place. The girls had blossomed after that.

But that didn't change the cowardice of what Anna had done—or the scar Jody wore as a result.

"Oh, Jo, *I* should have saved Mom. I was your big sister. I sacrificed you instead of protecting you." Anna's voice came out as a whisper at Jody's neck. She thought of Laprea, dead in the garbage heap behind D'marco's apartment building. "I can't protect anyone. I'm worthless."

"Enough of that!" Jody's voice was firm but gentle as she pulled back to look at her sister.

"I could just quit and move back here," Anna said quietly. "They need lawyers in Flint, too."

"No way!" Jody's face was serious. "You made it out of here! And you're gonna get through this. I've always been proud of you, and so was Mom. You made something of your life. I brag to my friends about you: big-city lawyer, fighting crime in the nation's capital."

"That's over now. I can't go back there."

"Who are you and what have you done with my sister?" Jody frowned sternly at Anna. "You didn't get where you are by feeling sorry for yourself. So you fucked up? Guess what, you're human. They didn't fire you, right? They gave you a crappy job. So go back and do it, and do it great. Eventually your office will see how talented you are, and you'll be back on track. And maybe you can still do something to help on that case."

"I owe it to Laprea's family."

"You owe it to yourself, Annie."

Anna took a deep breath as Jody hugged her. Jody's forgiveness felt like a blood transfusion, making Anna suddenly stronger and more alive than she'd been just a few moments before. She felt the return of the sense of purpose that had been missing since she'd been kicked off Laprea's case. Anna smiled through her tears.

"I feel like Maria, back at the abbey after Captain von Trapp got engaged, and you're the Reverend Mother singing 'Climb Ev'ry Mountain.'"

"That's right, baby. Ford every stream."

"Okay." Anna laughed, and pulled back to look at her sister. "But, Jo, what can I do about Jack? I hurt him, and he's such a good person. You should see him with his daughter. He's warm and patient—everything our dad wasn't. And he's an amazing lawyer. Sharp, great in court, and he really cares about the people he's fighting for. He trusted me. I think he was falling for me. And, God, did I ruin it."

"It'll be okay, Annie," Jody began. "There are plenty of fish in the sea."

"No," Anna protested. "I know all about the D.C. dating scene—and my own warped radar. The guys I pick, like Nick, they're hot, they've got an edge—and they always turn out bad. You know what I mean. I never would've been attracted to Jack if I met him at some party or a bar. But working with him, I really got to know him. And he's wonderful. I should have cut Nick out of my life completely, just focused on Jack. But I didn't."

"Well," Jody asked, "is that what you want? Are you sure you're through with Nick?"

Anna paused before answering. Her connection to Nick had been immediate and intense. He was rich, clever, and gorgeous. But that connection had stretched thinner and thinner with the pull and tug of Laprea's case. And Anna was beginning to realize that it was the damaged part of herself that was attracted to the bad-boy side of Nick.

"I think I'll always have a soft spot for Nick," Anna admitted, "but I know he's not the right guy for me."

Then Anna thought about Jack, sitting across the war room table with her, discussing some legal issue in his low, quiet voice. She remembered him bursting through her front door when D'marco was in her apartment. She pictured Jack in the foyer of his house, swinging Olivia in the air. Anna admired him. She trusted him. He made her laugh. It had been such a healthy feeling to actually want to be with a good guy for once. And, Anna realized now, her days felt empty without him.

"Every day I don't see Jack feels like a day I've wasted."

"Then you don't have a choice," Jody said. "You have to go win him back."

"Do you think I can?"

"It may take years and cost thousands of lives," Jody joked, "but you have to try, don't you?"

Anna took a deep breath as she and Jody hugged tightly. Jody was right, and Anna knew what she had to do now. She might not be able to get back her old job or convince Jack to trust her again. But she wouldn't spend the rest of her life wondering what would have happened if she'd only done something. If she failed this time, at least she was going down fighting.

32

Anna crouched before the old Xerox machine and stared at its tangled guts. Way back there, hidden behind a dozen black plastic knobs and tubes, she could see a suspicious white spot that might be the paper jam. She squeezed her fist through the plastic innards, groped blindly toward the spot, and sent up a quick prayer to the copier gods. She needed to get this done soon, or else she would miss the opening statements. She felt a promising, papery texture and grasped blindly at it, pulling out a handful of crumpled papers. Bingo. Her arm was covered in black toner powder, but she might have fixed it. She pushed the plastic door shut and the copier roared to life, sending papers flying through the machine.

Dan, the paralegal assigned permanently to the Papering Room, looked up in surprise and applauded. He'd given up on the copier. Anna clasped her hands above her head like a prizefighter who'd just won a big fight.

She felt like anything but a winner these days, though. Since returning to the U.S. Attorney's Office after visiting Jody in November, she'd spent almost four months here in the windowless Papering Room in the courthouse basement. No more hearings, trials, briefs, or arguments. It was all papering, all the time.

She'd been at this job for so long, she was the fastest lawyer on the two-hole puncher, a genius at data entry, the only person the fussy Xerox machine seemed to respond to. These were not accomplishments she had ever hoped to achieve.

EPO had conducted their ethics investigation. Although their report contained several sharp words about her conduct, they had cleared her of any ethics violation. Technically, she could go back to being a real lawyer. In reality, she was still an outcast. The office wasn't letting her out of Papering anytime soon.

She'd had even less success with Jack. He didn't pick up her phone calls anymore. She'd tried going to his office a few times, but his door was always shut these days, and his secretary always told her—kindly, pityingly, unconvincingly—that he was in a meeting. They worked in different buildings now—Anna was in the satellite office in the courthouse basement while Jack was based in the U.S. Attorney's Office—so they rarely ran into each other. On the few occasions when Anna did pass Jack in the halls, he would nod politely, but he wouldn't slow down. Anna had been unable to prompt any type of connection with him; in fact, she hardly saw him anymore. But she would see him today.

She hurried the copies back to her desk. The officer whose case she was papering had fallen asleep in the chair. His head lolled back against the mint green cinder block wall and a thin line of spittle dangled from his slack mouth. Poor guy was working midnights. Anna two-hole-punched the papers, impaled them on the metal prongs, snapped the file shut, and tapped the policeman with it.

"You're all set," she said, trying to keep her voice as cheerful as Dan's. If he could keep it up, she could, too.

The cop blinked awake, murmured his thanks, and shuffled off with the file.

Anna turned to her computer and noticed an envelope sitting on her keyboard. It wasn't unusual to have a piece of mail delivered to her workstation here in Papering, since she didn't have her own office anymore. She was about to toss it aside when she saw the return address. That was odd, she thought. She wasn't expecting anything from the FBI.

She ripped open the envelope and scanned the paper inside. Her eyebrows dipped in confusion. The letter was full of scientific jargon, peppered with charts listing a series of apparently random numbers. She had never seen anything like it before. After the third read, Anna finally understood its meaning. She sucked in her breath.

Holy shit, she thought.

Why was she getting this? Hadn't Jack canceled the test? And why was she getting this *now* of all days?

A moment's thought explained the timing. The FBI's DNA testing was driven by the date of the trial in the case they were doing the testing for. They were constantly backlogged—doing the DNA testing for everything from neighborhood robberies to war crimes in Iraq and Afghanistan—and local cases often got pushed to the last minute. The lab promised to get the report done by the first date of trial, which was usually plenty of time. The initial trial date almost never turned out to be the date that the trial actually started. Someone—usually the defense attorney—asked for a continuance for one reason or another, and the trial was postponed. In D'marco's case, though, no one had moved to continue it, and the trial was actually starting on the first scheduled trial date. If a prosecutor had been following up on this paternity test, she probably could have asked the DNA lab to send the results a few weeks before the trial. But there had been no one attending to it here, and the lab had gotten it done just under the wire.

Anna stood up. D'marco Davis's trial was starting any minute. She had to find Jack before he gave his opening statement.

"Dan, can you cover for me for a while?" She inclined her head toward the line of officers. "I need to go to court."

"Sure."

"Thanks. I owe you both." There was one other lawyer in Papering today, a new woman who'd just started last week. She looked panic-stricken that Anna would be gone. "Don't worry. Dan knows everything."

Anna strode out of the Papering Room and ran up three flights of escalators, squeezing her way around the people standing on them. She'd hardly spoken to Jack in the four months since the debacle at her house—but she needed to talk to him right now. And he wasn't going to be happy to hear what she had to tell him.

She jogged to Judge Spiegel's courtroom and paused for a moment to catch her breath in front of the thick double doors. Then she yanked one open.

Almost every seat in the spectator section of the courtroom was filled. There were friends and relatives of the Davis and Johnson families, journalists covering the now notorious murder case, interns and other lawyers simply there to see Jack Bailey and Nick Wagner go head-to-head. Several extra marshals stood lining the walls to make sure the escape-prone prisoner wouldn't try to run again. The courtroom was remarkably quiet for a room so packed with people. This is not good, Anna thought. Proceedings had already started.

A few people turned to look at her as she walked in, but most of the audience was focused on what was going on in the well of the court. Judge Spiegel was sitting in her high seat at the helm of the crowded, silent courtroom. She was wearing lipstick, Anna noticed, and her curly brown hair was blown out straight. Anna smiled at the realization that the stern judge suffered from the usual female vanities, and was not immune to the presence of the sketch artists sitting in the front row.

Nick sat at the defense table, his head cocked toward a clean-cut young man who was whispering in his ear. With his tailored suit, strong profile, and thatch of dark hair, Nick looked not so much like a lawyer as a Brooks Brothers model of what a lawyer should look like.

Anna wondered fleetingly if the other man at the table was Nick's paralegal—until she realized that it was D'marco Davis. He was nearly unrecognizable. D'marco had had a good shave and a haircut, and his cornrows were replaced with a neat, conservative fade. He wore a light blue sweater over a blue button-down shirt and tie, and a pair of trendy plastic-rimmed eyeglasses.

She should have known it was D'marco from the glasses. OPD attorneys always had their clients wear glasses for jury trials; Anna suspected they kept a bin of nonprescription frames just for that purpose. Somehow, glasses made even the toughest thug appear harmless and intellectual, as if the trial were keeping him from reading the biography of Winston Churchill he was in the middle of. Dressed up like this, D'marco looked like a large but mild-mannered orthodontist who just happened to have stopped by the courtroom on his way to a church supper.

Anna looked for Rose, but didn't see her. She was probably in the witnesses' waiting room. Anna hadn't spoken to Rose in months. She'd been forbidden to contact witnesses after she was kicked off the case. She wondered what Jack had told Rose about her absence. Anna couldn't believe that her first contact with Rose after all this time would be this.

Across the courtroom, fourteen men and women of varying sizes, ages, and colors sat in the jury box. They were the twelve jurors and two alternates. They couldn't be too far into the trial, because they all looked so fresh and attentive. Juror number six was giving D'marco a motherly smile. The orthodontist getup was working.

Jack appeared from behind the witness stand, carrying a large piece of posterboard. He looked completely at home in the well of the courtroom, relaxed, confident, and ready for the fight ahead of him. He set the posterboard on an easel. It was a blown-up photo of Laprea Johnson, smiling radiantly.

"Ladies and gentlemen, this is Laprea Johnson," Jack said.

With a sinking heart, Anna understood what was happening. She was too late. The trial had started and Jack was in the middle of his opening statement, introducing the jury to the person they would spend the next several days hearing about. The prosecution always used a photo of the victim, looking as sweet as possible, as Exhibit A.

Anna sank down in one of the few empty seats. There was nothing she could do except sit and watch what Jack said, and fervently hope it wasn't anything too damaging in light of the report she was holding.

"In August of last year," Jack was saying, "Laprea Johnson was a hardworking, twenty-one-year-old mother of four-year-old twins. She got up every morning at four thirty a.m. to go to work at the Labor Department's cafeteria, where she was a cashier. Outside of work, she enjoyed going to church and spending time with friends. She had a good life, a quiet, simple life that she had carefully built for herself and her family. On August sixteenth, D'marco Davis cut that life short, when he killed her in a fit of jealous rage."

Jack's words were surprisingly soft. His height and broad chest suggested a booming oratory, which made his gentle words seem all the more powerful. The jurors were paying attention, Anna saw. They liked him already.

"But I'm getting ahead of myself," Jack said apologetically, as if he hadn't planned exactly what he was going to say. "Let's back up. Because this story really started five years ago, when Laprea first met the defendant."

Anna nodded in appreciation of Jack's skill. He had gotten them to care about the victim, given them enough information to get them hooked. Now they listened attentively as he went through the details of

Laprea and D'marco's long, violent relationship. Jack wove the details expertly, stitching the fabric of Laprea's life thread by thread. He described how Laprea and D'marco had met, the puppy love that turned bittersweet, the escalating cycle of violence.

He didn't mention every time that D'marco had beaten Laprea—many of the prior assaults were not admissible—but even the small pieces that did come in sounded pretty damning. Anna thought the opening was going perfectly—until Jack mentioned how Officer Bradley Green would tell them about an incident that took place the day after Valentine's Day. *Oh no*, she thought, as he named Green as a witness. *I'm sorry, Jack.*

"You'll hear that as time passed, the defendant was growing more jealous, more suspicious, more violent. He accused Laprea of dating other people. And just a few months before her death, he told her he would kill her if he ever caught her with another man." Jack paused to let that sink in.

"That brings us to a night last summer: the night of Saturday, August sixteenth. You'll hear evidence that on that night, Laprea Johnson was pregnant with another man's child."

The courtroom murmured collectively. Jack waited calmly as the spectators shushed each other. The audience and the jurors were leaning toward Jack, eagerly awaiting his next words. Even the courtroom clerk had stopped playing computer solitaire and was looking at him.

Seeing Jack standing there, completely in his element, the courtroom eating out of his hand, Anna felt both admiration and an ineffable sadness. She'd once thought she would be sitting next to him today, sharing their easy camaraderie, ready to take on the world together. Now she could just watch him from her seat in the back.

"On that night, the defendant knew or suspected that Laprea was involved with someone else. That night, August sixteenth, is the night the defendant killed her.

"The defendant's neighbor, a sixty-year-old janitor named Ernie Jones, was on his way to work around nine thirty p.m. Mr. Jones was in the hallway outside of the defendant's apartment when Laprea came running out of the defendant's home. Her clothing was in disarray, and her face and arms were already covered in bruises. Mr. Jones saw the defendant follow Laprea into the hallway; and he saw that the defendant was extremely angry. The defendant screamed at Laprea and accused her of cheating on him. Then he punched her in the face. Mr. Jones heard her cheekbone crack when the defendant's fist slammed into it. The medical examiner will tell you that blow fractured her left cheekbone, although the fatal blow came later."

Despite the drama of what he was saying, Jack's voice remained soft, his gestures restrained. The facts were dramatic enough. Any attempt to dramatize the story would just cheapen it. But as he spoke, he walked slowly back and forth in front of the jury box so he could make eye contact with each one of them, making each juror feel as if he were telling his story especially to them.

"You'll hear that although Mr. Jones is smaller and

a good deal older than the defendant, he tried to intervene, to stop the violence in a fatherly way." Here, Jack allowed a note of anger to creep into his voice. "In response, the defendant punched that sixty-year-old man in the face."

The spectators murmured a chorus of disapproval, and Anna saw several jurors shoot daggers at D'marco.

"Laprea Johnson used that opportunity to try to flee from the defendant. She ran down the stairwell. As she ran away, she yelled that she was calling the police. She said that the defendant would never see his children again. Mr. Jones watched the defendant run down the stairs after her. It was the last time anyone would see Laprea Johnson."

Jack paused and took a sip of water. The pause was strategically placed here, allowing the jurors to fill in with their minds what happened after D'marco and Laprea were out of sight.

Jack went on to describe the nine-year-old boy who found Laprea's battered body the next day, in the wooded lot behind D'marco's building. He talked about the search warrant, how Laprea's purse was still at D'marco's house, her bloodstains on his carpet. He described the medical examiner's findings and the medical evidence, which showed she died of blunt force trauma to the head on the night Ernie Jones saw D'marco hitting her.

"Now, you might wonder: What was the defendant's reaction when confronted by the authorities? You'll hear that he ran. He ran from the police officers searching his home a few days after the murder. He was so desperate to escape, he jumped across rooftops, three stories up, to get away from them. And he continued running, one week later, when Officer Green found him lurking behind Laprea Johnson's house. That day, the defendant was so eager to flee, he tried to run Officer Green over with a car, and then he led the officer on a car chase through a residential neighborhood. Luckily, Officer Green caught him. And so the defendant sits before you today."

Jack listed the charges against D'marco, briefly explaining their elements. He didn't mention D'marco's escape and assault on Anna, which the judge had ruled was inadmissible here. That was a separate case, set to go to trial several weeks from now. Jack listed all of the witnesses the government was going to call, briefly stating their roles. When he mentioned Officer Brad Green, Jack described him as a good cop and a neutral eyewitness.

Anna sank further in her seat. This was going to be a disaster.

"After you've heard all the witnesses and seen all the evidence, you will come to one inescapable conclusion. D'marco Davis killed Laprea Johnson. I will ask you to hold him accountable for that. Thank you."

Several of the jurors nodded at Jack as he sat down. The courtroom was quiet; the jury was grim, feeling the weight of the case settle on their shoulders. A few women in the audience—Laprea's friends and family—were softly crying and holding each other.

It was a difficult silence for Nick to walk into. The crowd was feeling sadness at the lost life, and anger at the man who took the young mother from the world. Nick would have to counter those emotions. If anyone could do it, Anna thought, Nick could. As he stood in front of the jury, he exuded charisma, his boyish good looks and perfect smile making the female jurors take double, and a few triple, takes of him. Anna knew how they felt.

Anna expected him to come out swinging. Most OPD lawyers started their openings by passionately asserting their client's innocence. "Mr. Smith is innocent! He was innocent the day of the crime, he was innocent when the police arrested him, and he sits before you today, an innocent man!" Anna anticipated something similar from Nick. Especially since his client had claimed he was actually innocent when he'd broken into Anna's house.

Instead, Nick opened with a rather professorial lecture. "A bedrock principle of American law is the presumption of innocence," he began. "Mr. Davis is presumed to be innocent. What the prosecutor just said, however confidently he says it, does not change that."

Instead of declaring his client's innocence, Nick was imploring the jury to follow the legal principle that he was *presumed* to be innocent. It was a subtle but important distinction. He wasn't vouching for his client.

"As you listen to the evidence, keep an open mind. Don't come to any conclusion before you've heard everything. Remember that the government has the burden of proving Mr. Davis's guilt. That burden never shifts to Mr. Davis. The defense doesn't have to do anything. We could just sit back and see what evidence the government has. It's up to the government to meet its burden of proof: beyond a reasonable doubt, the highest burden in American law."

Nick didn't make any charges of police misconduct or prosecutorial overreaching. He didn't say there was an alibi, or that his client did it in self-defense. He didn't suggest that someone else did it.

What he did say was a mild and academic recitation of the law. It was a perfectly acceptable opening statement. But many criminal lawyers thought that the best defense was one that put forth their own theory of the case. Just arguing that the government hadn't met its burden was risky. The jury didn't just want to measure some technical evidentiary threshold; they wanted to know what had *really* happened. Nick wasn't suggesting any alternative story to counter the government's.

Anna was surprised that Nick's opening wasn't more aggressive. Why didn't he talk about the fact that Laprea was pregnant with another man's child? He could really spin that for the defense: there's this other man out there, intimately involved with the victim, and we don't know who he is. Where's the mystery man? Isn't he a suspect? That alone could be his "reasonable doubt." Anna knew the omission had to be a deliberate tactic on his part. She wondered what he had up his sleeve.

When Nick sat down, Anna saw that a few of the jurors were openly glaring at D'marco. Nick's plea for them to keep an open mind hadn't worked.

"This is a good time for our lunch break," Judge Spiegel announced. She turned to the jurors. "Please return at one o'clock, when we'll begin hearing from witnesses. Do not discuss the case with anyone in the meantime."

The courtroom stood in respectful silence as the jurors filed out, then burst into a subdued roar. A marshal led D'marco back to the holding cell. He cooperated, docile as the orthodontist he resembled. Anna walked toward the front of the courtroom against the wave of people filing out.

Nick was leaving as she was coming up. They met at the front of the audience section. He stopped in front of her, searching her face, wondering if she was there to see him.

"Hey," he said softly.

"Hi, Nick." She stepped around him.

Jack watched her interaction with Nick. A look of satisfaction flashed across Jack's face as she bypassed the defense attorney, but it was gone by the time she crossed the short space to the prosecution's table. Jack's expression reassembled itself into the mask of cool politeness he always wore around her now.

"Hello, Anna." Jack's posture was formal, almost military. "How have you been?"

"Hi, Jack," she said, feeling nervous warmth to be talking to him. "I've been fine. That was a great opening."

"Thanks." A small smile fought its way through the mask. He knew he'd given a great opening statement, and he was glad she had seen it.

"But," she said softly, turning so no one in the audience could hear, "I think you'd better see this."

She handed him the paper she'd been clutching throughout the speeches. He looked at her suspiciously, then skimmed the report. He was familiar with the format and quickly understood what it was saying. When he was done, he looked up at her, his green eyes narrowing with anger.

"Fuck."

"That pretty much sums it up."

"Anna, I told you to cancel the paternity test." His voice was quiet, but the anger was there. Anna's stomach clenched.

"The night we were at Ben's Chili Bowl? The night before I was fired off the case? Jack, I was kicked out of my office the next morning and told to have nothing to do with the case. I couldn't cancel any tests or do anything else. I thought you were going to cancel it."

He paused, staring at the paper. After he'd instructed Anna to put a stop to the testing, he'd checked it off his mental to-do list. Even when Anna had been fired from the case the next day, it hadn't occurred to him.

"You're right," Jack said at last. At this point, it didn't matter why the testing had continued. It had. Now he had to deal with the results.

33

Jack burst into the witness room, where Rose Johnson, Ernie Jones, and a bunch of police officers sat in the chairs lining the walls. He scanned the room until his eyes landed on Officer Brad Green. Jack glared at Green for a moment, just long enough for the officer to see Jack's fury and swallow nervously. Then Jack turned to the other people in the room.

"Officer Fields," Jack calmly addressed a young woman in an MPD uniform. "We have until one o'clock for lunch. Could you make sure Ms. Johnson and Mr. Jones find a good place to eat?"

The officer nodded and stood up with Rose and Ernie. Rose smiled quizzically at Anna as the officer ushered her out into the hallway, where a gaggle of women waited to enfold her into their clucking, loving circle. As the door was closing, Anna saw Ernie standing uncertainly to one side, until Rose reached through her people and drew him into the group.

Jack turned to the other police officers. "You're released until twelve forty-five." His eyes lasered back to Green. "Except you. And you, McGee. I need you here for this."

When the room was cleared, Jack turned to Green,

who was sitting in his chair and straightening his clip-on tie, smoothing it over the paunch of his belly.

"I just gave my opening statement," Jack said slowly. It was the very softness of his voice that alerted Anna to how furious he was. "I told the jury you were a good cop, a neutral eyewitness, a man with no dog in this fight." Jack paused. "Is that true?"

"Of course," Green said. Fear was plainly visible on his face. "What's going on?"

Jack tossed the report contemptuously on Green's lap. The policeman reluctantly looked at the paper. He didn't understand exactly what it was saying, but he understood that it was from the FBI's DNA laboratory in Quantico and that it involved him, Laprea Johnson, and her unborn baby.

"I—I think I need a lawyer."

"You're damned right you need a lawyer!" Jack roared. "Nick Wagner is right outside! You can lawyer up right now, and in a month, I'll see you in the case of the United States versus former officer Bradley Green!"

"If I talk to you, you'll charge me anyway." Green seemed to shrink into his seat. A wave of crimson crept from his round cheeks to the roots of his close-cropped hair.

"Maybe so, maybe not. But I guarantee that if you do not tell me the truth right now, you're done."

"I didn't know she was pregnant!" Green looked up at Jack. "Until I heard about the autopsy."

"It was your fucking baby!"

"It could be anybody's!"

"Anybody with your DNA! You were sleeping with the goddamn victim!"

Green's hands went slack and the FBI paternity report fluttered to the ground. Jack turned to McGee. "Detective, take his gun," he instructed.

McGee nodded, stood up, and walked over to Green. Green looked up at him in shock but didn't move.

"Brad, I need your weapon," McGee said apologetically.

Green still didn't react. McGee unbuttoned his suit jacket and deliberately put his hand on the gun holstered at his side.

Green stood up suddenly and put his hand on his gun. He rested his palm on the grip as he looked at the three other people in the room. Anna recalled that Green had been a college football player. Now he looked like he wanted to tackle—or shoot—McGee. Anna heard the soft click as McGee unsnapped his holster. The two policemen stared at each other, their hands poised on their revolvers. Anna half expected McGee to say, "Go ahead, make my day."

Green pulled his gun out slowly and handed it, muzzle down, to McGee. McGee nodded, ejected the magazine, and made sure there was no round in the chamber. Then he tucked it into the back of his pants. Anna exhaled, and Jack started pacing the small room.

"Let's take a minute to decide what to do now." Jack was talking more to himself than to anyone else. Anna heard the exhaustion that saturated his voice. She understood the effort it took to gear up for this trial: the lunches of Clif Bars eaten at his desk, the late nights working after he'd put Olivia to bed, the single-minded focus that allowed him to push through his own sleep deprivation. This morning, he'd been running on the energy of finally presenting this case to a jury. The paternity test results sliced through that energy to the core of his fatigue. He looked at his watch and rubbed the bridge of his nose. "I need to disclose this to the judge and Wagner. I obviously can't use Green as a witness anymore."

"Wait," Anna spoke up for the first time. She understood that Jack's mind was still on the trial, going down the path he'd been treading for almost a year. But there was one more thing she needed to know. "Officer Green, when was the last time you spoke to Laprea?"

"Ever?"

"Yes."

He looked at his feet and answered in a whisper. "On the night she was killed."

"You're fucking kidding me!" Jack balled his hands into fists and he strode over to the officer. "We've been investigating this case for months! We did a time line of every minute of the night she was killed. You sat there and didn't say a thing!"

Green backed up to the wall as Jack yelled in his face. They were inches apart.

"I couldn't tell you—I'd get fired. I'm sorry, Jack, but I didn't think it mattered. You put the case together great without my information."

"You coward! That's obstruction of justice!"

"Jack, please." Anna put her hand on Jack's arm. He looked at her hand, then at his own balled fists. He nodded, unclenched his hands, and retreated to the other corner of the room. Anna turned to Green and gestured for him to have a seat. He sank into a chair and put his head in his palm. Anna sat next to him.

"Officer Green," she said softly. "Tell us what happened. I think you'd better tell us everything."

He took a deep breath and exhaled deeply, a sigh that almost sounded like relief.

"It wasn't as bad as it looks now. I was just trying to help her. After that Valentine's Day assault, I'd check in on her and the family, I'd sometimes go have lunch where she works and talk to her. Davis was in jail pending trial, and she appreciated somebody coming by, you know?

"One night she was leaving work about the same time I was heading home. So I offered to give her a ride. One thing just led to another."

He looked both ashamed and a bit proud of his conquest.

"How long did your relationship last?" Anna asked.

"We only got together a few times. It never got serious. I mean, we talked about where it was going, but I wasn't really ready for anything big. I guess we had that talk a week or so before the first trial." He wrinkled his nose. "I hope that didn't affect her testimony."

Of course that affected her testimony, Anna thought. But she contained her anger and concentrated on obtaining the information she needed.

"Did you hear from her after that trial?"

"No, I think she was back with Davis then. The next time I heard from her was the night she died."

"What happened?"

"I was on duty, doing routine patrol, and she called my cell phone. From a pay phone. She was hysterical. Said D'marco hit her again, said she was ready to prosecute him 'to the full extent of the law' this time, and could I come over and arrest him. I told her: sorry. You know, because of her testimony last time. Lying and all. I told her it'd be hard to *ever* bring a case against him again based just on her word. No one would believe her. I wasn't going out there to arrest him for a case that was just going to tank when she got back together with him again. I told her if she wanted to get him arrested, to call 911. Let them sort it out."

"Mm-hm," Anna murmured for him to go on.

"She called again about an hour later. I wouldn't have answered if I'd known it was her, but it came up from a number I didn't recognize. I guess it was Davis's house. She was hysterical again. Still ranting about wanting me to come over and make an arrest. I wasn't really listening this time. I told her there was a hot chase going on—all available units were on the lookout for two armed men who'd just held up the Circle B. I was driving through an alley, working the spotlight, trying to see if there was anyone hiding behind the Dumpsters. I just told her again I wasn't arresting D'marco Davis. And she said something like 'No, you're not listening to me.' She was right, I wasn't listening.

"Right then, a guy matching the lookout darted out from behind a Dumpster, and I started chasing him in my car. I told her to call 911, and I threw the phone down so I could drive. Hell, she might've even hung up on me before that. I dunno, I was in the middle of a chase. That was it, the last time I heard from her.

"I didn't think he would kill her!" Green looked at Anna hopefully, as if by coming clean he would be absolved of his prior mistakes. "I wanted to tell you, but how could I? I'd be suspended for having a relationship with her. But I never lied to anyone or refused to answer questions. I honestly didn't think it would be a problem for this case. Her calling me doesn't change what Davis did to her."

"Did you get the guy?" Jack asked quietly from the other side of the little room.

"Which guy?"

"The Circle B robber. The one you were looking for."

"Uh—no."

"Did you radio in your location?"

"I don't think so."

"Did you make a report of your chase?"

"No."

"Is there anything whatsoever to support your story?"

"What—what do you mean?"

McGee cut in, his deep bass voice vibrating in Anna's chest. "Brad, I do believe the man's trying to find out if you killed Laprea Johnson."

Green stared at him, then looked to Jack, who was glaring back furiously, and Anna, who shook her head. She couldn't help him—and she didn't want to. Green's face melted into an expression of naked terror.

Green stood up shakily. "No, I—I think I do need a lawyer."

He waited for someone to contradict him, but he was met with complete silence. He fled from the room.

34

As they sat in the little witness room, surveying the smoldering wreckage of the prosecution's case, Jack and Anna both understood that the murder case against D'marco Davis was over.

As a witness, Green was destroyed. He was dishonest and possibly guilty of obstruction of justice, a man who would protect himself and his own career rather than come clean. If he was willing to hide things from the prosecutors—his own teammates—how could the jurors trust him? And Green wasn't just a dishonest witness. He was quite probably a biased one, too. He and the defendant were potential romantic rivals, which meant he had a reason to want to get revenge on D'marco. The prosecution could never rely on his testimony. Of course, they had a duty to disclose all of this to the defense. If they were to put Green on the stand as a witness, he would be destroyed on cross-examination.

And Jack had just told the jury what a good, neutral guy Green was. There was no do-over. Jack would lose all kinds of credibility with the jury.

It wasn't just that the prosecution could no longer use Green in their case. Green now *was* D'marco's case. Anna remembered D'marco's insistence, when he was at her house, that a cop had killed Laprea. That story, absurd at the time, took on a new significance now that they knew that Laprea had been involved with a cop. A dishonest cop who didn't want to be bothered by a woman from Anacostia. A cop who wouldn't be happy with an illegitimate child who might jeopardize his career and his wallet. It was certainly enough to make the jury wonder if Green killed Laprea—and, frankly, it was making Anna wonder as well.

Anna still thought D'marco was the more likely killer. But did she believe it beyond a reasonable doubt?

A prosecutor has to be sure. Before she asks twelve people to send a man to prison, a prosecutor has to know that the man she is sending away is guilty of the crime. If *she* has doubts, she has no business asking the jury to convict.

The murder case was done. Both Jack and Anna knew it.

"Do you still need me here?" McGee asked.

Jack rubbed the bridge of his nose. "What do you have, Tavon, a pedicure appointment?"

"I'm going to talk to the lieutenant," McGee said. "I have Green's gun, but they'll have to take his badge and do the administrative stuff."

"Good." Jack nodded. "Then do me a favor and write up Green's statement. Keep in mind that defense attorneys, Internal Affairs, and the media will be poring over your report for years to come. Shit, I should have asked you to take notes."

"I've got you covered, Chief."

McGee pulled a small, spiral-bound notebook from his suit pocket. He flipped it open with a smile, showing off several pages of his neat round writing. He'd discreetly taken down Green's statement nearly verbatim.

"McGee, you're great!" Anna exclaimed.

McGee looked at her impassively. "Humph," he said, and walked out. Apparently, she was not yet back on his good side.

She found herself alone in the witness room with Jack. He looked more exhausted than she'd ever seen him. She glimpsed his isolation, the loneliness of being at the top of the food chain. If something like this happened in one of her cases, she would have called back to the office to talk to a supervisor who could advise her on how to handle it. But the buck stopped with Jack; there was no one he could look to for cover. She wanted to put her arm around his shoulders and rub his back. Of course, she didn't dare.

"I have to disclose all of this," Jack said, more to himself than to Anna. "And talk to Rose and Ernie Jones."

"Right," Anna murmured. As the victim's surviving family, Rose had the right to be informed and consulted about major developments in the case. Ernie Jones, who was a victim of one of D'marco Davis's assaults, had the same right.

As if on cue, the door swung open, and Rose, Ernie, and their lunch group filed in. Rose and Ernie were chatting easily as they sat down. Anna looked at her watch: 12:50. The lunch break was almost over.

"Ms. Johnson, Mr. Jones," Jack said formally. Rose and Ernie stopped talking. "May I have a moment with you alone?"

"Course," Rose said.

The rest of the crowd filed back out, murmuring about what was going on. Rose and Ernie looked at Jack quizzically. Jack quickly told them what was going on, and what the prosecution might have to do at this point. Ernie nodded sagely; Rose looked shell-shocked. Both agreed that whatever Jack thought best was okay with them. Anna squeezed Rose's arm before following Jack out of the room. In the hallway, Anna saw the case advocate.

"Can you go in there and be with Ms. Johnson?" Anna asked the advocate. "I think she could use some support."

The advocate nodded and walked into the room where Rose was waiting. Anna knew Rose would be in good hands.

Anna followed Jack back into the courtroom, although she wasn't sure she was invited. The courtroom was filled with spectators again, but it wasn't as crowded as it had been for opening statements. Nick was standing at the defense table, looking through some papers. Jack strode up to him.

"We have to see the judge. In chambers."

Nick looked at Jack and then at Anna, who was standing a few feet behind the Homicide chief. "What about?" he asked warily.

"I'll tell you in there, on the record."

Jack approached the courtroom clerk and whispered a few sentences.

A few minutes later, Anna was sitting with Jack, Nick, and D'marco in chairs in front of Judge Spiegel's desk, like four children brought into a principal's office to discuss their detention. A marshal stood by the wall behind D'marco. A court reporter sat by the judge's desk, her hands poised over the keys of her stenographic machine, ready to take down the conversation when the judge came in.

Anna tried to ignore the fact that Nick and Jack were sitting on either side of her. She could see both men in her peripheral vision. She hadn't been this close to either in months. She glanced around the office to keep herself from looking at them.

Judge Spiegel's chambers had wide windows overlooking the appeals court across the street. The office was decorated with watercolor paintings, a colorful kilim, and the usual ego wall covered with diplomas, certificates, and plaques. A single framed photograph of a little white terrier sat on the judge's credenza. That lonely picture made Anna feel sorry for the judge, and consider her more human and vulnerable than she had before.

The judge strode in and sat behind her desk. She wore a bright yellow sweater set; the robe was reserved for inside the courtroom. The cheerful informality of her attire was offset by the reproof in her voice.

"This is highly irregular, Mr. Bailey. I hope you have a good reason for requesting this hearing. A courtroom full of people and fourteen sworn jurors are waiting for the trial to resume at the time I told them it would."

"Yes, Your Honor," Jack said. "What I need to discuss involves a likely grand jury investigation of an MPD officer, which cannot be discussed in public at this time. I need to disclose for the record some information I just learned." Although he spoke to the judge, Jack carefully articulated every word for the court reporter, whose fingers were flying over the keys of her stenographic machine. "After we broke for lunch, AUSA Anna Curtis approached me with paternity test results just received from the FBI. The test results show that Officer Bradley Green was the father of the unborn child Laprea Johnson was carrying when she was killed. Ms. Curtis, Detective Tavon McGee, and I then confronted Officer Green during the lunch hour. Officer Green confirmed that he had a romantic relationship with the victim, and he made additional disclosures. Detective McGee will be memorializing that conversation in a police report, and a copy of that report will be provided to the Court and defense counsel as soon as it is finished, no later than tomorrow morning."

Jack handed copies of the paternity report to the judge and defense attorney. As Judge Spiegel read it, she pursed her lips so hard that they disappeared from her now ashen face. Anna remembered the close relationship the judge was reputed to have with Green.

Anna looked away from the judge and found Nick gazing at her with surprised wonder. D'marco was grinning at her like a kid seeing Santa Claus. It was not a look Anna had ever hoped to elicit from a defendant.

Finally, the judge looked up from the paperwork and peered over her reading glasses. "How do you want to proceed at this point?" Anna detected a tremor in the judge's voice.

"I'd like to ask for a little more time, Your Honor," Jack replied. "I need a few days to investigate this issue and decide whether to go forward with the murder charge. I'm asking the Court to postpone the case until Monday."

"No sir." The judge shook her head. "You've had seven months to investigate this, and I've cleared my calendar, *this* week, for this trial. There's a jury that came back to this courthouse at one o'clock to hear your first witness. I'll give you until two p.m. Then you need to put on your first witness or dismiss the case."

"Can I persuade the Court to at least break the case until tomorrow morning?"

"Two o'clock, Counselor."

The slight downturn at the corner of Jack's mouth was his only visible reaction to the dilemma this created for him. The trial had started, which in legal terms meant jeopardy had attached. If he dismissed the case now, the Double Jeopardy Clause would prevent the government from ever bringing these charges against D'marco again. It would be like a full acquittal. And yet going forward with the case in its present state was not an option.

"All right then, I'd like to offer the defendant a plea," Jack said evenly. "The government will dismiss the murder charge if the defendant will plead guilty to the rest of the counts."

"Not a chance," Nick replied. "You know you're not getting murder now, and you'll be lucky if the taint of this doesn't destroy all your other charges. Let's go to trial with your star witness cop as the father of the victim's baby. I'd love to see that jury's verdict."

"I can drop the APO," Jack conceded. Green was the victim of the Assault on a Police Officer charge, from the day D'marco almost ran him over with the stolen Corolla behind Rose's house. "But he's gonna eat the UUV." Not that it mattered. Every felon in D.C. had an

Unauthorized Use of a Vehicle charge. "And he pleads to the Aggravated Assault on Laprea Johnson, and the Assault on Ernie Jones. I don't need Green for either of those. Jones saw your client hitting Laprea, cracking her cheekbone, before he clocked Jones. Jones is squeaky clean, and he's here today. I can make the Agg. Assault on his testimony alone."

Jack didn't mention the escape and assault on Anna. That was a separate case being handled by a different defense attorney.

"I'll take it," D'marco spoke up. "But only if it's a C plea."

Anna almost laughed. D'marco knew the system better than some attorneys. An agreement pursuant to Rule 11(e)(1)(C) was a type of plea deal that allowed the prosecution and defense to agree to the amount of prison time the defendant would serve, cutting the judge out of the sentencing process. D'marco suspected that Judge Spiegel would slam him if given a chance.

"Fine," Jack said. "Eight years."

"Two," D'marco countered, enjoying speaking for himself.

"Six and a half, and that's final."

"Done." D'marco smiled like a man who'd just won a round on *Deal or No Deal.*

"If you do a C plea, I'll accept it," Judge Spiegel warned, "but I'm going to sentencing right now. I'm not sitting through the fiction of a presentencing report, briefing, and arguments in a case where my hands are tied."

Nick leaned over and whispered briefly with D'marco. When they both sat back, Nick nodded to the judge.

"That's agreeable to the defense," Nick said.

"And to the government," said Jack.

A few minutes later, they were walking back into the courtroom. The spectators stood up and quieted down when the judge's door opened. Judge Spiegel strode up the few steps to her seat, while the lawyers filed over to their tables. Anna began to walk past the lawyers' tables toward the audience, but Jack motioned for her to stand next to him.

She hesitated, wondering if Jack meant this as a conciliatory gesture or as punishment. Her fifteen minutes of infamy had finally died down. Making an appearance in this case now would be like climbing onto the *Titanic* a few seconds before it hit the iceberg. In fact, people would say that she *was* the iceberg. But if Jack wanted her next to him for this, she owed him that. She stood beside him at the prosecution table, and heard the scratch of charcoal on paper as the sketch artists started to draw a new figure on their tablets.

The judge launched into the usual script for taking a guilty plea, generating a buzz from the audience as the terms of the agreement were announced. While a midtrial plea wasn't uncommon, dropping the murder charge at this point was a bombshell. The courtroom was buzzing with whispers by the time the judge reached the end of the colloquy and announced that she accepted the defendant's guilty plea. Judge Spiegel then called in the jurors, told them the parties had reached a resolution, and excused them from their jury service.

Anna looked back at the audience, where Rose sat in the first row. The advocate and a friend sat on either side of her, and both women were patting Rose's arms. Rose accepted their touch and looked stoically ahead.

"All right, Mr. Davis." The judge peered over her glasses at D'marco. "Do you want to make a statement before I sentence you?"

Nick leaned over and whispered some advice to his client. D'marco listened, then nodded and shuffled to his feet.

"I just want to say how sorry I am for everything I done," D'marco said. "'Specially to Laprea's mother." D'marco turned his back to the judge and spoke directly to Rose. "I'm sorry, Miss Rose. For real. I ain't never been good enough to Laprea. She deserved better, I know that. But I loved her, I swear to God I did. I want to make my kids' lives better now. I want them to know their father ain't killed their mother. I hope, Miss Rose, I hope you think about bringin' them to visit me in jail." His voice was cracking. "I know I don't even deserve that, but I'm still askin'."

Rose was sobbing softly. The advocate handed her a travel-sized package of Kleenex, and Rose dabbed her eyes. Her friends and cousins, sitting all around her, murmured and patted her, many of them crying themselves.

"Would you like to make a victim impact statement, Ms. Johnson?" the judge asked. "It's your right."

Rose shook her head no.

"All right. Then I'm ready to pronounce my sentence. The defendant will serve five years for the Aggravated Assault of Laprea Johnson. One hundred eighty days for the Simple Assault of Ernie Jones. One year for

Unauthorized Use of a Vehicle. The sentences will run consecutively."

Six and a half years total, with no chance of early probation. The marshal put his hand on D'marco's elbow and escorted him out of the courtroom. For a man who'd just heard that he would spend the better part of a decade in jail, D'marco wore a peaceful, Buddha-like expression. He'd just gotten out of serving life in prison.

The judge banged her gavel and walked out of the courtroom, setting the press free to jump up and crowd to the bar.

"Mr. Bailey, why did you drop the homicide charges?"

"Is anyone else under investigation for the murder?"

"Why was Ms. Curtis at counsel table again today?"

Jack responded with "no comments" as he packed up his briefcases.

Anna squeezed past the reporters and approached Rose in the audience. Rose looked exhausted as she gathered her purse and coat.

"Ms. Johnson—" Anna started.

"No." Rose held up her hand. "Not now."

Rose turned and led her friends and family out of the courtroom. A line of reporters trailed behind her.

Anna swallowed hard on the lump at the back of her throat. She felt sick imagining what Rose must be feeling.

Jack was walking down the aisle, and Anna fell miserably into step next to him. As she pushed out of the courtroom doors, she glanced back at Nick. He was standing at the defense table, packing his briefcase.

Their eyes met. It should have been a glorious moment for him. Murder charges against his client had been dropped; he was the victor in a highly publicized legal battle. Yet, as he watched her leave with Jack, Nick looked like a boy who'd just dropped a scoop of ice cream. Anna wondered what was going through his head. Despite the crowded courtroom, Nick looked very much alone.

Anna and Jack emerged from the courthouse into a damp, gray March afternoon. She walked next to him as he headed back to the office.

Anna broke the silence. "I can subpoena Green's phone records. That way we can confirm or disprove the phone calls he claims he received on the night of Laprea's murder."

"Okay, thanks." Jack was looking ahead as they walked.

"I could also pull his MPD duty records for that night."

"Good idea." Although he was apparently letting her work the case again, he still wasn't looking at her.

"Hey, Jack, I'm sorry about how this all happened. This came at the worst possible moment."

He exhaled slowly. "Don't apologize. It turns out your instincts were better than mine. You were right about Green. I just didn't see it coming." He slowed and finally looked at her. His green eyes were tired. "I didn't see a lot of this coming."

"Jack." She wanted to comfort him or find a way to carry some of his burden. The best she could come up with was "Let me buy you a drink or something."

He paused and slowed his step more. For a hopeful

moment, Anna thought he would say yes. Then he shook his head.

"Thanks for the offer. But I have too much work to do. Rain check, okay?"

"Sure."

Looking at him here in the dull gray light, Anna knew there would be no rain check. Jack had forgiven her to some extent, he had graciously commended her "instincts." But he didn't want to be with her. After everything she had put him through, she could hardly blame him. She had lost something very good.

She slowed to a sad stop. They had different destinations.

"Good-bye, Jack."

"Good-bye, Anna."

She turned back to the Papering Room.

35

While Dan continued to cover for her in Papering, Anna typed Green's cell phone number into an Internet database to find his service provider. Verizon. She quickly faxed a subpoena to Verizon's subpoena compliance center. Verizon would pull the phone records and send them to her; the process usually took a few weeks. But maybe . . . Anna sent an office-wide e-mail asking if anyone had a contact at the phone company. A few minutes later, she was sweet-talking a live person at Verizon, who promised to get the information to her that afternoon. Anna thanked the man and gave him the fax number of the Papering Room.

When she hung up the phone, she heard a familiar voice saying her name. She looked up and saw a tall figure standing in the doorway.

"Nick." Anna somehow wasn't surprised to see him. "What are you doing here?"

"Hoping to find you."

She glanced toward Dan and the new lawyer—and found them staring with open interest. She stood up and shooed Nick into the hallway.

"Defense attorneys aren't allowed back here."

"I know. I just need to talk to you for a second. Privately."

"Okay, come on," she said, and led Nick back into the public corridor. The hallway was busy, so she kept walking until they came to the back patio, where a portion of the basement was on street level. No one used this patio except the occasional probation officer on a smoke break. It was empty now.

The damp air smelled of spring; it brought Anna back to the day of Laprea's first trial, when Anna had come out here to decide whether to make Laprea testify. The air had smelled just like this. It was hard to believe that was almost a year ago. She let the painful memory pass, and looked at Nick. She hadn't seen him up close since she'd kicked him out of her apartment after his now infamous sleepover.

"What's up?" Anna asked brusquely.

"I wanted to compliment you. You got those DNA tests done, you suspected Green when no one else did, even when it ended up helping the defense. It was the right thing to do."

"I didn't do it for you."

"I know. Listen, I don't want to start a fight. I want to apologize. I said some things when we broke up—I wish I could take them back. I know you were doing what you thought was right when you prosecuted D'marco the first time. What happened to Laprea—that wasn't your fault."

"I know that." Anna found that she actually meant it. She no longer carried the guilt from that failure. She inhaled a deep breath, as if someone had unlaced a tight corset from her chest.

"Anna, I miss you," Nick said quietly. He looked at the gray sky, then back at her. "I'm getting out of this business. I put my notice in with OPD after the plea went through. I quit."

She blinked.

"Why?"

"Because of you. Why do you think? Seeing how all this hurt you—how it hurt us."

Anna stared at him. She knew how much his position meant to him, how he defined himself by his work. He loved his job. And he'd given it up. For her. It was what she'd hoped for—so long ago.

"I—geez, I don't know what to say, Nick."

"Say you'll have a drink with me. After work, tonight."

"Um . . ."

"Please."

She pictured Jack walking away from her this morning. He had no interest in being with her anymore. Meanwhile, Nick had given up his job for her. The least she could do was have a drink with him.

"Okay."

"Okay then." Nick smiled at her, his broad delight showcasing his perfect white teeth. "I'll see you tonight."

His smile was one of pure happiness, and she smiled reflexively back up at him. A current of electricity sparked between them as they grinned at each other. The chemistry was still there.

They went back into the courthouse and parted ways. As Anna walked back to the Papering Room, she played their conversation over in her head. It made her see Nick in a completely different light. She wondered if she'd been too hasty to write him off. Maybe there was more substance to him than she'd given him credit for. She wondered if it was possible that she and Nick might be able to have a happy ending after all. She still wore a small smile as she walked back into the Papering Room.

"Hey." Dan handed her a few sheets of paper as she came through the door. "This came in over the fax while you were out."

"Thanks." She sat down at her desk to look at the papers, although part of her mind was still back on the patio with Nick.

The guy at Verizon had faxed over the list of every telephone call Green had made or received in the month of August. Anna ran her index finger down the numbers until she got to August 16. There was an incoming call from a pay phone at 10:38 p.m., just as Green said. The next incoming call was at 11:26 p.m. According to Green, that was the second call he had received from Laprea on the night of her murder. Anna looked at the telephone number—and stopped breathing.

She recognized the number. She knew it by heart.

36

Anna closed her eyes, hearing the busy afternoon in the Papering Room continue around her. The tapping of computer keys, the whoosh of the copier, the voices of cops explaining last night's arrests. Eventually, the blood came back to her brain and the twinkling behind her eyelids dissipated. She opened her eyes.

Green had said Laprea called him twice the night she died, first from a pay phone and then from somewhere else. But he was hardly a reliable source; he hid the truth from them before. He could be lying now. His story just didn't make sense.

Because the second call to Green's cell phone came from Nick's home phone.

Why would Laprea have been at Nick's house that night? Did D'marco take her there? Nick and Laprea lived on opposite sides of town; Laprea and D'marco were seen in Anacostia the night she died; her body was found there. How could she have called Officer Green from Nick's apartment?

Even if Green were lying, *someone* called his phone from Nick's home that night. The telephone record didn't lie. But why would Nick call Green?

Her first instinct was to call Nick. There had to be

a simple explanation. She fished her phone out of her purse and scrolled down to his name. She paused with her thumb poised over the Send button. This was a criminal investigation. She couldn't just call and ask what was up. Nick had been D'marco's defense attorney; now it appeared he was also a witness.

She hung up and stared at the Verizon printout again. It wasn't going to give her any more insights. She needed more information, and she knew where to get it.

She stood up and grabbed her purse.

"Dan, I need to call on your goodwill again. I have to leave. I'm sorry."

"No problem." Dan looked concerned as she walked out of the Papering Room. "You okay, Anna?"

"Yeah. Sure."

Anna went up the escalator, rushed out the front doors, and caught a passing cab.

"Adams-Morgan," she told the driver. "Eighteenth Street."

As she rode to Adams-Morgan, more and more outlandish scenarios played out in her head. What if D'marco went to Nick's apartment and Laprea followed him there? What if D'marco had kidnapped Laprea and taken her to Nick's apartment? Could D'marco have killed Laprea at Nick's building? Is that why Nick stayed on the case for so long—because he was a witness? Had he been trying to protect himself?

Anna pointed the cabbie to the newest, most expensive building on 18th Street. She handed him some bills, took a deep breath, and walked up to the front door.

The receptionist buzzed her in to Nick's building. The lobby felt familiar and yet foreign, like when she'd visited her elementary school as an adult. She had forgotten how shining and modern the place was. The black granite floor, the towering steel sculpture, the floor-to-ceiling windows, all gleaming under carefully placed track lighting, were a contrast to her usual territory of basement apartment and basement government office.

Anna's clicking heels echoed through the desolate lobby as she walked toward the reception desk. There was Tyler, looking as male-modelish as ever in his all-black outfit, sitting behind his stone and glass command center.

Anna assured herself that the young millionaires who lived here were at work. They wouldn't start flooding back again until after five o'clock, and there was no way Nick would arrive before then. She had an hour. She hoped.

"Well, hello, Anna!" Tyler looked up from his *Us Weekly* magazine with delight. "Long time, no see! How've you been?"

"Okay, thanks. How are you?" She remembered that last time they spoke, Tyler had just moved in with his boyfriend. "How's . . . Brandon?"

"Great! We just bought a condo in Logan Circle; we're renovating."

He held up a handful of colorful paint chips. Anna pointed at a wasabi green swatch.

"Nice," she murmured.

"Thanks. For the kitchen, I think. Nick's not back from work yet. Do you want to wait for him here?"

"Actually, I know he's not here. I was hoping *you* could help me."

Tyler looked at her quizzically.

"I don't know how much Nick told you about why we broke up." Anna waited for him to reply, but Tyler shook his head. She lowered her voice and looked at the ground. "There was another woman."

"Oh, I'm sorry. Men can be pigs."

"I know. But we're trying to work things out. Maybe we can. But I have to know. That's why I need your help."

Anna leaned farther over the counter and looked at the switches, lighted buttons, and bank of televisions showing footage from the security cameras set up around the building. She could see what was happening at the front door, the garden, and roof deck. She could see herself in the lobby leaning over Tyler's desk. She glanced up at the receptionist.

"Tyler, are there tapes of what the security cameras are filming?"

"It's all stored on the computer. This is the best security system money can buy." He answered proudly before he understood what she was asking for. "Oh no, Anna, I can't do that."

She wished she'd thought to bring a subpoena with her.

"Please, Tyler," she said. "You're the only one who can help. I need to know if she came here."

Tyler shook his head—but started typing into the computer. "I'm going to regret this. Do you know the dates when you want to look?"

"Saturday, August sixteenth. Evening."

Tyler started scrolling through a page of files, oblivious to the sound of Anna's heart hammering against her rib cage. "It'll take a couple of minutes," Tyler said, typing some more.

To calm herself, Anna walked to the back of the lobby, where a wall of glass looked out over the Japanese garden. She watched the water flow down the little waterfall into the quiet pool below. Orange, black, and white koi swam in lazy figure eights below the canopy of a Japanese maple. The peaceful scene was a sharp contrast to the sensation that her chest was being wrung out like a dishcloth.

"This stuff only stays on the system six or seven months," Tyler warned. "It could have been overwritten by now. Whenever the memory gets full, the system recycles—wait." He stopped. "I've got it. You're lucky. Nine more days, and this'll be gone."

She hurried back to the desk and stood behind Tyler's chair, where she could see the plasma screen over his shoulder. The big screen was split into quarters, each showing a different scene: lobby, garden, roof deck, and outside the front door. He hit Play, and the four pictures began moving simultaneously. The images were sharper than the grainy black-and-white screen shots police typically retrieved from convenience store cameras.

Anna watched a couple have a beer on the roof deck and people walk through the lobby—seven months ago. A time stamp in the bottom corner read 18:30. "Say when," Tyler said, hitting Fast-forward. The action sped up, five times actual speed. People scurried in and out of the lobby with bags of takeout food, like lines of ants bringing home crumbs from a picnic. Anna watched the video of the lobby carefully; there was nothing remarkable for a while. Finally, Anna saw a familiar figure.

"Stop!" she cried. Tyler rewound the footage and hit Play again. The time stamp read 20:09 as Nick walked out of the elevator and exited through the front door, alone. Anna motioned for Tyler to fast-forward some more. At 20:38, Nick reappeared carrying a Chipotle takeout bag. Anna recalled that she was at her book club the night Laprea was killed. Nick had apparently stayed in with a burrito.

"There you go. He was flying solo." Tyler smiled at Anna, hoping this would satisfy her.

"Can you keep going? I think there might be something later."

Tyler frowned but hit Fast-forward again. The video moved through 21:00, 22:00, 23:00. Now the residents going in and out were dressed up for a Saturday night on the town: the women in high-heeled sandals and slinky tops, the men in carefully untucked Armani shirts.

Even though she'd been expecting it, it was still a shock to see the familiar figure walk up to the front door. The time stamp read 23:17.

"Stop," Anna said shakily. "Rewind. There." She pointed at the quadrant of the screen. "Is there sound? Can you play it?"

Tyler hit a few buttons and maximized the quadrant that showed the front door. The picture filled up the entire screen. He started the action again, now with muffled sound.

Anna watched in horror as Laprea Johnson stormed up to the front door of Nick's building. Anna recognized the petite figure, the long, quivering braids, and the black pants and shiny shirt Laprea was wearing—the same clothes she had on when her body was found behind D'marco's house.

Laprea was obviously upset. She tossed her hair back and forth in agitation, and was sniffling like a girl who'd been crying her heart out. She was hyped up on anger and pain, teetering on the brink of hysteria.

"Hey!" Laprea yelled, pulling on the lobby door. "Can somebody let me in? Hello?"

"Is there a receptionist working that late?" Anna asked without taking her eyes off the screen.

"No. There's no one after ten p.m. Visitors have to call directly up to the resident's unit."

No one answered Laprea, and she turned around, leaned back against the door, and let out long choking sobs of pain and frustration. To Anna, the woman's convulsions seemed to last for hours, but the time stamp showed just a few seconds. Finally, Laprea straightened up, put her hands on her hips, and looked around her. She walked toward the intercom and studied it. Now she was facing the camera, and Anna could see that Laprea had dark bruises around both eyes. One was swollen completely shut.

Laprea read the instructions engraved in the intercom system, then punched in a few numbers. The intercom rang several times.

Don't, Anna thought, grinding her teeth so hard they made a dull squeaky sound. *Oh God, Nick, don't answer. Just let her walk away.*

The line was picked up with a click.

"Hello?" Nick answered through the intercom.

"Mr. Wagner? It's Laprea Johnson. I'm at your front door and I gotta talk to you."

Nick's response was staticky, something about making an appointment at his office. Laprea stared at the intercom in disbelief.

"Appointment?" Laprea raised her voice. "You never needed no appointment to come to *my* house!"

A few seconds went by before Nick's voice responded. Anna could make out the words "very busy now" and "another time."

"Hell no." Laprea leaned down and spoke deliberately into the machine. Her voice dropped several decibels, and her softer speech was more ominous than her yelling. "D'marco just beat me up again, Mr. Wagner. I got black eyes and a split lip and I don't know what else. But you know what? I don't even blame him. I blame you." Laprea's voice started to rise again. "You said if I lied for him, this wouldn't happen again. Now I find out I can't even press charges, 'cause nobody's gonna listen to me no more. So now *you* gonna listen to me, and you gonna do something about this." She paused, then played her trump card. "Or I'm gonna report that you told me to lie for D'marco."

Oh, Nick, Anna thought. What did you do?

The intercom buzzed. Laprea yanked the door open and stalked into the building, her hair swinging with the beat of her angry footsteps. Tyler clicked a few buttons and the four-way screen appeared again. They watched Laprea storm through the lobby and into the elevator. The time stamp read 23:21 when the elevator doors slid shut. Whatever happened after that was off camera.

Tyler looked back at Anna, his eyes full of puzzlement and sympathy. He didn't know what was going on, but he knew that it wasn't good. Anna realized that she was squeezing Tyler's chair so hard that her fingernails had cut four little crescents into the black leather. She let go and forced her hands to relax at her sides.

"Tyler," she managed to say, "can you tell if they left the building that night?"

"Anna," he said miserably.

"Please."

He paused a moment, then fast-forwarded through the rest of the night. People came and went through the lobby, but there was no sign of Laprea, D'marco, or Nick.

"That doesn't mean she spent the night," Tyler explained. "They could have left through the garage."

"Is that recorded?"

"I can't tell when somebody leaves the garage in a car. The weight of the car opens the gate automatically. But I can tell when people come in. You need a key card." He opened another screen, full of columns of numbers, and scrolled down through the entries. "Here we go." Tyler pointed to the screen. "Nick swiped his card to get back into the garage at four fifteen."

"In the morning."

"Yes."

Anna felt nauseous. The walls of the building felt like they were closing in on her. She had to get out of here. Thanking Tyler through clenched teeth, she strode to the front door.

"Anna," Tyler called after. She turned back to look at him. "I don't know what's going on. But I know

Nick cares about you. I don't know what he was doing with that lady, but for what it's worth, I never saw him bring her here again. I haven't seen him with any other woman since you stopped coming around."

She nodded wordlessly and pushed her way into the cool spring air.

37

Anna headed south on 18th Street, down the big hill leading downtown. She was on autopilot. Her legs carried her on her normal path toward the Dupont Circle Metro. To the casual observer, she was just another young woman in a suit hurrying down the street. But she was shaking with shock. She hardly saw the neighborhood in front of her, instead replaying the image of Laprea standing in the elevator as the steel doors closed in front of her battered face.

At Connecticut Avenue, Anna's feet automatically steered her toward the Metro's escalators. She should go back to work, find Jack, and tell him—what? She needed to think. And she didn't want to go down into the subway. She wanted to stay in motion. She would walk. She took long, cleansing breaths and tried to find her center, as if this were a yoga exercise.

Anna veered around the subway entrance and kept walking, past the busy coffee shops and stores, crossing over the traffic circle and through the grassy park that was Dupont Circle. The cheerfulness of the crowds sitting on benches around the marble fountain, enjoying one of the first days of spring, contrasted with the empty coldness in her chest.

First Green, now Nick—was every man she had

relied upon a liar? What terrible secret must Jack be hiding? No, Anna told herself. Jack wasn't perfect, but he was honest. That wasn't much of a consolation now that he hated her.

Anna walked even faster, venting her frustration on the pavement. As she reached the posh shopping district in the Golden Triangle section of Connecticut Avenue, Anna slowed in front of the twinkling showcase windows of the Tiny Jewel Box. Engagement rings were on display, their diamonds scattering the sunlight into a million tiny rainbows. She had to admit, she'd thought about rings like this earlier this very afternoon, when Nick told her he was quitting his job.

Was it just this afternoon? It seemed like months ago.

She'd thought she knew who Nick was. A competitor, but fair, she had thought. Could he instead be someone who would tell a crime victim to lie under oath to protect his client? Could he have let Laprea in, talked to her, and then driven her home, where D'marco killed her? Or could the truth be worse? Anna remembered the animal hair found on Laprea's body; could it have been from Nick's alpaca rug? She recalled the way that Nick had encouraged his client to take a plea at the beginning of the murder case, and how his opening statement this morning had seemed unusually bland. She wondered about the fact that D'marco's trial had taken place so quickly, without the usual defense continuances.

Maybe Nick had *wanted* his client to be convicted.

Then Anna thought about how Nick looked at her when he was inside her. The contrast between that memory and the terrible things she was imagining made her dizzy.

Connecticut Avenue ended at Lafayette Park, a square of grass and tulips in front of the White House. Anna took the sidewalk that sliced diagonally through the park, and then followed the black metal fence around the White House and down 15th Street. If she turned left on F, she would be at her office in a few minutes. After a moment's hesitation, she kept walking south on 15th, cutting through the Mall, ignoring the joggers and children flying kites. At the end of the long grassy field, she crossed another busy road, and then found herself on the path ringing the Tidal Basin.

The cherry blossoms were just budding, creating a fluffy pink halo of trees around the wide pool. The Jefferson Memorial stood at the edge of the water, its white marble dome and Ionic columns contrasting with the purple dragon-shaped paddleboats dotting the water in front of the monument. It was almost five, but the sidewalk ringing the water was still crammed with tourists snapping pictures, pushing strollers, and picking a few unlucky blossoms. Anna was relieved to join the crowd flowing along the sidewalk.

When she got to the Jefferson Memorial, she sank down on one of the marble steps. The beautiful view of the Tidal Basin and its ring of blossoming trees was wasted on her. She thought instead about picnicking here with Nick last summer, how he'd teased her when she fed the fat ducks, the soft press of his lips skimming hers as he kissed her in the dappled sunlight.

She just wanted Nick to be a good guy.

She realized that she was in a position similar to that

of many of the domestic violence victims she worked with. She had the power to destroy a man she loved, with just a few words.

Anna finally understood why so many of the women couldn't bring themselves to do it.

Her cell phone rang, interrupting her reverie. She looked up and saw that the sun was setting, leaving streaks of pink in the darkening sky above the cherry blossoms. She'd been sitting here for an hour. The crowd had thinned and all the paddleboats were docked. Most of the tourist families had headed back to their hotels for dinner.

Anna looked at her phone. It was Nick. She obviously couldn't have drinks with him tonight. She would cancel their plans and hang up.

"Hi, Nick," Anna answered, surprised at how normal she was able to keep her voice.

"Hey, beautiful," Nick said. "It's good to be able to call you again. Where do you want to meet?"

"Actually, I can't see you tonight. I'm sorry."

"Why? If you're working late, I'll just swing by your office."

"No, I left already."

"Then I'll come to your house."

"I didn't go home," Anna interrupted. "I took a walk to the Jefferson Memorial. I needed to think."

"Great. I'll meet you at the Jefferson."

"No! Nick, don't come here—"

"I'll see you in an hour."

The line clicked as Nick hung up.

Anna stared at the phone as the sky continued to darken.

She sat there for several minutes, wondering what to do. Finally, she slid her cell phone open again and dialed Jack's office. She got his voice mail. "Dammit," she cursed under her breath. Was he still avoiding her? She pressed "0" and got his secretary.

"Hi, Miss Vanetta, this is Anna. Can I talk to Jack?"

"Sorry, hon, he stepped out for a moment, but if you want to leave a—"

"Listen," Anna interrupted. "I'm sorry, but this is an emergency. Whatever he's doing, I need you to tell him it's me—and that it's urgent. Please."

"Hang on a sec," Vanetta said doubtfully.

A moment later Jack picked up the line.

"Hi, Anna." His voice was coolly professional. "What's going on?"

Anna took a deep breath. Then she told him everything she'd found out since they'd said good-bye outside of the courthouse.

As she spoke, her view of the cherry blossoms became blurred, and she felt a cool wetness on her cheeks. She brought her hand up to wipe away the tears streaming down her face, and tried not to let Jack hear that she was crying as she told him all the details. But it was the hardest conversation she'd ever had. By turning this information over, Anna was betraying a man she had once loved—and might have loved again if things had been different. She was doing what she had asked so many DV victims to do: to tell the truth, even though it meant the end of her own relationship and the possible imprisonment of a man who, whatever else he had done, had at times made her very happy.

She wasn't just doing it for a principle: truth or justice for their own sakes. She was doing it for Laprea. For Jody. And for herself, to restore her own sense of honor.

As she came to the end of her story, Anna bit her lip in an attempt to steady her voice. Then she said out loud the words she'd been thinking and dreading. "Jack," she said hoarsely. "I think Nick was involved in Laprea's death."

She hung her head with the relief of unburdening her story, the grief of having learned it, and a feeling of vicarious shame, as if she were also to blame for whatever Nick had done, because she had loved him. At least she had done the right thing now, she thought miserably. The truth was out.

But she knew that simply turning over what she'd found wasn't enough at this point. She needed to do more.

"I want you to wire me up," she said, wiping her eyes with the back of her hand. "Right now. Nick is coming to meet me at the Jefferson Memorial in an hour—around seven o'clock. He's the one who insisted on meeting me here. He won't think it's a setup. Let me see what I can get from him."

There was silence on the other end of the line.

"Jack? Are you there?"

"Yeah." He cleared his throat. "Anna, listen. I appreciate you coming forward with this information. And your willingness to wear a wire. But . . . I don't like the idea of sending you out there. It's dangerous. You could get hurt."

"This is a homicide investigation, not a bake sale,"

she said wryly. "Come on, you use cooperators all the time—you wire people up for a living. This is a great opportunity. You *know* it's a great opportunity."

He paused uneasily. "I'm not even sure we can get there in time."

"I have faith in you, Jack. I'll see you soon."

She hung up before he could come up with any more excuses. She was touched that he still cared enough to be concerned for her safety. But physical safety was the least of her worries. This was about finally making things right.

She just hoped Jack would get there in time.

38

Tyler sat behind the reception desk, flipping through an issue of *Architectural Digest*. The front door opened and Tyler looked up from his magazine as Nick walked in. The receptionist's hands tightened guiltily on the glossy pages when he saw who it was.

"How's it going, Tyler?" Nick called as he passed the front desk.

"Nick," Tyler said tentatively.

"Hm?" Nick didn't slow his step.

"I did something I probably shouldn't have."

"What's that?" Nick paused with his hands on the elevator call button. He turned back to the receptionist. Tyler wore a tortured look.

"Anna came by this afternoon," Tyler started.

Nick walked slowly back to the receptionist and stood in front of the desk. He raised his eyebrows, waiting for more. Tyler hurried on.

"She . . . well, she wanted to look at some security tapes from a night awhile back. She was looking for another woman."

"Jesus. You didn't let her, right?"

"I was sure there wasn't anyone else, so I didn't see

the harm! I shouldn't have. Anyway, I want to give you a heads-up. She was pretty upset when she left here."

"What was the date you looked at?"

"A night last summer. Um . . . August sixteenth."

The blood drained from Nick's face, leaving his skin a sickly gray.

"Are you okay?" Tyler asked.

"Yeah, I'm fine." Nick choked out a reply. "Did she give you a subpoena?" Tyler looked puzzled. "A piece of paper. Did she say anything about an investigation?"

"An investigation? No. What do you mean?"

Nick turned away. He hurried toward the front door, paused, then turned back around and walked to the elevator bank.

"Nick, I'm really sorry!" Tyler called as Nick got onto the elevator. Nick didn't reply.

The elevator deposited Nick in the underground parking garage. He walked over to his BMW, parked in its usual spot, and clicked the key fob, unlocking the car with a chirp.

Before Nick could open the door, his body convulsed. He turned to the concrete wall and vomited. First his lunch came up, and then that ran out and he was retching bile, and then even the bile ran out, and he was dry-heaving at the pavement. Finally, his convulsions subsided. He put a hand up on the wall to steady himself, and stared at the mess by his feet.

After he'd caught his breath, Nick got into his car and found a napkin to wipe his mouth. He didn't start the car immediately. Instead, he leaned his head back and closed his eyes. After several minutes, he opened them and looked at the glove compartment. He popped the latch and reached inside for the black handgun. Nick turned it over in his hands, measuring the weight of the cold metal. He ejected the magazine, looked at it, then reinserted it—the gun was fully loaded. He slipped the gun into his coat pocket and started his car.

39

Anna watched the last traces of red and purple fade into the indigo of the city night. The Jefferson Memorial was lit up against the dark night sky, its glowing white pillars and dome mirrored in the black waters of the Tidal Basin. The place was nearly deserted. Standing at the edge of the stone patio by the water, Anna could see the ghostly outlines of cherry blossoms on the other side of the Tidal Basin. The trees reflected the light of the monument the way the moon reflects the sun. She could make out a small white light across the water, and she used it as a focal point, centering her gaze on it to calm her nerves.

As she waited for Nick, Anna rubbed her arms for warmth. She knew it wasn't the temperature giving her goose bumps. Her black suit and white blouse were adequate protection from the springtime cool. She was nervous.

She heard purposeful footsteps behind her and turned around to see Nick walk out of the shadows. He smiled, but a wild look in his eye spoiled his trademark grin.

"Hi, Anna." Nick stood in front of her, his hands in the pockets of his trench coat. He greeted her with a smile, but didn't reach out to touch her. "Thanks for waiting for me."

"Sure, Nick. How are you? You look—actually you look kind of pale."

Nick choked out a short laugh. "I want to talk to you, Anna. But only to you. Do you understand me?" Anna looked at him but didn't respond. Nick scowled, then gestured across the patio to a grassy area next to the monument. Under a tree, beside the marble wall, it was dark. "There."

Anna swallowed, then let him lead her across the patio.

They stood in the darkness of an old oak tree. Nick studied Anna with wary eyes. He reached out one gloved hand and caressed her cheek. Then he ran his hand down the side of her face, to her neck. Suddenly, he grabbed the lapel of her blouse with both hands and ripped it apart.

"What are you doing?" Anna cried, trying to push his hands away. Nick grabbed her wrists and held them tightly behind her back.

"Shhh," he said.

He tore the front of her blouse open, popping several silk buttons. His hand skimmed over her breasts, then around the waistline of her pants. He spun her around and frisked the small of her back. When he didn't find what he was looking for, he loosened his grip. Anna yanked herself out of his grasp.

"Jesus, Nick, what the fuck?" She tried to fill her voice with righteous indignation.

But she knew what he was doing. She looked down

at the lacy white underwire bra, the only hardware on her body.

Nick shook his head. "I'm sorry," he mumbled. "I had to see if you were wired."

"You could've just asked me," she snapped. She tried to close her blouse, but too many buttons were gone, and it hung open, exposing her cleavage. She tugged the fabric over her breasts and crossed her arms to keep the shirt in place.

Nick shook his head. "I had that in a case once. My client walked up to a snitch and whispered, 'Are you wired?' Right into the microphone. The jury loved that tape."

"What the hell is going on, Nick?" Anna tried to sound angry, but she felt a blossoming fear.

Nick put his hands in his coat pockets. "The surveillance video at my apartment," Nick stated flatly, confirming Anna's fears. "What did you see?"

Anna exhaled slowly. "I don't know what I saw. Maybe you'd better explain it to me."

Nick looked around. The memorial was deserted except for a few random couples around the Tidal Basin.

"This isn't exactly how I imagined our conversation would go when I came to talk to you this afternoon," he began. "I wanted to tell you that I still love you."

Anna nodded, but said nothing.

"I wanted to know if there was any chance you still had feelings for me," Nick said.

"Nick," Anna sighed, "of course I still have feelings for you. Why do you think I agreed to meet you tonight? For the past year we struggled with

I'm-a-prosecutor-you're-a-defense-attorney. We gave each other up for our jobs. So when you told me you were quitting, I thought this could change everything—maybe we can have our happy ending after all. But . . . I need to know what happened with Laprea Johnson."

"Don't ask me that, Anna."

"I deserve to know what happened."

"I agree. But don't ask."

"Nick." She stepped forward and met his eyes. "I can help you. Did you know that the video recording system in your building recycles? The tape from that night will be gone, overwritten, in nine days. I'm the only one who's seen it. If I wait a few days to send a subpoena, there'll be nothing tying you to Laprea that night. Do you get it, Nick? I can help you. But I need to know the truth."

Nick paused, staring out at the water. When he finally turned to Anna, his voice was calm and emotionless. "It was an accident, Anna. D'marco beat up Laprea that night, and I guess she blamed me. She was furious, crazy. You must have seen that on the tape."

Anna nodded.

"I never should have let her upstairs like that, but I was afraid of what she might do. She wasn't any better up in my place. I tried to calm her down, but she just got wilder. I couldn't get her to leave my house. Then she grabbed my phone and said she was calling the police. Calling the police—on me! I had to practically rip the phone out of her hands. And then she's kicking and swinging at me.

"I hit her, but I swear, I didn't mean to hurt her. She

was attacking me. But she fell back, and her head—her head hit the stones. The fireplace." Nick started to choke up. He forced his next words out between ragged breaths. "There was a cracking sound. God, Anna. And the blood. There was so much blood."

Anna swallowed a wave of nausea. Nick was no longer looking at Anna, but above her. He wasn't seeing the trees or the Tidal Basin, but the picture in his mind.

"I tried to do CPR. But it didn't matter—she was dead. I still kept trying. I was in shock. Literally, medically in shock. Do you see, Anna? It was an accident."

"Why didn't you just call the police?" Anna asked softly.

Nick blinked and turned his gaze back to Anna.

"God, the fucking police—they hate me! Can you imagine me calling the police? Hi, this is Nick Wagner from OPD, this crazy bitch just fell and died in my apartment. They'd have loved it."

Anna slapped him, hard.

"You asshole! You killed Laprea Johnson—you orphaned her children—and you talk about her that way! You pinned her death on your own client!"

"I'm sorry!" Nick knew he'd gone too far. He held up his hands in a conciliatory gesture and lowered his voice. "I'm sorry. But Laprea was out of control. And D'marco Davis was just getting worse. That's why you tried to get him locked up in the first place, right? Fact is, he would've killed her eventually. And he would've gone to jail. All I did was accelerate that."

Anna stared at him in wonder. She remembered what Nick had told her about his father's hit-and-run. Nick had deliberately shaped his life to avoid becoming his father. But when it really mattered, he'd done exactly what his father taught him.

Her silence seemed to encourage Nick. He took a step toward her and kept talking. "I just panicked, Anna. But it's okay now, see? D'marco is in jail for what he did, not for killing Laprea. There's no more murder case. And I'm done with criminal law. We can go on with our lives. It's all over."

He put his hand lightly on her arm. "I love you, Anna."

She flinched away, repulsed.

"You love me, too." The arrogance in his voice was gone, replaced with a soft pleading. "Right?"

She shook her head and pulled her torn shirt tighter across her chest. She didn't love him now. She never would again.

"It's over, Nick."

The wild look in his eyes grew brighter. He was fiddling with something in his pocket.

"Don't say that! We're in love. It can be like it used to be."

"I'm sorry. You're not the man I thought you were. I'm not the woman I thought I was."

"It's *him*, isn't it?" Nick spat. "Jack."

He gestured with his left hand while his right hand stayed in his pocket.

"This isn't about Jack."

"The hell it's not!"

Nick slowly drew the gun out of his pocket and pointed it at the ground. Anna stared at the dull black metal. She fought the urge to flee. She couldn't outrun a bullet.

"A gun." She spoke slowly as she eyed the weapon. "Is that the same gun you promised to get rid of?"

A shade of hysteria tinged his laugh. "Seems pretty minor compared to everything else, doesn't it?"

"Nick, take it easy. You're only making things worse for yourself."

"No, Anna. There's no way things could get any worse."

Nick racked the slide, chambering a round in the weapon.

"I'm sorry," he said.

Across the Tidal Basin, Jack held a set of earphones to one ear as a police officer pointed a parabolic microphone at the monument. The mike was the size and shape of a large round serving platter, curved toward the sound it was picking up. Jack had anticipated that the defense attorney might suspect that Anna was being taped, so he'd used this microphone rather than equipment that would go under clothing. The parabolic microphone couldn't work everywhere, but the Tidal Basin was the perfect site. With the mike focused across the clear space of the water, Jack and the police team had recorded the entire conversation between Anna and Nick.

Anna's calm announcement that Nick had a gun made Jack's stomach clench into a knot of terror.

"Go!" Jack yelled to the group of SWAT officers standing behind him. "Go! Go!"

The officers ran through the forest of pine trees that surrounded the cherry blossoms.

Jack shoved his earphones at an officer staying behind with the microphone and—although it wasn't protocol—ran with the arrest team, through the trees. He cursed himself for letting Anna put herself at risk. As a prosecutor, he felt it had been the right call—look what they'd gotten, a full confession! As a man, he felt sick with regret.

Jack pushed himself to run even faster. Somehow he stayed on his feet, despite the uneven ground and jutting roots. He didn't feel the branches clawing at his body, tearing bloody little creek beds into his arms and face. He had to get to Anna before Nick hurt her.

Anna stared at Nick. He was still pointing the gun at the ground. Her initial fear from seeing the gun subsided. She realized Nick wouldn't hurt her. She'd always known that about him. But she knew what he planned to do, and it filled her with dread.

"Easy, Nick, take it easy." She used her most soothing voice. "Look at me. It's gonna be okay. Just put the gun down."

"I'm sorry for everything," he choked. "I can't live with this."

"You can make amends. We'll find a way."

"How can I make amends? Can I bring Laprea back? Can I give those kids their mother?"

"You can't fix things if you're dead!"

"I deserve to die."

He placed the muzzle of the gun under his chin.

"Nick, no! You don't deserve a death sentence! You wouldn't give that to any of your clients. Don't do it to yourself. Please."

"What do I have to live for? Waiting for you and Jack to indict me? A trial, the press circus, prison?"

He wanted her to convince him that things could be okay. He wanted her to say she wouldn't turn him in. It was too late for that. She tried to think of anything she could say that would make a difference.

"If you ever cared about me, you wouldn't do this."

It sounded so trite, she was surprised to see him lower his gun.

"Anna—" he started.

The arrest team came crashing through the trees right then. A dozen thundering, panting men in black paramilitary uniforms pointed their guns at Nick. Jack was among them, waving his arms and shouting.

"Don't shoot!" Jack yelled to his men. "Don't shoot! She's too close! You don't have a clear shot!"

Nick looked at Anna, his face twisted with the shock of her betrayal. Then his eyes cut to Jack. Nick raised the gun and pointed it at the Homicide chief.

"Fuck you," Nick whispered.

"Jack, get down!" Anna screamed. She lunged at Nick and grabbed his wrist with all her strength—just as he pulled the trigger.

The gun fired: an earsplitting blast, a spark of orange in the dark night.

And then everything went black.

40

Jack clenched his stomach, bracing himself for the shot. But nothing hit him. He looked wildly around to see if anyone else had been hit. The officers were all standing.

Then Anna swayed and collapsed at Nick's feet.

"No!" Nick howled, and reached for her.

Jack was on him in a moment, yanking the defense attorney to the ground. Jack moved with a savagery he hadn't known he possessed.

"Don't you touch her," Jack growled.

The rest of the team ran over. Jack shoved Nick at McGee.

"Arrest him," Jack ordered. He sank down to Anna's side.

McGee kicked Nick's gun away from his feet and slapped on a set of handcuffs. Nick was sobbing and calling for Anna as McGee led him to a squad car.

Anna lay motionless on the grass. Jack put his hand down by her head and felt warm wetness. Blood.

"Anna?" Jack asked quietly. She didn't move. The remaining officers gathered in a quiet black circle around her. Faces grim, they quietly lowered their guns. Their silence was unnerving. It took something really serious to hush a bunch of fired-up SWAT cops. "Call an ambulance!" Jack ordered. A couple of the officers pulled radios from their belts and stepped respectfully away to make their calls.

Jack turned back to Anna. He put a hand lightly on her chest. She was breathing shallowly. That was better than nothing. He tried to see where the bullet had gone in, but didn't see an obvious wound. He knew he shouldn't move her body until the paramedics got here.

He held her hand as he stroked her hair. He started talking to her, hoping his voice would help her find her way back from whatever dark place she was in.

"Anna, you did great. You were incredible." He prayed she would hold on until the paramedics arrived. He could hear their sirens, approaching in the distance. "You saved my life."

She was as still as the ground she was lying on. Jack's heart skidded in his chest.

A bunch of people came crashing out of the trees: a handful of policemen leading two paramedics holding medical bags. The officers standing around Anna parted for them.

"Over here," Jack yelled, pointing at Anna.

The paramedics bent down next to her. Jack stayed by her side as they began examining her.

He realized now—he admitted it in a way he hadn't allowed himself before—that he was in love with this girl. This woman who had squared her shoulders, walked out here, and, with courage and dignity, done the right thing. He loved her. And he had squandered the short time he'd been given to be with her. Jack lowered his voice to a whisper.

"Come on. I can't lose you. I need you, Anna. I love you."

Seconds passed. Then Anna blinked her eyes open and grinned weakly.

"I thought so," she whispered.

EPILOGUE

It was late on a Saturday morning, and the courthouse was quiet. Anna used her left hand to insert her motion in limine into the time-stamp machine. The little device hummed as it thumped the date onto the upper corner of the paper. She slid it into the slot for after-hours filings.

Anna was getting more adept at doing things one-handedly. She still wore a blue sling on her right arm, and her right shoulder ached. But the bullet hadn't hit bone. Although Anna had lost a lot of blood that night, the doctors said that her injury would heal up cleanly. That was one thing she had in common with D'marco Davis.

Anna didn't mind working while injured, or on the weekend—not one bit. The office had reassigned her to a trial section. Now she was prosecuting felony domestic violence cases. It was what she'd always wanted to do. Anna had a trial coming up, and a slew of pretrial motions to file. She was finally back to doing what she loved.

She walked out of the courthouse's big glass doors onto the wide brick patio at the front of the building. Jack was waiting for her, leaning against the edge of the concrete flower box. He stood up when she walked out.

"You work too hard, Ms. Curtis."

"Just taking a page from your book, Mr. Bailey."

They walked to his station wagon, parked at the curb a few steps away. Anna peered in the backseat. Three children's booster seats were filled with three lively five-year-olds. Olivia, Dameka, and D'montrae were playing with a set of plastic dinosaurs. They waved when they saw Anna at the window.

Jack held the door open and she climbed into the passenger seat.

"Hi, Anna!" the children called in singsong unison. She turned back to them with a smile.

"Hello, cuties."

"Can we see the pandas?" Dameka asked excitedly.

"Please, please?" Olivia begged.

"Absolutely."

As Jack drove, the children quizzed Anna about the animals they would see that day. Anna answered as best she could, wishing she'd spent more time watching Animal Planet. Was a gecko a reptile or an amphibian? She had no idea. But she loved spending time with these little ones. Since Nick's arrest, Rose had softened toward Anna, and allowed Anna and Jack to see Dameka and D'montrae occasionally. Olivia and the twins loved playing with each other.

The twins were still adjusting to life without their mother. It would be a long process. Anna's office had helped Rose get them into a good counseling program. Their father had gotten a five-figure settlement from the city for being shot in jail; he'd signed it over to Rose. The money would help Dameka and D'montrae avoid the financial problems that affected many of their friends. But Rose told Anna that both children had nightmares that woke them screaming many nights. D'montrae had started acting out in school, which he'd never done before. Anna didn't spend as much time with the children as Rose did, but even she could see the clouds pass over their faces sometimes. At least the children had Rose, Anna thought. Their grandmother was devoted to them. In that way, the twins were far more fortunate than many children in the city.

The drive to the National Zoo took ten minutes, and soon Anna, Jack, and the kids were walking down the redbrick walk. It was a warm early-summer day, sunny without the stifling humidity that would come later in the season. The children ran ahead of the adults. Anna was glad to see the twins at play. From a distance, they looked like normal, happy children, untouched by tragedy.

Olivia paused at the head of the Asia Trail and turned to instruct her father to hurry up.

"Go ahead," Jack said. "Just stay close enough that we can see you."

He took Anna's hand as they walked behind the children, past the clouded leopards, fishing cats, and sloth bears. Finally, they reached the big panda yard. Two pandas were playing in the grass with a sturdy red ball; the pandas were flipping over each other to get the toy. The children squealed and shoved their way through the crowd of taller people to get a spot near to the front.

"Say 'Excuse me'!" Jack called to them.

"Excuse me!" they yelled, continuing to push through the crowd.

Anna laughed. "It's hard to be polite when there are pandas."

The kids wiggled into a space at the fence and watched, enraptured, as the pandas knocked each other and the ball around the yard.

Jack put his arm around Anna's shoulders, and she leaned into him as they watched the children watching the bears. She savored the feel of his solid chest against her shoulder, and she let her head lean back until her temple rested against his chin. He brushed his lips over her ear, sending a delicious shiver of warmth into her belly. She turned to Jack and gazed at him with a silent rush of love and happiness. Jack met her eyes and smiled.

"Me too," he said softly.

She reached up and pulled his head down to hers. They kissed for a few moments longer than people should kiss in the middle of a zoo.

ACKNOWLEDGMENTS

I am deeply thankful for the love and support of my parents, who are nothing like Anna's. My father, Alan Harnisch, is one of the nicest men in the world, and my mother, Diane Harnisch, is a bit of a local legend for her energy, guts, and organizational skills. Any success I've had has been built on the foundation they gave me.

Many thanks to my beautiful sisters, Kerry Hughes and Tracey Fitzgerald, my two best friends. Much love goes to my amazing grandmothers, Bertl Reis and Gertrude Breidenbach. Thanks to Laurie Harnisch for her thoughtfulness and enthusiasm.

The huge, loud, unconditionally loving Leotta clan is a force of nature, and I'm lucky to be part of it. Thank you to John, Carol, and Barbara for being my second family. Often, whether I'm writing or raising my boys, I try to be guided by what Mom Eileen would have done.

I'm incredibly grateful for the advice and support of Diana Amsterdam, a talented writer and my literary fairy godmother. Her early guidance jump-started this story and made it publishable.

Thanks to my steadfast friends and early readers, Jenny McIntyre, Jeff Cook, Eric Gallun, and Lynn Haaland. Your cheer, counsel, and laughter (with and at me) were critical. And thanks to Michelle Zamarin, Steve Spiegelhalter, and Meg McCoy for making me look good.

Thank you to Dr. Edward Uthman for sharing his expertise on autopsy procedures. Thanks to Long Nguyen for his talented eye and remarkable generosity. Thanks to Julie Buxbaum, author of *The Opposite of Love,* for her inspiring writing and kindness to strangers—I will pay it forward.

The men and women who work at the D.C. U.S. Attorney's office and the Metropolitan Police Department are real-life heroes. I'm proud and honored to be part of that team. Thank you to Kelly Higashi, chief of the USAO Sex Offense and Domestic Violence Section. Crime victims couldn't ask for a more devoted advocate, and I couldn't ask for a more generous boss. I'm also grateful to Channing Phillips for his equanimity and patience.

My story involves a fictional defense attorney, but D.C. is blessed to have two excellent public defenders' offices. Some of the best trial lawyers in America forgo lucrative law-firm salaries to work there representing indigent clients. Their work is true public service.

Thank you to my fabulous agent, Elaine Koster, and her indefatigable colleague, Stephanie Lehmann. Your tireless devotion made this a better novel and me a better writer. Thanks also for putting me in the gifted editorial hands of Touchstone Fireside's Lauren Spiegel, who combines sharp literary insight with bubbly and genuine warmth. Lauren, you polished up this book while making me smile, and I've loved every minute of working with you. And I'm thrilled to be working with Stacy Creamer, the woman who makes it all happen.

This novel wouldn't exist without the participation of the smartest, most honorable man I know, my husband, Michael Leotta. His unflagging support, insistence on excellence, and wise editing transformed my idle daydream into this book. Mike, you did so much, in so many ways, to bring this to life. There aren't words enough to thank you, so I'll just say: You've made every one of my dreams come true. I couldn't have done this without you. I love you.

Keep reading for a sneak peek of
the next Anna Curtis novel from
Allison Leotta

A GOOD KILLING

COMING SPRING 2015!

1

When I was fifteen, my favorite place in the world was the high-jump setup at the school track. The bar provided a simple obstacle with a certain solution. You either cleared it or you didn't. In a world of tangled problems with knotty answers, that was bliss.

I guess it all started out on that field, the summer before my sophomore year. That's when I fell in love with Owen Fowler. I never could hide how much I wanted that man.

That's why everyone immediately thought I murdered him. Watch any TV crime show, and the person who says "I couldn't have killed him—I loved him!" is the one who did it. Nothing fuels hate like love gone wrong. So when the coach went up in flames, people naturally looked to see if I was holding the match. But I swear: I didn't kill him.

You don't believe me, Annie, I can see it in your eyes. But I'll tell you everything, exactly how it went down. You probably won't agree with what I did. You definitely would've done things differently. But by the end, I hope you'll at least understand.

So—ten years ago. The athletic field was the most beautiful place in Holly Grove. A girl could feel like she was part of something good on that rectangle of perfect grass, surrounded by bleachers shining silver in the sun. Come fall, the football players would own the field, and the stands would hold ten thousand screaming fans. But in July, the stadium was empty, and the kids who went to Coach Fowler's sports camp got to use the spongy red track that circled the field. The air smelled of fresh-cut grass, the clean sweat of a good workout, and the occasional whiff of Icy Hot. To this day, I still love the smell of Icy Hot.

And I loved the feel of the high jump itself. That moment at the peak, as my back sailed over the bar and I looked straight up at the sky—suspended above the earth, touching nothing but air. Like I could detach from the physical world with all its problems. For a second, at least. I was free. It was my little piece of heaven.

You know what I mean, right? You were a pretty good sprinter yourself. What'd you place in the two hundred meter? Eighth in the state? But track didn't mean the same to you. You'd found another way out. By the time I turned fifteen, you'd already accepted that scholarship to U of M. That summer, you were just killing time before college, hanging out at the track a lot. You told Mom you went to watch me, but you were really there to flirt with Rob. Don't fuss, you know it's true. He was a hottie. And not just because he'd been starting quarterback that year—king of the town! He was objectively hot. Guess he peaked early.

You know why he suddenly got interested your senior year, right? After all those years of not knowing your name? No offense, but. You finally grew some boobs. My own chest didn't show signs of catching up any time soon. The high jump was the one place where my resemblance to a wall was still an advantage.

I was aiming to break your school record for high jumping. Six feet, one inch. I thought if I broke it, people would finally start calling me "Jody" instead of "Anna Curtis's little sister." I remember the day I first believed I could do it: July 15, 2004.

I was trying to figure out why my jump had stalled. I was doing everything right, but it just wasn't taking. I tried again: stood at my starting place and sprinted toward the bar. I hit my mark and rounded the turn toward the mat: five strides, pivot, jump! I flew backward, arched my spine, and kicked my feet up. But something was off, I knew it even before my butt knocked down the pole. As my back hit the mat, I heard the bar clatter to the ground, and Rob laughing in the distance.

I said, "Fuck."

"Watch your language, young lady."

Coach Fowler stood next to the mat, which was a surprise. He was the head of the whole camp and mostly stayed with the football team, leaving the lesser athletes to the lesser coaches. The thrill of him noticing me was canceled by the fact that it was when I'd messed up.

"Sorry, Coach!"

I jumped off the mat and fetched the pole. We set it on the risers together. He was tan and tall, with an athletic build and that aura of authority. The sun threw golden glints off his blond hair. He must've been forty at that point, but he was way cuter than the teenage boys he coached.

"You're a good jumper," Coach said. "You could be great—but you have to really want it. Do you really want it?"

I looked over where you and Rob were sitting. Rob was tugging on the tie of your hoodie. The coach followed my gaze.

"Your sister's a good runner. Fast, determined, scrappy," he said. "Jody—you're better."

I blinked with surprise. He knew my name. And . . . not many people thought I was better than you at anything. He reached over and pulled my hand away from my cheek. I hadn't even realized I was touching my scar.

"It's barely noticeable," he said. He cleared his throat and pointed to my pink chalk mark on the ground. "The problem is your approach. Your mark is too close. You shot up this spring, so your stride is longer. You need room to stretch out those long legs."

I tried not to blush at the implication that he'd noticed my legs. Coach took a piece of blue chalk out of his pocket and drew a line on the ground, about three feet behind my pink mark. He also moved back my starting mark. "Try that."

I trotted to the new starting place, feeling the blue nylon of my team shorts brushing against my glamorously long legs. I looked at the coach's marks and wasn't sure I could do it. I glanced at him, and he nodded. You and Rob stopped talking to watch me. I took a deep breath, squinted at the high-jump bar, and sprinted toward it. I reached the coach's mark and counted off my curve, demanding my legs cover as much ground as they could with each stride: one, two, three, four, five. Pivot. Go!

I jumped. And I flew.

I knew it was perfect the moment I took off. I felt it in my legs, my hips, my spine. I soared back over the pole with inches to spare. Suspended in the air, I looked at the bright blue sky and the soft white clouds and felt a moment of perfection.

I landed on my shoulder blades and let myself somersault backward. A few runners broke out into applause. You yelled, "Go, Jody!"

I jumped on the mat. "Yes!"

"There it is!" Coach yelled. "Good girl! Do that at a meet, and we'll be putting your name up in the gym."

I bounced to the edge of the mat, and Coach met me with a high five. Then he held out his hand to help me down. I took it, feeling honored, shy, and electrically happy. His grip was steady and strong. Dad had never held my hand like that. Coach's fingers tightened around mine as I stepped down, then opened to release me. But I didn't want to break the connection. I kept holding on to his hand for a few seconds after he let go.

2

Anna felt a gentle nudge on her shoulder but kept her eyes closed. Another nudge followed, more insistently. She smelled fresh-brewed coffee and heard morning birds chattering, but all she wanted was to stay curled in warm oblivion. She closed her eyes tighter, determined to hold on to her sleep. It was like trying to hold on to water; the harder she squeezed, the faster it slipped away. She cracked an eye.

The unfamiliar bedroom was bright and lovely, decorated in expensive neutrals. Her black pantsuit was draped neatly over an ivory chair. She glanced down and saw that she was wearing only her bra and panties from the night before. She became aware of a dull headache, throbbing with each beat of her heart. Blinking, she pulled the blanket to her chest, sat up, and tried to remember how she'd gotten here.

A pair of warm brown hands handed her a steaming mug of coffee. Anna looked up at the hands' owner. Her friend Grace smiled down at her.

"You look like your hair got caught in a blender," Grace said.

"I feel like it was my whole head."

At least she understood where she was: Grace's guest room. The night before came back in a series of images that grew blurrier toward the end: placing her engagement ring on the table at the Tabard Inn; walking through Dupont Circle with tears streaming down her face; meeting Grace, Samantha, and the detectives at Sergio's restaurant to toast the jury's verdict in the

MS-13 case. And wine. Endless glasses of wine, which, despite Anna's wholehearted efforts, had succeeded in blotting everything out for only a few short hours.

And left her with a massive hangover. She groaned and rubbed her temples. Grace handed her two Advil, which she gratefully swallowed down with coffee. It was sweet and milky, which coaxed a smile through the blur. Her life was a mess, but at least she had a good friend who knew how she took her coffee.

Anna spotted her cell phone on the nightstand. She had two "unknown" calls from a Michigan area code, and a string of worried texts and calls from her fiancé. Correction: her ex-fiancé. She let the phone thump back down.

"I would've let you sleep longer," Grace said, "but you have a phone call."

"Jack?"

"Who else?"

Anna shook her head, which was a mistake. She wondered how long it would take for the caffeine and ibuprofen to kick in. "We're done."

"He tracked you down here," Grace said. "That doesn't sound 'done.' That sounds kind of romantic."

"He's the Homicide chief. If he can't locate his ex-fiancé, he should resign."

"I didn't want to hit you with this, but . . . he's distraught. And you know he's not the distraught type."

Anna plucked unhappily at the blanket. She wanted to talk to him—she wanted it like a dieter wants cupcakes. But there was nothing left to say. She knew Jack loved her. He loved another woman, too.

"Please tell him I'm fine, and I'm sorry, and I can't talk to him now."

"Okay, sweetie."

Grace handed her a box of Kleenex and left. Anna

banished a rogue tear, as her phone buzzed from the nightstand. It was the "unknown" caller from Michigan again, the same 313 area code as her sister. She blew her nose and picked up.

"Hello."

"Hi, Anna? It's Kathy Mack. From Holly Grove High School?"

That was another world, and Anna needed a moment to get there. She stared at the ceiling until her memory caught up with the conversation: Kathy was an old friend of her sister's. Anna saw her occasionally, when she went home to visit Jody in Michigan. They'd never traded phone calls.

"Kathy—hi! Is everything okay?"

"Actually . . . no. There's a lot going on here. I don't know where to start. I guess I should start with this: Coach Fowler died. He— Some people are saying he was killed."

"Oh—that's terrible."

Anna sat back against the pillows. Since she was a kid, Coach Fowler had been a major figure in her hometown, leading Holly Grove's football team to the state championship several times. He was the most successful member of their community, and one who gave back. His recommendation helped Anna get a college scholarship and out of their small, rusting town.

"It is terrible," Kathy said, "but that's not exactly why I'm calling. See, the police want to question Jody."

"What? Why?" The coach had mentored Jody in high school, but that was ten years ago. As far as Anna knew, they hadn't been in touch since then.

"I have no idea," Kathy said. "And no one can find her. The police went to her house, but she's not answering her door. I've tried her number; she's not picking up."

"Thanks for calling me," Anna said. "I'll try her now."

They hung up and Anna dialed her sister's number. She got an automated message she'd never heard on Jody's phone before: "The person you're trying to reach is no longer available." It didn't let her leave a voice mail.

Anna's chest tightened. She was always vaguely worried about her little sister. For the last few months, they hadn't spoken as often as usual. If Jody were in trouble, Anna might not even know.

She welcomed a reason to get out of town for a while. Get away from Jack, D.C. Superior Court, and the inevitable sympathy from everyone she'd have to uninvite from her wedding. She could take a couple days off. Prosecutors often did after a big trial.

She swiped through her phone, tapped the Expedia app, and clicked on a last-minute deal to Detroit. Then she called Kathy back. "Thanks for calling, Kathy. I'm flying to Michigan this afternoon."

3

As soon as the airplane screeched to a halt on the runway of Detroit Metro Airport, Anna powered up her phone and tried to call her sister again. No luck. Her headache was receding, but the worry in her stomach grew.

She got off the plane and hurried past a wine bar, golf shop, and day spa—besides the casinos, the airport housed the most sophisticated commerce in Detroit—and took the escalators down to baggage claim, where she looked for Cooper Bolden. Kathy had arranged for Cooper to pick Anna up. He'd been a friend in high school, a sunny, bookish kid whose family owned a farm on the outskirts of the county. She hadn't spoken to him in ages. Last she heard, he'd become an Army Ranger and gone to Afghanistan. She scanned the area for him now, looking for a tall, skinny boy with knobby knees and flapping elbows.

Standing against a pillar, scrolling through his phone, was a man with a chest like a Ford 350. He wasn't wearing glasses, and his black hair was shorter, but under a couple days' worth of stubble was a familiar lopsided grin.

"Cooper?"

He looked up and she could see his eyes: light blue rimmed with indigo. She rushed forward to hug him. He stumbled, laughed, and hugged her back.

"Anna. Hi! Easy."

"Easy? You're three times as big as you were in high school."

Cooper laughed. "Maybe only twice as big." He pulled up the jeans on his left leg, lifting the hem. Below was a silver prosthetic limb. "Compliments of the Taliban."

"Oh, Coop. I'm sorry."

"It's okay. They didn't get the best part of me."

"Your spleen?"

"No. My enormous"—he held his hands two feet apart—"intellect."

"Of course."

"You look great," Cooper said. "Just like I remember you. Except more . . ."

"Weary?"

"No. Grown-up."

Anna grabbed her suitcase off the conveyor belt. When she packed it, two days earlier, she thought she'd spend a few nights at Grace's house, in the process of moving out of Jack's. Now she had the dizzying sensation of being a nomad, with no true home anywhere on earth. For the last year, she'd lived with Jack and his six-year-old daughter in their pretty yellow Victorian. After their engagement, Anna started calling it "our house." At Jack's urging, she'd begun to make it her own: rearranging where the mugs were kept, registering for silverware. But now she'd have to find her own apartment. She had to go to that pretty yellow Victorian and pack everything up, deciding which things to take and which to leave forever. She'd see all Olivia's toys and first-grade artwork and know that she had no claim to them. Because, much as she wanted to be—as often as she'd gone to parent-teacher conferences, braided the girl's hair, pored over parenting books trying to figure out the right answer to every six-year-old question—she wasn't Olivia's mother. Without Jack, she was nothing to Olivia. She was just a woman with a suitcase and a hangover.

Cooper took the bag from her hands. "I got it," he said.

She came back to the present and glanced at his leg. "But—"

"Can't stop me from being chivalrous."

She'd had a hard breakup, but he'd lost a limb for his country. It put things in perspective. Normally, she'd insist on carrying her own luggage, but now she just said, "Thanks."

As they walked toward the parking lot, she saw that Cooper's gait had changed too. It used to be a long, loping bounce, like a frisky colt finding his balance. Now his stride was shorter, more deliberate, and with a little hitch that could be interpreted as a swagger if you didn't know better.

"Have you heard from Jody?" Anna asked. "I still can't get ahold of her."

He shook his head. "All I know is the police want to interview her."

"I wish she'd called me. I'm a lawyer."

"I expect she knows that," Cooper said with a smile. "And she doesn't need a lawyer. She'll be glad to see her sister, though."

"I hope so. Can we go right to her house?"

"Sure."

In the parking garage, she followed him to a handicapped parking space and reached for the door to a gray sedan. He shook his head. "That's not mine." He walked to the other side of the sedan, where a huge black Harley-Davidson sat in a motorcycle spot. She glanced at the bike and then at Cooper's prosthetic leg.

"Don't worry. There's a double amputee riding across America." He strapped her bag to a luggage rack and handed her a helmet. "He was fine when he started, but he lost both legs in a motorcycle accident."

She laughed, weighing the risk to her life versus the risk of hurting his feelings. She'd never ridden a motorcycle before and was mildly terrified. She reached for the helmet. Cooper opened a saddlebag and pulled out a black leather jacket, similar to the one he was wearing, and held it out to her. But it was mid-June, warm and balmy.

"No thanks," she said.

"It's to protect your skin if we have a crash."

"Oh, that's reassuring."

She put on the leather jacket. It smelled of cedar, cherries, and the faint hint of another woman's perfume. Cooper straddled the front seat. She climbed onto the seat behind him and grabbed the metal handles on the sides of the seat, leaving a wide berth between their bodies.

Cooper glanced back. "Don't be shy. Scooch up nice and close and hold on to my waist."

She hesitated, suddenly wary. Who picks someone up from the airport on a motorcycle? What if she'd had more luggage? She met his clear blue eyes and found only earnestness there. She slid forward and put her arms around him.

He started the engine and pulled forward. As the motorcycle drove past the parked cars, her heartbeat quickened. She was very aware that she had a large man between her legs, her breasts pressed against his back, and a giant engine humming beneath her. She could feel Cooper's lean muscles beneath his leather jacket. She wasn't cheating on Jack, she reasoned. First: she was just getting a ride. Second: she and Jack were done. Third: she hoped she didn't die.

Anna tried to pay for parking, but Cooper beat her

to it. He pulled out of the parking structure and onto the service road. Anna could reach out and touch the car in the next lane—which would take her arm off. As he pulled onto the highway's on-ramp, Cooper yelled, "Ready?"

"Yeah," she lied.

The bike roared up to Michigan's 70 mph speed limit. She held tight to Cooper's waist. The motor filled her ears and the pavement flew under her feet. She wondered how it would feel if her body hit it. The bike angled low into a curve, and Cooper swung between her thighs. Her adrenaline surged. She was scared and thrilled and very aware of being alive.

Halfway between Detroit and Flint, Cooper slowed the bike and took the exit ramp marked "Holly Grove." Anna's grip relaxed, but her chest tightened. She'd been relieved when she left this town, and she never liked coming back. The only thing she really loved here was her sister.

Cooper passed through the historic downtown. It must have been charming once, but it wasn't used for much these days. The courthouse and city hall still looked respectable enough, but the storefronts in between were mostly vacant and dilapidated. With each auto factory that closed, the town took a hit. And the commerce that still remained in Holly Grove was in the suburbs. Cooper continued out there, passing subdivisions anchored with strip malls, big-box stores, and massive parking lots. He turned onto a smaller cross street, leaving the commercial strip behind.

As they came up to the curve before Holly Grove High School, Anna noticed an acrid smell, growing stronger. The football stadium came into sight, and she stared at it in shock.

A burned-out car was smashed into the center of

a blackened circle at the bottom of the stadium's cement wall. The ground beneath it was an oily scab of scorched earth. The top of the stadium appeared unscathed, with the word *BULLDOGS* still gleaming in blue and silver. The charred smell was so strong it was like sticking her head into a recently used barbecue grill. Yellow crime-scene tape surrounded the area. A few police officers lingered around the perimeter.

Cooper pulled the bike to the shoulder, put down the kickstand, and took off his helmet. The roar of the engine was replaced with the chirping of insects. She took off her helmet, too, smelling fresh-cut grass, ashes, and gasoline.

"What happened?" she asked.

"This is where Coach Fowler died," Cooper said.

"How?"

"He came around this turn. Guess his car was going pretty fast. Crashed right into the stadium. His car went up in flames. He didn't make it out."

She climbed off the bike and walked to the edge of the yellow tape. A cop on the other side glanced over but didn't shoo her away. She guessed the crime-scene work was done and they were just waiting for a tow. Cooper stood next to her.

The car was a classic Corvette. A few spots of blue paint were still visible, but most of the outside was burned black. The hood was smashed in so far, the car looked like a pug. A circular web cracked the windshield in front of the driver's seat.

Anna looked at the ground between the road and the stadium. There was a dirt shoulder, a section of grass, and then a cement apron abutting the concrete wall. There were no skid marks.

"You know what's weird?" Cooper said.

"Other than Coach Fowler crashing right into his

stadium, without making any apparent attempt to stop?"

"Cars don't generally explode on impact. I mean, it happens sometimes, but it's not like the movies. It's rare. And when cars do catch fire from a crash, there's usually a more heavily burned area where the fire started, like around the battery or gas tank, and then some less burned parts. But the coach's car is blackened all around. To me, cars look like this when someone has taken serious steps to make it happen."

"How do you know so much about burning cars?"

"I saw a lot of them in Afghanistan." Cooper ran a hand through his short black hair. "I was in one."

Anna glanced up at his face. He was looking at the stadium, but seeing something else. Before she could respond, a police officer came up to them. "Help you?"

"Actually, yes, sir." Cooper straightened and put a hand on Anna's shoulder. "We're looking for my friend's sister, Jody Curtis. I understand you are, too. Do you know if she's been located?"

"She's at the station now."

"Is she okay?" Anna said.

"Seems so."

"Thank God." She was flooded with relief. "What's she doing at the station?"

"Being interrogated," the officer said. "In connection with Coach Fowler's death."

That made Anna pause. *Questioned* was one thing. *Interrogated* sounded a lot more adversarial.

"Thanks, Officer." She turned to Cooper. "Can we head to the station?"

"Let's go."